E X T R ▲ C T E D

ALSO BY RR HAYWOOD

The Undead Series

The Undead Day One-Twenty

Blood at the Premiere: A Day One Undead Adventure

Blood on the Floor: An Undead Adventure

Demon Series

Recruited: A Mike Humber Novella

Huntington House: A Mike Humber Detective Novel

Book of Shorts Volume One

EXTRACTED

EXTRACTED BOOK 1

RR HAYWOOD

Text copyright © 2017 RR Haywood
All rights reserved.

Published by 47North, Seattle

www.apub.com

Amazon, the Amazon logo, and 47North are trademarks of Amazon.com, Inc., or its affiliates.

ISBN-13: 9781503941861
ISBN-10: 1503941868

Cover design by Mark Swan

Printed in the United States of America

Prologue

By twenty sixty-one the digital age of ownership and possession of almost intangible products is significant, but consumers still want physical goods. They still want to buy physical objects. They go online. Peruse the selections. Make the purchase and let the retailer do the rest.

Those retailers at the forefront of technology use drones and advanced logistical networks run by supercomputers. They excel in taking that product from warehouse to recipient, but as good as they get, they still have to rely on the physical carriage from point A to point B, which takes time, and time is money.

The research those retailers and tech companies invest in is called many different things. No matter the names they use, they are hoping for teleportation and the ability to take an object and move it from manufacturer to customer instantly.

If the technology could be developed for the *instantaneous delivery* of objects then perhaps, given time, research and understanding, it could also be used for the movement of people. *Instantaneous travel.*

The problem of course is that teleportation is not possible. It is a thing of fiction, of stories, of imagination. The theoretical science can theorise as much as it wants, but it is not, and nor would it ever be, possible. Everyone knows the dangers of monkeying around with the fundamental laws of nature. Anyone who has ever read popular science fiction knows what can go wrong. So the companies say it is purely research and development theory. They say they are forward planning for a hypothetical future because teleportation is not possible. It is a thing of fiction. It does not exist. It will never exist.

Then a whisper starts. The source is unknown but it grows and spreads through the intelligence community. Someone has done it. Someone has made a device, but not for the transit of goods over distance. The device is for the transit of goods *and people* across space *and time*.

Time travel.

All eyes turn to the retailers and tech giants. To the last, they deny knowledge and are as surprised as everyone else.

The virtual world becomes infested with advanced intrusive codes written to monitor the billions of social networking accounts and the written and spoken word in any and all forms. Secretly of course, because the wider public could never be told such a thing.

The quest starts. The hunt begins, but without a specific location, without a starting point, they are fishing in the dark in an ocean the size of a planet using a few rods in the vain hope of catching the one fish in the water.

2046

He looks down at his almost naked body trying to decide if he should remove his boxer shorts. The symbolism of walking naked into the sea conflicts with his desire to maintain standards. He decides that dying naked is not something he wishes to do and lifts his head to look out at the mirror sea reflecting the full moon. Stars overhead. So many of them. So bright too. A calm night. Peaceful. Fitting. The sand moves softly between his toes as he places the note on the neatly folded clothes stacked tidily atop his shiny black business shoes.

It is time. Time to go.

Control has been lost. Dignity and pride taken away, but all from his own actions. Now he must pay the price and in choosing this fate, he can best serve his family.

'Okay,' Roland mutters, nervously tapping the sides of his thighs. 'Right, okay.'

Still he waits. Unable to take the first step. His mind desperate to find reasons to stay another moment. He looks round to check his clothes and the handwritten letter are still there. What if a breeze gets up and blows the note away? It shouldn't. The forecast was fine for the next few days. He bends down to adjust the pile of clothes and takes the shoes to place on top of the paper. Another adjustment to make sure the note is visible. Then another to alter the gap between the shoes. Should he put one shoe on the note or both of them? What if one shoe is under the pile of clothes and the other is on top? Will that make a difference? Will it be analysed later as the final loss of cognitive function? Will experts decide that he was stark raving mad to put one shoe on top and one underneath before walking into the sea in his executive-style boxer shorts?

At this point, the placing of his shoes becomes extremely important. It is his final act as a human being and it needs to be right. A fleeting obsession is born. A myriad of thoughts flood his mind about what each adjustment will mean later. For a second he even considers putting the note inside one of the shoes but then worries someone might steal the shoes.

'God's sake,' he says under his breath, standing upright to smooth his dark hair flat against his skull with trembling hands. He glances back down at the shoes, frowning as he fights the impulse to stay and make more adjustments.

He gives a determined nod and stiffens his resolve. He is British. He will go with dignity and a stiff upper lip. The first step is firm and solid. A man taking control back. A man forging ahead to make his own future, albeit a very limited one.

The short journey across the soft sand seems to take hours but then, as with all things, it is over and as his left foot slides into the cool water of the ocean so the tear falls from his eye to roll fat down his cheek. His lips tremble. His legs start to weaken. A shiver runs up his back. His mind whirls frantic and desperate. His vision closes in. His heart thunders. His breathing becomes short, shallow and close to hyperventilating.

Onwards he walks deeper into the sea until the first splashes hit his knees, his thighs, his groin, his stomach, and for each one so the tears run faster, thicker, and he whimpers soft and terrified. For his family he will do this. For their sake he *must* do this.

'Don't go.'

The voice is jarring in the silence of the beach. Sparking a guilty reaction in Roland, who turns quickly in the chest-high water to stare at the lone figure on the beach, bathed in blue from a shimmering, iridescent square of light.

'Is it you?' the man calls out in a voice choking with emotion. A stranger but something familiar about him, the voice and the way he is standing.

'Do I know you?' Roland asks, his eyes flicking between the strange light and the man.

'It's me . . .' the man says, gulping to swallow his sobs.

'I . . . I don't know you,' Roland stammers while his brain screams for the connection to be made.

'I need your help.' The man's voice breaks as he walks fully clothed into the sea towards Roland. 'It went wrong . . . I . . . I broke it . . .'

'I don't know you, go away,' Roland says, stepping back deeper into the water in alarm, but there is something about the man. Something about the voice and the way he walks. The plaintive tone. The emotion. All of it is jarringly familiar.

'I broke it . . . I . . . don't go . . . please, don't go . . .'

A magic eye picture. A jigsaw finished wrong. The feeling you get when you see identical twins dressed in different clothes. That jolt of the eye at seeing something that the brain cannot process.

Roland is scared. Terrified. He is walking into the sea to die with all the emotion that brings but this man walking towards him is broken beyond compare. Fear and misery etched into every line of the man's face. A young man too. The jawline. The hairline. The colour of that hair. The way he walks. The voice.

With a wrenching drop of his stomach, Roland makes the sickening connection of recognition of something that cannot be possible.

He staggers back. His hands slap the surface of the sea. His eyes wide and unblinking.

'No . . .' Roland whispers, flicking to the blue square of light then back to the man he knows so well but not as a man. As a child. He knows him as a child. His own child that is at home in his teddy bear pyjamas.

'I broke it,' the man sobs. 'I need you . . . help me . . . please, Dad . . .'

One

2015

'Steph,' Ben shouts up the stairs. 'Steph? I've got to go . . .' He checks his watch then heads up, muttering under his breath that he's running late. 'Steph?'

'Huh?' She drops the phone on the bed as he walks into the room. 'You off?' she asks with a sudden beaming smile of white teeth and blue eyes that flutter as she walks towards him. Wet hair hanging down on slender shoulders and a soaking wet towel cinched tight over her breasts.

'Yeah,' he replies and glances again at his watch as she comes in for a kiss. 'I might be late tonight—'

'You said,' she cuts him off and leans in for a peck to avoid pressing her wet body against his clothes.

'Did I?' he asks, bending forward at the waist.

'Underground? Electrocution?' she says, pulling her head back and staring at him before blinking and looking away quickly.

'When did I—'

'Last night,' she interrupts with that beaming smile and quickly pulls the towel off to stand naked.

'Shit,' he mumbles, staring at her perfect breasts and down to her long legs. She comes in for a hug, filling his nose with the womanly scents of shampoo, conditioner, deodorant and creams. His mouth finds her neck, kissing down to her shoulders. She murmurs in pleasure but pulls away.

'Your train,' she says, placing an open palm on his chest. 'You'll be late.'

'I'll be late then,' he says with a grin.

'No,' she laughs, 'sod off . . . go on . . .'

'You've turned me on now.' He reaches out but she's gone to grab the towel, which gets wrapped round her body with one deft movement.

'You'll survive,' she says with a brief smile, then darts round as her phone vibrates on the bed. She thumbs the screen and turns away. Which is clearly an invite to come up behind her and continue the neck kissing and maybe steal a glance at the screen, but the second his hands touch her waist she steps away, deactivates the phone and glares at him. 'Ben, you'll be late.'

'I don't mind. We can do what we did last night . . .'

'I said no. Stop being a pervert.'

'Eh?' He comes to a stop at the harsh tone.

She turns away to the dresser to grab her hairbrush. 'I hate being pawed. You know that.'

'Pawed? You took your towel off . . .'

'Said the rapist to the judge.'

'What the fuck . . . ?'

'Don't swear at me, Ben.'

'Ah now,' Ben says, smiling apologetically with one hand on the back of his neck as he dips his head and looks up at her.

'Oh no,' she snaps, shaking her head at him angrily. 'Don't do that.'

'What?' he asks.

'That *ah now* with the hand on your neck. Look, I'm running late now,' she huffs. 'I'll see you tonight.'

'Steph, hang on . . .'

'I said I will see you tonight,' she snaps.

'Okay okay.' He backs away, feeling jarred from the sudden mood switch. She's been doing that a lot lately, but then they *are* planning a wedding and both of them work demanding jobs in the city. He heads down the stairs and pauses at the door. His face pensive. The urge to ask her now is strong but her mood is already dark and it risks an argument which will make them both late for work. Sometimes things are best left. 'I'll see you tonight then,' he calls up gently.

'Yes, Ben,' she shouts in that irritated tone.

He sighs and heads outside to drive to the station where he parks up and rushes on to the platform towards the kiosk then curses when the front of the train comes into view down the tracks.

'Ben.'

He looks over and sees Judith leaning out of the kiosk window holding a large disposable cup. She smiles kindly, a face of wrinkles, grey hair and twinkling eyes. 'You're late this morning.'

'Yeah, rushing about. Thank you so much though . . .' he says, grabbing the cup and delving a hand into his pocket.

'Pay me tomorrow,' she says, waving him away. 'You'll miss it.'

'Thanks, Judith.'

'Steph on her way is she?' she calls out as he moves across the platform.

'Yep, drying her hair about now I think.'

'I'll have one waiting for her.'

'Thanks, Judith.'

```
Hey love, can you pay for my coffee if you
have time, I almost missed the train? Judith
said she'll have yours waiting x
```

He clicks 'Send' and settles in for the forty-minute journey but his phone vibrates within a few seconds of sending Steph the message.

Ok

He notes the distinct lack of kisses or any term of endearment. That has been going on for a while now too and it adds to the feeling of discomfort, like a worrying nagging sensation at the back of his mind. You know when someone is turning off from you. The lack of cuddles or kissing with her eyes open. She is having an affair. He knows it now. Not from any feeling of possessiveness or insecurity but simply from an assessment of the evidence all taken together to reach a logical conclusion. It will be her boss. Steph used to speak so highly of him and talked about how cool he was all the time. Ben didn't mind any of that but he did notice when she suddenly stopped talking about him so much, which was the same time as the affection stopped and the bad moods started. The subtle changes in her appearance. The perfume she uses all the time that she had told Ben how much her boss liked. Little things. Lots of little things, but that is what Ben does. He takes the little things and works them through to find the logical conclusion. The only difference is that this is about *his* life and not an insurance claim. He hasn't said anything for fear of sounding like a jealous control freak, and it's making him feel like shit, with an ever-tightening knot in his gut.

He'd asked Steph what was wrong a couple of times. She said she was okay. He even asked her, just once, if she still wanted to get married, but she snapped and told him to stop being so insecure and needy.

Strangely, it was last night that finally made him realise there was something very wrong. They had sex for the first time in ages but it was different. Very different. It was the early hours and he woke up to find her hand on his penis and her mouth in his ear.

'Fuck me,' she demanded almost angrily.

Ben rolled over and started to kiss her neck but got pushed roughly away.

'I said fuck me,' she hissed and pulled him on top while rubbing his cock. The second he was rigid she thrust it inside, bucking, grunting and raking at his shoulders while demanding to be fucked harder. It was over quickly then she stared up at him in the moonlight coming through the blinds for a long minute before rolling over and going straight back to sleep. She was different. So angry, and she seemed so full of spite too. Ben didn't recognise her.

They live outside London. Close enough for property prices to be staggeringly high but far enough to be classed as a Home County.

Forty minutes later he's bouncing along the platform and jogging across the busy roads with veins full of caffeine.

'Morning, Ben.' The receptionist greets him with a smile as he bursts through the door and runs across the tiled floor towards the lift.

'Hello, Tracy,' he calls out with a wave and runs the last few steps into the packed lift being held open by a man in a suit with swept-back dark hair who nods and steps aside to let him in. Ben's firm has the fifth floor. The chap who held the door open for him stays in as the doors close on the fourth.

'You going to Hallows?' Ben asks politely.

'Yes,' he replies, matching Ben's politeness and raising it several notches with the strong cultured tone of the very well educated. 'Do you work there?'

'I do. Ben Calshott. Nice to meet you,' Ben says, offering his hand.

'Very nice to meet you, Mr Calshott. What do you do?'

'Insurance investigator,' Ben says, wincing like it's a bad thing. Everyone has a bad story of insurance companies ripping them off or not paying out. 'Not a loss adjustor though,' he adds quickly, as most people get the two roles confused.

'Ah, very interesting,' the man says, taking a long look at Ben's jeans and open-necked checked shirt.

'I'm on-site today, hence no suit,' Ben explains. 'You here for a meeting?'

'Indeed I am,' he says with perfect politeness as the doors ping open. 'Nice to meet you, Mr Calshott.' He walks out and heads straight to the reception with a confidence in his movements. Ben watches him for a second, trying to work out why the man is here. The suit is expensive and well-tailored but something about it looks out of place. People very rarely come for face-to-face meetings too. Not with Skype, conference calls and email so easy to use. He puts it to the back of his mind and rushes on with a glance at his watch.

'Morning morning.' Ben bustles into the already full conference room. 'Am I late?'

'You're fine,' the boss says. 'Grab a coffee.'

'Anyone else?' Ben asks, looking round at the shaking heads and people raising their mugs to show they've already got one.

Ben gets a coffee and snags a croissant from the basket before taking his seat at the round table for the Monday morning weekly brief. The boss insisted on a round table as she said firms that use square tables promote unnecessary ranking and hierarchical structures that lead to division. A round table means anyone can sit anywhere, and the boss is always first to get in, which means she can choose a different place to sit every time. A clever woman is the boss.

Ben waits his turn knowing he has time to eat the croissant and brush the crumbs from his shirt as big Todd rolls his eyes at him with a smirk. Ben flicks his middle finger at him and gets a chuckle in response. Ben likes Todd. He likes everyone here really. The boss is as careful about recruitment as she is about table selection.

'Ben,' she says, 'you had the fire last week? All finished?'

'Yep, the report's all done.'

'Conclusion?' she asks.

'Ah.' Ben pulls a face. 'Big house in the country, worth a fortune. Wife, husband, two kids and two dogs. Bad times financially. Husband's firm going down the pan which leads to a loss of income which means they can't buy the very latest Chesterfield sofa to put in the drawing room. She set the fire on the existing sofa and I reckon . . .' He pauses, holding his pen up for effect. 'I reckon she intended to burn just the sofa at first but then got greedy and figured that if a few more bits got damaged she could claim on them too . . . which is why she left the windows open on a cold day . . .'

'To fan the flames,' someone mutters.

'Exactly. Cigarette left in an ashtray, cigarette falls out, rolls across the fire-retardant material and lands on the carefully placed broadsheet newspaper left on the floor . . . fire starts . . . burns the entire bloody house down and kills the dogs . . .'

'Shit,' Todd says. 'What a bitch.'

'Oh, she's cold, mate,' Ben says to him. 'Cruella de Vil but with less emotions.'

'Accelerants?' the boss asks.

'Had the wooden floors varnished the day before,' Ben says.

'Was the fire intense?'

'Very,' Ben says, holding a look on his face that the boss knows only too well. 'Destroyed all the evidence.'

'I see,' the boss says, arching an eyebrow at him. She sighs for effect. 'Go on then,' she adds with a grin. 'I know you've got something by the look on your face.'

'Ah now,' Ben says, smiling wryly with one hand on the back of his neck as he dips his head and looks round the room.

'Here he goes,' Todd says and laughs, shaking his head as the others all start chuckling. The boss leans back and folds her arms with an amused expression.

'Well,' Ben says, 'the floors were varnished six months ago. All of them were done by a specialist flooring company. Big house. Lots of rooms. All of them have wooden floors so the cost to get them redone is huge. Why would you get them done again within six months?

Especially if you're having a hard time financially. The average for a domestic house is every five to ten years. Commercial properties or those with lots of foot traffic might do every three to five years, but six months? Even the Queen doesn't get her floors redone every six months. Now, I did consider maybe some damage to one room which could require the floor to be repaired, but she had the whole house done again and, get this, even the flooring company told her it was unnecessary. That is enough to show preparation for fire and will undermine the insurance claim . . . I've got a copy of my report ready for the police once it's signed off.'

Smiles round the table. Nods and mouths turning down in recognition of good work.

'Well done,' the boss says, smiling warmly at Ben. 'Your hundred per cent success rate continues.'

'Thanks,' Ben says, shifting uncomfortably from the sudden attention.

'You've got the Underground next?' the boss asks, already knowing the answer as it was her that gave him the case to work on.

'I have.'

'What's in the Underground?' someone asks.

'Trains,' Todd says with a grin, looking round the table. 'What? That was funny.'

'It wasn't funny,' Ben says, deadpan.

'You're funny,' he says.

'You look funny,' Ben says.

'Boys, please,' the boss says with a good-natured smile.

'Worker was electrocuted,' Ben explains to everyone.

'From the rails?' Claire asks.

'No, an electrical switch. He's claiming faulty wiring,' Ben replies. 'Dark space, confined, he's saying his batteries in his head torch were too weak and the circuits or wiring hadn't been correctly maintained.'

'Double liability then,' Claire says. 'Contractor?'

'Yeah, his firm are subcontractors so he's claiming on them for the supply of dodgy equipment and Transport for London for failing to maintain their electrical circuits. Very big potential payout as he's got the union behind him making noises.'

'So that's you tucked up for the next couple of days crawling about rat-infested tunnels,' the boss says lightly. 'Good luck,' she adds with a big grin. 'Claire, how was the flood?'

'Wet . . .'

Ben feels his phone vibrate in his pocket and the temptation to check it is overwhelming, but that's a fate worse than death. The boss is an incredible person but woe betide the person who crosses her, and not checking your phone during Monday morning prayers is inscribed in scripture. Instead, he sits through the meeting and is first out the door with phone in hand when they finally finish.

```
We need to talk tonight
```

The words are portentous and foreboding, giving Ben a tight knot in his stomach. He thumbs a quick reply while walking back to the lift.

```
That doesn't sound good. What's up? X

We'll talk tonight.

I'll be late home tonight . . . What's up?
Can you talk? X

No. Busy. We'll talk tonight.

I love you Steph but you're acting weird
lately. What was that about last night? I can
tell something is wrong x

Last night?
```

The sex. What was that about?

Did you like it?

Yeah course I did but it was a bit strange.
I hate text conversations. Can you talk?

From his office to the Tube station, with that knot in his gut growing harder with every reply. Even the delay of her replies spoke volumes. There was a time the replies came almost instantly, but now they didn't, like he was an afterthought or an irritation.

The signal goes as the carriage doors on the Underground train seal him into the packed masses. He stares down at his phone seeing his future disappear as quickly as the signal bar fades on the screen. In the end he pockets the phone and stares round as glumly as everyone else. His mind filling with images of his fiancée in the arms of another man. He'd kept those thoughts away but with the reality of the situation growing starker by the day it couldn't help but start to creep in. He clears his throat and blinks rapidly to rid himself of the thoughts. His fist clamping hard on the safety rail.

He crosses London to the meeting point at Holborn. It's early summer, every station and train is packed with a riot of cultures and languages. The winter coats are gone now, replaced with lightweight jackets, shirts and blazers. He gets to Holborn and waits for the site manager at the ticket kiosk. This is the preliminary meeting for Ben to get a first visual inspection of the site, and the works manager is under orders to meet him alone with no union reps or senior managers present. He checks his phone continually but there are no new messages. Steph will be at her desk now but maybe she'll text him at lunchtime. The knot in his gut twists and drops. Anxiety in his face. He pushes it away to focus on the job at hand and looks round casually then double takes as he spots the man in the nice suit from the lift this morning on the other side of the road. By the time the flotilla of buses has gone he's lost from view. It's a small world sometimes, even in London. Ben looks again thinking maybe he has something to do with this meeting today but he was too well dressed to be a works manager and looked more like a top-line executive. A crowd of men and women brush past Ben rushing into the entrance. A tall ginger man turns to glare at Ben from the shoulder contact but this is central London so Ben smiles to show no offence is taken.

'Ben Calshott?'

'Oh hi.' Ben turns to see an overweight man wearing a crumpled suit glaring at him.

'Works manager,' he says brusquely with a distinct London accent. 'You got the short straw then did ya?'

'Yeah, something like that,' Ben replies.

'Got overalls have ya?'

'Er, no . . . I was hoping I could borrow some?' Ben asks, pulling a face as though to say he forgot to bring his own.

The fake grin on the works manager's face fades instantly. 'Nope.' He walks off without another word. Ben falls in behind him as he paces through the terminal towards a service door at the back. The tall ginger man is still there with his group and Ben figures they're tourists from a western country. Dark hair, light hair, pale and olive complexions and all of them wearing *I Love London* jackets and carrying bags. They don't look happy though; mind you, no one ever looks happy on the Underground.

Ben follows the works manager through the service door, which cuts the thrum of noise from the terminal the second it closes. Plunging them into a weird silence broken only by the rumble and vibration of trains as they go through a catacomb of corridors, doors and stairs leading down.

'Where did it happen?' Ben asks, knowing exactly where it happened.

'Aldwych,' the works manager says as gruffly as before. 'Silly prat,' he mutters. 'Oops, not allowed to express an opinion,' he adds pointedly.

They reach a room full of workers having a tea break. Orange over-alls, safety hats and head torches everywhere and all conversation ends the second they walk in. One set of large overalls rest on the back of a chair that the works manager starts putting on.

'Hi.' Ben says, looking round at the grimy, expressionless faces. 'How's it going?' No response. 'You work for the same firm as the bloke who got electrocuted?'

'Are you questioning my staff?' the works manager asks sharply. 'Cos they got union reps who should be present if you're doing that.'

'Ah now,' Ben says, smiling apologetically with one hand on the back of his neck as he looks up at the works manager. 'Are they your staff then?'

'Eh?'

'You're the works manager, aren't you?'

'Yeah.'

'So you're employed by Transport for London.'

'I am.'

Ben can see the overalls worn by the men are not Transport for London issued, which in turn means they are not Transport for London workers. 'These are subbies,' he says with a nod to the still quiet workers. 'So they're not employed directly by Transport for London.'

'What?'

'Just saying.' Ben shrugs casually. 'You know . . . technically they're not your staff. They're subcontracted so they're employed by someone else who you pay to do certain work.'

'We're going,' he says with a rapidly reddening face.

'Thing is,' Ben says, holding his ground and not walking after him, 'these blokes are covered by the same safety regulations as everyone else working down here . . . but they're not covered by Transport for London employment rules.' Ben holds his gaze as though talking directly to him but knowing everyone in the room is listening intently. 'So they can talk to me if they want to, you know . . .' He pulls a few business cards from his back pocket, 'if they want to tell me anything they can.' He drops the cards on the table. 'Safety breaches . . . unnecessary risks . . . fault reports not being actioned . . . you know, the sort of thing insurance companies get payouts for . . .' He lets the last few words hang in the air and feels the change in atmosphere as the works manager looks like he's about to have a heart attack.

'We need to get on,' he growls.

In the next room, the works manager issues Ben with a safety helmet, an orange vest, a head torch and a safety guide to read through, then makes him sign for a laminated visitor's card. Ben's office is full of protective clothing they can use but it's always interesting to turn up without anything and see what rules they break. Everything here is done properly.

'You'll stay within sight of me at all times and do as I say when I say it.' The works manager reels off the instructions. 'Walk directly behind me and do not touch anything without asking first. We are not going anywhere near the live rails but there are still dangers inherent with an underground rail service. Do you understand, Mr Calshott?'

'I do and you can call me Ben, mate.'

The olive branch is ignored so they walk in silence through the next maze of corridors until they're in the high-arched tunnels with their footsteps echoing. Ben feels the vibration of trains passing through other tunnels and stays close behind the works manager until they reach a lit platform adorned with an old-style sign proclaiming they're at Aldwych. Ben recognises it from movies and knows they keep it for film and television locations and guided tours. They get on the platform and head into the main tiled corridor once used by the public. The manager unlocks a side door and they go into a dark room complete with a bank of electrical switches and circuits.

'In here?' Ben asks.

'Yep.'

'What happened?'

'I wasn't here was I? I didn't see it.'

'Fair enough. Has anything been touched since the accident?'

'Sparky came down and made it safe.'

'An electrician?'

'S'what I said.'

'An electrician has been in here since the accident?'

'S'what I said.'

'Who? I wasn't told anything about that.'

'Not my responsibility.'

'Who then?'

'Personnel manager.'

'Which wire did he say caused it?'

'Dunno.'

'Yes you bloody do, you're the works manager. Which wire?' Ben snaps, showing a level of firmness instead of an easy-going smile.

The manager huffs and walks to the second bank of switches. 'This one.' He points to a wire leading into a switch.

'What does that do?'

'It provides electricity to the switch.'

'Not the wire, the switch. What does the switch do?'

'Operates the lights on the stairwells.'

'Why was he working on it?'

'It's booked for filming. They want to change the lighting for a period film.'

'And?'

'And what?'

'What was the purpose of the visit by the worker to this room?'

'Ask him.'

'I am asking you.'

'He was tasked to check the fittings in accordance with the instructions of the production company so they could arrange manufacture of the right size of lights and equipment.'

'He's saying he touched the switch and got zapped,' Ben says, pointing at the switch. 'Which suggests the wiring within the switch was loose and made the whole casing live. Did the electrician who attended find anything?'

'Dunno.'

'Know what,' Ben snaps, 'I am not your enemy, mate. I am not employed by the insurance company . . . I am independent. I just find out what happened and report back.'

The manager looks away with a distinct lack of interest. A company man through and through and, like a stick of rock, you could break him in half and see the Tube logo running through his core. Ben knows the type and gives up any hope of winning cooperation. The few stabs at humour and firmness have failed, which tells Ben anything short of a briefcase full of unmarked bank notes will also fail. Instead, and with a sigh for effect, he pulls his phone from his pocket and activates the camera.

'I am taking pictures,' Ben states slowly as he thumbs the screen to fill the room with the irritating noise of the fake shutter clicking, 'to make sure nothing is tampered with between now and when I return with the claimant.' He takes more pictures to make more shutter noises and changes the angle a few times, turns the flash on, turns it off and does it all again for good measure. The works manager remains stoic and devoid of expression but even he can't prevent the physiological reddening of his cheeks, flushing with unconcealed anger.

'Done?'

'Yes, thank you,' Ben says, pocketing his phone. They go through the same game as before. Walking in silence down the platform and through the disused tunnel before going back into the maze of corridors. They reach a door. The manager stops to take the hard hat, vest, torch and pass from Ben before opening the door and politely stepping back. 'After you.' He ushers Ben through and for a second Ben thinks maybe he's had time to think or mellow until he says, 'Nice meeting you,' and slams the door in Ben's face, leaving him on the Holborn station platform. He goes to bang on the door but gives up as soon as the thought forms. What else could you expect?

He starts moving through the dense crowds towards the arched entrance and catches sight of the tall ginger man in the *I Love London* rain jacket standing with his back to the wall further down the platform. He figures he must have got isolated from his group but then Ben spots the dark-haired man with olive skin wearing the same *I Love London* gear kneeling on the ground as he goes through a zip-up bag. Then he sees another one from the same group standing by the edge of the platform. It gets Ben's attention and he turns round slowly, picking out the jackets and the faces of the group he saw bustling through the entrance. The woman with blonde hair and the pink *I Love London* coat is there too, also going through a bag on the floor. It's weird how they're all separated. Ben looks back to the ginger man wiping his forehead with a trembling hand and staring fixed at the brown-haired woman by the platform edge, who has her eyes closed while muttering as though praying.

The realisation hits at the same second as her right hand comes up to her waist and shoves into a side pocket of her waterproof coat.

'FOR THE EARTH . . .' A screeching voice as her left hand shoots into the air with a clenched fist, then the whole of her disappears in an explosion of pink mist with a dull bang that detonates in all directions, taking out swathes of people standing nearby. Hot wet spray hits Ben's face. People scream on the platform and on the tracks. Bodies writhe with injuries and convulse with limbs locked out in spasm from the electric current of the live rail.

Time slows to a state of mind Ben had once before. Everything in front of him is in perfect clarity to the smallest of details and he can see everything as it is about to play out.

The ginger man lifts his arm to shove into the side pocket of his waterproof jacket. Ben looks round but it's like everything is in slow motion. He spots the dark-haired man pulling a sawn-off shotgun from a bag then the woman with the pink top rising to her feet with a black pistol gripped in each hand. More of the *I Love London* brigade on the platform. People screaming. People dying. Blood and bodies everywhere. Everyone will die if he does nothing. That is fact. Everyone here will die.

Ben starts running, instinct pushing him to react. The ginger man has a bomb. Stop the bomb. That's all Ben thinks. He aims for the ginger man, who thrusts his right hand into his jacket. Nothing happens. His hand fumbles as a puzzled look floods across his face. Two huge booms from the entranceway as the dark-haired man fires both barrels of the sawn-off shotgun at the commuters running to escape. The effect is devastating with pellets spreading to lacerate flesh and muscle.

Ben veers and dodges through the terrified people trying to run away or find somewhere to hide, but the only exit is blocked by the man with the shotgun. Gunshots boom loudly in the enclosed space as the woman with the pistols starts firing them one after the other, aiming directly into the crowds of innocent passengers. The sawn-off shotgun snaps open as the dark-haired man nods and turns towards Ben while bringing two new cartridges from his pocket.

The ginger man presses at the thing in his pocket that must be a detonation switch for a bomb. The man with the sawn-off is reloading but that only gives him two shots. Everything in perfect clarity like it was before. There is no panic within Ben. Just an icy coldness that tells him what must be done. In that second he sees the woman as the most dangerous one and veers hard to smash into her from behind. They go down amidst a tangle of limbs just as the shotgun fires pellets over his head.

'SHOOT HIM,' the woman screams as the dark-haired man cracks the shotgun open again. Ben feels her bucking underneath him. Fighting to get his weight off her. The danger is immediate. The threat is obvious. The man is reloading the shotgun. The ginger man is trying to detonate his bomb. They have to be stopped or everyone will die. The woman twists to aim one of the pistols up towards Ben. He grabs the back of her head with two fistfuls of hair and slams her down into the concrete ground with barely a flicker showing on his face. He lunges at the black pistol in her right hand as another huge explosion comes from the tiled entranceway and more people scream, shout and yell out in pain from the pellets striking them.

He wrenches the pistol from her grip, stands up and fires down once into her head. The recoil sends him staggering backwards, tripping and sliding over body parts. Ben looks over at the dark-haired man snapping the shotgun closed and holds the pistol with both hands, points and squeezes the trigger. The first bullet hits the dark-haired man in the stomach so Ben fires again and again. The man smashes backwards into the wall behind him, pulling the triggers to fire both barrels of the shotgun into the ceiling before slumping down, leaving a thick smear of blood on the shiny tiles behind him.

A scream to Ben's left and he turns to see a woman in an *I Love London* top running at him with a huge bloody knife in her hand. He turns and fires, ice cold and perfectly calm. The bullet hits her chest, spinning through her heart.

Within that chaos of noise Ben detects a variance in the screams and spins around to see the ginger man kicking a woman to send her over the edge of the platform on to the tracks below. He wrenches another by her hair with a vicious strength that belies his lean frame. She goes down too, landing inches from the live rail. Ben runs towards him knowing that everyone will die if that man detonates his bomb. Another *I Love London* T-shirt lunges towards Ben. He stops, aims and fires two shots. One misses. The other hits the man in the face. Ben turns, his boots sliding on the blood-soaked ground. He looks to find the ginger man now holding a black stick in his hand, frantically hitting the top of it. The ginger man stops with a sudden cessation of movement and slowly lifts the stick to stare at the wires coming out of it with an almost comical expression on his face as he spots one wire hanging free. Ben points and shoots twice while running and misses with both shots. The gun clicks empty. The ginger man grins with victory and shoves the wire back into the stick as Ben grits his teeth, snarls and drops his shoulder to drive him off the edge of the platform down on to the rails with a sickening crunch. Ben's head spins. Stars and strobes flash in his vision. He slams fists into the ginger head again and again.

A rumble vibrates through the ground. A rush of hot, dry air blasts past Ben. A train coming down the tracks with a driver completely unaware of the carnage unfolding. Ben glances at the rapidly emptying platform. Bodies everywhere. The people on the tracks scream as they try to climb back up.

The ginger guy hisses beneath him, his hands fumbling at the black stick. Ben rips the man's waterproof jacket open to see a thick black waistcoat, like a paramilitary thing but with wires and big square chunks of plastic.

Without thinking, Ben stands up and stamps his foot down hard on to the man's head, ending the struggle instantly. The body can't stay here. If the train hits it, it could detonate the explosives and there are still too many people. Ben knows nothing about bombs but he does know there is electricity everywhere and a single spark hitting the bomb could cause the detonation.

Ben drags the man as fast as he can. Glancing from the body in his hands to the mouth of the tunnel at the far end. One foot after the other but the progress is too slow. The reflection of the train lights shows on the walls and Ben feels another gust of wind blast past him and the vibration of brakes being applied.

It's not enough. The dead man is too heavy and his feet kept tripping, causing Ben to lose momentum. He clenches his jaw and tries harder. The train comes into view. Two bright lights like the eyes of a snake as the driver finally notices the smouldering corpses on the tracks. He hits the brakes, which screech and send a deeper vibration through the ground. A young female police officer runs on to the platform, sweeping her gaze over everything until catching sight of Ben. They lock eyes for the briefest of seconds before she turns and shouts at the driver but the train hits a body that bursts apart like a ripe melon spraying blood and gore everywhere. Sparks shoot out from metallic objects trapped between the wheels and the metal track. Ben lifts his head to stare at the showering sparks getting closer as the train closes the gap.

'GET HIM.'

Words shouted in a second of absolute confusion. He snaps his head round and instantly screws his eyes closed at the dazzling blue light filling his vision in the darkness of the tunnel mouth. An impact from the side. People grabbing him hard, forcing him across the tracks. The ginger man is ripped from his hands. The train comes in fast. Too many sensations at once. Too many things happening. A second later the detonation sends a massive shock wave through the tunnel. Bricks and dust fall from the ceiling. Everything vibrating and shuddering. The noise is indescribable. A solid wall of intense sound. Fire. Flames. Twisting metal. Voices screaming. Smells of chemicals and heat all overwhelm his senses. He hits out, punching and raging at whoever is attacking him. Chaos and confusion. Torches shining in his eyes. Sounds everywhere. He's taken down to the ground and dragged into a world of silence that his mind cannot comprehend.

'Jab him,' a voice grunts. 'Fuck's sake . . . jab him . . .' Ben fights hard, driving his fists into bodies that yelp out in pain.

'Have you got him?' another voice asks from somewhere a bit further away.

'Please . . . stop hitting me!'

'Malcolm, I suggest you inject him now . . .'

'I'm trying! But he's fighting like a . . .'

'Ben, calm down. We're here to help.' Ben recognises that voice somewhere in the layers of his subconscious thought but the front of his mind is filled with people in *I Love London* jackets and a country lane in the middle of nowhere. Dense smoke seeps into the room. Bricks and debris fly past, bouncing off walls.

'Turn it off!'

'Bloody trying . . . Boss . . . turn it off . . .'

'Ben, just calm . . .'

People saying his name over and over again. He grabs something and bites into it. Someone screams so he bites harder and kicks into something else that also screams out in pain. Two men holding him down. They scrabble about trying to grab his arms while a third voice, the one Ben recognises, gives instructions from further away.

'That's it, hold him down now . . . get his arm, Malcolm. Konrad, you grab that other wrist . . . quickly now chaps . . .'

'I'm trying,' one of them squawks, then yelps when Ben punches him.

'Ben, just calm down . . . we're here to help you . . .'

'He got me in the face. I think he's bust my nose . . .'

'Just knock him out, Malc.'

'Is it broken?'

'Not now, Malc! Jab him . . . I can't hold him.'

'That's it chaps. You're doing well but do hurry it along . . .'

A heavy weight smothers Ben's upper body as one of the men lies across him, trapping his arms. 'Got him! Malc . . . jab him . . . jab him . . . Malc . . . jab him . . .'

'I am trying, Konrad,' Malcolm says tightly as Ben surges up to sink his teeth into something warm and fleshy.

'AARRGHHH,' Konrad screams. 'HE'S BLOODY BITING ME AGAIN . . .'

'Shush now, Konrad . . .'

'But he's biting me . . .'

'Yes, I can see that, but there's no need to scream so loudly. Do man up.'

'Got it,' Malcolm shouts as something sharp is jabbed into Ben's neck that sends a warm feeling spreading through his body. His head becomes too heavy to hold up and he sinks down, with his teeth sliding from the flesh he was biting into.

'Thank God,' Konrad groans.

'Is my nose broken?'

'Not now, Malc. He's still fighting.'

'Give it a second. Christ, the program isn't wrong with this one!'

'Why isn't it working, boss? He should be out by now.'

'Because he's Ben Ryder, chaps, which is exactly why we want him.'

Ben Ryder? I'm not Ben Ryder now. I'm Ben Calshott. Birmingham. The gang. They've found him. They'll kill him. He explodes and fights with renewed strength, gouging, biting, hitting and bucking like mad, but that spreading warmth sinks deeper and pulls him down like he's falling slowly. The air is too hot and feels too thick. His ears ring. Every inch of him hurts and he tries to stay awake but the pull is too great and he goes down until the last thing he hears are several relieved voices.

'He's out.'

'Sure?'

'Well he's gone limp, Malcolm, which does suggest that he's out considering he was fighting like crazy a second ago.'

'Don't be sarcastic, Konrad. Check his pulse.'

'I can't do that if he's going to buck about. Hold him down . . .'

'I am, just check his pulse.'

'I am, Malcolm! His pulse is slowing . . .'

'Check his pupils too, Konrad,' the posh voice says.

'I'm not a bloody doctor, boss. Hang on, yeah . . . yeah they're dilated. He's out.'

'Oh my God that was hard, is my nose broken?'

'Hang on, I'll have a look . . .'

'Don't blind me!'

'You told me to look at your nose.'

'My nose, not my eyes, you twat.'

'Your nose is in-between your eyes and, yeah, it's bent and bleeding.'

'Bent? My nose is bent?'

'Yeah, bent, like . . . like broken . . .'

'It really hurts.'

'Well done, chaps! Right, stop dithering about now and get him away . . . and don't forget the other meds.'

Two

1943

The sentry coughs into the night, exhaling a plume of hot air that steams and hangs before evaporating. He bends his legs to stimulate the circulation. His gloved left hand rests on the barrel of the machine gun while his right holds the cigarette.

Harry watches him from the shadows of the verge not more than twenty metres away, knowing the wooden guard hut behind the sentry gives cover from the biting wind. He also knows the sentry has nothing to do for the next two hours but smoke and stamp his feet and look up at the million stars shining in the blackness of the night. In two hours, the sentry will report using the radio in the hut and he will do the same thing every two hours until he is relieved. After that, he will go to the mess, get some hot food and then report to his section head before getting some sleep. When he wakes, the young soldier will get hot food from the mess and report to his section head before coming back to what must be the worst sentry position any soldier has ever been allocated.

There is a war going on. Country against country and a world being conquered by the power of the Third Reich. Brave men earning medals for acts of outstanding bravery while the sentry gets hot food and reports to the section head before coming back to stare at the same bloody stars every night. Harry can sense the frustration in the sentry. The way he huffs and grips his machine gun and sighs with boredom. A man who dreams of being in firefights killing English and American soldiers.

The sadness of it becomes even more striking when the young German soldier curls his lips and pretends to fire his machine gun and by that single action he shows just how young he is and why he is being used as a sentry instead of a front-line soldier. Harry waits for the sentry to light another cigarette, knowing the sentry's night vision will be momentarily ruined by stupidly staring at the lit match. He goes forward. Slowly at first, then bursting up to a hard sprint.

The steel against the sentry's throat is sudden and the blade bites deep. He would scream but the hand over his mouth clamps too hard. He would turn and fire but the strength in the arms holding him is too great. He would kick out but the knee in his back drives in with such brutal force that he's ripped from his feet and slammed down into the ground as the dagger is stabbed through his throat and he catches one final glimpse of the night sky before the huge foot smashes down, rendering him forever silent.

Harry pauses and holds still. A glow catches his eye. The still-burning end of the cigarette dropped from the sentry's hand. He stubs it out, twisting his boot into the hard surface of the unmade road, and drops down to wipe the blade of his dagger on the tunic of the dead German soldier.

The mission was voluntary. The British Army did not order men to undertake suicide missions. They asked politely and got volunteers instead. The whole regiment volunteered but every man there knew who they would pick.

'You understand there is no planned extraction,' the captain told Harry gravely. 'We can get you in but not out, you need to be absolutely clear on this.'

'Aye, sir,' Harry replied, standing at ease in the small office, staring at a point on the wall directly ahead of him. The captain was a good chap. Harry knew he would never send a man to his death if he did not consider the prize to be worth it.

'If you can get to the boats then you might, and I emphasise you might, get out, but they are under orders not to wait and to only do what is required.'

'Aye. Understood, sir.'

'Harry,' the captain said in such a tone that Harry knew he was required to look at the captain instead of the spot on the wall. 'This has come from the top. They want destruction. Total destruction of everything. You have absolute permission to cause absolute carnage.'

'Sir,' Harry said with a firm nod.

In the wooden sentry hut, Harry finds the short-wave radio. A clipboard fitted with a single sheet of paper hangs from a hook but it holds no value and is simply used as a record for units entering the deep-water harbour of the Norwegian fjord.

Two miles from here to the harbour. Two miles that need to be covered before oh-two-thirty hours, when he can give the signal. Two miles on rough terrain in the freezing cold of a Norwegian winter, but still far easier than the training regime of yomping ten miles with a backpack full of bricks into a live firing exercise.

He sets off and instinctively veers to the grass verge, which softens the tread of his boots. His thick black beard protects his face from the cold. With the dark navy fisherman's coat over a thick knitted jumper he looks every inch the Norwegian fisherman indigenous to these parts. That he cannot speak a word of Norwegian does not bother Harry. The disguise is to make him look natural to any passing patrol.

Fifteen minutes later, he crests the top of the hill and starts the descent towards the dark harbour. No lights show for fear of the RAF.

Blackness against a sea of blackness but the harbour is here, and in that harbour are U-boats and those U-boats are the target. Five of them reportedly brought in for service and repair. There will be guards, patrols, dogs, searchlights and rapid response units ready to mobilise instantly, but the element of surprise and sheer audacity might just see him through.

He drops down to one knee, letting his breath recover while picking out the darker silhouettes of the buildings and smiling at the first slivers and cracks of warm yellow lights showing in the windows and door frames. It's no different to England or any other base he's been on. Soldiers believe they are invincible and, despite the constant warnings, they cannot help but get lazy. Doors not quite closed properly, curtains not drawn tight enough. Soldiers need to drink and move about. Who would attack here anyway? Norway in the middle of winter? Against the army of the Third Reich? Not a chance. Anyway, an RAF pilot flying thousands of feet in the air cannot possibly see a tiny yellow light on the ground.

The next sentry post is manned properly with alert guards under the watchful eye of an officer. Harry stays low then drops on to his belly to snake over the freezing, stunted grass to the high-wire fence surrounding the town. In the shadows, he stops and pulls wire cutters from his pocket and sets to work. Each clunk is dull and seems to reverberate in every direction and he stops frequently to scan the vicinity and listen.

He works steadily, biting through the links before peeling back the fence and creating a hole big enough to squeeze through, but he backs away and belly-crawls along the fence to the sentry hut while keeping his head tucked low in the high collar to prevent the moonlight reflecting from the skin round his eyes, cheeks and nose.

Five metres out and he is close enough to hear the muted conversations of the guards and see the steam of their breaths. He pulls the explosive charge out, several sticks of dynamite wired to an electric timer. He turns the dial to set fifteen minutes and places it on the floor before belly-crawling back to the hole in the fence and through into the town.

He gets to his feet, dusts his clothes off and walks casually. There will be a curfew in place but the tide will be high soon and the German soldiers need fresh fish to eat. Another hour will see the local fishermen getting ready to set out. With luck, he will be taken as an early riser.

He stops to light a cigarette at the corner of a building, closing his eyes against the flare of the match. Nothing is less suspicious than a bearded fisherman in a fishing village smoking a cigarette. He checks his timing, pauses for a couple of seconds and then sets the next charge with a ten-minute delay, dropping it into the shadow of the building.

He strolls down a side road towards the harbour, smoking casually while picking a stray bit of tobacco from his tongue and showing no reaction to the sound of heavy boots from a night patrol marching nearby. Every commando knows the score if they are caught by the enemy. The Geneva Convention no longer applies to them and already the brass back home are getting reports of captured commandos being executed by firing squads. He is in disguise too so the luxury of being transported somewhere else before being executed is also highly unlikely. He will either be shot on sight or tortured to death. He should have been given a cyanide capsule but the mission was scrabbled together so fast no one had time to get them.

He stops at the corner of the next building showing a sliver of yellow light through the gap in the curtains and the voices of soldiers talking inside. He places the third charge with five minutes and change on the timer and walks on. With three minutes to go, he heads purposefully towards the harbour. With two minutes to go, he makes out the dark shapes of the U-boats in the water. With one minute to go, he reaches the old wooden huts used to store the nets and gear for the fishing boats.

With thirty seconds to go, he shakes his head at the poor level of security within the town. Twenty seconds and he stands in the deep shadows rocking on his heels while his right hand grips the first grenade. Ten seconds left and the first alarm sounds from the night patrol finding the hole in the fence. A shrill whistle taken up and returned by every other guard until the general alarm warbles through the town, rousing every soldier to his feet.

The explosions are not perfectly synchronised but are bloody close. The first detonation is the second charge placed. The second explosion is the dynamite placed by the main gate and the last is the closest, but all are within a few seconds of each other and it only serves to increase the level of confusion and mass panic within the town.

The diversion is under way. The German soldiers think the attack is coming from within the town and it's that misdirection that has to be sustained to give the other commandos the chance to place the charges on the submarines in the dock.

One life to save many. The devastation wrought by the U-boats on the Allied fleet will be significantly slowed with five taken out of service, and the psychological effect against the Germans is a price worth paying. No matter where you are, the British Commandos *will* find you and they *will* kill you.

He draws a deep breath and pulls the pin from the grenade but holds it clamped in his left hand while his right tugs the service pistol free from his waistband. A snort of derision as he glances down at the now live grenade and thinks of the deadly little cyanide pills. Who needs a pill when you've got a grenade?

In the maelstrom of chaos, order is formed. The German army is the enemy but one given respect for the discipline they show, and already the officers are shouting orders.

He steps out of the shadows and walks steadily back towards the town, knowing it is time to earn his nickname.

Two soldiers run towards him still blinking the sleep from their eyes. For a second the disguise works and they pay no heed to the bearded fisherman until he fires from the hip. They both drop with looks of utter shock etched on their young faces. Belly shots. Not immediately fatal and they scream and writhe with burning agony in their guts from the heavy slugs. Harry moves forward, firing twice at point-blank range, instantly killing them. Pistol ditched, grenade from left hand to right and in one smooth motion he turns to launch the grenade into the air towards the town. He grabs the machine guns from the fallen soldiers and, clutching one in each hand, he sets off as the grenade detonates to a chorus of screams and shouts.

He strides into a wide road packed with soldiers forming up as an officer gives curt orders from the high step of a house. Moving sideways across the road Harry opens up, firing both weapons into the dense ranks. Bullets spew from the barrels, shredding men apart. A twitch of aim and the officer is sent spinning from the step with his chest ripped open. They return fire but Harry is away, running into an alley between the buildings. Ditching one of the machine guns, he pulls another grenade, bites the pin out and flings it over his head in the direction he came from.

Harry glances to the sky, longing to hear the roar of the engines. From the alley, he barrels into a four-man patrol running from the opposite direction. He shoots two, feels rather than hears the gun click empty and rams the stock into the head of the third. The fourth spins on the spot, bringing his weapon to aim just as Harry steps in and drives the dagger through his neck. Wrenching the blade free, he punctures the chest again and again as the soldier grips the trigger of the machine gun, firing blindly into the air. He quickly turns to finish the dazed soldier on the ground. Four down and he slinks back into the shadows between the buildings.

Searchlights sweep the town. The sound of heavy-calibre and small-arms fire coming from the harbour front tells Harry the Germans have spotted the fast boats moving towards the U-boats. Explosions erupt with sheets of flame scorching the air as the Germans start throwing grenades into houses, believing there to be multiple attackers.

Harry bursts from the alley into the wide main road of the town, firing at the soldiers running in every direction. He runs behind a building, counting to three before stepping back out to fire into the ranks chasing towards him. Several go down. He moves away, running crouched as he pulls the final grenade from his pocket, bites the pin out, stops, turns and rolls it back to the corner of the house before dropping to lie flat. The soldiers reach the corner to fire round with arms extended before running into the path of the grenade that destroys their small squad.

On his feet and running, firing from the hip while engines roar in the sky and the fires of the town light a path for the pilots of the RAF bombers.

In the harbour, the first U-boat blows with a ground-shaking explosion that brings Harry down again to his stomach. Burning fragments spin in every direction, with the secondary detonations creating a noise that becomes a thing of unimaginable terror. Fires raging, engines screaming, bombs falling, guns firing and the cries of the dying. *You have absolute permission to cause absolute carnage.* Carnage is caused. Devastation is wrought.

The second U-boat explodes. The first bomb dropped from the planes strikes and the chaos of the tiny fishing village perched on the edge of the Norwegian fjord becomes hell with hundreds killed instantly.

A soldier on fire runs past Harry screaming for his mother. Two more chase after him, desperate to save their comrade. Harry fires from the ground, killing the two, but leaving the burning man to draw more of his comrades out. Another bomb drops. Harry grins at the bravery of the pilots flying into the barrage of anti-aircraft fire that must be rattling them in their seats. That grin freezes in horror as the leading plane is hit with an explosion of flame high in the sky and a shriek as the aircraft breaks apart to plummet down through the air.

The third U-boat detonates and this time Harry feels the rain of seawater coming down. Three boats destroyed. The town is already on its knees. No matter what happens now, this is victory. This is testament to training, fortitude and a willingness to hold your nerve. Thousands of Allied lives saved and the ships bringing food and supplies will get to British shores, bringing desperately needed resources to the starving population.

The only problem is Harry is still alive. He was not meant to get this far. No one actually said it was a suicide mission, but it was obvious. The fourth U-boat blows. He grins while trying to think of what to do now. An idea forms. *If you can get to the boats then you might, and I emphasise you* might, *get out.* He goes for it. Grinning with the audacity of the attempt. Running flat out, he jumps over the dead bodies and veers round the still-burning man. Booming anti-aircraft guns firing. Lights strobing the sky. Small arms still give battle and in that noise is the unmistakable sound of Sten guns. British Sten guns firing short, staccato bursts. How the hell the commando teams on the boats are still alive is beyond Harry. The U-boat explosions should have got them. The returning fire from the Germans should have got them. But that noise is unique.

Ditching the German machine gun, he works to strip the heavy coat from his frame, letting it drop in his wake. His arms pump. His feet pound the ground as all around him houses blow apart from bombs falling from the sky. Flames everywhere. People screaming orders and through them all he runs with a wry grin that maybe, just maybe, he can get away and get that pack of smokes Tom owes him.

In the water only two of the commandos' wooden-hulled fast boats remain from a fleet of seven sent in and those two boats whizz back and forth giving the Germans something to aim at while the divers freeze in the water, fixing the charges to the last U-boat.

Harry runs down the steps on to the lower wall and through the Germans kneeling to return fire.

The boat powers through the still waters towards the stern of the U-boat as Harry runs alongside and vaults the gap to land heavily on the metallic flank. He sprints past the jutting tower hardly daring to believe no one has shot him then curses foully as the bullets start pinging near his feet.

A burning desire propels him on. That absolute need to reach the fast boat as it stops to collect the divers who set the charges.

He wants to scream out to wait but every bit of air is needed to fuel his lungs that beat his heart that drives his muscles to keep working. Through tear-streaked eyes caused by the freezing air whipping past his face Harry watches the two divers being pulled from the sea while two more commandos change the magazines on their Sten guns. Only a few metres to go now and he powers on. The first commando completes the magazine change and yanks the bolt back before aiming at the dock and the look of surprise on his face makes Harry want to burst out laughing. The commando pokes his mate in the arm and points dumbly at Harry. The second commando blinks and grins with a slow shake of his head.

'HARRY, YOU FAT BASTARD,' he shouts, waving a pack of cigarettes in the air. 'YOU TIGHT SOD,' he yells, laughing, as he yanks the bolt back on the weapon. 'RUN, YA CRAZY GIT,' he adds, as though Harry isn't shifting at all.

The commandos fire past Harry at the harbour wall, giving what small cover they can. The men urge him on, shouting and waving for Harry to go faster and put some bloody effort into it. The man at the wheel revs the engine, aiming for the corner of the submarine to give Harry a chance to jump in, except the angle is off. The commandos firing don't realise and lay down whatever fire they can muster and Harry watches in horror as the boat starts to veer away in tiny increments that increase the gap. With a rare tingle of fear coursing through his veins Harry leaps from the submarine but the distance is just those few inches too far and even the outstretched arms of the commandos can't reach him as he splashes down into the freezing water of the fjord, which rips the air from his lungs.

Blackness everywhere and the shock strikes him to the core. The shock at missing the boat. The shock at seeing it edge away and the shock of the freezing cold water filling his boots. They become anchors, pulling him down deeper and deeper. His lungs demand air and the transition from hot to instant cold overwhelms his senses. Training kicks in. Don't panic. Lock it down and work to swim up.

With a final kick, his head breaks the surface and he sucks the too cold air into his lungs, which spasm with a violent cough. Something hits him from behind. He jolts away, turning to see the burnt bodies of dead German sailors in every direction.

One last charge to go and he swims through a sea of corpses while his chest tries to cough the rancid water from his lungs. The dull thud of the last explosion reaches his ears and he knows it's too late. A second later and the shock wave hits, sending him surging high on a wave of death.

An instant later, he feels the gut-wrenching change of direction caused by the sucking void trying to fill the hole created by the U-boat surging into the air from the force of the explosion. Rip tides swirling in every direction, spinning him round and pulling him under. Gravity overcomes force and the boat reaches the apex of its climb into the sky before sinking back down as more explosions rip through the hull. When it lands, the displacement expels the water that had been pulled back into the explosive suction, pushing it out with raging tsunamis to the sides. Waves metres high surge over the harbour wall, ripping men from their firing positions as flaming debris rains down.

All sense and meaning are gone. Harry is unable to swim with or against the flow so he relaxes to let the water take him.

It is over. The battle is done. He stood a chance at getting away and if nothing else his mates will go back saying Mad Harry Madden almost made it back for that pack of smokes Tom owed him.

Five U-boats taken out with hundreds of enemy soldiers killed and this night will be remembered forever. Better to die now in the freezing water than be tortured at the hands of the jackboot-wearing SS and executed later by firing squad.

With the booming retorts of the anti-aircraft guns still firing, Harry opens his mouth and purposefully sucks in the retch-inducing water. Instant panic sets in as his body fights to rid his lungs of the liquid, but vomiting only induces an urge to breathe in and Harry keeps his head down, forcing himself to overcome the panic to suck the water in again and again. Images of his life flash through his mind. From a child playing in the woods to the stories of the comet streaking overhead on the day of his birth. Through school, working, dating and then the army. Training in the Scottish Highlands. Running. Swimming. Laughing and fighting.

No regrets now, old chap. No looking back. You did your bit. That's all anyone can ask. Sleep now. Wait for Edith.

Edith. Her face in his mind and that single image is what he holds closest as the warming hands of death start easing him from this mortal world.

'Where is he? Is that him?'

'Christ, there's loads . . . how we gonna find him?'

Edith so fair and small. The way she laughs at the difference in their size. His huge hands dwarfing her dainty fingers.

'Harry? No, it's not him . . . check that one, Malc . . . quick!'

'Which one?'

'No, try that one . . . he's got a beard . . . yes! Harry? Harry?'

Hands grab his shoulders as the beckoning becomes so powerful it cannot be denied, but denied it is and the hands pull him roughly from the warm waters.

'It's him!'

'Get him in . . . *NEIN, ER IST TOT . . .*'

'What did you say, Konrad?'

'I told them he's dead . . . get him in before they realise . . . Harry? Stay quiet . . .'

'It's a bit handy you being German, Konrad.'

'Thanks, Malc.'

'Don't bother you then?'

'What?'

'You know, being here . . .'

'In Norway?'

'Yeah, you know . . . never mind.'

Confusion now. Edith still in his mind but fading away at the English voices speaking German, or are they German voices speaking English? He's pulled over the side of a boat and lands heavily with hands gently slapping his cheeks.

'Here, Konrad, don't hit him . . .'

'I'm trying to rouse him, Malc.'

'He might do what Ben did and I ain't getting beaten up twice in one night. Hang on. Is he even alive? He doesn't look too good.'

'He's going into shock . . . his lungs are full of water . . .'

'Give him that epinephrine, I'll get the defib charged.'

'I'm doing the defib.'

'Just give him the eppy pen. I'll get it charged.'

'We said I was doing the defib . . . the boss said I was doing it.'

'Alright, Konrad! I'll just charge it.'

'Don't zap him, Malcolm.'

'I said alright, Jesus Christ, it's only a defib. Just give him the eppy.'

'Which one is it? This one?'

'That's the sedative. The other one . . . the other one . . . oh my God, Konrad, the bloody other one, you twat.'

'Got it. Right, Harry . . . you're going to feel a burst of energy now. What if he starts fighting, Malc?'

'Just give him the bloody eppy before he dies.'

Whatever residue remains from death beckoning is banished the instant the adrenaline shot is administered and a surge of power and strength floods Harry's battered system. Dying from drowning to unquestionable consciousness in an instant, his mind cannot cope with the transition as he tries to grasp the fleeting image of Edith. He bucks and writhes from a spasm that purges the seawater from his lungs and stomach out through his mouth and nose. Gasping for air, puking, writhing and all the time freezing from the icy water clinging to his clothes.

'Cor, that stuff is strong, Konrad.'

'You ever tried it?'

'Epinephrine? Nah, you?'

'Yeah,' Konrad snorts. 'It's bloody awesome stuff. Get some oxygen into him.'

Harry feels a mask pushed on his face and sweet oxygen flowing down his burning throat as someone starts cutting his clothes off. He tries feebly to bat them away.

'It's okay, Harry. Stay calm. We're here to help you.'

Pulsing with energy but freezing cold, his body starts shivering with the first danger sign of hypothermia and his skin, now exposed to the air, feels like razor blades are being pulled over it.

'Hypodermic shock, where's the thermal blanket?' Konrad says.

'By your feet, dickhead. And it's "hypothermic" not "dermic" . . . "hypodermic" is a needle thing,' Malcolm says.

'Needle thing? Good explanation.'

'At least I know what it is,' Malcolm huffs.

The hands roll him on to his left side and push a thin material over his back before rolling him over on to his right side, cocooning him within the blanket.

'Is it on?' Konrad asks.

'I don't know, I'm driving the bloody boat now,' Malcolm replies.
'It's on. Oh, it feels so nice and warm, my hands are freezing.'

Instant heat surrounds Harry but the shivering continues as the blanket works to raise his core temperature. Not vomiting now, but his lungs hurt with each breath and his throat burns. Exhaustion saps at his mind as the adrenaline burns off. The sweet oxygen and the heat of the blanket lull him down from frenzied consciousness back towards sleep.

'Hey, I think he's alright now,' Konrad says.

'Good work, just got to get the hell out of here now,' Malcolm mutters.

'Harry, can you hear me? Nod if you can hear me. He's nodding.'

'Is he? Wow.'

'Sarcastic twat,' Konrad says.

'You just proved an English bloke can nod when you ask him . . . well done for that.'

'Harry, just rest. We're getting you somewhere safe so don't panic. Everything will be okay. Rest now, Harry. I'll give him the sedative now, Malc. He's out. Christ, that town is ruined. Have you seen it?'

'Seriously?'

'What?' Konrad asks.

'You're asking me if I've seen the town? The town that's just had the shit bombed out of it . . . the town with the massive fires . . . the town we're going away from . . . that town?'

'Shut up.'

'No, really. Did you mean that town or is there another one?'

'Such a sarcastic dick. We ready to go yet?' Konrad asks sulkily.

'Almost, we're still in visual sight. Give it another minute.'

'Mad Harry, eh?' Konrad says. 'Christ, we've got Mad Harry . . . the actual Mad Harry . . . at least I hope it's Mad Harry. Do you think it's Mad Harry? What if we got the wrong one?'

'He's not the wrong man. The program matched him,' Malcolm says.

'No, I mean what if *we* got the wrong one, like . . . picked up the wrong bloke.'

'Oh, I see. We'll just bring him back if we have and do it again.'

'Yeah, I suppose. I'm bringing gloves if we come back again.'

'I'm bringing earplugs so I don't have to listen to you.'

'Pardon?'

'Funny!'

'I try.'

'You're very trying. We're here, you ready?'

Three

2020

'Listen up.' The sergeant waits for the conversations to stop. 'Duties. Smith, front door, Carter and Lamb on the main gate, Pilkington, you're at the rear, and Patel, you're upstairs.' He rattles through the roster, glancing up to get a visual check that each officer understands their posting. 'Nothing new intelligence-wise. It's Friday night so hopefully he will retire to his rooms and you shall have a peaceful and pleasant shift. Patel, you cover the main corridor in addition to upstairs.'

'Will do.'

'Questions? No? Good. Five minutes then we take over from the day shift.' The conversations spark up again as handguns are checked, boots polished, hats brushed, hair tidied, ammunition fed into magazines and utility belts adjusted.

'Safa,' the sergeant calls out, 'a word in my office.' He walks off ignoring the low calls of the other officers as Safa flicks them a middle finger and walks after the sergeant across the corridor and into his office. 'Close the door,' he says, taking a seat.

She does as told and pushes the door closed before standing easy and watching as the sergeant activates the screen on his tablet, thumbs across and hands it over without saying a word. She hesitates for the briefest of seconds then reaches out to take the device.

'Read it,' the sergeant says.

'It's headed confidential,' Safa says, wondering if this is an integrity test.

'It's about you, read it,' he says.

She scrolls down the screen, glancing at the email addresses and dates and times until getting to the main body of text. With a heavy heart she scans the text until reaching the bottom, then blinks and reads it again. Glancing up she notices the grin on the sergeant's face.

'Accepted?' she asks. 'Seriously?'

'That's what it says,' the sergeant replies. 'I tried to stop it going through of course,' he adds wistfully. 'I told them you were the laziest, most bone-idle copper I've ever worked with and you couldn't hit the side of a barn with a shotgun *and* you were rude, obnoxious and just generally shit at your job.'

'So they ignored you then?'

'Everyone bloody ignores me,' he grumbles. 'Might as well not be here for anyone actually listening.'

'Sorry, what did you say?'

'Very funny,' he says, standing up and holding a hand out. 'Well done, Safa.'

'Finally,' she says, taking his hand.

His expression softens. 'Got a month to do,' he says gently. 'I can maybe speed it up by a few days or a week . . .'

'It's fine.'

'It's not fine. It's not bloody fine, Safa.'

'Sarge . . .'

'Go to the federation,' he urges. 'Speak to someone.'

'No.'

'Safa . . .'

'No,' she says with a firm edge to her voice.

'Safa, you know I could do it without your consent.'

'You won't,' she replies bluntly. 'You can't.'

He sags down into the seat, shaking his head as she gently places the tablet down on his desk. 'Such a nasty, vile prick. Go on the gate . . .'

'Sarge, we've been through this.'

'Sick? Go sick for a few weeks.'

'Not a chance.'

'You look sick,' the sergeant says hopefully.

'Sarge,' she says softly. 'I appreciate it but . . . I won't go sick and I can't do the gate or the front door. Three weeks. I can do three weeks.'

He sighs and holds her gaze. 'Okay, but if it gets worse then tell me.'

'With respect,' Safa says, 'I won't. I'd better get upstairs.'

'Yeah. I'll come up as much as I can. Go on.'

Closing the door behind her, she walks down the main corridor and pauses at the full-length mirror by the security door. Black trousers pressed and clean. Boots shiny. Hair scraped back into a tight bun. White shirt and black tie. The pistol on her belt is checked. She turns her radio on before popping the earpiece into her ear with a wishful glance at her ballistic vest hanging from the hook. The officers on the main gate and front door wear their vests but those posted inside are not allowed as it is deemed too aggressive to visiting dignitaries and heads of state.

The vest would have hidden her shape and worked to take away the appearance of femininity. It might have helped, but then the vest would never hide her eyes and face.

Three weeks. I can do three weeks. Twenty-one days, and with days off that makes it fourteen days. Seven of those fourteen days are eight-hour shifts and the other seven are nine-hour shifts, so that makes one hundred and nineteen hours. God, that sounds even worse when you think of it like that. Fourteen days is the one to keep in mind. Just get through it and move on.

Steeling herself, she steps out from the police offices and into the main corridor with her head held high. She takes the service stairs to the top floor and down the corridor to take over from the day-turn officer.

'Sorry,' she whispers. 'Sergeant wanted to see me.'

'It's fine. You okay?'

'Yeah, great. Got the heads-up,' she says quietly.

'Yeah?' the day-turn officer asks as he hands over the duty tablet. 'You going then?'

She nods quickly, swiping the screen to sign in on the device. 'Three weeks, maybe a month.'

'Wow,' Mark whispers. 'Diplomatic to royalty, eh?'

'Yeah,' she says. 'Much going on?'

'Nope, he's due back in an hour.'

'An hour? Is he out tonight?'

'Not heard anything,' Mark says. 'He stays in on Fridays, doesn't he?'

'Normally,' she replies, keeping her tone carefully neutral.

'Oh well, I'd better go. Promised I'd take the kids swimming.'

'Yeah, see you tomorrow.'

The duty starts. The corridor falls into silence. She walks down, checking each door is locked, the windows are secure and, taking the scanner from the discreet cupboard, she checks the side tables and vases for placed listening devices or bugs and goes through the same ritual every officer does at the start of the duty and several times during their shift. When he gets back she will repeat the sweep through the rooms of his apartment and then again as many times as he deems fit.

Transfers are not uncommon. The skill sets are the same. Diplomatic protection officers guard politicians and dignitaries, which is much the same as the royal protection officers guarding the royal family. Transfers within six months of being posted are uncommon though, so her request was initially refused. The problem was not having sufficient reason to request the transfer, but she could not use the real problem, she could never use the real problem. Only the sergeant knew the real problem and even he did not know just how bad it really was. In the end, a discreet suggestion that one of the aides was showing undue attention was enough for the transfer to go through. After the debacle of her one-day posting on the door, they realised it was the safest option to prevent any negative PR.

Safa loves the job. All British police are armed now so being an armed officer is nothing special, but to be a Close Protection Officer is still to be the cream of the elite. She had only been in the job for two years when Holborn happened. She was first on the scene and the last person to see Ben Ryder alive before the train blew him apart. She already knew who Ben Ryder was. Everyone did, and it was because of him she wanted to be a police officer in the first place. Then Holborn happened and that touch of fate or destiny or simple staggering coincidence sparked her desire to achieve the best she could. Besides, she hated investigation-based police work. She was too headstrong, too physical and detested the slow, plodding world of gathering evidence to compile court files and write reports of who did what to who and why.

This world is by far the best. The military and police cross-over skills are fantastic. The knowledge of weapons, strategies, tactics, combat, both armed and unarmed. The level of fitness required, the constant training, house entry, VIP escort, static guarding and high-speed vehicle manoeuvres. It is so far removed from normal policing she is amazed she is still able to call herself a police officer.

Over an hour passes before the update comes through the secure radio into her earpiece. He is on his way back now. She checks her watch. Just gone sixteen hundred hours, which means he will be downstairs for a while until early evening. A few more hours until it starts. The tension increases. In her mind she plays out the dream of going Mad Harry on him. She could physically destroy him in seconds just with her bare hands but that knowledge only makes it worse, that she *could* stop him but she *can't* stop him.

She does not wear make-up now and never uses perfume. Even her deodorant is unscented. A sports bra keeps her chest as flat as possible, the cost of the discomfort weighing off against the reduction in attention. The trousers are good, they hide the shape of her curves, but the tight utility belt only serves to show the narrowness of her waist. Most of the other female officers look severe and imposing with their hair scraped back, but Safa only looks more alluring as it opens the shape of her face and those eyes. Shaped and hued like an Egyptian goddess. The kind of eyes technicians spend hours doctoring photos of models to achieve. All of that and her dusky skin tone and high cheekbones are what made the national press so frenzied on the one and only occasion she'd been posted on the front door.

They had seen female officers before but no one like Safa. Within a few hours she was removed from post as the Internet became inundated with her image. The attention was staggering and threatened to destroy her career within the Diplomatic Protection Squad. Close Protection Officers were faceless, expressionless, devoid-of-emotion sentinels posted to do a serious job. The top brass went into meltdown. They couldn't remove her from the squad as that would render them liable to charges of discrimination, but under the mandates of national security, officer safety and the role profiles of discretion they could impose an order banning her from any forward-facing roles.

She accepted the order as everyone knew what the requirements of the posting were. Two other officers on the squad had already been removed from forward-facing roles. One due to a scar on his face and the other for having complete heterochromia, which was something else picked up by the ever-watchful vultures of the press pack outside. You couldn't really blame them, they were bored and spent hours waiting in a deserted street for something to happen, so the arrival of an armed officer with one blue eye and one green eye gave them something to look at, and photograph, and film, and discuss on websites and rolling twenty-four-hour news channels.

Once posted inside she took the jibes and comments in good humour. The aides, staff, visitors, politicians and even the man himself all recognised her from the coverage but she thought the attention would pass. Only it didn't pass. It got worse.

'Mobile to gate, we're on your channel now for approach.'

'Static gate receiving, waiting order to open.'

'Static control to mobile, that's received and understood. All static units be aware of approach from mobile.'

Safa moves to the stairwell heading down to the ground floor corridor and her position beside the main lift.

'Mobile to static gate, open now please, code alpha alpha nine seven.'

'Code alpha alpha nine seven received, gate opening.'

She listens intently, processing the movements in her mind. The code means there are no issues and a normal approach is expected.

'Mobile to gate, we're through. Comms to you.'

'Static gate to front door, approach to you now, confirm visuals.'

'Front door to gate, visual clear approach to me now. Mobile slowing. Mobile stopped. Door open. Transfer under way, hold positions, he is answering questions from the press. Hold. Hold. Hold. Transfer back under way and safely through front door.'

Safa waits with her left hand closing to activate the press-to-talk switch as the front door swings open and the man himself walks through, waving back at the press.

'Inner post,' Safa transmits softly. *'Inside now, door closing . . . secure.'*

The front door closes with a horde of aides waiting to rush forward the second the view outside is gone. She watches everything, everyone. Eyes sweeping over the aides as they hold tablets and sheets of paper, but more than anything she watches the man himself to see if the smile given to the press fades when the door closes. It doesn't and her heart sinks because to her a good mood is worse than a bad one. He grins round at the aides, making jokes in his blustering, seemingly permanently confused way that won so many millions of people over during the last election.

'Bloody day,' he booms down the corridor. 'Is it clock-off time yet?' he asks a senior aide, who shakes his head gravely.

'No, sir, unfortunately you have one further engagement.'

'One more?' he blusters. 'Good God man, you're working me to death.'

'My apologies, sir,' the senior aide says.

'If I'd known what a taskmaster you were I'd never have taken the bloody job, eh Carmichael? Taskmaster, ain't ya?'

'I am, sir.'

'Does he boss you about too?' he asks a junior aide. 'Bet he does,' he adds, with that wry grin the nation loves so much. 'I bet he's a right mean bastard and a secret Labour voter to boot no doubt. Eh, Carmichael? Vote Labour, do you?'

'The Green Party, sir,' Carmichael replies with a deadpan expression.

'THE GREENS!' he booms round at the smiling sycophants. 'Bloody Greens he says, did you hear him? He said the Greens! Carmichael is a bloody Green . . . what about Mrs Carmichael? She a Green too?'

'Unfortunately not, sir. The good Mrs Carmichael cast her pledge towards the presently incumbent government.'

'A Tory!' he shouts with victory. 'Pass on my heartfelt thanks to your good lady wife, Carmichael, and tell her I said her husband is a bloody evil taskmaster.'

'Will do, sir.'

'What have we got left then?' he asks with a heavy theatrical sigh.

'Private business, sir,' Carmichael replies, knowing not to give the identity of the caller away in a corridor full of aides.

'Which one?'

'Sir.' Carmichael passes the tablet over, taking care to angle the screen solely towards his boss.

'Ah right,' he says, reading the screen. 'How long?'

'Ten minutes, sir.'

'Right, bring him straight down and can someone get me a mug of tea please?'

He sweeps past, ignoring Safa, who in turn ignores the look of utter distaste sent her way from Carmichael. Voices clamour as the aides rush down the corridor and past the base of the famous yellow stairs.

'Safa to static control, corridor clear.'

'Understood.'

She waits, standing easy next to the lift as aides and staff bustle about. One more meeting to go. With luck it will be a long one and delay him finishing work for the evening.

'Gate to front door, private business caller en route to you. Search complete and negative.'

'Front door received, visual on the private business caller now. Confirm white male, dark hair, blue suit with dark red tie.'

'Gate to front door, confirm visuals. Yes yes.'

'Front door receiving caller now, transfer under way. Caller at the door.'

An aide bustles past Safa towards the door, pausing only to straighten his suit and adopt a suitable countenance.

'Good evening, sir. Please do come in.' The aide holds the door open just enough for the man to step through. 'Follow me.' The aide moves off down the corridor as Safa sweeps her eyes over the private business caller.

Safa looks ahead until he has gone past and resumes the visual inspection, now examining his back, her eyes running over the folds of his clothes looking for anything that should not be there.

'Safa to control, private business caller inside.'

'Understood.'

She waits. That's all this job is really. Waiting. Lots of waiting and watching. The dread builds. Tension in her shoulders, which she rolls gently. Every second that goes by is a second closer to him coming down to the lift and the evening of utter shit that lies ahead. *Fourteen days. Just fourteen days.*

She cannot do a thing to stop it or make it not happen. No one would listen. The man is adored by tens of millions with a popularity not known since Churchill during the war. Every little factor has been taken into account. She is British by birth but born to an Egyptian mother and an Indian father. She is young and female. She is physically beautiful and a police officer on a salary that will never really be that high. In contrast, he is the Prime Minister. Enough said. There is no evidence and there never will be. The only option is to get away and that option is under way now. Fourteen days and she will be protecting the royals instead. Old, infirm, rude and incredibly wealthy, but it is not here and that is all that matters.

'Pilkington to Safa, private business caller towards you for exit.'

'Safa received.'

The aide comes first, leading the way with the man walking behind. The man smiles at Safa as he ventures down the corridor towards the door and nods politely as he passes. She stares back without expression.

'Have a good evening, sir,' the aide gushes as the man walks through the opened front door.

'Safa to front door, private business caller with you.'

'Front door received, caller on way to gate.'

'Gate received, visual on caller now.'

A gentle rise in her heart rate and her stomach tenses. Eyes forward. Firm and resolute. She steels herself in readiness.

The Prime Minister appears within a few minutes. Blustering along the corridor with Carmichael following in his wake and a muted conversation under way. They stop to talk quietly before Carmichael nods and walks off.

Exhaling noisily through his nose, the Prime Minister walks briskly to the lift and waits for Safa to key the code. A visual check inside and she steps aside, letting him enter before walking in after him. The doors close with a gentle hiss, sealing them into the dead zone. No electronics will work in the lift. No CCTV. No audio devices and even her radio will not transmit. After the bunker, the lift is one of the most secure rooms within the building. A gentle vibration and the lift starts to ascend and she stares ahead, praying they go straight to the top, but the hand moves past her shoulder and presses the button, bringing the lift to a gentle stop between floors.

'How are you, Safa?' he asks gently.

'Fine, sir,' she replies dully.

'Friday night.' He breathes the words out, letting the back of his hand press against the material of her trousers with just enough pressure for her to feel it. His breathing quavers. He steps closer, exhaling a blast of air on the back of her neck. She stares ahead with thinly pursed lips and her left eyelid strums with the revulsion running through her body. 'You're transferring,' he says, and her stomach tightens again. 'Leaving me,' he breathes into her ear. 'I could block it. You know that. I'm the Prime Minister. I can do anything.' He draws the words out and steps closer. 'Raghead.' His mouth hovers so close to her ear. 'Dirty raghead.' His breathing gets faster with his excited state. 'My raghead wants to leave, does she?'

She could beg but that's what he wants. She could tear him apart and beat him to a pulp but she would be shot on sight. She could shoot him, then herself, but that would shame every member of her family, as no one would ever know why. She cannot tell anyone or do anything so she stares ahead with her left eyelid beating a drum that only gets worse when she feels his erection pressing into her hip.

'Can you feel that, raghead?' He exhales the words, bringing a hand up to her ribs. 'I can block your transfer . . .' The hand rises an inch. 'I can deport you and your raghead family . . .' The hand brushes over her shirt as it goes up another inch. 'Maybe the police will find something in your father's office.' The tip of the forefinger on his right hand presses against the bottom of her sports bra. 'My dirty little raghead . . .'

It consumed her life. She did not go out and never wore make-up. She did not date but wore baggy clothes and felt shame towards herself and her family. The pride they all had at the job she achieved that so quickly turned into the worst nightmare imaginable. She never cried or wept but locked it down inside and kept coming to work to protect the man who did this to her.

'Undo them.' His trembling breath seeps into her ear. 'Quickly.' She swallows, knowing that any option of doing anything other than she is told bears a consequence too severe to contemplate.

'Now.' He hisses the word out and her hands lift to work at the buttons of her white shirt. He never does it himself. He never touches her for fear of leaving any DNA trace that could not be accounted for. If she delays he gets angry, and his power is too great to risk testing him. He knows everything about her. The universities her father and mother teach at. The careers of her brother and sister.

'Wider . . .' He peers over her shoulder, staring through the gap in her shirt to the plain white sports bra underneath. His breathing gets faster as the stiffness against her backside pushes harder.

Over the last six months she's considered every angle. That maybe his trousers pressing into hers like this would leave trace fibres. They would but it would never be enough to show anything other than normal transference of people moving in close proximity to each other.

'Whore.' The blunt voice at normal volume makes her flinch visibly. 'Get dressed,' he sneers, reaching past to press the button on the lift, and she rushes with hurried hands to re-clasp the buttons on her shirt. He steps back, humming to himself as the lift comes to a stop and the doors open.

'Remember what I said,' he whispers behind her as she gets to the door to his apartment rooms. She does not reply but unlocks the door and enters first with a visual sweep through the bathroom, kitchen, dressing room and bedroom.

'Clear, sir,' she reports dully.

'Thank you, constable.' He nods affably. 'A sterling effort as always. Dismissed.'

She walks towards the door, passing by his shoulder as he whispers quietly, 'Think about it.'

He did not need to whisper and he did not need the pretence of acting normally either. His apartment is almost as secure as the lift.

Outside she transmits to control that he is within his apartment. The message is relayed to a house of staff breathing a sigh of relief.

The evening draws out. An aide brings food. A silver tray of the Prime Minister's favourite fish and chips. She is brought coffee and relieved by the sergeant for a toilet break, but in such close proximity to his apartment they speak only muted words of a professional nature.

The shift in time heralds the greatest danger. The meal has been served. The toilet break given and with nothing else planned, she knows he will be in there, drinking, scheming, planning. She stares at the door, tensing at every sound from within. The shadows grow longer, deeper, and the soft glow lamps come on at the appointed time. *Fourteen days. Fourteen days.* She repeats it over and over. Imagining herself working within the royal households and away from here. She shows no visible reaction when the door to his apartment opens.

'Can you do a bug sweep, please,' the affable voice calls out.

'Sir.' She moves to the cupboard and takes the long wand, forcing herself to take a deep breath and hold steadfast with courage in the face of adversity. He will not beat her. He will not win. *Fourteen days.* 'Sir, which rooms?' she asks, smelling the whisky in the air.

He turns with a smile. 'All of them, please.'

She nods and starts in the kitchen. Sweeping the device over every surface and object, knowing it will detect anything transmitting or receiving a signal. With the kitchen clear, she walks into the bathroom, catching sight of him in his study, sitting at his desk and staring at the multiple computer monitors. The bathroom is abject luxury. A deep corner bath fitted with hydromassage jets and a wet room bigger than the living room of her own tiny flat. All clear, and she moves out and decides swiftly to do his bedroom while he is in the study. Everything clean and tidy. The drawing room clear. The lounge area clear and with the last room to go she freezes at the sight of his half-erect penis clearly visible through the open flies of his trousers while he stares at the monitors as though unaware of his appendage on display.

Fourteen days. You cannot do anything. He is the Prime Minister. You are a police constable.

'Sir?' she calls out, forcing her tone to remain neutral.

'Finished?' he asks, still staring at the monitors.

'Yes, sir.'

'Really?' he asks lightly. 'Have you done in here?'

She hesitates, thereby passing tiny measures of victory his way. 'No, I have not,' she says quickly.

'Better do it then,' he says thoughtfully, picking his glass tumbler up to take a big mouthful of the amber liquid.

She enters with a firm step and her hands show no tremble as she commences the security check. Working down the wall, checking the frames of the paintings and prints on the walls. The lamps on the tabletops, the underside of the surfaces and working round towards the desk. A glance over and her left eyelid flits at the four monitors showing images of naked Arabic-looking women. Her mind processes fast with the possibility of finally having evidence then realises that his computer will be one of the most secure in the world. The Prime Minister can access anything without leaving a trace and anyway, if the Prime Minister wants to wank at porn then he can, everyone else does it.

She has to scan the desk. She swallows, gripping the wand.

'Sir, the desk?'

'Yep.' His voice is hoarse and rough with anticipation. What did he think? That she would see the images and be so turned on she would throw herself at him? That the sight of his cock would make her drop down and open her legs? He is not married but famously single and quite possibly the most eligible bachelor in the world. He is relatively young too, not yet fifty.

Oh God, he is erect now. Fully hard with the thing standing to attention in his lap. He smiles, turning his head with a slowly spreading grin. 'Am I in your way?' he rasps and clears his throat with a chuckle. 'Too much whisky,' he explains. 'Want me to move back?'

'If you don't mind, sir.' Forcing that neutral tone is near on impossible but she does it. Standing resolute as he pushes the wheeled chair back a few inches and leans back with his hands behind his head while opening his legs a few inches as though proudly displaying his swollen member.

She kneels down, working the wand along the desk legs, the underside and the external casing of the computer, freezing when he shifts position and resuming when he goes still again.

She works from bottom to top, trying to ignore the erotic images of dusky-skinned women.

'They look a bit like you,' he says pleasantly and waits as though expecting a reply. 'That one does,' he adds, leaning forward to press a manicured finger against the screen on the left. 'Don't you think?'

She does not reply. To verbalise anything now would be to give away her fear.

'I said don't you think?' he asks again. 'That one.' He jabs the screen. 'Looks like you . . . do you know her?'

Still she does not reply but works the back of the monitors.

'Figured you all know each other,' he says with the faintest of slur to his words. 'I'm not racist though,' he adds quickly. 'Love all the ragheads,' he sputters with a laugh and stands up. She holds perfectly still with the wand an inch from the rear of the last monitor and his form in her peripheral vision.

'I can have the police find extremist material in your father's office,' he says quickly. 'He'll be arrested and questioned under terrorism laws.

A leak will take place telling the media that your family are linked to Islamic extremism . . . do you understand?'

Her heart hammers in her chest and her mouth goes dry. She swallows with a visual show of her nerves and the knuckles on the hand holding the wand go white.

Later, when the investigation concludes, the report will show that the fast jet entered UK airspace on a planned flight path provided to the authorities. The report will detail how the scanning stations did not detect anything of concern because the jet engines did not show a military signature, thereby causing the aircraft to be perceived as civilian.

'You carry gloves. Put them on,' he orders, pulling a pair of tight-fitting latex gloves from his pocket.

The report will detail how a crude missile system was fitted to the executive jet with a basic laser guiding system operated by the pilot on line of sight.

She has no choice. The threat is real and everyone knows that behind the genial, blustering persona there is a core of ice running through the Prime Minister.

The investigation will reveal the jet descended from fifteen thousand feet to five thousand and finally down to two thousand feet as it thundered towards the capital. It will detail that the alarms sounded within Heathrow, Gatwick and Stansted, who all received the alerts and tried desperately to make contact with the aircraft they all assumed was plummeting from the sky.

His gloves are tight. Carefully chosen to prevent transference of DNA but to be tight enough and thin enough for him to feel every ridge and bump of her flesh. Her own gloves are not that carefully chosen and simply taken from the boxes in the first aid room. *You do what it takes to protect your family. You do what it takes to get by in this world.* He will not hurt her, as any injury will show, so she pulls the gloves on and finally lets the utter distaste show on her face, but that only feeds his perception of power gained. He nods at her shirt. An order given without words required. She complies, glaring at him balefully while working to open the buttons, her movements not hesitant now but forceful and determined. Courage in the face of adversity.

The air traffic controllers fail to make contact and, as dictated by protocol, they send an emergency message to the police, fire and ambulance services of Greater London as they work to track the likely impact point of the jet they still believe is coming down for a crash landing. When the final destination shows Downing Street to be the likely crash site the only response left is to alert the RAF, who scramble their own rapid-response fighter jets.

Her shirt is undone. The sports bra showing clearly. He touches himself with an almost drunk look on his face, which flushes red from the lust surging through his body. He takes a square packet from his pocket, bites the corner open and pulls out the condom, which he fits with shaking hands and eyes that cling to the sight of her.

He nods again, another order given, and she stands almost to attention, grips the bottom of her sports bra and tugs it up to show her breasts. He gasps with lust and steps closer, a fumbling glove-covered hand reaching out to grab and squeeze. She glares at him, unmoving, unflinching, uncowering.

The rapid-response fighter planes, as fast, as modern, as agile and as capable as they are, cannot bend time and space and still have to rely on human beings running from mess rooms to climb into cockpits that have to be sealed while they press physical buttons and prepare for take-off. It takes only a moment but every second delayed sees the incoming jet holding that flight path as the pilot scans the ground ahead for the target premises.

It is timed perfectly and the unmarked white vans nearby are parked in the darkness while the men within clutch their assault rifles to their chests. It has been two years in the planning and is the most sophisticated attack ever to strike at the heart of British politics.

What the report will not reveal is that at the time of the attack, the Prime Minister was in his private study of his private apartment drunk on whisky while sexually assaulting the armed female police officer assigned to protect his life. His right hand pumping and his left hand squeezing while his eyes dropped down to the belt on her waist.

The pilot gains visual sight. The laser system activates. The order is given for her trousers to be pulled down. The men in the vans tense. The pilot locks on. Her hands move to her belt as the realisation of the situation worsens. The laser holds steady. The thumb presses on the fire button, releasing the lock, which fires the ignition on the missile, which blasts away from the jet to roar across the sky. Every alarm in Downing Street screams out as the attack is finally realised. Drunk on lust, the Prime Minister's eyes stay fixed on her hands gripping the clasp of her utility belt.

The piercing whine reaches her ears. Every second of training kicks in as she lunges forward, taking him to the floor to cover him with her own body as the missile strikes the wall just above the front door. Eviscerating the guard standing outside. The night-turn press pack are blasted apart and reduced to molecular form.

She holds him down amidst the rumble of the house. A booming explosion rips the air apart. Everything shaking and vibrating and the Prime Minister screaming in fear as Safa glares round at the pictures falling from the walls and the tables juddering across the floor. Her earpiece fills with voices that go unheard from the noise of the screams and the fireball ripping through the ground floor. On her feet, she grabs his arm, heaving him up and forcing him bodily across to the front door of the apartment. Pistol out. She leans into the corridor, checking the view before forcing the cowering politician down the corridor to the stairwell door.

A hole in the front wall. The door is gone. The windows obliterated with smoke billowing out and flames licking high. The plane has already gone, screaming away into the night as two RAF jets thunder overhead giving chase and already locking on to the aircraft and the pilot giving prayer inside.

The vans start with powerful engines roaring to life. The lead van goes first, building speed with the others. A reinforced chassis with oversized bull bars on the front. The driver grips the wheel behind the bulletproof glass that is peppered with shots from the single surviving officer at the main gate. Her colleague lies dead with his skull fractured from the house brick sent sailing through the air from the missile strike.

The van hits the gate. The second van hits the first and together they power forward while the men inside cling to the grab handles welded to the ceilings. The gates give way, screaming in agony from the twisted metal forced apart. The engines of the vans rising in pitch and the gates give enough for the driver of the first van to give an order. Both vans reverse and the doors slam open to black-clothed figures wearing respirators dropping down to run sprinting through the gap formed in the gates with weapons already up and aiming.

At the top of the stairwell, Safa holds position, listening intently to the orders on the radio squawking in her ear. The systems are failing. Officers are dead but more are on their way. She listens to Pilkington clambering through the debris of the main corridor on the ground floor telling everyone the front wall is breached and giving calm updates as he fires one-handed at the incoming figures, who slay him on the spot with the distinct clatter of assault rifles.

The Prime Minister whimpers, cowering on the ground behind her with his lust as forgotten as his now flaccid penis still hanging free of his trousers as Safa takes advantage of the wait for orders to do her shirt buttons up.

'Safa . . . BASEMENT.'

'On it,' she replies, thumbing the press-to-talk button. 'On your feet now.' She grabs the politician by the arm, heaving him to his feet. 'Down to the basement.'

He whimpers, crying like a child as she harries him down the flights of stairs, working to get ahead of him as they pass the doors to the middle floor. Smoke thick in the air, chemicals too. Fires burning. Gunshots. Heavy-calibre assault rifles and suddenly the nine-millimetre pistol in her hands feels very small. She gets him safely past the middle floor and heads down for the total security of the bunker, built to withstand a direct cruise missile strike.

On the ground floor, the black-clad figures move like professional soldiers. Two pacing forward to hold at doorways as two more sweep into the rooms, opening fire as they go and pausing only to place the explosives pulled from their tac vests. Opposition is given, with police officers firing pistols and submachine guns drawn from the armoury. One attacker is shot through the head but the officer is shredded within a split second by several assault rifles tearing him apart. The emergency lights flicker and strobe, bathing the rooms in a flashing red glow mixed with the orange of the flames still blazing at the front of the building.

In the stairwell, Safa listens to the transmissions of the other officers. *The attackers are professional. They are firing burst shots and covering each other. Multiple fatalities. One attacker killed. Officers down. Officers down.*

She rushes past the ground floor door knowing the control room would have initiated the locking mechanism on the stairwell doors but not knowing the figures on the other side are placing explosive charges round the frame. On the next flight down towards the bunker, she hears the sizzle before the explosion and ducks down as the door behind her blows apart. The Prime Minister screams again with his hands covering his head and sinks into the corner of the stairwell with a jet of piss squirting down his trousers.

Safa holds position, aiming with a double-handed grip and waiting for the first charging body to come through the ruined door. Firing twice and the rounds from her pistol slam the man back against the wall. She plants another shot in his head and twitches to fire at the next one rushing in. Her face a mask of focus and concentration. Two down, shot and killed outright. Voices from the corridor shouting orders in a language she does not know. A shout and an object rolls in. She grabs it quickly, throws it back and drops as the grenade detonates in the packed enclosure. An advantage taken and she presses the attack home, leaning round the ruined doorway to empty her magazine into the screaming bodies in the corridor beyond.

Counting the shots, she knows when the last bullet is fired and ducks back to eject the magazine from the grip and ram a fresh one home. Her eyes glance down at the assault rifle next to the fallen body and the second the idea forms so the weapon is grabbed. Military grade, high specification. Expensive hardware designed and built for professional soldiers. In training they teach not to use dropped weapons as you can never be sure if the weapon has been properly maintained, but right now she needs more than a nine-mill pistol can give. She checks the rifle magazine and slams it back in. She test fires once into the screaming body of a black-clad man. With the recoil and weight noted, she shoulders the weapon and runs back down the stairs, gripping the screaming Prime Minister by his hair. *If the shit hits the fan it doesn't matter how you do it but get him into that basement.*

At the bottom, she shoves the Prime Minister against the steel door of the bunker and holds position with the rifle pointing back up the stairs. A camera checks the view, the door opens to the duty military intelligence staff clutching their own sidearms. She shoves the crying man inside as the stairwell behind is sprayed with automatic fire. Turning quickly, she fires up and paces a step forward to keep the attackers suppressed. The door closes behind her with the brutality of protocol. The Prime Minister is safe. Nothing will get through that door and into the bunker. She glances back with barely a reaction showing on her face but knowing inside that the soldiers would have seen the Prime Minister crying like a baby and covered in piss with his dick hanging out. Worth it. So worth it.

She goes up, trained to defend but designed to attack. One foot after the other. Rising to meet the threat. Intense heat wafts down from the blaze burning through the house. The acrid smoke burns her eyes. She ducks down at the rounds ricocheting on the walls ahead and waits prone on the stairs for the next attacker to come into view. She fires the heavy rounds up into his stomach and chest, sending him staggering back. On her feet and she executes him with a shot to the head and tugs a magazine free from his belt to replace the one in her weapon. Up again she goes, ascending while aiming for the ground floor door of the stairwell with a decision made to hold that position until reinforcements can arrive. The radio traffic blasts through her ear. Officers still being killed and a few confirmed kills on the attackers but many more still at large.

She reaches the ruined door of the ground floor and presses her back against the wall at the same instant as two black-clothed men clutching assault rifles burst through. She drops her assault rifle and lunges between them, knowing their own forms and big guns will hamper their movement. She throat punches one and slams her elbow into the face of the other. They both stagger from the ferocity of the attack that she presses home. Grabbing the bulging section of the respirator of the closest she pulls down hard, making him bend over at the waist and using her knee to slam up into his head while forcing him round in a circle into his comrade, pressing them both into the wall.

She anticipates the moment the bent-over attacker surges up and moves round his body, getting her right arm across his throat. With a grunt she tenses and snaps viciously to the right, breaking his neck. A step away as she draws her pistol, turns and fires into the one just pushing off from the wall. He goes back from the power of the rounds slamming into his chest. She twitch aims to fire one through his head, killing him instantly. Movement in her peripheral vision. She adjusts to aim and fire into the doorway at the black-clad figure charging through.

'REAR GARDEN,' the sergeant's voice screams in her ear with gunshots in the background. Safa moves out from the doorway, striding down the smoke-filled corridor, stepping on and over the bodies. *'MULTIPLE TARGETS . . . I'M HIT . . . I'M HIT . . .'*

She grabs a new magazine from a body, reloads and runs towards the firefight in the enclosed rear garden. Pistols, submachine guns and assault rifles. Grenades exploding. Flames burning. Smoke billowing. Staff dead in every doorway and room. Carmichael slumped down with the top of his head missing.

Safa pauses outside the room leading to the rear garden. Two men ahead of her kneeling in a doorway firing into the garden. Both of them dressed in black and she hesitates, not knowing if they are attackers or the first response teams. One of them turns, showing the respirator on his face. She opens fire, killing them both instantly. She holds still for a second then runs to take their position at the doorway with bullets slamming into the walls.

Chaos everywhere, people screaming in pain, bloodstains on the ground and smeared up the walls. The cacophony of noise drowns out the rushed words coming over the radio. She aims into the garden, scanning left and right as her eyes work to adjust from the red flashing lights within to the darkness outside.

'Safa?' She turns quickly to see two uniformed police officers running towards her but recognising neither of them. Both of them with bruised faces and one has a thin strip of white material across his recently broken nose.

'GET DOWN,' she shouts, waving for them to take cover.

'Safa Patel?' one of them asks, dropping to his knees beside the door.

'Which division?' she barks at them, noticing neither of them are armed and turning back to face the garden. She locks aim on a black-clothed figure running a few metres away and guns him down as the two new officers cower back from the noise of the rifle.

'Are you Safa Patel?'

'Yes,' she snaps. 'Which division are you from? Shit . . .' She flinches at the rounds slamming into the wall and frame. She fires back but the weight of the attack coming at her is too great. The attackers are too many and advancing while throwing grenades and firing with controlled bursts.

'GO BACK,' she shouts at the two unarmed officers. 'GET OUT . . .'

They are winning. Christ, the attackers are winning. Her heart sinks at the sight of them. So many left and still they fire, killing anything that opposes them. Gunfire behind her at the front of the house and more attackers shooting towards the gate and the officers trying to get inside the street. Trapped. No way out. The Prime Minister is safe in the bunker below but anyone left up here is dead.

'Go up the stairwell and into the lift,' she says to the two men, not thinking where they came from or how they got into the house. She grabs another magazine from one of the bodies. 'Stop it between floors . . . they'll never get you there . . . Go,' she spits when they don't move.

'Okay,' the police officer with the white strip across his nose says with a glance to the other one. 'Er . . . you going to be okay here?' He edges closer as though trying to peer through the door.

'Just bloody go,' she shouts. 'Now . . . go . . . they're coming . . .'

'Sorry.' The man whips an arm out, jabbing a needle into her neck before pulling her down. 'Now, Konrad,' he shouts.

The other man nods, pulling an object from his pocket. He yanks a pin out and throws it through the doorway, a split second later the flash-bang explodes with a sustained burning phosphorous light, blinding everyone in the garden. Safa fights to free herself, kicking and bucking, but the man is heavy.

'Stay calm, Safa,' Malcolm urges. 'Please, we're here to help.'

'Fuck off.' She fights to tug her pistol free but finds a hand gripping her wrist so headbutts up instead and slams into his already broken nose, which bursts apart with a shower of blood.

'My bloody nose!' Malcolm cries out as hard fists start raining punches into the sides and back of his head. 'Bloody hell, she hits hard . . .'

The spreading warmth permeates through her body from the neck to the shoulders and down her arms and torso and into her legs. She feels herself slowing but fights it, hitting, kicking, punching, biting, gouging, and all the time trying to get her pistol free.

'This is worse than Ben,' Malcolm sobs as he takes another beating.

'They're coming back,' Konrad shouts, throwing another flash-bang into the garden. 'Don't look outside, Malc.'

'Eh? OH MY GOD THAT'S SO BRIGHT.'

'I said don't look outside.'

'I can't see a sodding thing,' Malcolm bleats.

'You bloody idiot,' Konrad groans.

'Jab her again,' Malcolm shouts as his head gets another hard punch. 'She's taking longer than Ben . . .'

'You can fuck off, Malc, if you think I'm going near her.'

'Just bloody jab her . . .'

Safa bucks and writhes but the drug is strong and the adrenaline released soon pumps it round her body that starts to sag and soften as the blows become ineffective.

'Oh thank God,' Malcolm says as the woman underneath him starts going limp. 'Drag her, quickly . . .'

'I'd love to,' Konrad hisses, 'but your fat arse is on top of her.'

'I'm bloody blind,' Malcolm points out.

'Whose fault is that? I said don't look outside . . . I said that . . . I said don't look outside . . .'

'Just get her up before they blow the house,' Malcolm says, rolling off Safa. 'How long have we got?'

'Less than a minute,' Konrad says then yelps and ducks as the room is sprayed with bullets. 'STOP IT YOU BASTARDS,' Konrad shouts and chucks another flash-bang into the garden, which explodes with phosphorous light blazing into the air. 'Been beaten up and got bloody freezing in NORWAY AND NOW YOU'RE SHOOTING AT US . . .'

'Konrad, that's not helping, is it?' Malcolm says, trying to squint through eyes still hurting from the flash-bang.

'Made me feel better,' Konrad mutters. 'Right, come on then . . .'

'That would be fine if I could actually see anything . . . and my nose is broken again . . .'

'God, you whine so much!'

The last sensation Safa feels is being dragged by two men bickering. She tries to open her eyes and gains a fraction of a view that is filled with blue light before the drugs take hold and she sinks down into oblivion.

The black-clad figures press the attack home, running in to find no one there. An order given and as one they run to the front and clamber through the debris into the street, running towards the gate and the firefight taking place. With greater numbers and higher-powered weapons they force the newly arrived police officers at the gate to fall back and once a safe distance has been gained a button on a device is pressed and the terraced house above the bunker holding the Prime Minister detonates, torn apart by the combined explosive forces of the charges set within. Every corpse inside the house is obliterated. Walls are blown out and floors collapse as the fireball spreads down the street giving day to night while the Prime Minister whimpers in his bunker covered in his own piss, surrounded by military personnel wondering if they should tell him his dick is out.

Four

Konrad and Malcolm walk stiffly down the concrete corridor and pause outside the door. Both of them covered in bruises with split lips, black eyes and swollen faces.

'Ah,' Roland says, rushing to the doorway on hearing their shuffling feet. 'How did it go?'

'How did it go,' Konrad mutters, looking away.

'Come in, chaps,' Roland says, moving back into the room dominated by a huge rough-hewn wooden desk. 'Safa Patel?' he asks, staring from one to the other.

'In her room,' Malcolm says, wincing at the pain caused in his mouth when he speaks.

'Really?' Roland asks, his face showing genuine delight. 'All three in one night. How marvellous! My, we have been busy, haven't we?'

'Some of us have,' Konrad mutters again.

'Yes,' Roland says slowly while shaking his head as though not quite believing it. 'So how did it go?'

'Go?' Malcolm asks, glancing at Konrad. 'Well, we got her here.'

'No no, did she put up a fight?' Roland asks eagerly.

'Seriously?' Konrad asks. 'Have you seen our faces?'

'I have and it's wonderful,' Roland announces, then stops at the thunderous looks coming back. 'I mean yes, yes of course I have and, er, well chaps. I am indebted to you. Indeed I am. I would have loved to have been there for Harry and Safa but, well, yes.' He rocks back and forth on his heels, placing his hands behind his back to look serious and studied. 'But all three!' he booms again with a big smile. 'So? Did Safa fight you did she?'

'Yes,' Malcolm replies flatly.

'How much?' Roland asks.

'Loads,' Konrad says as flatly as Malcolm.

'Well now,' Roland says, grinning at both of them. 'Very well done, chaps.'

'Boss,' Malcolm says with a worried glance at Konrad. 'Er, what you gonna do when they wake up?'

'Pardon?' Roland asks.

'They ain't gonna be happy are they?' Malcolm says.

'And we've already had the shit beaten out of us,' Konrad adds.

'You didn't get your nose broke,' Malcolm mutters.

'You didn't get your nose broke,' Konrad mimics.

'Twat,' Malcolm huffs, then looks at Roland. 'They're hard as nails . . . we've kidnapped 'em, pumped 'em full of drugs and we really ain't gonna stop 'em if all three go nuts.'

'Nuts?' Roland asks, smoothing his dark hair back.

Malcolm looks at Konrad, who looks back at Malcolm. 'Have you thought this through?' Konrad asks.

'Of course I have,' Roland replies brusquely. 'But yes, I will admit there is an element of, er, well, winging it as we go . . .'

'We?' Konrad asks.

'Hmmm,' Roland says. 'I was rather thinking they would wake up and I would explain what has happened and . . . well . . . that would be that . . . I mean, they are Harry Madden, Ben Ryder and Safa Patel and the program has matched them for honour and integrity as well as bravery and courage.'

'No,' Malcolm says quickly.

'No?' Roland asks.

'No,' Konrad says firmly. 'You're gonna need more men.'

'More men?' Roland asks with a look of alarm.

'In case they go nuts,' Konrad says.

'*When* they go nuts, not *if*,' Malcolm adds.

'Right. More men, eh?' Roland says, grimacing at the prospect. 'Er, perhaps you chaps could find some?'

The two men exchange a look. 'Fine,' Konrad groans.

'Great!' Roland booms. 'Get some big ones.'

'Big ones,' Konrad says with an exhausted nod.

'But don't tell them what . . .'

'Yes, boss,' Malcolm sighs. 'Don't tell them anything. We know.'

'They can't see the door thing,' Roland says.

'Door thing,' Konrad mutters.

'Portal,' Malcolm says.

'Yes, that portal door thing. They can't see it . . . or outside! Christ, don't show them outside.'

'We won't.'

'Offer them money,' Roland says, holding a finger up.

'Well, they ain't gonna work for free,' Konrad says.

'But not too much money,' Roland adds quickly with a look of panic. He stares at the two bruised men. 'Well, off you go then.'

'What, now?' Konrad asks.

'We've only just got back with Safa,' Malcolm says.

'But they might wake up and go nuts,' Roland says. 'We need some big men here.'

'Yes, boss,' Malcolm sighs again.

'Great stuff,' Roland says. 'Well done chaps!'

Five

Three austere sterile rooms. Concrete walls. Concrete floors and ceilings. A single metal-framed bed in each room. Two of the rooms have metal shutters indicating the placement of a window.

Ben stirs, sighing and breathing heavily. 'Can you turn the light off please?' he mutters, squeezing his lids closed from the glaring light of the single bulb hanging from the ceiling.

Harry opens his eyes and closes them immediately, waiting for the retina burn to pass before trying again with tiny increments to lessen the pain and increase the transition from darkness to light.

Safa wakes and immediately rolls over to bury her head in the pillow at the glaring light as she becomes acutely aware of the pounding headache in the back of her skull.

Ben tries again and slowly peers round at the room. He must be in a hospital. A really horrible hospital run by stretched staff too busy to actually provide care for their patients. Maybe if they bought lower-wattage bulbs they would have enough money left to pay nurses. These things could illuminate a football pitch.

Harry looks round his room too. Noticing the shutter and the door first. He checks his own body for injuries, twitching limbs and tensing muscles to see if anything is broken. He listens too. He must be in a German camp. The Boche must have dragged him from the water and brought him to wherever this is. They'll know he is a commando from what happened in the fjord. He wipes his nose with the back of his hand that comes away with a smear of blood. His head is pounding. It feels like when he was training to dive and he came to surface too fast from deep water. He must have sunk down deeper than he realised in the fjord.

Safa stares round at her cell. It must be a cell. There is no doubt in her mind that it is a cell. Bare concrete walls, floor and ceiling. A single metal-framed bed and a single solid, metal-riveted door. No tables. No obvious cameras. No alarm cords or tablet screens anywhere. They think she had a part in it. The Prime Minister must have ordered her to be detained under the terrorism laws. His threat was real. She grips the rising panic and forces it back down as another possibility presents itself. What if the attackers got her? What if she is being held by the terrorists ready to be killed and put on the Internet?

Ben feels like shit. His head is pounding and he has to forcibly peel his tongue from the roof of his dry mouth. His throat hurts too. He checks to see if he is injured and wiggles his hands, legs, arms and feet but everything feels okay. Then he remembers that people who lose limbs still feel the lost limb and thinks maybe he is limbless and feeling ghost limbs. He pushes the blanket off, a weird synthetic thing, and looks down at the grey tracksuit covering his seemingly intact body. Concrete walls? Grey tracksuit? Is he in prison? He looks again at the shutters on the wall and over to the solid metal door with a fresh worry pushing into his mind.

Harry fingers the material of his tracksuit, nodding to himself at the quality of the garment. It feels like cotton but it's not cotton. It's thin, soft and strong too. He does the same with the blanket, rubbing it between his thumb and fingers. He nods again in respect. The Boche do make good stuff.

Safa sits up too fast and grips the bed with a wave of dizziness that sweeps through then eases away. She takes deep breaths. Inhaling through her nose that feels wet like it needs blowing. She wipes it with the length of her thumb. It comes away smeared with blood, which she squints at in confusion. She must have been hit hard during that last fight. That thought makes her look up and round again for cameras. She can't see any but that doesn't mean they aren't watching. Whoever *they* are. This feels professional. It feels too well put together to be the terrorists. If she'd woken up chained in a shit-covered room on top of a filthy mattress she might have accepted it, but this is too good. Must be the police then, or one of the other agencies. They think she had a part in it. That's a good thing. Stay calm and let the investigation run. She's clean. She knows she is.

Ben gets up and immediately sits back down from the wave of dizziness moving through his head. His vision darkens until he feels like he will black out. He takes short, shallow breaths until it passes, but it leaves a crushing pain in the back of his skull. Something hot drips on to his hands resting on his lap. He looks down to see a thick drop of blood on his knuckles. Another drop lands, making him realise it's coming from his nose. He looks round for tissues but even that motion makes him feel sick. Like his head is struggling to catch up with his eyes. He pinches the bridge of his nose, tilts his head back a bit and rises gently to his feet, giving his blood pressure a chance to catch up. How long has he been unconscious for? Would they put an unconscious prisoner in a room on his own? What if he swallowed his tongue or drowned from his own nosebleed? He knows they have different laws for terrorism, but this is England, not America. He looks round for a camera or dome but sees nothing other than the bare concrete walls and bare concrete ceiling. No mirrors and nowhere for a concealed camera to be situated.

He staggers towards the door, feeling pain in his head with every step. It's warm, muggy and close. He knocks on the door and waits for a prison officer to open it, and when nothing happens, he knocks louder.

Still no response, so he bangs the side of his fist, listening to the dull echo sound on the other side.

'Hello?' he calls out with a hoarse voice, wincing from the pain in his throat. 'Can I have some water please?' This is bad. You can't leave an unconscious prisoner on their own without medical care or water.

'Hey.' He bangs again louder and longer. 'I wasn't one of them . . . check the CCTV . . .'

Harry looks up at the first bang coming from outside his door. Must be more cells. He slides from the bed to stand up and feels a wave of nausea sweep through him. He teeters for a second and grips the bed but stays upright. Breathing heavily and simply waiting for the effects to pass. An English voice calls *Hello*. Harry staggers to his door. His hand automatically going for the handle that he turns to pull the door open. Another solid riveted door opposite with someone banging on the other side asking for water.

Safa hears the bang and the voice too. Now standing in her room feeling weak and ready to pass out again. Hearing other voices is worrying. Especially a male voice. She should not be in a mixed-gender prison or holding centre. She holds still, staring at the door and listening as the voice asks for water.

Ben jumps back at the bang on the other side of the door. The handle goes down and it swings inwards to reveal a huge bearded man with a smear of blood on his nose glaring at him through bloodshot eyes.

'Not locked,' Harry says with a voice as hoarse as Ben's.

'Are you a guard?' Ben asks, looking but not seeing the soft grey cotton tracksuit Harry is wearing.

'No,' Harry rasps. 'Regiment?'

'Eh?'

'Regiment?' Harry asks. 'Rank?'

'Do what, mate?' Ben shakes his head and feels a fresh wave of dizziness. His vision goes dark again as two strong hands grip his shoulders to keep him upright.

'I'm fine . . . honestly.' Ben steps through the door, squints round and spots three weird-looking institutional blue armchairs, like moulded from one object without seams or armrests. Low, too, but they are better than falling on the hard concrete floor. He staggers over to sink down, much to the relief of his swimming head. Harry watches him for a second before deciding that sitting is indeed much better than standing right now. He sinks down into the third chair, leaving the empty one between them.

'Harry,' Harry says quietly in a rough-sounding voice.

'Ben.'

'Rank?'

'Rank?' Ben asks, glancing over at him. 'Oh . . . you in the army or something?'

'Army,' Harry says, rubbing a hand through his bushy black beard with a confused look.

Ben shakes his head. 'Investigator with . . .' He stops with the sudden thought that everything is not right. This is not right. 'Where are we?'

'POW camp,' Harry says with a heavy shrug.

'POW? What, like prisoner of war?'

Harry nods and that confused look starts to morph into a suspicious glare at Ben, who pats his trouser legs searching for pockets.

'They take your phone?' Ben asks him, but Harry just narrows his eyes. 'Mobile,' Ben says. Harry remains silent and watchful.

This room is the same as the ones they woke up in with concrete walls, floor and ceiling and a too-bright light. Three chairs and five doors.

'What's through those?' Ben asks, motioning at the closed doors.

Harry doesn't reply. Ben glances over to see him shrug but staring hard.

'Investigator with who?' Harry asks.

'Pardon?'

'You're an investigator. Who with?'

'Insurance . . .' Ben's words cut off with his stomach lurching as he looks back to the open door leading to the room he was in and the name Ben Ryder stencilled on it in black letters. Ben Ryder. Why didn't they put Ben Calshott? Who told them he is Ben Ryder? How do they know? He gets a memory of someone saying his name when he was grabbed and held down. They said Ryder, not Calshott.

Safa checks over the room again but spots nothing other than the bed and the door. She weighs her options quickly, both of them. Wait here or try the door. She is smart but also not one to hold back, especially with the risk of her family being threatened by the Prime Minister. She moves silently to the door and tries to listen. Two voices. Both male. One is very deep, which forms the mental image of a big man. She can't hear the words but she catches the tone and short sentences like they don't know each other. It must be a prison. She wipes her nose again and ignores the blood still seeping out.

Ben looks round to the other open door and the name stencilled in the same black letters. Harry Madden. That rings a bell. Harry Madden. Where's that from? Ben knows that name. Harry Madden. Bloody hell, the soldier from the Second World War. The famous one who destroyed a U-boat depot. *Mad Harry Madden*. Ben glances at Harry thinking he even looks the same as the pictures from the school textbooks.

'Did you say you're in the army?' Ben asks.

Harry still does not reply but just stares without expression. He's a huge man, broad with a big chest and thick hairy wrists that poke out the end of the tracksuit top. Legs like tree trunks and the tops of his feet are as hairy as his face and arms.

'Any relation?' Ben asks with a forced smile.

Harry cocks his head, unspeaking but interested.

'Harry Madden,' Ben says. 'Mad Harry?'

Harry's eyes flick to his name on the door then over to Ben and up to the name Ben Ryder on the other door. Ben watches him, expecting a reaction at his old name being seen but Harry shows no reaction. Instead he leans forward to look to one of the closed doors. Ben tracks his movement and reads the third name stencilled on the bare metal. Safa Patel. Ben looks to Harry and shrugs.

'Someone else,' Ben says and starts to rise.

'Where you going?' Harry asks with a hard glare.

Ben points at one of the unmarked doors. Harry nods as though to give his agreement and rises to follow. Ben walks slowly to the door and tries the handle. It yields to reveal a bathroom of sorts. One shower unit at the end. One stainless steel toilet. One basin fitted to the wall. Three neatly folded grey towels each with a new toothbrush inside a large clear plastic cup. 'Bathroom,' Ben says to Harry, who moves to peer over his shoulder.

Ben goes inside, grabs the first cup and twists the tap to run the water. He rinses the cup, fills it up, sips then gulps the contents down greedily. The water is like nothing he has ever tasted before. Cool, fresh, light and purer than any water he has ever drunk.

Harry watches from the open door. He moves in to take the cup from the second pile and holds it under the running water. The suspicious look stays on his face until the first sip is taken, then his eyes come alive and he drinks it down in one long gulp followed by a noisy belch and a new suspicious look, but this one directed at the cup. He fills his again, drinks it down then holds the cup in front of his face and taps a fingernail against the side.

'What's this?' Harry asks.

'Plastic,' Ben says obviously.

Harry glances at him. 'We got plastic but nowt like this,' he says, switching the glare from Ben to the cup.

Ben looks out of the room to the name Harry Madden stencilled on the door. 'You taking the piss?' Ben asks him, then realises he just asked a very big man a rude question in the bathroom of a prison. 'I mean, like . . . you know . . . it's totally cool if you are.'

Safa hears them move across the room on the other side of her door. Low conversations. Another door opening and what sounds like running water and it's that sound that makes her decide to go out. Her thirst is immense. Her mouth and throat feel bone dry. She needs water. With a deep breath, she pushes the handle, not expecting the door to open. When it does she has to step back quickly, which causes the dizziness to sweep through her again. She grabs the door frame and fights the sensation with her eyes closed. The voices stop talking. She detects the sound of motion and snaps her eyes open as Ben walks towards her in concern at her falling.

'Get the fuck away . . .' she snarls and steps back with her vision blurred and threatening to close in.

'Okay,' Ben says quickly, softly. 'You'll be okay. The dizziness passes . . .'

'Leave me alone,' she mutters fiercely and waits for her eyes to clear to see the two men staring at her. One of them is huge and bearded. At least six foot four and standing in the door to the bathroom while holding a plastic cup. He looks familiar but she shifts her gaze to take in the one that moved towards her then blinks again as her mouth drops open.

'You okay?' Ben asks gently.

She watches him. Taking in the dark blond hair and features. Recognising him instantly. Knowing him instantly.

'I'm Ben,' Ben says. Safa glares harder. Her eyes fixed on his face, tracing along his scar, and then down to the grey tracksuit.

'You're Safa?'

She glares back at his face until he slowly lifts a hand and points behind her.

She turns and reads her own name stencilled in thick black letters. Safa Patel. She looks back at Ben then past him to Harry, who also looks so familiar. Like she knows him but cannot place him. She edges forward to the threshold of her doorway and peers across the room to the opened door on the other side and the name Ben Ryder stencilled in the same thick black letters. Her heart hammers, thundering in her chest.

'Do I know you?' Ben asks, staring intently at her. 'You look familiar.'

She swallows and forces herself to look past him to the big man. 'Who are you?' she asks as Ben points to the door next to hers. She has to step out from the room to see but that means leaving the perceived safety of her room. Ben and Harry both detect the fear and move back at the same time to show they are not a threat. She edges out and peers round to the door next to hers and the name stencilled in thick black letters. Harry Madden. She shoots a hard look at Harry as her heart starts jackhammering again. He looks like Harry Madden. The other one looks like Ben Ryder. Harry Madden and Ben Ryder? They are both dead. She looks at the names then at the faces, trying to process what she is seeing and reading.

'Mad Harry Madden,' she mutters to herself and shakes her head. This is a dream. A nightmare or a hallucination brought on by the drugs. Maybe some kind of psychosis designed to unhinge her mind so she will blab about the terrorist attack. 'Ben Ryder,' she mutters and stares at Ben, locking eyes in the same way she did five years ago. It is the same man. She saw him. It was Ben then and it is Ben now. The same face she has thought about nearly every day for the last five years. The same man that made her want to be a police officer.

'You're dead,' she whispers.

'Feels like it,' Ben says, pulling his head back an inch.

'Water, miss?' Harry rumbles from the bathroom doorway, seeing the blood drain from her face and wondering why they have put a woman in a POW camp.

'Easy.' Ben shoots forward as she sways on the spot and starts to buckle. 'Sit down, it's right here.'

She lets him guide her and giggles drunkenly at the thought of Ben Ryder helping her to a chair. 'Ben Ryder,' she slurs and looks at him again. 'You're Ben Ryder.'

'It's Calshott,' Ben says.

'Pah!' Safa bursts out laughing as she sinks down and points a trembling finger up at him. 'S'not Calshott, it's Ryder.' Her hands grip his face. That he shows instant alarm is lost in the fug of her mind. 'Ben Ryder,' she says again, stroking his cheeks and staring into the soft blue eyes. Her own eyes fill with tears that spill down her cheeks. 'Ben Ryder . . .'

'Calshott,' Ben says, seeing the drunken, slack look in her eyes. 'Miss, just rest. I'll try and get help.'

She saw him. She was the last one who ever saw him. Ben Ryder. The last decent man to have ever lived. Her mind fills with images of the Prime Minister leering and grabbing her. His filthy whisky-tainted breath in her face and the months she took the abuse while knowing there were decent men in the world who did brave and good things. But it's too much. The shock of it is too much and the last traces of the drugs in her system pull her back down into sleep.

Six

'Bloody hell,' Ben says when she finally lets go of his face and slumps back in the chair. She does look familiar. He knows her from somewhere. He looks at the name on the door again. Safa Patel. That's a distinctive name. He would remember a name like that and especially a woman like this. She is beautiful.

'She okay?' Harry asks.

Ben shrugs and steps back. 'She's breathing,' he says. 'Is there an alarm or something? Maybe we should get an ambulance . . .'

'Ambulance?' Harry asks, going straight back to that suspicious glance again. 'She knows you.'

'Er.' Ben pauses and thinks about what he should say and even if he should be saying anything, but Safa stirs in her chair and groans softly as her eyes open again.

'Water, miss,' Harry says. There is something about his manner, the way he moves clutching a tiny plastic mug and obviously trying not to scare her by ducking down and holding his hand out to offer the drink. Never before has Ben seen a man trying to appear less threatening.

Safa takes the cup slowly as her eyes start to focus again. She does the same as the other two and sips first then gulps the water down in one long, thirsty drink.

'Another one?' Harry asks politely, reaching out for the cup. She hands it over, staring up in wonder at the attentiveness of such a huge, hairy man mountain and again reads the name on his door. He brings her another drink and backs off to hover nearby as she watches him and Ben over the rim of her cup.

'Water?' Harry asks Ben.

'Er, yeah, yeah thanks.'

'Ben Ryder,' Safa murmurs in a voice now firmer and more normal. 'You look like him and you've got the scar too,' she adds, leaning forward in the chair to look at the faded cut down his right cheek. 'But you're not him.'

'Can we sit down?' Ben asks when Harry comes back with water and a handful of toilet tissue. Two white tufts of paper already poking from his nose that make Safa and Ben blink at him in the utterly surreal confusion of the moment.

'Stops the bleeding,' Harry says, handing them both a section of toilet tissue as Safa realises they both have nosebleeds. Drips of crimson on the fronts of their tracksuit tops. She looks down, seeing the same on her front, and takes the tissue. Two chunks torn and fashioned to be pushed carefully into her nostrils. Ben watches her then looks at Harry. His head still struggling to catch up.

'Stops the bleeding,' Harry says again, still holding a chunk of tissue for Ben.

'I know you're not Ben Ryder,' Safa says, as Ben stuffs tissue up his nose. 'I saw Ben Ryder die. I was there,' she adds. 'On the platform . . .'

It hits Ben hard. The sudden recollection of the uniformed police officer running across the platform screaming at the driver. The shape of her eyes. The angle of her head. The poise in her manner. Ben swallows, gripping the cup harder.

'I need to sit down.'

'And you?' she says, turning her attention to Harry. 'Are you meant to be Harry Madden?'

'Aye. Harry,' Harry replies and seems to think for a second before moving to the last chair.

'Not *the* Harry Madden,' she says clearly. 'Not *the* Ben Ryder either.'

They fall into a heavy silence. All three with white toilet tissue poking from their noses, staring at each other suspiciously.

'Heard about this, I did,' Harry says in a deep, rumbling voice.

'About what?' Ben asks.

'Mind games,' Harry states, looking at Ben benignly.

'What about them?'

'This,' he says.

'What?! What mind games? Where are we? Who are you two and what the fuck am I doing here?'

'You'll not be cussing in front of a lady now,' Harry says in a low, warning tone.

'Fuck that,' Safa says. Harry blanches and looks away as though embarrassed. 'I agree, who the fuck are you two and what am I doing here? You are not Ben Ryder and you . . .' She points at Harry. 'I don't know who you are.'

'I am Ben Ryder,' Ben says. 'You were the police officer on the platform at Holborn station.' Her head snaps to face him. 'I saw you . . . you were running and waving at the driver to stop . . . I was pulling the ginger man down the tracks.'

'What was his name then?'

'Who?'

'The ginger man.'

'I don't know! How would I know?'

'Exactly, you can't know because Ben Ryder blew up with the train.'

'No, no I didn't. Two men pushed me into a side room and . . .'

'And what?' she demands.

'And . . . I don't know . . . I can't remember . . . I blacked out then woke up here.'

'Yeah, okay then, you been asleep for what . . . five years?'

'Five years? It was a few hours ago. What're you on about?'

She shakes her head at him in disgust. 'Stop it.'

'Find the works manager . . . or the men on tea break I saw . . . or my office! They'll tell you I was sent there for the worker that got electrocuted in Aldwych . . . I didn't know those people . . .'

'Mind games,' Harry says, tutting. 'Dirty.'

'I'll tell you what mind games are,' Safa says. 'Mind games are being suspected of being a terrorist just because you've got darker skin, which is racism. I was doing my job. I hope to hell you've got every copper from the house in here because if you've singled me out on the basis of my ethnicity I will go bloody Mad Harry on . . .' She stops, realising what she's said, and glares through narrowed eyes at Harry, who just blinks and tilts his head.

'I got him down to the bunker,' she continues. 'I got him down there . . . if I was part of it, why didn't I kill him or hand him over? I didn't even go in with him . . .'

'With who? Where?' Ben asks. 'What are you talking about? Holborn?'

'He said he'd do this,' she mutters darkly. 'He said it,' she says louder into the air as though someone else is listening. 'He said he'd put extremist material in my father's office if I didn't . . .' She stops again, breathing hard through her mouth. 'I am not a terrorist,' she shouts.

'Neither am I,' Ben shouts at whoever is listening.

'I am,' Harry says almost cheerfully. 'Harry Madden. British Army. I were dropped a few miles out from the harbour. I blew the town to light a path for the bombers so the charges could be set on the U-boats.' He speaks matter-of-factly without any trace of humour or deceit. 'So . . .' He pauses, staring from Safa to Ben. 'You can pack it in. You don't need to do the mind games cos I admit who I am.' He drains his cup and places it gently down at his feet. 'Oh, and I was in civilian clothing too, so that makes me a spy. I won't fight or struggle if you execute me now, but if you hold me here, I will consider it my duty to try and escape.'

Silence follows. Safa and Ben unmoving as they watch him settle back in the chair and stretch his legs out. 'You've done well with your cups anyway.'

'Cups?' Safa asks.

'Aye, your plastics,' he says. 'Good stuff. You might be the enemy, but credit given where credit's due.'

'Oh my fucking God,' Ben stammers. 'What the hell is going on?'

'Good English. Study in England?' Harry asks.

'In England?' Safa asks.

'Before the war,' Harry says.

'What year is it?' she asks him with a quizzical look.

'Nineteen forty-three,' he replies.

'Of course it is,' she says witheringly. 'And you're the real Harry Madden and he's the real Ben Ryder.'

'I am,' Ben says to her. 'But he isn't the real Harry Madden. You think they think you had something to do with the attack on Holborn? I can tell them I saw you trying to stop the train.' Ben speaks out to the room while pointing at Safa. 'I saw this police officer running on the platform, she was in uniform and tried stopping the driver by running towards the train . . . I think that's important.' He pauses as she glares at him. 'No, I really do think that's important. Think about it, why would you run *towards* the train if you knew it would blow up?'

'I didn't know it would blow up,' she says angrily. 'And that was five years ago.'

'You blew Holborn up?' Harry asks with a pained expression. 'That's not military. Civvies would've been down there. That's not on.'

Three conversations going on at cross-purposes. Ben and Safa feel like they're drunk and out of sync with everything else. A feeling of confusion with a sense of panic starting to rise. It's too hot, too close and they have tissue stuffed up their noses.

'You can't treat people like this,' Ben says. 'What about the Human Rights Act?'

'Oh, nice touch.' Safa offers a humourless smile.

'What?'

'Human Rights Act? The one that was abolished in twenty eighteen? That one? Like I said, nice touch.'

Safa's hands tremble. Harry looks genuinely confused. Ben keeps swallowing. They all take turns to stare at each other, as each thinks the others must have been drugged to make the side effects look real. This is a test designed to cause stress and confusion so they will spill the beans about Norway, Holborn and Downing Street. Safa and Ben equally worry about how to convince the others. Harry just sits quietly.

'My name is Ben Ryder and I had nothing to do with what happened at Holborn . . .'

'Five years ago,' Safa says.

'Yesterday.'

'Five years ago . . .'

'Yesterday.'

'Five years ago.'

'Yesterday . . . my name is Ben Ryder. It was changed to Ben Calshott after what happened when I was seventeen. I am engaged to Stephanie. We are getting married. I work for Hallows Insurance Investigations.'

Safa smiles coldly and shifts position to face him. 'What happened when you were seventeen then, Ben Ryder?'

Ben hesitates, not wanting to give voice to the thing he buried for so many years.

'Go on then,' Safa says, goading in tone. 'What happened when you were seventeen, Ben Ryder?' she adds mockingly.

'I killed five people . . .' Ben says.

'Who?' She cuts across him as Harry looks at Ben with renewed interest. 'Who did you kill, Ben Ryder?'

'Please stop.' Ben looks away as the memories flood back.

'Oh, you look all hurt,' she says in a mock soft tone. 'Come on, you're Ben Ryder. Who did you kill?'

'Carl Pocock, Daryl Evans, Umbassa Ubedi, Sean Harris, Matmoud Hussein. We were in Lovell Lane in a village thirty miles from Birmingham . . .'

'Yeah yeah, you can get that from Wikipedia.'

'Yes you can,' Ben says, having Googled his own name before. 'But it won't say that our names were changed to Calshott or that we moved to Surrey, or that my father was given a job in NatWest or my mother was the payroll clerk for the local Tesco's. Or that we had a dog called Bobo . . . does it say that? Does it say I went to Littlehill Comprehensive? Does it say that the last investigation I worked on before I was sent to London yesterday—'

'Yes.'

'And does it . . . what?'

'Yes it does.'

'What?'

'Wikipedia says all of that. That at the time of your death you were engaged to Stephanie Myers. Oh, don't give me the all-shocked look now, everyone knows it, lightning striking twice? Ben Ryder killed five drugged-up gang members and saved a woman and her child . . . then years later saved hundreds on the London Underground. All there. Every word of it.'

Ben's heart races, booming in his chest, and his mouth goes dry. Breathing faster, he looks at Safa then at Harry. 'This is fucked up. Who . . . I mean . . . who are you then?' he asks Safa.

'Safa Patel,' she states as though speaking to the room again. 'I am a police officer with the Diplomatic Protection Squad.'

'And?' Ben asks weakly as Harry simply watches on with interest.

'Oh, you want the rest?' she asks scathingly. 'My turn is it? Oh, okay then. I'm so happy to comply and do as you want, Ben Ryder.'

'I don't—'

'PC 01899 Patel,' she cuts him off. 'I was on duty yesterday. Do you want the names of the other officers on duty?' she asks lightly. 'No? Got them already? Well, let me proceed then. I commenced duty and first went upstairs to relieve the officer on day duty. I then remained on the top floor until the Prime Minister came back, at which point I moved downstairs to the static point beside the lift. I then remained at that static point until the Prime Minister had concluded his business and at no time did I see anyone other than the normal Downing Street staff . . . no, hang on . . . there was a private business caller . . .' The overly sarcastic voice goes as she becomes serious and earnest.

'He was only there for half an hour and there was something odd about him. Have you checked him? We didn't have his details, only that he was a private business caller . . . check him.' She nods at Ben and Harry as though they can arrange for that to happen. 'Then he . . . the Prime Minister I mean, I took him up to his rooms and, er . . .' she hesitates. 'I stayed in the upper corridor until he called me in for a bug sweep . . . I was, er . . . we were in his study when the first explosion came. I got him down the stairwell, I engaged the attackers on the ground floor and know I killed three, possibly four. I got the PM down into the bunker then went back upstairs. I definitely got six more confirmed kills.' Harry leans closer. 'Then I heard the firefight in the rear garden and went there until the . . . shit,' she spits. 'The two police officers . . . there were two police officers that came in but they weren't armed! Christ, how did I not notice? They came from the front of the house and asked me my name. They asked me two or three times like they wanted to be sure or something then one of them attacked me. Yes,' she blurts with an apparent fresh memory recall. 'He jumped on me and stuck something into my neck and the other one was throwing flash-bangs into the garden . . .'

'In your neck?' Ben interrupts as her words spark a fresh memory.

'Must have been a sedative,' she says, looking down at the ground between her feet as though struggling to remember. 'One of them had . . . he had a broken nose and black eyes . . . he said something about . . .' She looks up at Ben. 'About Ben breaking his nose . . .'

'Me?' Ben asks, recoiling. 'I remember being stuck in the neck but . . .'

'In the neck?' she asks.

'Yeah, this side,' Ben says, reaching up to place a hand on the right side of his neck. 'Still tender.'

'Let me see,' she asks, leaning forward.

Ben twists round and holds his hand over the sore spot. 'Here,' he says.

'Move your hand,' she says, pushing his arm down. 'Here?'

'Ow.' He flinches and glares at her for jabbing a finger into his neck.

'Puncture mark,' she says.

'Have I? Let's see yours then.'

'This side.' She touches the left side of her neck. 'See anything?'

'What, there?' Ben asks, jabbing his finger into her neck. She recoils, giving him the same glare he gave her.

'Yes,' she says through gritted teeth. 'Is it punctured?'

'Yeah. Harry?' Ben asks.

'I were out of it,' he says, staring at them like they are both crazy.

'Let's see your neck,' Safa demands as he leans forward in the chair. 'Is it sore anywhere?'

'Sore everywhere, miss,' he mutters.

'Here?' She presses into his neck softer than she did with Ben and he flinches slightly with a nod.

'Really?' Ben gets up to look closer as she holds her finger gently on his neck. A tiny mark like the one on her neck.

'I did break someone's nose,' Ben admits, sitting back down. 'When they grabbed me . . . I thought they were the terrorists or something . . .

I mean, it was pitch black and they had these head torches on blinding me but I hit out and I heard one of them say I'd broken his nose.'

It strikes Ben that Harry is the only one to have admitted doing something and looks the most relaxed while he and Safa are both protesting and trying to convince the others of their innocence.

'Harry? What happened to you?' Safa asks him.

'Told you,' he says. 'I got into the base and set charges to light a path for the bombers to cause a distraction for the U-boats to be attacked. I'm a British Army commando.' He stops and looks away without a flicker of expression. 'I knew what I was getting into.'

'And that was in nineteen forty-three?' she asks.

'Aye,' he says stoically. 'It *is* nineteen forty-three.'

'And you' – Ben looks to Safa – 'were at Downing Street during a terrorist attack in twenty twenty.'

'Yes.'

'And I was at Holborn when something happened in twenty fifteen. Great. Got it. Makes perfect sense now.'

They both look at Ben with raised eyebrows. 'Does it?' Safa asks.

'Nope.'

Another silence. They take turns to wipe the sweat from their faces while the rain beats a solid rhythm on the shutters behind them.

'If you're from the future,' Harry says slowly, breaking the silence, 'who wins—'

'We do,' Ben replies quietly.

'The Germans?'

'No! The British . . . or rather the Allies.'

'What happens?' he asks with such open emotion the other two think he really believes he *is* Harry Madden.

'We won,' Bens says with a shrug.

'How?'

Ben looks down while Safa clears her throat. The legend of Harry Madden was taught in every school for years. Movies, books, television series. Even coining the phrase 'Mad Harry'. This man is not Harry Madden, but the belief he projects is overwhelming.

Harry doesn't say anything but just turns and stares ahead, nodding slowly. 'What's through there?' he asks, looking at the door.

'Dunno,' Ben says. 'Way out maybe?'

Harry sighs heavily and looks at Safa. 'I'm going to escape now.'

'Okay,' she replies slowly.

'I'll do my best not to hurt you if you try and stop me.'

'I'm not going to stop you.'

He looks at Ben.

'Oh, I won't try and stop you either,' Ben says quickly.

Harry walks slowly to the door and pauses with his hand stretched out as though expecting some kind of reaction.

'Nowt?' he asks without turning round from the door while Safa and Ben exchange a glance. With an almost disappointed tut he slaps his hand down noisily on the handle, clearly not expecting it to open and stepping back in surprise when it swings in towards him.

'Shit, it's open?' Ben asks.

'Wikipedia said Ben Ryder was a good investigator,' Safa says, proving a point.

'Yeah? Wikipedia also said Harry Madden was a commando in the Second World War . . .'

'Empty,' Harry says from the doorway as he looks left and right.

'Really?' Ben asks, going over with Safa to join him at the door. Harry steps out, allowing them space to move into a wide corridor in the same design as their rooms with concrete walls, floor and ceiling. Harsh strip lights overhead and the same solid, metal-riveted doors on both sides.

'See this?' Safa says, pointing at the outside of the main door and their names stencilled in black. *Harry Madden. Ben Ryder. Safa Patel.*

'Feels warmer in here,' Ben whispers, tugging at the collar on his grey tracksuit top. 'Which way?'

'No names on these doors,' Harry says, walking down the corridor to the first door on the opposite side.

'Are they open?' Safa asks.

Harry pushes the handle down and steps back to swing the door open. 'Same,' he says. Safa and Ben walk down to stare into a replica of the rooms they just came from. A main room with three pale blue moulded armchairs. A bathroom with three towels, three cups and three toothbrushes. The doors from the main room lead to the same austere bedrooms, each fitted with a single metal-framed bed. They go down the corridor, taking it in turns to open the doors. Each set of rooms is the same and the stress rises as quickly as the sweat prickles their faces and necks. Dark patches form under Harry's armpits. Bare feet slap gently on the concrete floor and the feeling of being unable to catch up increases by the minute. At the end of the corridor they stop and stare at the double doors fitted into the wall.

'Listen,' Harry whispers, bending his head closer to the door to listen to the voices coming from the other side. 'People.'

'We've got to be in a prison,' Ben whispers.

'No locks,' Harry says, shaking his head.

'Maybe it's a weird prison then, like a special terrorism prison?' Ben says, feeling completely out of his depth. 'Maybe . . . er . . . we should stay together?' Blank looks from both of them and he bites his lip, trying to think how to form his words. 'Safa, you're a copper right?' Ben asks.

'Yeah, so?'

'I thought they didn't like coppers in prisons . . . and, er, lady coppers especially?' Ben adds with a wince.

She blanches, glaring from Ben to Harry with her lips pursing.

'Stay together?' Ben asks them both. Harry nods, looking down at Safa.

'Miss?'

'I can handle myself,' she says firmly.

'Fine, sorry I was—' Ben starts.

'Stay together then,' she says, cutting him off. 'If *you* want to, that is.'

'I do,' Ben says. 'I mean, look at the size of him.' He motions at Harry. 'I don't want to get done in the showers.'

'Done?' Harry asks innocently.

'We've got our own showers,' Safa says.

'Done for what?' Harry asks again.

'You know,' Ben says to Harry. 'In the showers in prisons . . .'

'Beaten?' Harry asks.

'Yeah, something like that,' Ben says meekly as Harry rolls his eyes.

'That was a joke,' Harry says. 'I know what they do in prisons.'

'Fuck's sake,' Ben groans.

'They steal from each other, right?' Harry says, holding that poker face perfectly.

'Let's just get in,' Safa orders with a grim expression, pushing past Harry and through the double doors.

Seven

The room is big and square with bare concrete on all sides. Metal shutters run down the length of one wall with a long wooden table underneath. Harry nudges Ben and Safa to look at the bowls of fruit on display.

Bananas the size of . . . well . . . very big bananas, and round orange things that cannot be oranges because they are the size of melons. Large wooden bowls hold other things that look like apples, pears and berries, but so much bigger and in different shades of colour. The objects are clearly fruit but like nothing any of them have ever seen before, with an array of vibrant colours seeming more vivid in the otherwise bland grey room.

A dozen or more men stand conferring quietly at the far end of the room next to a set of doors. Several rough-hewn tables and chairs lie scattered about.

The difference of perceptions and of what the eye sees and matches to the experiences of life and the knowledge held by the viewer.

To Safa, the sights are jarring and only increase her already heightened anxious state. Prisons do not have fruit on display and they do not have wooden chairs and tables that can be smashed up to make weapons from. Prisons do not have mixed-gender communal rooms. Prisons do not require a female detainee to share a bathroom with a male detainee. They do not have open doors. This is not a prison, but it still feels like a prison. That alarms her. It upsets the black and white in her head, which has no room for grey uncertainty.

To Ben, the sight means a myriad of things. His mind is more open than Safa's and less confined to the world of law and order. He sees nutritional food laid out, which tells him there is some effort put into providing care for the people meant to stay here. The rough-hewn tables and chairs tell him this is more building site than anything else, but again some effort has been made to provide at least a place to sit and eat. He sees open doors and a sense of security, but cannot fathom if they are secured within or from something without. The whole of it taken thus far speaks of a thing as yet unfinished.

Harry sees a POW camp. Enough said.

They look over to the dozen or more men. Safa sees security personnel dressed in paramilitary-style coveralls and wearing assault boots. She sees wide shoulders, straight backs, clean-shaven chins and military-grade haircuts.

Ben catches obscured glimpses of a tall, dark-haired man dressed in khaki talking to the men, but pausing after every sentence as though someone is translating his words. He sees the men staring from the man in khaki to someone else as they track the conversation.

Harry sees guards.

Safa looks round again. Still jarred. Still uncertain. Her proactive mind tells her to do something and take control.

Ben sees people and figures who will know what is going on. He can hear them talking and snatches of words in English and German. The dark-haired man he glimpses is speaking English, but someone else is translating into German. Why German? His mind reaches the conclusion that he must be in a European detention centre. Which explains the weird set-up.

Harry sees German guards speaking German in a German POW camp.

Just as Safa is about to take control by calling out, and just as Ben is about to whisper his thoughts to the others, Harry nods once, smiles and sets off striding towards the German guards speaking German in the German POW camp.

'Er . . . where's he going?' Ben asks, pointing after Harry.

'Harry Madden. Sergeant. Second Commando Unit . . .' Harry booms across the room, snapping the head of every German guard towards him, who see a huge man in a grey tracksuit with toilet tissue poking from his nose.

'Holy fuck,' Safa mutters. 'He really thinks he's . . .'

'Parachute Division. British Army . . .' Harry shouts, his voice deep and proud. He rolls his shoulders as he walks and flexes his wrists while making fists, telegraphing his intent to fight. 'I am a commando. I was dressed as a civilian . . .'

Ben tries to snort a dry, humourless laugh and sends the tissue from his left nostril shooting out. Safa shakes her head in disbelief but clocks the formation as the men in the coveralls suddenly disperse from a tight group to one that ranges out in a flanking manoeuvre. She takes a step forward. Her eyes reading the tiny visual nuances in the men, who check their immediate space and slide feet to keep one forward and one back in a basic combat stance.

'Harry!' a man calls out in English, striding from the back of the group. A tall man with dark hair. The same one Ben could see in the crowd. Ben gets that jolt of déjà vu again. The same as when he saw Safa and Harry. The same weird, unsettling sensation that is rapidly becoming too familiar. His mind races to remember how he knows this person, but he cannot find the context or place in his mind.

'Sir.' Harry comes to a sudden stop and snaps a smart salute. 'Are you the CO in the camp?'

'The what in the what now?' Roland asks, blinking in response.

Harry lowers the salute, instantly absorbing that this man is not an officer. He rolls his shoulders again. Makes fists and looks round at the guards. 'Come on then,' he says mildly. 'Get it over with . . .'

'Get what over with?' Roland asks as Ben searches his mind and tries to shake the fug of confusion spinning inside his head. Safa stares on. Watching and listening and still seeing the men in coveralls moving out in a circling motion. Hands away from bodies ready to lunge and fight and she notices the way they glance to each other too, confirming placement and positions. She takes another step forward.

'Dirty Boche,' Harry says, his voice dropping to a dangerously low tone. '*Kampf mich* . . .' he adds with relish.

'Oh fuck,' Konrad whimpers.

'*Kampf mich*,' Harry says, louder and harder. '*KAMPF MICH* . . .'

'Ah no . . . no no no,' Konrad wails, waving his arms at the men in coveralls, now glaring angrily at Harry.

'What's he saying?' Malcolm asks.

'Harry, let me explain,' Roland says.

'What the fuck?' Ben says.

'No idea,' Safa mutters.

'Oh no,' Konrad whimpers again. 'He's telling them to fight him . . .'

'I bloody said he would do this,' Malcolm says. 'We said it. We did. Roland, we said he . . .'

'Now now, Harry,' Roland says, trying to show an assured calmness but his voice quavers with sudden worry.

'*KAMPF MICH*,' Harry bellows, lunging a step at the closest man, who jumps back a step. Harry sees only German soldiers. He sees blond hair, blue eyes and arrogant sneers. He sees Bert, Jack, Billy, Dick and Wozzer and the rest of his mates all killed by these Nazi bastards. He sees his country in flames with women and children dead from bombing raids. He sees the horror of war and the enemy in front of him. They will kill him. He is a commando. They will execute him by firing squad or worse. He will go out fighting and by God he will take a few with him on the way. He can see the guards are close to fighting him. He can feel the tension almost ready to explode. He boots a chair at one of them and feints towards another. They circle him and lower into fighting stances. He smiles grim and full of malice. '*Kampf mich*,' he says again, waving them to come at him. '*KAMPF MICH* . . .'

'Harry, please let me . . .' Roland stammers as the situation spirals rapidly out of control. 'Konrad! Do something . . .'

Harry hears the name Konrad. Konrad sounds like a German name. The English man is on their side. He sneers and stands upright, knowing his final words will ignite the touch paper. '*Fick . . . deine . . . mutter . . .*' he says with malicious delight. That does it. Tell any soldier in the world to fuck his mother and watch what happens.

'*NEIN NEIN NEIN*,' Konrad screams.

'Oh bugger,' Malcolm yelps.

Harry smashes a fist into the first one coming at him. Pivoting from the hips with a tremendous blow that shatters the man's nose and sends him flying back off his feet. The next two are battered away. Blood and teeth flying out but these are tough ex-soldiers hired as muscle and used to scrapping. They learn from the downing of the first three and form up to lunge in groups. Harry dances back. Punching hard and kicking out with surprising agility for such a big man. He grabs the arm of a man trying to punch him and snaps the elbow joint over his knee. The man screams and drops. Harry boots him hard, sending him sliding back into the feet of the next man.

'*GEHEN*,' someone roars. The rest rush as one. All of them ploughing in to land punches on Harry, who staggers back from the onslaught. He rallies to fight, smashing fists into faces and headbutting others but there are too many. Two go for his legs to try to take him down but he stays upright. Roaring to fight on and hurt them before they kill him.

Ben watches on with his heart hammering and his vision closing in. The sound of the arm breaking was sickening. The blood flying about. The teeth scattering across the floor. The chairs and tables overturning and the noises of the punches. He winces as the fight moves across the room.

Safa watches too. Taking small steps towards Harry as the grey in her mind slowly recedes. This is black and white. This is fighting. She does not know who Harry is but only that he cannot be Mad Harry Madden, so therefore she holds no loyalty to him, but right now he is fighting a dozen men on his own and that isn't right. Not right at all. She takes another step. Then another. Her eyes tracking every movement and motion. An urge inside to help Harry but a voice telling her none of this right. She twitches and flinches like Ben. One of the men gets punched hard by Harry and staggers back with blood streaming down his face that twists with rage as he grabs a chair and swings it up overhead ready to slam into Harry.

'That'll do.' Safa is off. Running in and aiming for that man. 'HARRY, WATCH OUT . . .'

Harry turns as the chair slams into his chest. He goes down amongst a shower of broken wood and men diving in with kicks, punches and stamping feet. Safa goes in fast. Her eyes locked on the man that hit Harry with the chair. He turns to face her. The rage on his face morphing into a puzzled expression as she sidesteps as though to go past him but then hooks her arm out across his neck, slamming him down into the ground. She follows through with a fist ramming into his nose, breaking it instantly. She twists as she rises. One step into the maelstrom of violence centred on Harry and she leg sweeps one away and throat punches another, who drops back gargling for air with his hands clutching his neck. She hits two more away before the mass realise what's happening and go for her. She's fast, though, and tough too. She hits hard and ducks to weave and bob, using her knees and elbows to hit and strike anything that comes at her. She is brutal. She is efficiency of training in doing a thing she excels at. Every move is calculated. Every punch is aimed. An arm comes round her neck from behind. She drops instantly on to her back to kick up with the heel of her foot into the man's face. She rolls over and away before rising swiftly as Harry surges up, sending men sprawling as he roars to fight on.

Ben just watches. His mind now empty. His eyes watching, but his head detaching from the present reality. In that chaos he almost calmly takes in just how bloody tough Safa is. She's vicious. Totally and utterly vicious.

The fight gets worse. The violence increases. The men are hurt and angry. They grab staves of wood from the broken chairs and rush at Harry and Safa with weapons. In return they get broken arms, dislocated shoulders, snapped fingers, fractured wrists and busted noses. Still it increases. Still it gets worse. Safa is struck by a fist hammering into the side of her face, snapping her head over as a blond-haired man slams a length of broken chair into the back of her legs. She goes down hard and tries to roll away as Harry is taken down by two men launching at his legs and a third grabbing him round the neck. Safa rolls and tries to rise but the blond-haired man runs at her, battering her down with the length of wood with a wild, raging scream.

For Ben, time slows the same as it did twice before. Once when he was seventeen and the other just a few hours ago on the platform at Holborn. Everything in perfect clarity. Every move predicted and laid out.

Safa lashes out with her legs and trips the blond man with the piece of wood. He sprawls out over her as yet more rush in to kick and batter down at her. Men grab her arms. Others punch her face. Harry tries to rise but more men dive on top of him. The blond man gets up on to his knees and with a flash of pure spite he drives a fist down into Safa's face with such force it hammers the back of her head into the concrete.

Ben goes in hard and low with his arms spread out to sweep them off Safa. They land in a heap of tangled limbs but he moves faster than they and rises to rain a barrage of punches on the blond man, driving his fists into his nose, eyes and mouth. The blond man fights back for a few seconds but his nose breaks, his jaw dislocates and his eye socket fractures. The blond man goes limp and suddenly unconscious as another man wrenches Ben away, sending him spinning across the floor. Safa rises to take him down, tripping him from behind and slamming a fist into the back of his head as he falls.

A fist hits Ben on the side of his face so he hits back. He gets hit again and he hits out again. Safa on the floor rolls from one before springing to her feet with eyes on the man coming at her. A sidestep and she drives the blade of her hand into his throat then spins behind him to slam vicious little punches into his kidneys.

Harry back on his feet with two men unconscious on the floor. Another one goes at him from the right but gets swatted away by a stinging backhand.

An arm comes round Ben's throat from behind. Safa is punched hard but she rallies and drives a knee up into the stomach of the man that hit her. He sinks with a blast of air as she spins round, locks eyes on Ben being choked from behind and charges.

'Drop your legs,' she hisses. Ben does as told. Letting his body weight sink down, forcing the man to lower with him as Safa starts hitting the heels of her hands into the sides of his head, snapping it side to side. The man releases Ben, dropping him to the floor, where he twists on to his back and kicks up into the man's groin as Safa keeps hitting him back and away. She goes like a demon but gets swarmed by men coming at her from the side. Ben rises quickly but two grab his arms.

He tries kicking one away and gets his right hand free but someone hits him in the back of the head. He staggers forward, feeling the dizziness, then is ripped from his feet.

Harry goes down again. A mound of human forms pinning him to the floor. Safa the same. Screaming madly but held down. Still she fights. Kicking, bucking and biting, but they hit hard and keep her down.

Sharp pricks in necks. Plungers sunk down. Warmth spreading from drugs that add to those already in their systems. They fight on but slower now, weaker and with failing energy. The fight ebbs from limbs as they are pulled down once more into chemically induced sleep.

Eight

He backs the van up, stops the engine and grabs the plain black brief-case before dropping down to walk in through the main doors to the reception desk.

'Can I help?' the receptionist asks in German.

'I have some injured men,' Konrad replies in fluent German, biting his bottom lip with nerves.

'Okay,' the receptionist says, leaning to look past Konrad. 'Where are they?'

'Outside.'

'I see. How many do you have?'

'Twelve.'

'I see.'

'I heard you don't ask questions.'

'Payment?' the receptionist asks, still without a flicker of reaction.

'This do?' Konrad hefts the case on to the desk and turns it so the locks face the receptionist. He clicks it open and lifts the lid enough to allow the receptionist a good view of the banknotes stacked inside.

'Fine,' she says, standing smoothly. She closes the lid and swings the case under the desk. 'Bring them in.'

'I can't,' Konrad says, heading for the doors. 'Have you got cameras here?'

'No cameras,' she says.

Konrad nods and rushes outside, leaving the unmarked van where he parked it. Keys in the ignition. Unregistered and bought with cash. The same van he used to collect the men and take them to the bunker. Untraceable and no doubt it will be used towards the medical costs of the private clinic that specialises in giving treatment to conflict-injured private security personnel.

Three are dead. Three more will probably die. The rest have severe injuries of broken bones, concussions, fractured eye sockets, torn ligaments and tendons, broken wrists and fingers, and all done by three people still suffering the effects of strong sedation.

◆ ◆ ◆

Those men worked for Hans Markel and it was Herr Markel that drew the attention.

It was his security company Konrad contacted to hire a dozen men. Now six of them are dead and the other six are severely injured.

The clinic would not divulge information other than the fees had been paid in advance. In truth, it wasn't about the money. The owner was paid a briefcase full of money when Konrad hired the men and, as far as the owner knew, the job was to assess the security of a prototype underground detention centre, but he did not know where it was.

The twelve hired men were blindfolded then driven round Berlin for a few hours before being led downstairs to a cellar, where the portal was open against a wall covered by a thick curtain that gave the impression they were moving from one room to another through a standard doorway.

None of those survivors could say who hurt them other than it was two men and a woman. One of the men was called Harry and he was

English. That was it. They didn't know where they had been taken or who ran the prototype detention centre.

Herr Markel put the word out. His men were tough. They were all ex-military. They were professionals and now six were dead. Who did this?

The security services in Berlin react in the manner of a close-knit community, reeling from the impact of six operatives killed in one unknown job. That catches the attention of the local intelligence services. In turn, that feeds into the immensely heightened state of surveillance currently under way.

That attention instantly shifts to Berlin. They have a location. They have a start point. Berlin is immediately geofenced. Hundreds of analysts from dozens of organisations are put to work scouring every social networking account, every email, every text message and every voicemail going into or coming out of Berlin.

Agents are despatched to put boots on the ground. Airports become thick with countermeasures to lay false trails.

The secret, silent hunt begins in earnest.

Nine

Three austere, sterile rooms. Concrete walls. Concrete floors and ceilings. A single metal-framed bed in each room. Two of the rooms have metal shutters indicating the placement of a window.

'Shit,' Ben mutters at the pain in his retinas. Pain in his face. Pain in his knuckles and pain that seems to be coming from every part of his body at the same time. The memories come back quickly. The attack on the Underground. Waking up in here. Meeting Harry and Safa. Going into that big room, then the fight.

On his feet and again the dizziness rushes through him but he makes it to the door before his vision closes and he slides down the metal rivets into a crumpled, groaning heap on the floor.

Harry wakes the same as before. Opening his eyes slowly to adjust to the glare from the light. He tenses his limbs, feeling pain but knowing nothing is broken. He rises gently to sit on the edge of his bed, compensating for the wave of dizziness by moving gradually. The images of the fight swarm through his mind. The German guards he attacked. Why didn't they shoot him? He did not expect to wake up again. With a grunt he remembers seeing Safa fighting and pushes a hand through his bushy beard. He's never seen a woman fight like that before.

Safa wakes the same as before too. Grunting and rolling over to stop the light burning her eyes. She remembers instantly where she is and what happened. She rises too fast, dizziness surges through her mind, but she staggers to the door to grab the handle and hold on for a second.

Ben groans on the floor.

Harry rubs his beard.

Safa sways.

Ben gets to his feet and yanks his door open as Harry opens his. They both stop on sight of the other and stand swaying and silent for a few seconds. Ben looks to the third door that's still closed.

'Safa?' Ben lurches to the next door and lurches in as she lurches out, making him lurch back. She sags into his arms that are too feeble to hold her, and they both sink down into one bigger crumpled, groaning heap. A big hairy hand grips an arm of each and up they go as the blood drains from Harry's face from the exertion of pulling them both up. They stagger apart, separating and aiming for the blue chairs, which they sink into with much more moaning and groaning.

In silence they sit. Heads feeling heavy and light at the same time. Eyes not quite working properly or sending the right signals to their brains.

'Sorry.' A low voice, distinct and deep, but Ben and Safa still have to look over to check it's Harry speaking and not someone else. The big man lifts a hand an inch from his lap then lets it fall back down. 'Sorry,' he says again.

'Ah,' Ben says for lack of anything else to say. He squints at Safa. 'You okay?'

She shrugs and immediately winces. 'How do I look?' she asks, and Ben pauses while trying to find the sarcasm where there isn't any.

'Yeah,' Ben says slowly, looking at the bruising on her face.

'That bad?'

'Yeah.'

They both look at Harry and wince at the sight of the bruises and welts on his cheeks and forehead, his swollen lips and black eyes. He just shrugs.

'Had worse,' he says in a voice like an old bear.

'Worse?' Safa asks, still squinting from the harsh lighting.

'Forty-two. Portsmouth . . . Canadians . . .'

'Oh,' she says, as though that explains everything.

'Fight like bastards they do,' he muses quietly.

In silence they sit again with bruised faces, staring down at cut knuckles.

'Well,' Safa says with an almost reflective tone. 'That went well.'

Ben snorts a dry laugh from his sore nose. 'You think?'

She smiles, suppressing a laugh. 'Maybe.'

'Nah, it's fine,' Ben says. 'Love getting the shit kicked out of me . . .'

She snorts her own dry laugh as Harry tuts then chuckles with a groan.

'Don't,' he says.

'What?' Ben asks, turning to look at him and wincing at the pain in his neck, which makes Harry chuckle again, which in turn makes Ben snort again.

'Stop it,' Safa says quietly, trying to suppress the urge to giggle. There is nothing to giggle at but thinking of the word 'giggle' makes her giggle again, which sets Harry off, which makes Ben snort again.

'So.' Ben looks at them both in turn. 'Did we win?'

That sets them off again. All three giggling and desperately trying not to as it hurts so much.

A grunt of a pig comes from Safa, who freezes at her own sound as Harry and Ben both stare then start laughing again.

'What was that?' Ben asks.

'I don't know,' she says. 'Stop . . . it hurts . . .'

'Your fault,' Ben gasps, looking at Harry.

The tension, the fear, the confusion, the pain, the utter incomprehension of where they are or why they are there. Drugged twice, beaten up once and it's enough for that tension to need a release and so it does, with tears rolling down bruised faces as they all try not to look at each other.

They don't speak. They can't. Any word spoken comes out wrong, which sets them off. So instead they sit and chuckle until the mist clears from their eyes.

'I'll get the water,' Harry says, rising up slowly and holding the wall in expectation of the dizziness.

'You should,' Safa says after him.

'Don't make me laugh again,' Ben says. They wait while he goes in, pours the water and comes out with three cups held together in a triangle within his huge mitts. They take the cups and start drinking as Harry lowers back down into his chair. He downs his water and looks over at Safa.

'Thank you. I didn't expect your help.'

'Said we'd stick together,' Safa says, looking back at him.

'Who taught you to fight?'

'Metropolitan Police,' she says.

'Did well,' he says, tilting his head with a show of respect.

'Me?' she says, shaking her head. 'You were amazing, Harry. Like . . . you had so many.'

'Aye,' he says as though it was nothing.

'You think we killed any?' she asks.

Harry nods. His face impassive. 'Two at least,' he tilts his head, 'maybe one or two more.'

Safa tuts and winces with a dark look before glancing at Ben. 'You okay?'

'Huh?' Ben asks, blinking at her. 'You killed some of them?'

'Aye,' Harry says, still as though it was nothing.

'What, like, dead?' Ben asks, still feeling like he's drunk.

'Aye.'

'Fuck,' Ben mutters, staring down at the cup in his hands.

'Who taught you to fight?' Harry asks.

'Me? I've never learnt anything about fighting,' Ben says as Safa watches him closely.

'It shows,' he says. 'Natural ability.'

'Natural ability,' Safa mutters. She doesn't look away when Ben glances at her but studies him closely. 'Ben Ryder killed five men once,' she says softly as though talking just to Harry. 'He was seventeen,' she says, 'walking home on a country lane . . .'

'Seventeen?' Harry asks.

'Five men from Birmingham stopped and attacked a woman and her daughter . . . Gita Choudhry . . . the little girl was called Meera. She was six,' she continues as Ben shifts uncomfortably from the intense scrutiny. 'Puncture in the rear nearside tyre. Gita was trying to change the wheel when the men stopped . . . they were going to rape the woman but *Ben Ryder* intervened . . . a seventeen-year-old kid got the knife from one of them and used it to kill five hardened gang members.' She pauses while Harry stares at Ben with the same searching gaze. 'Then years later he was on the London Underground when it was attacked and he killed again . . .' She stares at Ben. Remembering the footage from Holborn she'd watched hundreds of times.

'You believe me now?' Ben asks gently.

She hesitates and narrows her eyes before blinking and looking away. 'No. Ben Ryder died.'

'I am Ben Ryder,' Ben sighs heavily. 'I was . . . I'm Ben Calshott now.'

'You fought like Ben Ryder,' she says, bringing that look back.

'You saw him fight before?' Harry asks.

'CCTV,' Safa says, looking from Ben to Harry. 'The cameras at Holborn captured everything. Our Ben here moved exactly the same way Ben Ryder did . . . five years ago.'

'They have cameras at Holborn?' Harry asks.

Safa tuts and rolls her eyes. 'Full-colour high-definition real-time recording.'

'Safa,' Ben says. 'I am Ben Ryder.'

'I am Harry Madden,' Harry says.

She snorts and turns away again. 'Mad Harry Madden . . . whatever.'

He draws breath to exhale through his hairy nose. 'They called me that on the base,' he says. 'I did missions that I weren't expected to survive . . .'

'So you must be Safa Patel then,' Ben says once Harry trails off with a finality that tells them he isn't going to continue. 'But if you're really Harry Madden then that means Safa is ahead of us both . . . in years I mean.'

'Are you an idiot?' she asks coldly.

'Sometimes,' Ben admits ruefully. She smirks, then tries to hide it by scowling. 'Guess you became famous then,' Ben says as she looks over questioningly. 'Harry is famous for what he did. I know I was famous from when I was seventeen—'

'And after,' she cuts in. 'From Holborn.'

'So you must be the same, from what you did at Downing Street.'

She nods, thinking. 'The press knew who I was. I was posted on the front door once . . . just once . . .' she adds sourly.

'Ah,' Ben says, realising what she means.

'What?' Harry asks.

'They keep loads of reporters and photographers outside the Prime Minister's house,' Ben explains. 'Safa is, er . . . well, forgive me being blunt, but she's very attractive . . . I don't mean that to sound weird . . .'

'It's fine,' she says. 'I'm not vain but I get it all the time. My eyes.'

'Beautiful eyes,' Harry says without any trace of weirdness.

'Press went crazy when they saw me. I was in the papers and on the Internet for ages . . . the Cleopatra Copper,' she snorts humourlessly.

'The inter what?' Harry asks.

'Give it a rest,' Safa groans.

'The Internet,' Ben says to Harry. 'Er . . . do you know what computers are?'

'Are you really explaining the Internet?' she asks.

'Computing devices?' Harry says.

'They got much smaller and a lot more powerful,' Ben explains as Safa once more rolls her eyes and huffs. 'They pretty much ran the world . . . someone figured out how to connect them all . . . like telephones, I guess, but each computer could hold information, lots and lots of information, and every other computer could have access to all of them and the information they hold. We put satellites in space too . . .'

'Ach,' Harry says disbelievingly.

'We did,' Ben says. 'Space shuttles that took communication devices into low orbit around the planet. That meant we had phones and computers without wires.'

'Like radios?'

'Yeah, kind of,' Ben says. 'Mobile phones that use cellular technology . . .'

'You were asking for a mobile,' Harry says, looking at Ben. 'Didn't understand it . . .'

'Everyone has a phone now,' Safa adds, then blinks. 'Why am I telling you?' She scowls, but Ben knows what she means. It's the sense of self emanating from Harry. Like an utter belief that he is who he says he is. He isn't panicking or trying to convince them but is just calm and resolute. Just how Harry Madden would be in such a situation.

'So what now?' Safa asks. 'We going back out for round two?'

'Door will be locked,' Harry says, getting gingerly to his feet and walking over to the exit door, which he rattles a few times. 'Aye, 'tis.'

'Fair enough,' Safa says. 'I'd lock it after that. What I want to know,' she adds with a look down at herself, 'is who changed our clothes?'

'Oh yeah,' Ben says, looking down at his own clean clothes. 'No bloodstains . . . and we've been washed too, by the looks of it.'

'Better be a woman that's done me,' she says, scowling.

'I'm sure it was,' Ben says quickly. 'They wouldn't do that, would they?'

'Depends on who *they* are,' Safa says. 'Who were those men anyway?'

'Guards,' Harry says as though the answer is obvious.

'Well, yeah, but . . .' Safa says then stops. 'Not German guards though . . . I mean . . .'

'They were German,' Harry says. 'German guards.'

'Yes, but not World War Two German guards. Just . . . oh bollocks. I have no idea.'

'Oh shit,' Ben says suddenly, leaning forward on his chair. 'That man . . .'

'Er, which one?' Safa asks.

'The man in the room,' Ben says quickly.

'And again which one?' Safa asks.

'The dark-haired one . . . the English bloke. Him. I saw him!'

'Yeah,' Safa says slowly. 'We all saw him, Ben.'

'No! I saw him in London. At work. Before . . . I saw him before . . . the morning . . . in the morning before Holborn . . .'

'What?' Safa snaps as Harry looks on with interest.

'At my work,' Ben says. 'He was in the lift when I got to work but he had a suit on. Er . . . he asked me if I worked at Hallows and . . . that's the name of my firm,' he adds.

'I know it is,' Safa says flatly. 'So does half the world.'

'It was him. It was. We spoke and he . . . yeah, it was him. Fuck! What's he doing here?'

'Maybe it's his house,' Safa says, then stares back at the looks coming from the other two. 'That was a joke.'

'It's not a house,' Ben says.

'I said it was a joke,' Safa says.

'Did either of you see him?' Ben asks.

Harry shakes his head. Safa just stares at Ben. 'Holborn was five years ago . . .'

'Yesterday.'

'Five years ago.'

'Yesterday.'

'Five years ago.'

'Yester—'

'Stop,' Harry says.

'So what did he say to you?' Safa asks. 'Five years ago.'

'Oh, you mean yesterday? Well, I said hello and he said hello. Then I asked him if he was going to Hallows and he said he was but didn't say anything else . . . no, he asked me if I worked there, yeah, that's right, we shook hands and I gave him my name but he never said his . . . he did look at the way I was dressed though.'

'Why?' she asks.

'I was in jeans and a shirt instead of a suit, for going down the Underground later.'

'Did you tell him you were going into the Underground?' Harry asks.

'Er, Christ, I don't remember but probably not . . . I didn't know who he was so I wouldn't say anything about a case or investigation.'

'Five years ago,' Safa mutters.

'Think mine's bad?' Ben asks. 'Harry's from nineteen forty-three,' he adds with a nod to Harry.

Another silence, but this one is filled with the sound of cogs turning in heads at the implication of all three being from different times. Ben glances at Safa, who lifts her eyebrows and looks over at Harry, who shrugs.

'I'm not saying it,' Ben tells them both.

'One of us has to,' Safa says.

'You do it then,' Ben says.

'Me? No way. Harry?'

He sighs and looks round as though completely disinterested. 'We're in a Boche POW camp.'

'What?' Ben asks.

'Spoke German. I heard them,' Harry says.

'Yeah,' Ben says slowly. 'That's not what I was thinking.'

'What then?' Harry asks.

'Ben?' Safa asks, prompting him.

'You're the copper,' Ben replies, trying to evade saying it.

'Doesn't make any difference,' she mutters. 'Fine, I'll say it then.'

'Go on then,' Ben says when she doesn't say it.

She looks away, rolling her eyes. 'Feels stupid.'

'Fuck's sake,' Ben groans. 'Time travel . . . there, I said it.'

'What?' she says, screwing her face up. 'Time travel?'

'Eh? Wasn't that what you were thinking?'

'No! I was going to say we're dead.'

'Dead? What . . . dead? Like, actually dead?'

'Yeah.'

'What kind of being dead is this?'

'I don't know. I've never been dead before.'

'It's a shit afterlife if we're dead.'

'Harry died in Norway and you died in Holborn and I must have died in Downing Street . . .'

'Yeah but we aren't actually dead.'

'How do you know?'

'Well, like, we got in a massive punch-up for one thing. And I don't see any angels flying about or pearly gates or devils with pitchforks or clouds or the baby Jesus singing hymns with Moses while explaining how his mother was a virgin. And my face hurts from being punched repeatedly. And although I haven't actually read the Bible or any other religious book I don't think it mentions anything about being punched repeatedly . . .'

'Vikings?' Harry adds helpfully.

'But . . .' Ben stammers. 'No . . . bloody no . . . just bloody no . . .'

'You don't think we're dead then?' Safa asks.

'Oh my God! What kind of copper are you? We wake up drugged and you instantly think we're all dead?'

'Well,' she says defensively. 'What, then?'

'I just said it . . .'

'Time travel?'

'Well yeah.' Ben shrugs, but feels instantly stupid. 'Or kidnapped and drugged and, like, brainwashed so we actually believe who we think we are.'

'That's a better one,' she says quickly.

'Yeah? Better than being dead too?'

'It's more likely,' Safa says. 'The brainwashing thing, I mean.'

'No it's not,' Ben says, hardly believing their reactions. 'It's least bloody likely . . . I'd choose the being dead afterlife shitty dream before I chose that one.'

'Why?' she asks. 'Time travel is made-up. It's fiction . . . like zombies or . . . or vampires or . . .'

'You can't drug someone and then make them believe completely and wholly that they're someone else . . . with that person's memories and feelings and . . . and knowledge and . . . and stuff . . . you couldn't do it once, let alone twice.'

'Schizophrenics?' Safa asks.

'Seriously?' Ben says, shaking his head slowly. 'No, that's not . . . just no. I am me. Do you believe you are you?'

'Yes.' She nods instantly.

'Harry?'

'Been through this.'

'So who is drugged and brainwashed? I know I'm not . . . so that can only mean you two are . . .'

'Well—' she goes to say.

'And,' Ben cuts her off, 'we're not talking about two normal people either but two people with exceptional memories and knowledge . . . you'd have to be already vulnerable and susceptible to even remotely suggest anything like planting a memory . . .'

'People get false memories all the time,' Safa says. Silence again as she reflects on a lifetime of memories and experiences. 'Okay,' she says. 'I'm not brainwashed.'

'Nor me,' Ben says.

'But it's not time travel,' she says.

Ben sighs and sinks down into his chair. 'I dunno what's going on,' he admits. 'What other—' He gets cut off by Harry waving his hand and moving swiftly to the door.

'Someone's coming,' Harrys says, moving back a few steps from the sound of footsteps getting closer, the steady dull thump of boots on the bare concrete in the corridor outside.

'Er, hello? Are you awake in there?' a male voice calls out, followed by a gentle knock on the door. Harry turns, looking from Ben to Safa almost as though he's waiting for orders.

'We are,' Safa calls back, wincing as she stands up.

'All of you?' the man asks.

'All of us,' Safa says.

'We don't want any trouble,' Ben calls out. 'We just want to know what's going on.'

'Nor do we,' the voice says meekly. 'If we open the door, will you attack us?'

'No,' Ben calls out.

'Mr Ryder? Was that you?' the voice asks.

'Yeah it's me.'

'What about Miss Patel and Mr Madden?' he asks.

'They're right here,' Ben says.

'Cor, fuck me,' the man mutters. 'I don't want to do it. You do it.'

'Me?' another voice says. 'Sod off, my nose has been broken three times in the last—'

'So it's already broke then. Go on, Malc. You do it.'

'No!' Malc hisses. 'You do it.'

'I can't. I'm scared,' the other voice says.

'We won't attack you,' Ben calls out, looking at the other two. 'Will we?'

'Er, no,' Safa says.

'I will,' Harry says.

'Harry,' Ben groans.

'Sod that. I ain't opening it,' one of the voices mutters.

'We're not opening it if Mr Madden is going to attack us,' the other voice calls out.

'Harry,' Ben says. 'I just want to get out of here.'

'We're in a Boche camp,' Harry says, rolling his shoulders to prepare for the fight. 'They get what's coming to 'em.' He turns to look at Ben and Safa. 'You two get back against that wall . . . or go in one of the other rooms. Right, you dirty Boche, Ben and Safa don't want to fight so leave them out of it . . . just me . . .'

'We're not in Germany,' Malcolm calls out. 'Mr Madden, none of this is what you think it is.'

'Mind games,' Harry tuts.

'Do the window,' the other voice whispers.

'We can prove it,' Malcolm blurts. 'But please stay calm.'

'I'm calm,' Harry says, dropping into the same low voice he had yesterday.

'Shit,' Ben mutters as Harry gets ready to fight whoever is about to come through.

'Harry,' Safa says quickly. 'We're not at war with Germany.'

'You coming?' Harry calls out.

'We're going to show you,' Malcolm says.

'COME ON,' Harry roars at the door.

'Harry,' Safa says tightly. 'Come back from the door . . .'

They turn quickly at the sound of the metal shutter behind them starting to rise.

'They're coming in through the window . . .'

'We're not coming through the window, Mr Madden,' Malcolm calls. 'Please just stay calm. Everything will be explained.'

'What's going on?' Safa asks, glancing at Ben. Her face fixed with a grim expression.

'I don't know,' Ben replies. 'We'll stay together though, yeah?'

'Okay,' she says. 'Harry?'

'It might be a gas attack . . . they pump gas into the rooms . . .'

'We're not in Germany,' Safa snaps. 'We're not at war . . .'

The motor hums gently, pulling up the metal shutter that clacks noisily like a slow-moving train. Daylight spills through the narrow gap at the bottom that widens slowly. They stay by the chairs with Harry closest to the door. All three of them watching the sliver of light grow wider as the shutter pulls up to reveal a thick pane of glass. It keeps going up as Harry steps closer to Ben and Safa and pauses. A green splash of grass comes into view. Thick and lush-looking. The side of a hill with a steep turf bank on the left side. The shutter clacks and they stare motionless as the view opens up to show the bank stretching off into the distance and what looks like a steep drop to the right side.

'Blue skies,' Safa says, ducking down to see under the shutter. It goes higher until a gloriously deep blue sky comes into view with perfect white fluffy clouds sailing high. It looks normal, nice but normal.

'Go to the window,' Malcolm calls out. 'Look down the hill.'

'Trap,' Harry mutters.

'I'll go,' Safa says, moving towards the window.

'Miss, let me . . .'

'I said I'll go,' Safa says, waving a hand at him. She reaches the window and looks first to the left then ahead and finally to the right and down the hill. She freezes. Not a muscle twitches. She doesn't blink but just stares with her heart thumping so loud she swears the other two must be able to hear it.

'Fuck . . .' she whispers.

'What?' Ben asks.

'Oh my fucking God . . . fuck . . . fuck . . .'

'What?' Ben asks again.

'Look.' She barely breathes the word but lifts a shaking hand to point down to the right side. Ben glances at Harry and they both weave round the chairs to join her and look down into a huge, magnificent sweeping valley. They have the same reaction as Safa and both stare frozen to the spot, unable to move.

'What the fuck are they?' Safa eventually asks.

'They're . . .' Ben says, swallowing.

'Are they?'

'Er . . . they look like it,' Ben says.

'I see,' she replies calmly.

'Aye,' Harry mutters.

'Yes,' Safa says.

'Indeed,' Ben says.

'Aye,' Harry says.

'Fuck,' Safa says.

'Indeed,' Ben says.

'Aye,' Harry says.

'Outside,' she says, 'they're . . .'

'Indeed,' Ben says, and finally pulls his gaze away from the window to look at her. In the surrealness of the moment he takes in the cat-like shape of her eyes.

'Outside,' she whispers, 'they're dinosaurs.'

Ten

Extracted. Drugged. Waking up in a bunker. Fighting. Beaten. Drugged again. Waking up again. A slight shift in the perception of each in the belief that the other two believe they are who they say they are. Confusion. Fear. Anxiety. Disorientation and now dinosaurs.

'Actual dinosaurs,' Ben murmurs.

'Outside,' Safa whispers into the silence of the room. 'Actual dinosaurs outside.'

They stare through a thick pane of glass at a huge open vista of a view. Lush grass, long and vividly green. Everything is vivid and striking in colour and depth of hue. It could be the drugs in their bodies and that sense of disorientation, but right at that second they see the sky in a shade of blue none of them have ever seen before, so pure, deep and rich.

They look out from the side of a very big hill with flat ground outside that drops away in a long sweep down to a wide valley floor full of thickets of trees the size of which Safa never thought possible. Wide plains between the forests and the unmistakable sight of long-legged, long-necked dinosaurs. Hundreds. Big ones, smaller ones and what look like baby ones staying close to the rest.

They stay silent, staring dumbfounded out the window to the grey-coloured beasts in the valley below and Ben thinks of elephants. The same shades of grey and they also look peaceful like elephants do, like they're content to just plod about munching on grass and reaching up to eat the leaves from the trees. 'Shit.' Ben makes the connection as his eyes finally start sending the right messages to his brain. 'The trees. Look at the trees.'

'Huh?' Safa mumbles and cocks her head until she makes the same connection. 'Big trees,' she says slowly. 'Really . . . really big trees.'

That the creatures are enormous is beyond doubt. They are a great distance away, but even so they can tell the creatures are enormous but still lifting those long necks to reach the branches of the trees, which must also be gigantic.

'No scale,' Harry cuts in.

The door unlocks behind them but they don't move or do anything other than stare at the sight of a herd of dinosaurs at the bottom of a valley.

'Everyone okay?' a tentative voice asks as the door swings open.

'Ha!' Ben exclaims at Safa and Harry, who both flinch at his outburst. 'I was bloody right . . . what did I say?'

'What?' Safa asks. 'Oh . . . oh that . . .'

'Dead, are we?' he asks with a smug grin.

'Alright,' she groans.

'In a German camp, are we?' he asks Harry.

'Might be,' he rumbles.

'No,' Ben scoffs. 'They're dinosaurs. That means it's time travel.'

'No,' Safa says with a disdainful look. 'We could be in a park or something. Like Jurassic Park . . .'

'That's a movie,' Ben says.

'Park?' Harry asks.

'Jurassic Park,' Safa says.

'Is that in Germany?' Harry asks.

'It's made-up,' Ben says.

'Like time travel is,' Safa points out. She stands straight to rub her eyes. 'Right,' she says, looking at Ben then at Harry. 'Yep, still there,' she says, looking back out the window before turning to the door. 'Did you know you had dinosaurs outside?'

'Er, we did,' Malcolm, with a new white strip across his face, says nasally, as though he is either very congested or has had his nose repeatedly broken.

'They're very calm,' Konrad whispers.

Malcolm smiles nervously as the three of them turn to stare. 'Er, so . . . um . . . the boss is ready to explain and, er . . .'

'Is that the one with the dark hair?' Ben asks. 'The English one.'

'Er, yes,' Malcolm says. 'That's the boss . . . Roland.'

'Roland?' Ben asks. 'Is that his name?'

'Good question,' Safa says sarcastically. 'Well done, Investigator Ben.'

'Oh, we're dead, are we?' he asks her and gets a scowl in return. 'Got bloody dinosaurs in the afterlife then, yeah?'

'I think we should meet this Roland,' Safa says, ignoring his comments.

'Maybe he's dead too,' Ben suggests.

'Such a twat,' she mutters. 'Harry?'

'Yes, miss?'

'You don't have to call me miss, Safa will do. We going to meet this Roland?'

'Aye.'

Ben looks past Safa to Harry and spots that relaxed, benign *go with it* expression is back on the big man's features.

'Roland will explain everything,' Malcolm says carefully. 'But please . . . we really need your help,' he says, dropping his voice and edging closer into the room. 'All of you,' he adds, looking at each in turn. 'We can't get on without you and it was hard enough getting you three so we couldn't go back and get more cos, like, my nose is already broke loads and I told Roland I ain't going back any more and . . . like, it's desperate and . . . it ain't what you think, it really isn't . . .'

'I'm not going back either,' Konrad says, shaking his head emphatically. 'Please . . .' he adds with a pleading tone.

'For what?' Ben asks.

'Please,' Malcolm says. 'Let Roland explain it . . .'

'Fuck it,' Ben says with a sigh and moves towards the door. 'I'm going with them. I'm so confused.'

'Everyone is,' Malcolm says earnestly. 'But it'll be alright.'

'Now you three are here,' Konrad adds. 'Roland said that was the hardest part . . . getting you three.'

Safa and Harry follow behind Ben as Malcolm and Konrad go out into the corridor and move down towards the door at the end.

'Hello,' Harry says with a wry grin as he looks up and down the empty corridor, 'where's everyone else?'

'Er, they're in hospital, Mr Madden,' Malcolm says, casting a dark, worried look at Konrad. 'Some are, anyway,' he adds in a much quieter tone.

They go through the doors into the big room, now empty of other people but with broken chairs and tables stacked in a pile. The smell of chemicals hangs in the air and wet patches on the ground speak of blood being scrubbed away. Ben and Safa look at each other as though seeking reassurance. Harry does not seem fazed or bothered at all but moves along, staring hungrily at the table full of the fruit.

Through the next set of doors into another corridor much the same as the last with a series of metal-riveted doors along the sides and something about it all immediately makes Harry think of staff quarters. Three of the rooms they pass are filled with personal belongings strewn about.

They go through another set of doors into another corridor but this one is shorter with an open door on the left and a locked door on the right with a red light bulb fixed over the top. One more door at the end and that has a solid metal locking bar fitted across it and weird stainless steel panels bolted to the wall either side and above, forming a crude porch.

'Ah, Malcolm.' They snap eyes over to see the man with the dark hair standing in the open door.

'Roland,' Malcolm says with a relieved nod.

'Where are we?' Safa asks bluntly.

'I will explain,' Roland says gravely, with sincerity pouring from his every word. 'Please, do come in and sit down.' He leads them into the room and moves round to the other side of a large, rough-hewn wooden desk. Three wooden chairs of the same rough style rest in front of the desk, which he motions to with a wave of his hand. 'Do take a seat. Malcolm, Konrad, would you please get our guests some coffee.'

'Yep,' Malcolm says as they both scarper with obvious relief.

Harry goes first, taking the seat on the far right. Ben goes left, leaving the middle one for Safa.

'Right,' Roland says, looking over at Harry, then Ben, then finally at Safa. 'I owe you an apology.'

'Clearly,' Safa snaps. 'What the fuck . . .'

Roland blanches at her ferocity. His eyes darting to Harry and Ben. He smooths his hair back and slowly sits down. Harry stares at him, taking in the khaki shorts and short-sleeve shirt that look so much like the jungle uniform of an officer. Ben takes in the room, the rough wooden desk and chairs, and the plain fear pouring off the man. That it's the same man he saw in the lift is without doubt, yet the man in the lift was assured and confident. This man is the polar opposite. Safa just glares. She too can see the fear, but her impetuous nature wants answers and she wants them now.

Roland holds a hand up as Safa goes to speak. 'I did not predict your reactions, which was stupid of me, completely stupid. How I did not take into account your backgrounds is beyond stupid, so,' he says, spreading his shaking hands out, 'I am sorry . . . and I am also sorry for the . . . the bloody mess that ensued after, but we are rushing and doing things so fast that none of us really has any idea what we are doing.' He stops, blowing air out from puffed-out cheeks.

'I don't know how to explain it so you'll listen to the end and remain calm . . . truly.' He looks at them imploringly, his hands trembling as he rests them on the desk. 'We do not have the capacity to deal with you other than drugging you, and I don't think we can use that drug again. We have no real medical facilities here or medical professionals and the only way to get treatment is to go back, which really is not an option.'

Ben listens intently, registering the words *go back*. He looks at Harry then at Safa, his mind processing the time periods they are from, then to the view out the window to the dinosaurs. He touches his nose as though feeling for blood and realises his headache is still there, the dizziness, although lessening, is still there too. 'Oxygen,' he mutters, then looks up at Roland. 'Oxygen toxicity.'

'Ach,' Harry says, nodding as he makes the same connection.

'What is?' Safa asks.

'Very good, Mr Ryder,' Roland says, watching Ben closely. 'We are in the Cretaceous period. The oxygen levels here are far higher than anything humans are used to.'

'That can kill us,' Ben replies quickly.

'What?' Safa asks again.

'Like diving, miss,' Harry says. 'Have you heard of the bends?'

'Oh, right,' Safa says in alarm.

'We need to leave here,' Ben says, rising to his feet. 'Seriously . . . that level of oxygen will kill in . . .'

'You have all been medicated to prevent any toxicity,' Roland says, holding his hands out to offer reassurance. 'The effects will recede. Indeed, Malcolm, Konrad and I have been here for three weeks and we have no effects now.'

'Medication?' Ben asks, still standing. 'There isn't any medication for—'

'There is,' Roland says, cutting him off. 'Let me explain. Please, let me explain. Everything will become clear.'

Ben sits down, partly because he knows he needs to listen but mostly because he stood up too fast and his head is swimming again.

'Malcolm and Konrad are terrified of you,' Roland continues, unsure of where to start or what to say. 'It was a stupid, stupid thing to do, bringing people like you back without precautions . . .'

'People like us?' Ben asks. 'A soldier, a police officer and an insurance investigator?'

'Sounds like a joke,' Safa snorts to a suddenly interested, almost hopeful look from Roland. 'Where the fuck are we? Who the fuck are these two?' She thumbs towards Ben and Harry. 'And why the fuck have you got dinosaurs in your garden?'

'Time travel,' Ben says with a sideways glance at Safa.

'Piss off,' she mutters, returning his sideways glance as Roland watches on with that hopeful look still adorning his face.

'Thanks.' Ben smiles. 'Now,' he says, looking back to Roland. 'What the actual fuck? I mean . . . what the actual fucking fuck?'

'I'm with him,' Safa says, pointing at Ben. 'What the actual fuck?'

'Indeed,' Roland says with the faintest hint of a smile twitching the corners of his mouth. 'Humour in the face of adversity . . . yes . . . indeed.'

'Do I need to ask again?' Safa asks, cocking her head with a hard glare.

'Gosh no,' Roland says, removing the smile from his face. 'But I need your assurances that you will not react and that you will listen to my full explanation. Do I have that from each of you?'

'Sir,' Harry says smartly when Roland looks at him.

'Thank you, Mr Madden. Miss Patel?'

'Just spit it out.'

'Mr Ryder?'

'Fair enough.'

Roland takes a deep breath and steeples his fingers. The nerves once more showing as he clears his throat. 'You each died at the point we extracted you. Mr Madden, you died in Norway, Mr Ryder on the tracks in Holborn and Miss Patel died when they blew the charges on Downing Street . . .'

'Charges?' Safa asks abruptly.

'I will answer what I can later. Please, allow me to continue. I need you to first understand what I mean when I refer to a timeline. My timeline, for instance, is from the second of my conception to my death and then *beyond* my death.'

'Beyond?' Ben asks. Feeling that fug starting to come down again.

'The timeline of humanity is made up of every single living thing and every single thing done by every single living thing.'

'Eh?' Safa says, shaking her head.

'Your timelines ended when you were each killed. However, the effects of your lives on humanity's timelines continued *after* your deaths. Harry became famous as Mad Harry Madden. Ben became known as the man who saved Gita and Meera Choudhry then later went on to save hundreds of lives on the London Underground. Safa, you were also present that day on the London Underground and led hundreds of people to safety, plus, if not for your actions, the Prime Minister would undoubtedly have been killed. You became incredibly famous after your death and inspired many women to join the police and armed services. You understand the concept of timelines? Good, it's important you know that and always remember it because you can never go back.'

Ben flinches from the bluntly spoken words. Safa blinks at Roland while Harry just stares on as impassive as ever.

'You died in that world and you can never have those lives back. We cannot and will not ever return you and, once you know why you are here and fully understand the concept of timelines, you will agree you can never go back. Your presence would impact on hundreds, thousands, millions . . . countless tiny events in the history of humanity that could ultimately have devastating effects.'

Ben swallows, not comprehending and not absorbing the meaning of his words because understanding what Roland just said is not acceptable.

'The three of you could take over this place,' Roland says into the silence of the room. 'You're capable of doing that, but you have been very carefully chosen . . .'

'What for?' Safa asks in a voice choked and hoarse.

'In twenty sixty-one a young scientist working alone made a breakthrough that enabled time travel to become possible. I do not know how it works. Nobody here knows how it works. It has something to do with a mathematical equation and that is the entirety of my knowledge surrounding *how* it works. Suffice to say, it *does* work. There is a device that enables time travel.'

'Who made it?' Safa asks.

'Does it matter?' Roland asks carefully. 'This happened forty-one years after your death, Miss Patel. The inventor had no concept of security and because *he or she* never thought of the dangers, *he or she* never thought anyone else would either. The device became known,' he continues bluntly. 'The original has been secured but we know that another has been replicated and is now in use.'

'How do you know?' Ben asks.

'Because the timeline of humanity has changed, Mr Ryder. The inventor went forward fifty years and made observations on society. Non-intrusive and non-affecting. Merely observations done as part of a series of tests determined to prove accuracy of the device. Later, when the inventor went back to that same point, it had changed.

'The first trip fifty years in the future showed a society and species advancing as it should. The second trip, to the same point and location, revealed a post-apocalyptic wasteland. Cities in ruins—'

'Maybe he got the date wrong.'

'No, Mr Ryder. The date was not wrong. It was the same point in time at the same location previously used.'

'How can you be so sure?'

'The person invented time travel! I'm sure they could accurately record a date and location.'

'Mistakes happen,' Ben says. 'People get things wrong all the time . . . write down a date wrong . . . attack a room full of German guards . . .'

'I said sorry,' Harry mutters.

'My face still hurts,' Ben says pointedly.

'Be quiet,' Harry rumbles. 'The officer is speaking and I want to eat.'

'I'm not an officer,' Roland says into the stunned silence. 'Are you taking this in, Mr Madden?'

'Aye. Have you checked the Boche, sir? Sort of thing they'd do.'

'Er,' Roland says, clearly thrown off his train of thought.

'Check the Germans,' Harry says knowingly. 'Was that the mess back there, was it?'

'Mess?' Roland asks meekly.

'Are you hungry too?' Safa asks Harry.

'Aye.'

'Can we get some food and come back?' Safa asks.

'Come back?' Roland asks, then seems to snap back to life. 'Yes, yes of course. You must be famished. Er . . . you are all staying remarkably calm.'

'No point in panicking, sir,' Harry says.

'Quite,' Roland says. That hopeful look once more creeping back on his face. 'I say, shall we continue our conversation for a little bit more and then break for food? Would that be okay?'

'Sir,' Harry says with an air of disappointment.

'So fifty years from twenty sixty-one. So that's what . . . er . . . twenty-one . . . one one?' Safa says.

'That's correct,' Roland says.

'Twenty-one eleven?' Ben asks, working it out.

'Yes,' Roland nods.

'I just said that,' Safa says.

'You said twenty-one one one.'

'Which is the same as twenty-one eleven,' Safa says.

'Mine was cooler.'

'Two thousand one hundred and eleven,' she says. 'No' – she thinks for a second – 'twenty-one hundred and eleven . . .'

'Mine was still cooler.'

'Two triple one!' she states. 'That's cooler than twenty-one eleven.'

'Nah, twenty-one eleven.'

'What do you call it?' Safa asks, looking at a stunned Roland.

'Er, twenty-one eleven,' he says meekly. 'But two triple one is just as good.'

'Patronising,' Safa says with a huff.

'No, gosh no . . . not patronising but, er . . . I like them both,' Roland says.

'Harry?' Ben asks, leaning forward to look past Safa. 'Twenty-one eleven or two triple one?'

'Was that fruit back there, sir?' Harry asks.

'Yes . . . but could we please carry on?' Roland asks, shaking his head for a second before continuing. 'We—'

'So when does it happen?' Safa asks.

'Pardon?'

'When does the world end?'

'He just said,' Ben says to her. 'Twenty-one eleven.'

'No, he said they found the world was over in twenty-one eleven, not that the world ended in twenty-one eleven.'

'Good point,' Ben concedes, his mind whirling so fast he was missing some of the obvious connections.

'So when does it happen?' she asks again.

'We, er . . .' Roland starts to say in a voice much too slow for Safa.

'What you do,' Safa says, edging forward on her seat again, 'is go back to twenty-one ten and check the world. If it's all blown up then keep going back a year until you find when it isn't all blown up and you've narrowed down the year . . . then what you do is—'

'Safa,' Ben cuts through when she finally draws breath. 'Maybe we should just listen?'

'We did listen,' she says. 'He said the world blows up in two triple one and—'

'Twenty-one eleven . . .'

'Whatever,' she tuts. 'So what I'm saying is they should go back a year at a time until they find out when the bad guys do the bad thing and phone it in.'

'Germans,' Harry adds with a nod at Roland.

'Phone it in?' Ben ask.

'Yeah.' She shrugs, pulling a face. 'Phone the police or the Feds or the bloody KGB . . . I don't know who but . . . the point is it's not difficult to figure it out.'

'Exactly,' Roland says.

'Exactly,' Safa says, she sits back and crosses her legs as the room fills with a silence that grows heavier with the air of expectation. She shifts position, uncrossing her right leg from over her left and re-crossing with her left over her right as Harry coughs lightly and Ben stares at her. 'You want us to do that, then?' she finally asks.

'Yes,' Roland says firmly and very much relieved. The banter and use of humour at such a time of heightened stress is a good sign. It's what soldiers and professional security people do. *Black humour* they call it. A way to alleviate the pressure and show an air of non-intimidation. He expected it from Harry and to a certain extent from Safa, but the fact that Ben is also doing it is a very good sign. Plus they haven't gone mad and beaten him up either.

'Coffees,' Malcolm says from the doorway.

'We eating now?' Harry asks.

'I brought some little bread cakes in,' Konrad says, walking in behind Malcolm with a basket in his hands.

'Take a few minutes,' Roland says, standing up and heading for the door. 'I need to get something.'

Eleven

'Okay.' Roland comes back into the room, takes a coffee and heads round his desk with a glance to the now empty basket and Harry swallowing the last cake.

'Did you want one, sir?' Harry asks with a mouthful of bread cake. Ben and Safa sip their coffees from unpainted earthenware mugs. Both quiet, both pensive and both having just watched Harry demolish the entire basket of bread cakes.

'No thank you,' Roland replies in his cultured voice as he takes his seat and rests the large-screen tablet on the desk. 'Now. I am going to explain the rest. In twenty-one eleven the world has been destroyed.'

'We got that,' Safa says.

'Good. Now it wasn't like that before . . . when the inventor *first* went forward fifty years, so we know something has changed but we don't know what or by who, but we do know there was a replica device made.'

'By who?' Ben asks.

'We don't know,' Roland replies. 'Needless to say the inventor, on realising the danger, took steps to secure the device, which is why we are here. In the Cretaceous period.'

'I'm lost,' Safa says. 'What's this got to do with dinosaurs?'

'It hasn't,' Roland says, puzzled at the question.

'It's, er,' Ben says quietly, looking at his plain mug, 'a place to hide?' He glances at Roland, who nods. 'The Cretaceous period spanned tens of millions of years.'

'Got it,' Safa says. 'So we're hiding here?'

'Yes,' Roland says.

'How did you get the device here?' Ben asks, trying to fathom out how you would transport the thing made to enable time travel through time and scratching his head in the process.

'Good question,' Roland says in genuine admiration as that hope continues to grow. 'We didn't. The inventor made a second one, which was brought here through the first one. That first one has now been destroyed.'

'Okay, so let me get this right,' Ben says slowly. 'You built a time machine then fucked up when some other people made a time machine so you legged it into the very distant past to hide your time machine from everyone else?'

'Er, yes . . . that is spot on,' Roland says after thinking for a second.

'And now you've realised that whoever made a second time machine has done something and destroyed the world by twenty-one eleven. Right?'

'Yes,' Roland says, smiling at Ben.

'I've got that,' Ben says then looks at Safa. 'You?'

'Yep,' she says.

'Harry?' Ben asks.

'Aye, now I do,' he says, nodding at Ben, 'but I didn't get a word of what the officer said.'

'I'm not an officer.'

'So why are we here again?' Ben asks.

'Ah.' Roland pulls a face and steeples his hands over the top of the tablet on the desk. 'We realised that any impact on the timeline can have devastating effects on the future of humanity. We need you to find out what changed and stop it from happening and, if we are able, you will locate and destroy the other device.'

'That's great, but why are *we* here?' Ben asks again. 'Why us specifically.'

'We have a program. An advanced software program developed after your deaths that enables us to pick out people with certain skills and knowledge that will be able to assist us. Neither I, nor Malcolm or Konrad,' Roland says emphatically, 'have the required skills to do this. You see, we discussed whether we should get historians, scientists or other experts and then we discussed getting you three first, which of course would be harder given your propensity for violence and . . .'

'We're not violent,' Ben says, aghast at the implication.

'I am,' Harry says honestly.

'Yeah, I can be,' Safa says.

'I'm not violent,' Ben says, aghast at the implication.

'In the end we decided to risk extracting you three first.'

'Why don't you just use your soldiers?' Safa asks. 'You know, the shit ones from yesterday that can't fight. Those soldiers . . .'

Roland's face darkens. He shifts on his seat and drops his eyes for a second. 'You killed three of those men outright,' he says quietly. 'And it looks like a few more might die . . . they were seriously injured when they left here and—'

'And whose fault is that?' Safa asks scathingly.

'I know, I know,' Roland says quickly, holding his hands out.

'What the fuck did you expect? Two of us are trained to kill, you fucking idiot . . . you drugged us and let us wake up on our own!'

'I said I know,' Roland replies, the worry back in his features. 'We're already impacting on the timeline. Three men dead . . . more injured . . . this bunker . . . simply by being here is risking an impact on the timeline, but if we don't *do* something the whole world will end.

I've done the best I can. Nearly everything here is constructed from organic materials and . . .'

'Electric wires,' Safa states. 'The shutters. The bathrooms are made from stainless steel . . .'

'Yes, I said *nearly* everything. The walls are concrete and we believe they will erode without trace over the next hundred or so million years. They are not reinforced with steel but purely concrete. The wiring is a risk yes, as are the shutters, but extreme times call for extreme measures. Malcolm and Konrad have done what they can, but as I keep saying . . . there is no precedent for this and we cannot involve anyone else. Those men you fought with were hired help. They had no idea they were in the Cretaceous period. They thought they were in a prototype detention centre in Berlin. Good God! There are three of us doing this. Just three and we only started a few weeks ago. Everything has been done in that time. The blasted concrete is still drying. We had no idea of the effects of oxygen toxicity and had to research and source medications. We had no idea if any bacteria on us can kill anything outside or the other way around. Trust me. Please just listen and trust me when I say this is being done on the fly as we go along.'

Silence settles. Desperation and passion in Roland, who sinks back in his chair and lets whatever mask he held in place slip from his face. Pure worry shows. Pure, desperate anxiety etched into every line on his face.

'The program selected you,' he says, looking at each of them in turn. 'Of all the thousands of people that could have been chosen you three were the ones selected. Forgive my bluntness, but you have each killed several times, many in the case of Mr Madden. You have shown courage in the face of adversity and an ability to remain calm and cool at times of great pressure. You are intelligent, or at least competent in the skill sets required. Two of you are trained investigators . . .'

'Yeah,' Safa says slowly. 'I'm really shit at investigating . . . that's one of the reasons I went for Close Protection.'

'Insurance,' Ben points out. 'I investigate insurance claims.'

'We checked, Mr Ryder. Your skills are entirely transferable to the task required, and of course your actions when you were seventeen and again at Holborn.'

'There are thousands of people out there that would be better than me at this,' Ben says, shaking his head. 'Really, you've got the wrong bloke.'

'Same,' Safa says. 'You need soldiers, not coppers. Use Special Forces . . . there must be hundreds of them that would jump at the chance . . .'

'We need people we can extract without causing any damage to the timelines. One,' he says, holding a finger up, 'Special Forces soldiers are generally accounted for even at the point of death. Two, Special Forces soldiers would be even harder to extract than you. Three, current serving and most past serving Special Forces soldiers are not routinely known by software programs that we can access and know about. Four, the closest match to any Special Forces-trained soldier that we could find was Mr Madden and he is here with us.'

'What's Special Forces?' Harry asks.

'It's what you are,' Safa says, 'or rather what you became known as later. SWAT then, or FBI agents . . . CIA?'

'Same as Special Forces,' Roland says, 'you'd think there would be thousands, right? Wrong. There aren't. No, there are thousands, tens of thousands, but when you drill down to being honourable, honest, reliable, trustworthy, being able to kill, keep calm, resilient, trained, disciplined and then dying at a point where they can be extracted, the numbers drop down and down until we're left with a bare few . . . which is you three.'

'Point,' Ben says, holding his hand up. 'I am not trained. I said that. I am not trained. I am an insurance investigator . . .'

'The program matched you, Mr Ryder,' Roland replies almost apologetically. 'You had a one hundred per cent success rate, I believe.'

'Everyone knows that,' Safa says quietly, glancing at Ben, who blinks at her, then back to Roland.

'In insurance. I investigated insurance claims. I'm not a fucking detective.'

Roland nods at him, smiling sadly.

'What about our bodies?' Ben asks suddenly.

'Mr Madden's body was never recovered, which we all know,' Roland says softly.

'I didn't know,' Harry mutters.

'Miss Patel's DNA was found under the rubble but the ensuing explosions were so devastating it was recorded that she had been obliterated. In your case, Mr Ryder, again the explosion resulting from the front of the train striking the bomb vest was so contained within the tunnel that later collapsed that the heat within that confine destroyed all living tissue. Your DNA was never recovered, but then neither was the man you were dragging or the driver of the train. That was another factor in our selection methodology. There were others selected and, forgive me, but some were better, but their bodies, or parts of their bodies, were later recovered. To take them would be an impact on the timeline of humanity.'

'But building a fucking big house in the dinosaur times isn't?' Ben asks, glaring at him. 'Putting fucking electric wiring and shutters? You've probably got solar panels on the sodding roof. Are they going to erode? What if someone in the future finds a fossilised solar panel? What then?'

'But they haven't,' Roland says in that soft tone. 'We're in the past now, Mr Ryder, but we still have access to our normal time . . . or the future from here . . . so we know nothing has been found from this site.'

'But . . .'

'And we also know that this location is swallowed by the ocean long before the first person ever walks upright. I think . . .' he says, then pauses for a second. Emotion in the room. Raw emotion that is growing stronger by the second. He lifts the tablet and swipes the screen. 'I think now is the best time to show you this . . .' He thumbs an access code into the device. 'The inventor recorded some footage . . . I think it pertinent to show you that footage. It is somewhat impacting and, believe me, it is not my intention to further distress you, but I think it may help you understand the gravity of the situation.'

'What's that?' Harry asks, staring at the thin, flat object in Roland's hands.

'Like a TV,' Safa says, 'Ben said earlier about computers?'

'This tablet is actually 3D enabled but I think, given the presence of Harry, standard two-dimensional footage will suffice . . . now the actual film was captured by a drone . . .'

'A drone?' Harry asks, alarmed at the prospect of there being robot soldiers in the future.

'Small flying device,' Safa explains. 'Like a helicopter? Did you have helicopters?'

'I know what they are, rotorcraft?' Harry says. 'Saw one once, useless thing.'

'They got better,' Safa says. 'Much better . . . a drone is a very small one operated by a remote control. They put cameras on them to record the ground and the military use them to drop bombs and spy on stuff.'

Roland waits for the explanation to finish, detecting there is already the beginnings of a bond growing between the three people in front of him. He turns the screen to face them, leans over the top and presses the triangle to play the footage. Audio fills the room. A slight hiss, then the sound of the drone blades whirling. The screen comes to life, showing an unfocused grey blur and the distinctive motion of a camera lens trying to focus. Harry blinks and leans forward. His attention as much on the tablet as what's on the screen.

The noise of the drone blades increases. The engine rising in pitch and suddenly there is the sensation of lift being given by the camera.

Grey rubble underneath from a distance of a few feet. Less than head height. All three watch it closely as Roland watches them. Movement is gained, the drone goes forward and rises steadily. More broken rubble shows on the screen. It could be anywhere. It means nothing. Ben scowls, feeling like a cheap trick is being played. Safa more so, she lifts an eyebrow at Roland, who simply waits.

The drone lifts higher. The footage pans out. A half-burnt child's doll adds a dramatic splash of colour to the screen. Ben tuts. Safa rolls her eyes. Harry stares enraptured by the high-definition, pin-sharp footage.

'Seriously?' Safa asks.

'Just wait,' Roland says.

They wait. They see more rubble. The drone rises to show a ruined building. Dirty brown and grey bricks, a slate roof, window frames and household objects scattered in the debris. Something from the start of a movie. The drone continues the rise. More ruined buildings come into view and what looks like a bog-standard street that could be from any western country. Houses broken and falling apart. Roads buckled, broken and pitted. Trees now burnt stumps. A lack of life. A lack of anything living to be seen. It could be footage from post-Second World War bombing raids in Germany. It could be from any number of conflicts. It could also be a film set.

The shot widens as the drone lifts higher. More streets come into view in much the same state. Just rubble and debris everywhere. The scale starts to become impressive. A whole bunch of streets ruined and broken. Cars and vehicles are spotted but with the height of the drone it's not possible to see the make or style. Still the drone rises.

The residential view of streets starts to change. Bigger buildings come into view. Still broken and laid to waste, but more commercial in appearance. Railway lines appear at the top of the screen as the drone flies on. Loads of tracks laid side by side but all twisted and broken. A huge roof of something lies smashed next to the tracks. Ben and Safa both edge closer with the first twinges of recognition.

Beyond the tracks a tower block lies on its side. Debris smothers the roads. The scale of whatever devastation happened becomes more evident.

'Shit,' Safa mutters. The first capsule comes into view. Broken from the main spoke and lying away from the huge wheel that was once the London Eye. Capsules litter the ground everywhere. Some still attached to the spokes. Bricks, rusted steel girders, slabs of concrete everywhere. No grass though. No weeds sprouting through the gaps. A complete lack of any greenery. The edge of the river comes into view. The filthy brown water flows past sunken objects as the drone banks left. Westminster Bridge lies with the middle section submerged in the river. Chunks of buildings poke up through the surface of the water. The drone rises further still as the ruined Houses of Parliament come on to the screen. The iconic clock face of Big Ben lying amongst the masonry and spires. Everything broken. Everything ruined, filthy, dirty and lifeless.

Ben's heart hammers in his chest. Safa's mouth goes dry. Harry just watches the screen, any emotion hidden, but his eyes are sharp with understanding. Roland watches them. Seeing the same thing as when he showed the footage to Malcolm and Konrad and no doubt a mirror of his face when he first saw it.

London ruined. The capital gone. Iconic landmarks fallen and broken. No life anywhere. The whole of the vista looks barren. Not a blade of grass on the ground or a bird in the sky.

''We don't know how this happens,' Roland says softly. 'But we know it will happen. Which is why we need you. We need you to find out how this happens and stop it. I can't make you help me . . . I can only hope you will do so because you see the gravity of the situation. Other than the inventor, there is myself, Malcolm, Konrad and now you three that know of this. Just us . . .'

Safa flicks her eyes from the screen to Roland. Harry does the same. Impassive and centred without a flicker of panic or worry on either of their faces.

'If we help,' Safa says slowly. 'Can we go back?'

'Miss Patel,' Roland says, conveying a deep sadness. 'We can *never* go back. We have to . . .' He stops, flicking his eyes left and right, trying to find the right words. 'Detach ourselves from the lives we had . . . those lives are not ours.'

'Ours?' Ben asks.

'Yes, ours. I was extracted too, Mr Ryder. In fact, I was the first extraction.'

Twelve

'Berlin. Germany,' she says, looking over the table. Years of training show in the absolute lack of reaction on her impassive face. 'Private clinic. Dozen operatives taken in. Six dead. Six injured. That's the start point.'

'Understood,' he says. 'Team?'

'You plus four,' she says.

The man is highly trained but even he shows the tiniest of reactions in the safe dead-zone environment of the briefing room. A team of five was a big team in his world. They either worked solo or in pairs, rarely in threes, only in exceptional circumstances would they go for four, and five was unheard of.

'Five identification packets. Five passports. Five driving licences. Five legends to learn.' She places five unmarked brown envelopes on the table, pushing them towards him. 'You are Alpha, you will be *Alfie* during our communications. You will designate Bravo, Charlie, Delta and Echo. I am the controller. I am *Mother* for our communications.'

'This real, then?' Alpha asks. To generate five legends in such a short space of time that matched each agent took some doing and for *her* to remain as controller was also exceptional. He'd heard the rumours of course and had been waiting patiently for deployment but he didn't actually believe it. Time travel was not possible. It was fictional. It did not exist.

'Who knows,' she says, still impassive. 'But it's too big not to be at the front . . . and we are always at the front.'

He nods. Just once. A dip of the head. This is the top of the game, where every single nuance of body language is analysed to a depth greater than the ability to second-guess, creating in turn a breed of person that simply does not show reaction. It is safe here. It is safe with *her*, but even so, he has just shown one tiny reaction and he sure as hell will not show another so soon after the first.

'Budget?' Alpha asks.

'None.'

Again he suppresses any urge to show reaction. She watches him, looking for the reaction and seeing the suppression of the reaction. He is good. He is the best they have, apart from her of course.

'Any methods are sanctioned in advance,' she says, holding that level of scrutiny of him. 'You have freedom to operate but *we* will be at the front. Credit cards are within the packages. There is cash waiting for you downstairs. We do not require receipts.'

Fucking hell. No receipts? This is beyond rare. This is way past exceptional. This is groundbreaking.

'We do, however, require results either to confirm or negate. Questions?'

He stares, impassive. Cogs turning. 'No.'

'Have a safe trip, Alfie.' Mother smiles, beaming a grin full of warmth and humanity that changes her whole appearance and manner with an instant transition into character.

'Great.' He grins back, as happy as she at the trip he is about to go on.

'Let me know how you get on,' Mother says as he rises.

'Will do,' he says, grinning back, perfectly in character.

'I want pictures,' she says, gently chiding him as he heads for the door. 'And make sure you eat properly, not too much junk food . . . and no hookers . . .'

'Yes, Mum,' he says, rolling his eyes as though he has just been gently chided.

Thirteen

'Banana,' he says again. 'Definitely banana.' With the ruthless precision of a hungry gorilla he snaps the top and peels the first segment down the long body. 'Smells bananaish,' he says after sniffing the exposed fruit. He takes a big bite, chews for a second and pulls his head back in disgust. 'Not a banana,' he informs them with a mouthful of mush, which he swallows before taking a breath and then another bite.

'Why are you eating it then?' Safa asks at the look of horror on his face.

'Don't waste food,' he says while shoving the next piece in.

They watch him eat and his relaxed easy manner is in such stark contrast to the rush of emotions Ben feels. He felt okay earlier when he didn't know what was going on. The adrenaline was there. Now he just feels wretched.

'I don't think I'm right for this,' he says.

'What's the alternative?' Safa asks. 'Go back and get blown to bits on the Underground?'

'What about you?' Ben asks. 'Your family? Friends? Your life . . . I'm engaged to get married . . .' He thinks of Steph as the words come from his mouth. She was having an affair. She was having an affair while he got blown to bits on the Underground.

'Anyone got a knife?' Harry asks.

'You *were* engaged,' Safa says bluntly. 'You heard him. You're dead. We're all dead.'

'I'm not fucking dead. I'm here and so are you and Harry.'

'No knife, then?' Harry asks, looking round the room.

'Ben, you heard what he said. We can't go back . . . HARRY!' she cries out as Harry's fist smashes down into the big green fruit, sending chunks of sticky goo flying everywhere.

'Sorry,' he says sheepishly, staring round at the results of the mini explosion.

'It's in my hair,' she tuts, tugging a slimy green dollop from the black strands.

Ben peels a lump from his cheek and stares at it for a few seconds. 'What is it? Melon? No that's . . . is it lime?'

'Dunno,' Harry says, chomping away. 'Tastes nice.'

Ben licks the end of the dollop and waits for his taste buds to decide if they want it or not. Melon but with lime, or apple, or something else. It's nice but earthier than any other fruit he has tasted. He reaches out to take another wet dollop from the table.

'Maybe he's got it wrong,' he says between mouthfuls as Safa starts to dig in to the chunks of fruit.

'Got what wrong?' she asks while hungrily eating the fruit. 'Oh, the timeline. Everything he said made sense though. Hang on, Harry, can you smash that one?' she says, rolling another big thing towards Harry. Larger than the one he just smashed and a deep pink colour with streaks of green and orange radiating out from a thick stem.

'Take cover,' Harry says, raising his fist. Safa and Ben both duck as he smashes down, spraying the room in more sloppy goo. They sit back up and watch Harry picking chunks of fruit out from his beard while flicking his hand up and down, trying to shake the remnants off.

'Me first.' Safa leans over, scooping a handful of soft innards out from the broken shell. She does the sniff test then a tentative lick before shovelling it in her gob. 'Oh,' she says enthusiastically. 'Try that.'

'Yeah?' Ben asks, reaching over. 'What is it?'

'Like plum . . .' she says, spraying fruit. 'Sorry.' She covers her mouth, tasting the plum-like fruit that is deeper, richer and with hints of other things and different from the first one that was lighter and cleaner. 'Don't talk to me. My mouth is having an orgasm.'

'Miss!' Harry cries out with a crimson blush spreading through his cheeks.

'What?' Safa asks in mirth at his discomfort. 'It is,' she says.

'I . . . well, I just never—' Harry says primly.

'Never what? Orgasmed?' she asks as he blushes an even deeper shade of red. 'I only said "orgasm".'

'Stop it,' he huffs, looking away, but reaches back to grab another bit of the plum fruit.

'I forgot you were all sexually repressed back then,' she says goadingly as Harry starts to cough and splutter in response.

'Not repressed . . . just discreet,' he says between coughs.

'Anyway, what were you saying?' she asks Ben. 'Oh, you said he might be wrong about the timeline thing.'

'Yeah,' Ben says, eyeing another long, marrow-shaped object. 'Maybe he is.'

'He isn't, you know that.'

'I don't know anything . . . Harry, what's that one?' Ben asks as the ravenous hunger takes over his sense of misery.

'This one?' he asks, hefting the marrow.

'Yeah,' Ben replies, then looks at Safa. 'So you're just accepting it then?'

'What choice do we have?' she asks.

'Want it?' Harry asks them both, holding the marrow thing up.

'Can I open it?' Safa asks.

'Will you stop being vulgar?'

'Probably not,' she replies. 'Okay, yes, I promise to try and stop being vulgar . . .' she adds when he holds the marrow thing away with a smile.

'Heavy,' he says, placing it down on the table with a thump.

'I'm on it,' she says, standing up. 'Take cover.'

'Cover,' Harry says as he and Ben both duck.

'Shit!' Safa yelps in pain from her karate-chopping hand bouncing off the marrow thing. 'Trying again . . . ouch . . . fucking thing . . . ow! Fucking stupid . . . shit!'

'Miss, do you want me to . . .'

'No . . . ouch . . . oh, you piece of shit . . . right . . .'

'Stop hitting it then,' Ben says from under the table.

'Fucking having it,' Safa growls, hefting the marrow up over her head and slamming it down on to the table.

'Done it?' Ben asks, peering over the edge.

'Not a dent,' she says with a huff. 'Right, we're eating off the floor.' She hefts it up again and launches it down on to the concrete floor, the impact resulting in a wet splat as the skin finally breaks and the fleshy innards spill out. 'Fuck you,' she says in victory.

Being the closest, Ben leans over to grab a chunk of the new fruit but pulls back with a grimace at the disgusting stench. 'No way.'

'Really?' Safa asks, grabbing her own bit. 'Oh, that's disgusting . . . what is that? It's like feet . . . like cheesy feet . . .'

'I'm sticking with the plum thing,' Ben says, ditching the cheesy-feet marrow chunk and going back to the flavoursome plum thing instead. Harry drops down and sniffs delicately at the broken cheesy-feet marrow. A hand comes out, picking a tiny bit up, which he licks as Safa gags. He nods and pushes the finger into his mouth, nods again and takes a bigger bit.

'Harry,' she groans. 'That's disgusting.'

'Like the mouldy cheese we had in France,' he says.

'I might be vulgar but you're gross,' she says, screwing her face up at him bringing a big piece back to the table. 'The whole room stinks of it now,' she adds.

Ben eats the fruit and ignores the rising panic about his being millions of years in the past having been rescued from death by some men from the future. It's not real. It's made-up. It can't be real. Things like this don't happen in real life. Seventeen-year-old kids don't kill gang members in country lanes and seventeen-year-old kids don't then end up becoming so famous they have to be put into witness protection with a new identity. Those seventeen-year-old kids don't grow up to stop a terrorist attack on a train platform either.

This is happening. This is real. His guts lurch and the hunger fades instantly while his mind frantically searches for a punchline or a way of proving it isn't happening.

'What happens to Steph?' he asks so suddenly it makes Safa stop chewing and stare at him like a rabbit caught in headlights.

She swallows and holds still for so long he starts thinking she won't reply. 'Ben, once you know something you can't unknow it,' she says softly. 'Maybe it's best not to know.'

'No.'

She carries on chewing but looks away, deep in thought, before swallowing and glancing back at him with conflict etched on her face. 'What difference does it make?' she asks so gently even Harry picks up on it and looks over with interest.

'What happens to Steph?'

The softness fades like a switch pressed. 'I won't lie, not for you or anyone,' she says bluntly. 'Don't ask me. It's unfair.'

'Unfair? Are you taking the piss?'

'Seriously, we're not talking about it.'

'We bloody are,' he says, glaring at her. 'Tell me.'

'Roland said we have to forget about the past . . .' she says, her voice growing harder by the second.

'The past? The fucking past? It was yesterday . . . I want to know . . .' he says with his voice rising at the feeling of something being hidden from him.

'I've got family,' she says, speaking over him. 'I don't know what happens to them. Harry's the same. Just leave it.'

'We just fucking got here and I'm not you,' he snaps. 'I'm not a soldier or police officer. I work in a bloody office and investigate insurance claims.' Anger floods through him at the unfairness of it, at the pure, bitter unfairness.

'Let it go,' Harry says, holding a chunk of the cheesy-feet marrow in front of him.

If anyone else had said that Ben would bloody explode but that's Mad Harry Madden holding a piece of cheesy-feet marrow from millions of years ago and again the surrealness of it sinks deep into his gut.

'Eat some plum, Ben,' Safa says, pulling the carcass of the squashed fruit over.

'I don't want the fucking plum. How can you be so calm?'

She shrugs, non-committal and avoiding in the same gesture. 'You learn to lock it down.'

'How did you learn that? Why? What did you have to lock down?' he asks loudly, then flinches from the look of pure venom he gets back.

'Eat,' Harry says easily, breaking the tension. 'Both of you.'

So they eat. They eat plum fruit that isn't plum and lemon–lime–melon that isn't any of those things.

She focuses on the fruit in her hands, tearing pieces away and eating without a trace of emotion or feeling. He is Ben Ryder. The actual Ben Ryder. He was the reason she joined the police and the reason she chose Close Protection. Now he is sitting opposite her eating fruit in a bunker in the dinosaur times after being told they've got to save the world. Oh, and Mad Harry Madden is at the table too. She takes it in. The whole of it. The *all* of it and the one thing that forms in her mind is that she will never again have to be touched by that vile man again.

Not here and not for anyone, and what's more, although she doesn't know Harry, she already feels a bond with him and knows he will have her back, like she did for him during the fight. Downing Street was the first time she'd killed another person and she'd always wondered what it would be like to deal with something like that. To know you had taken life. As it happens, she feels nothing. They attacked. She did her job. Same with the men in this room. They could have done what they were told to do and restrained Harry but they attacked him with weapons, and used those weapons on her when she went to help. It is what it is. She looks round at Harry eating thoughtfully then across to Ben and her eyes linger on the faded scar on his right cheek. Ben Ryder. It's really him. She suppresses the smile that wants to form in memory of him running in to the fight earlier. He is completely undisciplined and without technique but he's brave enough. Smart too. Very smart. He's Ben Ryder. *The* Ben Ryder.

Harry eats the fruit. He's hungry and four years of warfare have taught him to eat when you can. None of this is surprising to him. His mind is desensitised from a life of seemingly never-ending missions, firefights, sabotage raids, guerrilla warfare, open warfare, hand-to-hand combat, dirty fighting in back streets and parachuting on to open fields to cover behind tanks as they laid waste to towns. If the fast boat had got him out of Norway he would have been patted on the back and sent back out. It is what it is. He likes Safa though. That she is a woman doesn't factor in his head. Plenty of the resistance fighters he worked with were women and she can fight. Blimey, can she fight. He muses inwardly and has to suppress the smile tugging at the corners of his mouth in memory of Ben flailing his arms about in the fight. The man lacks training and control but he is brave and has the right stuff. Clever too. Got a quick mind, he has.

Ben eats because the other two eat. His mind whirls. His stomach twists. His nerves frayed. He thinks of Steph and hates that he is not being told something. Safa was holding something back. His life is gone. He is dead but not dead. He is not a soldier. Not a cop. Not a detective. He is not what they need but yet he is here. Why did this program choose him? He had a one hundred per cent success rate in his cases but they were insurance claims, not murder investigations, and they certainly didn't involve trying to work out who blew the world up in the future. He glances at Harry, wishing he had that level of calmness. He looks at Safa, amazed at the smallness of the world and that she was the copper who ran on to the platform at Holborn. Even without make-up she is stunningly beautiful but she is hard as nails too. Seriously tough. Why can't he be calm like they are? Why can't he project that level of . . .

'The window might be a hologram projection,' Ben says, his brain engaging gear once again. His heart thrills at the possibility. He stops eating to stare at Safa then at Harry.

'Hologram?' Harry asks.

'Like an illusion,' Safa says quietly.

'No,' Harry says instantly.

'Technology has advanced from nineteen forty-three, Harry,' Safa says.

'We should go outside and look then,' Harry replies calmly.

'That valley is a big distance,' Ben says, thinking on the spot. 'It could still be faked somehow.'

'One way to know for sure,' Safa says and sits up to look round. 'We'll need to see it working. We need proof.'

Fourteen

'We want proof,' Safa says, bringing them to a stop in the corridor on seeing Roland in the doorway to his office.

'Yes, I had envisaged you would indeed require . . .'

Ben stands at the back and notices how tiny she is compared to Harry and he's amazed Harry is letting her take the lead the way she is. Maybe Harry is content to just stand back and watch for a bit, like assess and weigh it all up before making his own mind up. Ben prays the windows are hologram projections and Roland is a mad kidnapping wanker who is about to be beaten up by Safa and Harry. He ignores the fact that he already believes Safa and Harry are who they say they are. That bit isn't relevant to his desperate hope.

Malcolm thrusts a key into the door with the red light over the top of it and leads them in. A large square room again styled in that homely fashion of bare concrete walls, floor and ceiling. The only difference is there are two free-standing, long metal poles with solid-looking weight plates at the bottom giving them stability. Two sleek black boxes like music speakers are attached to each pole. The three stare at the poles. No wires anywhere. No weird contraptions or flashing lights. Just two poles with speakers. Ben looks for the magical doorway or portal but doesn't see anything and feels the hope rising that this really is all bullshit.

'Where is it?' Safa asks.

'Quite underwhelming, isn't it?' Roland says, walking past them to the poles.

'That?' Safa asks, pointing at the poles then looking at Konrad and Malcolm like she's about to start hitting them. Ben hopes she does. He'll even help. Not that she needs his help, mind.

'Let them set up, Miss Patel,' Roland says as Malcolm pulls a tablet computer from a pocket and starts thumbing the screen to life while Konrad moves apart the poles, which slide on castors to roughly the width of a doorway. He then loosens the holding bolt on one of the speakers and slides it up the pole, pauses, looks at Harry, then pushes it higher before stopping and tightening the bolt. He does the same thing on the other side until two sets of the speakers are opposite each other at the top and bottom, forming a square.

'Activating,' Malcolm says, looking up as a blue square of iridescent light comes to life formed between the four corners made by the positions of the speakers. It's beautiful, with shimmering hues of faint colours rippling across the surface.

'Fuck me,' Ben murmurs at the mesmerising sight. A solid wall of light of such a shade of blue but with every colour in the spectrum of light rippling through it. Perfectly blended too, and just that alone is a sight to see, but the way it bathes the room in colour instantly makes him think back to the light he saw in the tunnel at Holborn.

Konrad stares at it for a second then turns to them. 'You go through that and you're there,' he says simply.

'Are you being serious?' Safa asks them both. 'That is a time machine?' She points in disbelief while Harry folds his arms and starts gently frowning.

'Yes, Miss Patel,' Malcolm says, dropping his eyes back to the tablet.

'That is it,' Roland says. 'Simple, isn't it? But you wanted proof.'

'We go through that and we can travel in time?' Ben asks, waiting for Safa to start punching people.

'Yes, Mr Ryder.'

'Okay.' Ben shrugs and steps forward, ready to prove him wrong, but also with an awful sinking sensation that this is about to get a whole lot worse. 'Go on then.'

Roland doesn't reply but looks at each of them in turn. 'Before we proceed I will need a vow from each of you that you will do exactly as I say at all times. We are about to travel to a point in the timeline of humanity. Any interaction we partake in can alter that timeline. We will not talk to anyone. We will not speak within the hearing of any other person we see. We will do nothing at any time to draw attention to ourselves. If I say we abort then we come straight back through the door thing immediately—'

'Portal,' Konrad mumbles.

'Thank you, Konrad,' Roland says stiffly. 'We will spend less than a minute there but I am confident it will satisfy your desire for evidence. We cannot stay longer as we do not have adequate clothing for you to fit into the period of time we are going to. This is observation only and for the sole purpose of proving the device's capability. Do you understand?'

'Fair enough,' Ben says, itching to get it done and finished to prove this bloke is a freak so he can find a way out. The more he thinks about it, the more he believes the window was a hologram. But that other warning voice is there too. He ignores that other voice though, as he doesn't like what it's telling him.

'Mr Madden? Do I have your word you will follow the instructions I have given?'

'Miss?' Harry asks, which makes Ben blink in surprise at him giving way to Safa again.

'Okay.' Safa looks at Roland. 'But if anything happens to Ben or Harry I will come for all three of you. Are *we* clear on that?'

'I accept those terms,' Roland says with a nervous glance to his two workmen. 'This is a test of honour and integrity as much as a method of proving the machine.'

'Whose?' Harry asks.

'Both, I rather fancy,' Roland says with a tight smile. 'I think we are ready to proceed, Malcolm. We'll go for that room Konrad rented.'

'Okay,' Malcolm says, thumbing the screen with well-practised movements. 'Won't be a minute.'

'Room?' Safa asks with a questioning look at Konrad. 'How will a room prove anything?'

'It will,' Roland says simply.

Harry moves to stand in front of the device, looking up at the speakers then down to the floor before walking round behind the light.

'Can you see me?' he asks.

'No, mate,' Ben calls out.

'Same,' he says, coming back into view on the other side. 'Can I touch it?' he asks, extending a hand towards the light.

'Done,' Malcolm says.

'Please allow me to check first,' Roland tells Harry. He turns to the light and after a quick thumbs up from Malcolm he bends forward at the waist and shoves his head into the wall of light and disappears from the torso up. He's there but not there. Like he's been shorn off across the midsection. Harry quickly leans round the back of the light and shakes his head.

'No way.' Ben rushes round, the reverse is the same as the front, but with a distinct lack of Roland's upper body poking out. His brain struggles to process what his eyes are seeing. Roland is there. Leaning forward but not there on the other side.

'All clear,' Roland says after pulling back. 'Please, come straight through.' He steps into the light and is gone completely from the room. Roland is not there. He is gone. The three of them gawp with eyes wide open and try peering harder into the light but fail to see anything on the other side.

'It's safe,' Malcolm says, nodding at the bright blue doorway. 'Honest, it won't hurt or anything. Me and Kon done it loads of times.'

'Loads,' Konrad says, nodding at them.

Harry goes first. Holding his hand out to touch the light gently as though he's trying to stroke it with his fingertips but his fingers go through.

'Can you feel it?' Safa asks.

'No,' Harry replies. With a grunt he lunges forward as though to headbutt the light but sails clean through it. A second later he pulls back with the blood draining from his face, standing shocked to the core. 'Wait here,' he whispers and steps through.

'What the fuck,' Ben mutters, subconsciously stepping closer to Safa. 'Holy shit,' he yelps as Harry's head appears through the light as though he's leaning forward from the other side.

'Come through.' Harry grins wide and toothy then pulls back out of view again.

'Fuck,' Ben mouths again and looks at Safa, who stares up at him looking weirdly excited. She smiles, grabs his hand and nods at the light. He swallows and nods back.

'On three,' she says. 'One . . . two . . . three . . .'

The transition is instant and painless. Exactly like stepping from one room to the other with a distinct lack of any form of sensation or physical reaction. They half-expected it to feel cold but that's only because it's blue.

They take in the room in one swift look round. An old-style bedroom with an ancient-looking brass-framed bed against a wall that has had the worst plastering job ever seen. Lumps and bumps everywhere. Streaks of brown damp too, and the room smells musty. The blankets on the bed are rough wool and covered with stains. An old set of drawers, broken and leaning at an angle against another wall. Bare wooden floorboards. An old-style wooden-framed push-open window of single-paned glass is in the wall, through which natural daylight streams and catches particles of dust, which glint and hang in the air.

The smells hit them next. The scents of people, cooking, fires, horse manure, smoke, soot and a dozen other things all at the same time. The sounds of people talking nearby and a street outside full of life. The distinctive clip-clop of horse hooves and a man shouting out in a language they do not understand but recognise to be French. Ben recognises everything visually. The bed is a bed, for instance. The drawers are drawers. Everything is old yet it doesn't feel old in here.

'Ben.' Safa calls his name having gone to the window to stare out in silence with Harry at her side.

'Please do not stay at the window for long,' Roland whispers. 'And speak quietly.'

'Yeah, sure,' Safa whispers, complying instantly with his request. 'Look.' She nods as he steps over. The window looks down from the third or fourth floor of a building to a busy street crammed with people. It's so familiar yet so jarring at the same time. Ben and Safa have seen this in movies many times, but not like this. This is olden times and instantly recognisable from thousands of photos and Hollywood movies with elaborate sets dressed to perfection. Horses everywhere. Pulling carts or old-fashioned enclosed carriages that range from falling apart to gleaming clean with smartly uniformed drivers at the front in a riot of colours. Bright blues, reds, yellows and shades of gold. Some of the people walking are dressed in filthy brown and grey clothes. Others in vibrant colours and styles. Market-style stalls selling food, fish, meats, breads and other things they don't recognise. Smells waft in and this time they gain directional awareness and see cooking pots on glowing coals and an old woman spooning liquid from a pot into a bowl that she hands to a man, who starts eating it on the spot. It feels like spring or early summer with a clear blue sky overhead and that buzz you get when winter is finally over and the days become warmer and longer.

'Over there.' Safa nudges him. Ben follows her finger and reels back from the shock.

'Fuck me . . .'

'It's real,' she says, turning to grin at him and again grabbing his hand. 'It's fucking real, Ben . . .' A rush of emotions inside her. Time travel is real. Harry Madden is real and she's holding Ben Ryder's hand. Time travel is real. No one will ever touch her like *that* again. She's away from there. Away from that time and with two people who know what honour and decency is.

The thing she was pointing at is unmistakable. Even in the half-built state it's in now. The Eiffel Tower is one of the most recognisable structures on the planet and there it is. The four huge legs sweeping inwards and up to the already-built first platform, and even from this distance and seeing it across rooftops, they can make out the latticed framework.

'Paris, France. April eighteen eighty-eight,' Roland says from behind them.

'Can I open the window?' Safa asks eagerly.

'Yes, but please do not draw attention to yourselves. Miss Patel, you are somewhat distinctive in appearance. Might I suggest you do nothing to draw attention?'

'Sure,' Safa says, lifting the latch to push the window open. The air comes in. Real air. Real air full of soot and smoke that is almost choking in how dirty it is after the purity of the bunker, but it's wonderful all the same. Harry stares down to check no one is looking up then leans quickly out, takes a deep breath and comes back in.

'Konrad rented this room this morning local time and a week ago in our time reference but even so . . . I'm afraid we have to leave,' Roland says. 'We cannot risk being seen here and I always fear the blue light will be reflected or seen by someone.'

They back away like gentle sheep herded by a shepherd and go through the blue light back into the now dingy concrete bunker room to air that seems so thick, clean and rich. Roland comes through behind them and nods to Malcolm, who swipes his thumb across a big red square on the tablet, shutting the blue doorway off in the blink of an eye.

They stand in stunned silence. All three staggered at what they just witnessed. Malcolm and Konrad smile at each other. It was the same for them when they first saw it. Roland pauses, giving them a minute to absorb it.

Finally, he clears his throat. 'Was that, er . . . well, will it suffice?'

'Fuck no,' Safa scoffs with a huge smile that she fights to control. 'I mean, no,' she says more seriously. 'Totally not convinced . . . not convinced at all.'

'Pardon?' Roland asks in genuine shock.

'What else you got?' she asks.

'Got?' Roland asks.

'Yeah . . . what else? Where else? Not convinced . . . need more. Harry? Are you convinced?'

'No,' he says deeply, seriously, but with a glint in his eyes.

Roland tuts, rolling his eyes and huffing. 'It's not a toy.'

'No, it's a bloody time machine!' Safa states, the grin once more stretching wide. 'Come on, where else can we go?'

'There isn't anywhere and . . .'

'You drugged us,' she says bluntly. 'Twice . . .'

'I am aware of that, Miss Patel, but we took very serious measures just to garner use of that one room. We do not have any other safe periods that we can—'

'Ah now,' Ben says with a hand on the back of his neck as he looks up at Roland. Safa's head snaps to stare at him. Roland, Malcolm and

Konrad the same. Ben blinks at the sudden strange attention but holds the thought in his head. 'Thing is,' he says with an apologetic smile, 'that footage you showed us could be faked . . . computer generated.' He shrugs casually. Safa stares harder, seeing the glimpse of a predator in Ben's eyes. 'The dinosaurs were miles away and viewed from a window . . . so they could be faked. That room we just went into was just a room overlooking a street, which could also be faked. We were there for less than two minutes. What you have shown us so far is not evidence enough to convince us that—'

'Forgive me,' Roland says, interrupting. 'We cannot and will not take the risk of popping into random eras to satisfy your curiosity. The risk is too great. Any single infraction or . . . or' – he waves his hand in the air – 'interaction could be devastating to the timeline.'

Ben tuts and nods, still holding that casual demeanour. 'So I was famous for what happened at Holborn?'

'I do not see the relevance,' Roland replies stiffly.

'But you knew where I would be at Holborn? Right?'

'Well, yes, but . . .'

'So why come to my work in the morning? What *essential* need did you have? I mean, the risk to the timeline is too great, isn't it? You knew where I would be so why take that risk?'

'Ah. Yes. Indeed,' Roland sputters, smoothing his hair back as he pouts, frowns and rocks on his heels.

'Your toy, yeah?' Ben asks pointedly. 'Don't want to share it?'

'Gosh no. Not at all . . . I merely meant that . . .'

'Rio de Janeiro,' Ben says. 'Nineteen ninety-nine. The carnival ran from the thirteenth to the sixteenth of February. Over two million people on the streets. Lights everywhere. Go for the evening so that blue light doesn't show out . . .'

'Good Lord, we cannot do such a thing,' Roland sputters again.

'And you were on the other side of the road before I went into the station,' Ben says, still casually but far more predatorily. 'What *essential* need was that? London is covered in CCTV. Smartphones everywhere . . . you chose a date to show us. Now we choose a date. I'm not asking for ancient Rome, the birth of Jesus or the Battle of Hastings, Roland. Think about what you are asking us to do . . .'

'He's right,' Malcolm mumbles, glancing at Roland. 'You let us see the *Titanic* sailing out . . .'

'What?' Ben snaps as Roland groans. 'You let them see the *Titanic*? Are you fucking stupid?'

'Oh, we were at the back, Mr Ryder,' Konrad says.

'And we dressed in local clothes,' Malcolm adds.

'We didn't let anyone take our picture either,' Konrad says.

'We were, like . . . five minutes?' Malcolm says, looking at Konrad.

'Oh, less than that . . . more like four, three even . . .'

'And Roland liked it,' Malcolm says as Roland groans again, sagging on the spot. 'His suggestion actually, wasn't it, Kon?'

'You cheeky fucker,' Safa says, glaring at Roland.

'Okay okay,' Roland says, holding his hands out to placate them. 'Fine. Rio nineteen ninety-nine. We'll need a few minutes to get organised.'

'What for?' Ben asks immediately, the suspicion still strong.

'Er, we need the GPS coordinates, Mr Ryder,' Malcolm says.

'Ben, mate,' Ben says, still unused to being called Ryder after so many years. 'How do you get those?'

'They'll need clothes too,' Konrad says to Roland. 'We've got a place we use,' he adds, looking at Ben to explain. 'Take us a half hour. Any preference on clothes?'

'Street clothes. Jeans, T-shirts . . . casual,' Ben says before Roland can answer. 'Muted plain colours, nothing bright or patterned.'

'How do you know about covert clothing?' Safa asks him.

'Common sense,' Ben says bluntly, not wishing to explain anything to anyone right now. 'We'll wait in that big room.'

They file out of the room, leaving Roland, Malcolm and Konrad in silence. Into the corridor and back up through the doors towards the room with the fruit.

'That was bloody amazing, Ben,' Safa says, once more in the lead, but she turns to smile at him.

'Aye, good work.'

Ben doesn't reply. His clear head vanishes as those emotions plummet back down into despair and confusion.

Fifteen

Safa watches him. He's hardly said a word since they walked out to wait in the main room. 'You look good,' she says with a smile at his jeans and plain black T-shirt.

'Thanks,' Ben says, smiling tightly at her.

'Yanks wear denim,' Harry says again, tutting at the jeans on his legs in distaste.

'It's just for now,' she says.

'What's wrong with slacks?'

'Nothing, apart from nobody ever wears them now,' Safa says.

'Yanks wear denim.'

'Do they?' Safa asks. 'Do yanks wear denim?'

Harry tuts and smiles at her. Taking the jibe in good humour. The clothes are basic and, as requested by Ben, they're muted plain colours. Normal jeans, normal by any standard in the post-war western world. A black T-shirt for Ben, dark blue for Safa and dark grey for Harry. Three pairs of plain brown boots complete the ensembles. Ben takes the other two in and looks down at himself. They look like plain clothes police officers. Boots, jeans and almost matching T-shirts, but it'll do for now. He's surprised Safa hasn't picked up on their almost uniform appearance, but then she was from a Close Protection uniformed role so figures maybe she didn't have a background in covert work. Same with Harry really. He must have done stuff behind enemy lines before and he already said he was dressed as a civilian in Norway. Maybe they had people choose the clothes for them. That makes sense.

'Ready?' Safa asks, then tuts. 'Harry, pull your T-shirt out.'

'Why?'

'No one tucks their T-shirt into their jeans.'

'Why?' he asks, but pulls the hem out anyway. Ben was right. Harry has worked behind enemy lines but Ben was also right in that there were people to choose the right clothing for them. Experts and locals from those areas they were working in.

With Safa once more in the lead they head through the bunker to find Malcolm waiting outside the room holding the device.

'You coming with us?' Safa asks bluntly, seeing him wearing the same style jeans and T-shirt.

'Gonna wait by the portal,' he says, dropping eye contact from her.

'Fucking hell,' she says, walking into the room to see Roland and Konrad in jeans and T-shirts. 'So we're all going then?'

Roland stiffens at the rebuke in her voice, looking as uncomfortable as Harry in denim and a casual top. 'Malcolm will wait by the device. Konrad will stay this side but is ready to come through should the need arise. I, of course, am coming to ensure we minimise our contact with the timeline. When we do go through we will not talk to anyone or engage in—'

'You said that before,' Safa says, still blunt and direct. 'Get on with it.'

'Yes, but—'

'Ben, Harry, don't talk to anyone. Don't do anything. Got it?'

'Got it,' Ben says.

'Roger,' Harry says.

'Sorted,' Safa says, nodding at Roland. 'We going then?'

The blue light comes to life as Konrad operates the tablet. The room instantly bathed in the gorgeous blue, shimmering, iridescent shade that absorbs Safa, Harry and Ben again. Roland goes first, simply walking up to the light and leaning forward to look through. He pauses, holding position for a few seconds before pulling back.

'Spot on,' he says to Konrad. 'We're in an alleyway behind some buildings . . . the main road is directly ahead with the procession going past. It's very noisy and very bright,' he adds. 'Right, well, indeed. I shall go first.' He steps through without another word.

'Miss?' Malcolm asks politely, looking at Safa. She ignores him and walks through the light, stepping instantly into a back alley filled with sound and light reflected from the main road a hundred metres down the alley. Rubbish strewn everywhere. Hot, humid air thick with smells that once again contrast so sharply with the purity of the bunker. Drums booming. Beats sounding from samba bands. Music everywhere. The fast-paced, distinctive tunes so synonymous with this carnival. Voices. Flashing lights. People walking past the entrance to the alley dressed in increasingly outlandish outfits. Huge plumes of fake feathers ten feet high. Skirts billowing. Scantily dressed men and women gyrating and dancing as they go past. Ben comes through behind her. She moves forward to make space. Harry comes through, then Malcolm at the rear. None of them speak but simply stare out at the noise and lights and feel the heat and humidity. An instant transition from a sterile environment to one filled with sensations.

'We need to go up,' Ben shouts to be heard over the immense noise. He needs convincing properly. He needs to know this is fact. This is happening and this is nineteen ninety-nine.

Safa nods back and starts off down the alley. That she takes the lead again, despite both Roland and Harry being present, is not questioned. The natural authority she exudes is organic but very strong. Harry's competence is overt and strong too, but different to Safa's aura.

She reaches the mouth of the alley and stares out in wonder at the flotilla of vehicles, floats and human forms going slowly by. The music is incredible. Hundreds of drums. Hundreds of instruments. All fast. All frantic. The energy pulsates through them. An army of white-clad men and women dancing past. Giant headdresses, flowing capes and feathers on legs. All of them in time to the beat and singing out. Bystanders thick in number line both sides of the street. Thousands of people just in this one street. Safa's heart races. Not from fear or panic but simply in reaction to the transit from the bunker to this. The spectacle of it. The noises. The smells. The others get to her and stand each side watching with mouths open. Harry especially. Never before has he seen such a thing. Never before has he even imagined such a thing. The colours. The vibrancy. The clothing and the lack of clothing. The music and the dancing. His lips twitch with a tight smile at first that slowly spreads wide across his face, showing absolute delight.

The most beautiful woman he has ever seen dances by dressed just in her underwear with a plume of thick black feathers glued to her backside. Huge boobs, wide hips and swaying to the music. She goes past as Harry turns to see the most beautiful woman he has ever seen dressed just in her underwear with a plume of thick white feathers glued to her backside. On it goes. He shakes his head. He grins and laughs. Warfare is dirty. Warfare is nasty. This is what living should be. Just this.

Ben looks round. Seeing the same as Harry, but Ben's life was saturated with such things, and although the energy and pulse still get to him, the sights have less impact. Is this nineteen ninety-nine? How can he tell? He glances back down the alley to see the reflection of the blue light, which looks weak and paltry in comparison to the lights up here. He says something to Safa. She looks at him, grinning widely but shaking her head. *Can't hear you*, she mouths, pointing to her ear.

'NEWSPAPER,' Ben shouts into her ear.

She nods at him and looks round. She would just stand here watching if it were up to her, but she's already seen how smart Ben is and everything he said earlier made sense. All of that stuff before could have been faked, but this? This isn't fake. Not a chance. Still, he wants a newspaper to be completely convinced. She tugs at his arm, motions for Harry and Roland to follow her, and sets off, pushing through the crowd down the side of the street. Roland flinches in panic at straying from the portal but also knows there isn't a thing he can do to stop them. The noise is awful. The lights are so bright. A fish out of water, but unlike Harry, he hangs back and keeps his head down.

Safa looks back, checking the others are staying close. Ben right behind her. Sweat shining on his face, his dark blond hair starting to slick down in the humidity and heat. He smiles at her, nodding for her to keep going. This is incredible. Half of her switches on to the job at hand and looks round for threat perception, assessing everyone in view and automatically scanning people for weapons, a habit now ingrained. The other half of her wants to sway to the music and laugh out loud for the mind-blowing thing she is doing.

The building line on their left drops back. A big red and white striped awning stretches out from a bar front. People everywhere drinking bottles of beer as they dance and watch the carnival going past. She gets Ben's attention and nods at the bar. He nods back. She motions to Harry and Roland, indicating they are going to stop near the bar. She leads the route to find a space big enough for all of them a few metres from the entrance. The smell of beer mixes with the other scents of cooking food and body odour, but it's not unpleasant. Not to any degree.

Ben scours the ground all around them. All he needs is a single page from a newspaper that has the date on the top. Harry and Roland stop by Safa. Harry's eyes fixed on the most beautiful woman he has ever seen dancing by until he turns to grin and Harry realises, with a start, that it's a man in drag. Harry blanches, steps back and turns away quickly with an absolute look of shock on his face that makes Safa burst out laughing. Ben moves away from them, heading towards the front of the bar.

He gets barged and jostled with every step. Smiling faces everywhere. Someone pats him on the back. He turns to see a drunk man giving him a thumbs up. The inside of the bar is worse than the street. Jammed tight with people clamouring and waving money at the poor bartenders passing bottles of beer out and snatching money without looking at what notes they're being given.

He spots a small group standing together just down from the entrance. Men and women drinking beer, swaying and laughing as they watch the procession. A folded newspaper sticks out the back pocket of one of the men. Ben heads towards them, already smiling as he waves to get the man's attention. The man turns, happy but puzzled as to what Ben wants. Ben grins and points to the paper in his pocket and motions to ask if he can have a look. The man beams and laughs before pulling the paper out and handing it over.

'Thanks,' Ben shouts, wondering what the Brazilian is for 'thank you'. Don't they speak Spanish? Or is it Portuguese? '*Gracias*' or '*obrigado*'? '*Obrigado,*' Ben shouts, remembering the film *City of God*. The man laughs even more as Ben unfolds the newspaper. *O Globo* in bold print in the top centre. He scans the information bar underneath, seeing the edition number in Roman numerals and the date next to it. *14 Fevereiro 1999*. 14 February 1999.

A bottle of beer is pushed into his hand. He looks up, startled and shocked at confirmation of the date and that time travel exists, and that he died, and that he saw dinosaurs, and that the world ends in the year 2111. The man who gave him the newspaper laughs again and motions for Ben to drink the beer. Ben freezes. The music booming. The lights flashing. Noise and sensations everywhere. He died. It happened. The man moves in to lift Ben's hand up as though helping him to drink. Ben drinks. He drinks the beer as the man and his friends applaud in delight. Ben keeps drinking. He guzzles the warm, fizzy beer down because he is dead. He died. He will never see Steph again. He will never see his family or his home again. Homesickness hits. Despair sinks in. He drinks more. Suddenly so thirsty. He empties the bottle and lowers it from his mouth. The man takes it away and pushes another one in.

'*Obrigado*,' Ben shouts. The man says something fast, laughing and smiling. Ben laughs back at him. It's funny. All of this is funny. 'I'm dead,' Ben tells him. The man and his friends laugh. 'I DIED,' Ben tells them. They laugh again. Ben laughs too and drinks the beer as a single tear falls from his eye to roll down his cheek. A hand on his shoulder. Safa at his side. She leans over him to stare at the front page of the newspaper and spots the date. She doesn't know that *Fevereiro* is 'February' but the rest is obvious. She smiles at him, seeing the tear but thinking it's a bead of sweat trickling down.

A beer is pushed into her hands. She sees it coming and takes it with a smile and a nod, spotting the boxes of beer at the group's feet. She sips the warm liquid and stares round. Harry and Roland come over. Beers pushed into their hands as the group sees that the nice man who asked for the newspaper is joined by his friends. Roland frets. This is interaction. This could damage the timeline. Harry drinks his beer and stares suspiciously at the most beautiful woman he has ever seen dancing nearby.

Ben drinks. He drinks the beer in the hot, humid air of Rio de Janeiro on the fourteenth of February nineteen ninety-nine and knows he is dead. He died. He doesn't exist.

Sixteen

Three austere, sterile rooms. Concrete walls. Concrete floors and ceilings. A single metal-framed bed in each room.

They wake and squint at the glaring light overhead. Mouths dry. Heads pounding. Safa grunts and rolls over to bury her head in the pillow. Harry closes his eyes and starts squinting to let his vision adjust while going through his now habitual check to see if anything is broken. Ben groans, lifts his head and squints round at the awful room before dropping his head back down.

Safa rolls and twists to sit on the edge of her bed and waits for the dizziness to pass. Her mouth is so dry. Her throat too. She's sweating and feels dirty, grimy. Her hair is greasy too. She looks to her clothes on the floor where she left them last night. Was it last night? Does time even exist here? She blinks at her own stupid question and deliberates the possibility that she is still drunk. She tuts at the memory of Roland panicking and trying to make them leave Rio but being blatantly ignored as they drank beer with their new mates and got roaringly drunk.

She smiles and chuckles in that way people do the morning after the night before. Harry was dancing with the carnival girls. She snorts at that image. The huge bearded man stamping his feet while holding a bottle of beer over his head and linking arms with scantily clad women to twirl and dance. Roland was going apeshit by then, but their new friends shoved more beer into his hands.

She stands with a groan and realises she actually feels much better than the last time she woke up in this room. The pain in her limbs is easing and the groggy feeling is just a plain old hangover and not the sickening drugged sensation. She goes out into the middle room then dances back in realisation she is just in her bra and pants. She considers for a second, shrugs and moves swiftly for the bathroom. A simple, thin, sliding bolt on the inside. She uses the toilet, brushes her teeth and twists the shower head on. Cold water thunders out. She waits for it to get warm. It doesn't. She waits longer. It stays cold. Oh well. She steps in and immediately shivers with a yelp at the cold water spraying her naked body. With the immediate shock over, she relaxes. The air in this place is warm and muggy and the shower feels lovely as it blasts the hangover away. A new bottle of shower gel on the side. She lathers up and washes quickly, using the same product to wash her hair while making a mental list of all the things they will need. Whether they are staying is not a question that needs answering. The thing has been proven. Time travel exists. They are in a bunker a hundred million years ago. The world ends. They've got to stop that happening. The idea of it, the sheer overwhelming concept overshadows any trace of homesickness she feels. She loves her family. She misses them, but her mind is mission orientated. It always has been. Things are black and white to Safa. She *has* to do this and be here so therefore she *cannot* do anything about missing her family or home. Besides, she gets to work with Mad Harry Madden and Ben Ryder and that is enough to make her smile. She already adores Harry. The man is incredible and not what she was expecting at all. He's a squaddie through and through. He drank so much last night he was singing songs, dancing and was louder than all of them, but he has a deep respect in him too. Dignity and pride, and he clearly loves Brazilian women. She laughs again at the memory and wonders if Roland will still be sulking. Mind you, even he was tipsy and in the end he kept saying how glad he was they were all there. *I am so glad. So glad. Really so glad. Indeed, I am really rather glad.* He even admitted he didn't have a clue what he was doing, but he muttered that and she pretended she didn't hear. Sometimes an ace is best left in the sleeve.

Ben, though. She frowns in puzzlement as the cold water rinses the bubbles from her hair. She can't read Ben. One minute he seemed fine and the next he was morose, completely withdrawn. One minute he was laughing at Harry dancing with that carnival girl while Roland was having kittens and the next he was staring into space and drinking bottle after bottle of beer. He was drunk too. Completely drunk. She had to help him back to the portal with Harry, where Malcolm and Konrad were in fits of panic at how long they'd been away.

'Ah fuck off,' Ben slurred at them. 'Got a time machine . . .'

It was funny the way he said it but he didn't say it with humour. Shock. She nods to herself. It's just shock. She and Harry have an advantage in that their roles kept them away from home for long periods of time. Ben has never had that. He just needs to adjust.

She ends the shower and wraps a towel round her body before stepping out into the main room to snort a laugh at the sight of Ben and Harry sitting slumped in the blue chairs looking like shit.

'Shower's free,' she says bright and loud, moving into her room to get changed. She pushes her door to but leaves it slightly open. 'We need a team leader,' she calls out. 'Harry? You were a sergeant. You up for it?'

'No,' he croaks.

'Is that the hangover talking?' she asks from her room, wincing at having to wear yesterday's street clothes again.

'No,' he croaks again. 'You do it.'

'You sure? Can you handle a woman telling you what to do?'

'Yes, if you stop shouting.'

'Roger, I'm team leader then. I would have done it anyway . . .'

'I know,' Harry mutters.

'Ben, you'll need training.'

'Training?' he asks, his voice croaking much the same as Harry's.

'You've fired a weapon already,' Safa calls out. 'So that's a head start at least . . .'

'Eh? What? Why do I need training? What for?'

'Those two idiots didn't have a clue when they came for me. They need professionals. We're the professionals,' she says, coming out of her room now dressed to shake her head at them both still feeling sorry for themselves. 'We'll start training today but we need kit. You two get ready. I'll find Roland and give him the good news.'

'Good news?' Ben asks, completely confused and still feeling like his head is struggling to catch up.

'That we're staying,' she says. 'Come on. Get showered. You'll feel better. Drink lots of water. I'll be back in a few minutes . . .'

Ben and Harry watch her go then look at each other and shrug.

◆ ◆ ◆

'We're agreed,' Safa says, coming to a stop in front of Roland's desk with her feet planted apart and her hands clasped smartly behind her back.

'Oh, that is wonderful.' Roland sags into his chair, hungover and worried sick, but the relief washes over his face. 'Really, I cannot express just how . . . I am honoured, thank you, thank you and . . . well, when can you get started?'

'We need time to train,' Safa says bluntly, standing at ease while looking over his head.

'Train?' Roland asks, going instantly back to looking worried again as he stands up. 'How long will that take?'

'As long as it takes,' Safa says. 'You want this job done, then we'll do it properly.'

'Miss Patel, I understand what you're saying but we need to progress—'

'Fifty years from twenty sixty-one?' she asks. 'Which is . . . oh, about a hundred million billion years from now, so we've got time. We've got as much time as we need.'

'Okay,' Roland says. 'How long do you need?'

'I just said. As long as—'

'Yes yes, as long as it takes, I heard you.'

'Look, we've agreed to do this for you,' she says coldly. 'We've all got skills the others need. Harry is about eighty years out of date and Ben needs to start from the basics. Anyway, you've got a time machine, haven't you?'

'Yes, but only for the intended purpose.'

'Which is what?' she demands.

He blinks and shakes his head. 'So you can investigate and find out how it happened . . . so you can stop that happening. Also to extract anyone else you feel you need to help you. On that note, I have a list of people that—'

'So you'll be using the time machine for the mission, which may change as we progress.'

'Yes,' he says suspiciously to her. 'But we cannot manipulate time for our own purposes.'

'You already have,' she snaps back. 'We're dead, remember?'

'Okay, okay.' He holds his hands out, palms facing her. 'Fine, yes, I understand you need time to train, but please do so quickly. We have to make progress.' He stops and looks like he's expecting a show of gratitude. 'What?' he asks when it doesn't come.

'Equipment,' she says, as though it's obvious. 'Clothing, boots, weapons, radios, kit . . .'

'Weapons?'

'Harry was using bloody spears back in his day and—'

'Miss Patel, I do not envisage a situation where you will need to use weapons.'

'No?' she asks in mock surprise. 'Then why us, sir? Who broke the world, sir? Was it some bad people, sir?'

'Oh, for God's sake. What weapons do you need?'

'All of them, sir.'

'What?'

'All of them, sir.'

'What does "all of them" mean?'

'My team need to be able to use any weapon they pick up, sir.'

'Stop calling me sir!'

'Do you want a trained, disciplined unit?'

'Yes,' he sighs. 'Fine . . . Safa? Is this really necessary?'

'It is,' she says seriously.

'Okay, make a list and give it to Malcolm and Konrad. I'll be going back soon anyway. I need to make sure we didn't cause a catastrophe with last night's debacle.'

'It was a good night.'

'It was a foolish thing to do. We cannot, under any circumstances, do that again.'

'Roger . . . sir . . .' she says with a twitch of a smile. 'I thought you were glad we were here?'

'Pardon?' he asks, blushing slightly.

'So glad, so so glad, really rather glad,' she says, looking at the spot over his head again.

'Very funny. Is there anything else I can help you with?'

'No, sir. Thank you, sir. Am I dismissed, sir?'

He waves his arms. A monster created and now standing in front of his desk.

'Can we go outside?' she asks, dropping back into a normal tone.

'Yes,' he sighs, his head still aching from being drunk and wishing she would bugger off now.

'I thought you said about bacteria or something.'

'We researched it. Malcolm or Konrad will show you but there's a decontamination air-spraying thingy by the back door.'

'Technical,' she mutters.

'I am not a technician. Malcolm and Konrad do those things.'

'What do you do?'

'I get money to pay for all this. Now, was there anything else?'

'Er . . .' she muses, pulling a face. 'Not for now.' She nods, turns smartly and marches through the door to catch sight of Malcolm and Konrad trying to scarper down the corridor.

'You two,' she barks, bringing them to a stop as Roland winces in his office at her brutal tone. 'We need kit. Got paper and a pen?'

'Paper?' Malcolm asks ever so politely.

'For a list,' she says as though just this minor delay is causing her untold frustration that may manifest in extreme violence at any second. The two men literally quake in their boots, both of them shuffling and looking round nervously.

'Got a tablet,' Malcolm says, pulling a device from one of the many pockets in his cargo trousers. He slides a stylus from the side and activates the screen with a look of focused concentration. 'So, er . . . what can I get for you? Oh . . .' he says when she deftly plucks the tablet and stylus from his fingers and starts scribbling on the screen.

'You've got our sizes, right?' she barks at the two workmen.

'Sizes, Miss Safa?' Konrad asks.

She looks up slowly. 'Feet,' she says, pronouncing the word clearly.

'Oh, shoe sizes, yes, we have those, and clothes sizes and . . .'

'Who washed and changed me?' she asks casually.

'Pardon?' Malcolm asks as the blood drains from his face.

'Who washed and changed me?' she asks again. 'Because if I find out a man washed and changed me while I was drugged I will kill that man.' Malcolm doesn't reply but stands mute and terrified while Konrad shuffles back a few steps. 'Did a man change me, Malcolm?'

'No, Miss Patel,' Malcolm whimpers.

'I have not seen any other women here, Malcolm.'

'Roland got one here . . .' he stammers. 'A woman, I mean . . . Roland brought a woman here . . .'

'Roland?' Safa calls out. 'Is that true?'

'It is,' he calls from his office quickly, very quickly.

'You said no one else knows apart from us . . .'

'I promise you,' Roland says, appearing in his doorway. 'It was a woman.'

'If you are lying to me I will kill you all. Are we clear? Good. Now be quick. I expect you back in one hour.'

'One hour?' Konrad says, taking back the tablet to look down the list. 'But . . . they . . .'

'One hour,' Safa snaps. 'The world is depending on us so hurry up. One hour.'

'Yes, miss,' Konrad shouts as they run for the door.

She walks on, marching through the corridor to the main room to find Harry at the big table pouring coffee into three earthenware mugs while Ben rests his head in his hands at the one remaining intact table.

'They're on it,' she says brightly, her tone immediately changed. 'I gave them a huge list and said they had an hour . . . and I also said I would kill them if I found out they washed and changed me. Apparently they had a woman come here and do it.'

'Who?' Ben asks, lifting his head.

'Didn't ask,' she says, shrugging. 'You're the investigator, not me.'

'You're a copper,' he says.

'I told you already. I'm shit at investigating.'

'Whatever,' Ben groans as Harry plonks a mug of coffee in front of him.

'What did you put on the list?' Harry asks, sitting down heavily.

'Boots and clothes, nothing too difficult. Are you sure you're with us on this, Ben?'

'For now,' he replies honestly. 'How does Roland know we won't just do one on the first job?'

'Do one what?' Harry asks.

'Leave, just walk away,' Ben says.

'*Do one* means to leave?'

'Yeah, sort of, like slang. You'd say *do one mate* to someone you wanted to go away or you might say *I'm doing one* if you wanted to get out of somewhere. So anyway, how does Roland know we won't just walk off on the first job?'

'We do the mission,' Harry says with a stern look at him.

'This isn't a war now, Harry.'

'He said the world ends,' Harry says. 'We've got to stop that.'

'We've got to stop the world from ending.' Ben says it back quietly while his head spins.

'We did it before.'

'When?'

'The Germans. We stopped them.'

'Harry, this isn't like that,' Ben says.

'Don't overthink it.'

'Mate, this isn't about overthinking it. This isn't a war with planes and submarines . . .'

'Is that what you think it was?' he asks, smiling sadly. 'But you had the benefit of looking back. We didn't. We only knew what was in front of us and we trusted those that knew better. We're here. We do not *do one* on the first mission as that drops everyone else in the cackymess and you don't do that to your mates.'

'Cackymess?' Safa asks.

'I don't get it. I can't . . . fuck me . . .' Ben gasps and blows air out while looking frantically round the room. 'Why are you letting Safa take charge?' he asks Harry.

'What did you just say?' Safa snaps at him.

'No,' Ben groans. 'I didn't mean it like that. I meant that . . . like . . . Harry is a commando from the war, right, so . . . oh, fuck's sake. Safa, I didn't mean it in a negative way. You're awesome and I'd follow you anywhere but . . .'

'Just answered your own question,' Harry says easily.

'This is fucked. We're waiting for boots in a fucking bunker in the past . . .'

'Ben,' Safa says gently, reaching over the table to place a hand on his arm. 'Just take it easy and go with it, okay.'

'Okay. Sorry,' he says with a nod at her. 'Sorry, Harry.'

'No harm no foul.'

'We're here,' Safa says to him. 'It's happening. This is real and Roland chose us because he knows we're not the kind of people to run away or . . . or give up at the first hurdle.'

'But . . .' Ben stammers and tries to grasp at the words in his mind but it's hopeless. He feels hopeless. Completely and utterly lost.

'I saw what you did at Holborn. I know what you did when you were seventeen. That's why Roland chose you the same as he chose Harry and me. The only difference is Harry and I have been trained and prepared to accept things a bit better, that's all. Listen, Ben.' She speaks so softly that he hangs on every word she says. 'We'll get you through this. What you're feeling now will pass. I promise. I had it when I first joined the police and then when I joined the DPS and I'm sure Harry had it when he first signed up.'

'Normal,' Harry says. 'Man up. You'll be fine.'

Ben blinks and straightens his back from the mild sting in Harry's words. 'Okay.'

'Good.' She smiles at him. 'You'll be fine. I promise. You'll feel better once we're taking control for ourselves. Now, fancy some fruit? Or whatever that stuff is . . .'

Seventeen

'That was quick,' Safa says, turning round in her chair as Malcolm rushes into the main room carrying two huge black holdalls. 'Get everything?'

'Yep,' Malcolm says, dropping the bags to gasp for breath. 'Me and Kon went . . . was . . . we . . . yep,' he says again.

'Where's Konrad?' she asks.

'Oh, down there,' Malcolm says, waving his arm at the door. 'Wouldn't come up.'

'Why not? Did he change me?'

'God, no! No, Miss Patel . . . no no no . . . he, er . . . well, he . . . I got what you said.'

'Did you change me?' she asks, narrowing her eyes at him.

'No! I promise. It was a woman . . . honestly . . . I did Mr Ryder and . . .'

'What?' Ben snaps, rising to his feet.

'Oh shit . . .' Malcolm says, backing out of the room.

'Did you touch my willy?'

'No . . . no I didn't . . . oh God . . .' He stammers the words out, getting through the door and backing away down the corridor. 'We didn't touch your penis, Mr Ryder . . . none of us . . . I promise we didn't . . .' He scampers away as Ben turns round to see Safa chuckling and Harry with a broad grin. Suddenly the world swings back on its axis and it's not so bad being here.

'Did you touch my willy?' Safa says. 'Classic . . . Harry, do you know what a willy is?'

'Aye.'

'Right,' she says, still chuckling, as she grabs the bags. They head back down to their rooms. A fact which strikes Ben instantly. That he is already thinking of them as *their* rooms. *His room.* He has a room. He follows them in and immediately moves to drop down into one of the blue chairs.

'Let's see what we've got,' Safa says, unzipping the bags. She starts pulling things out, examining them in turn. 'Pair of boots for me . . . Harry I'm guessing these are yours,' she says, holding a huge pair up.

'What are those?' he asks.

'Boots,' she says, looking up at him.

'They're not boots,' he says.

'Oh right, yes,' she says, standing up to hold them properly. 'Synthetic material with breathable mesh . . . they're used by tactical police, soldiers, Special Forces . . . lightweight, breathable and the grip is incredible.'

'I want my boots.'

'Harry, these are excellent boots.'

'Good, keep them. I want my boots.'

'We don't have your boots, we have these boots.'

'The boots I was wearing, where are they?'

'I don't know. I was drugged the same as you.'

'I'm going to get my boots,' he says, walking towards the door.

'Harry, just try these, you'll love them I—'

'MALCOLM? WHERE ARE MY BOOTS?'

'Well,' she says, looking at Ben then down at the boots. 'They *are* good boots,' she tells him. 'Yours,' she says, pulling another pair out from the bag. 'We've got trousers . . . wicking tops . . . shirts . . . bags . . . belts . . . he's got everything,' she says, feeling impressed at the goods laid out on the floor. 'And everything is new too.'

'Did you ask for black?' Ben asks, staring at the clothes being stacked into three piles.

'Yep, why? Did you want another colour?'

'No, just asking.'

'Could ask for yellow or something if you'd prefer.'

'I said I was just asking,' he replies too quickly.

'Just banter, Ben,' she says, standing up. 'I didn't mean anything by it.'

He exhales slowly and closes his eyes for a second as the world turns back on its fucked-up axis. 'Sorry.'

'It's fine,' she says so gently and again in such contrast to how she speaks to Malcolm, Konrad and Roland. 'We'll get through this. I promise.'

'How can you know?'

'Because,' she says with a slow smile, 'you're Ben Ryder . . .'

'Ah don't,' he groans. 'Don't say that.'

'Trust me, you don't know what you're capable of.'

'I do, and being a soldier dressed in black isn't it.'

'They play that footage in police tactical training schools all over the world . . .'

'What footage?'

'From Holborn. What you did on the platform that day.'

'Why?'

'To show the level that's required.'

'Level? What level? I was fucking terrified. I must have tripped over like ten times and missed nearly every shot . . . it was awful . . .'

'Not that,' she says. 'That's training. Firing guns and fighting people comes from training, but what you did was from instinct. I bet it felt slow to you, right?' She smiles when he nods. 'It wasn't slow. It was over like that,' she says, clicking her fingers. 'Couple of minutes and it's done. That's how fast you were *and* you identified each target in order of priority. Yeah you were sloppy and yeah you fell over, but you didn't have lightweight, breathable tactical boots and months of hard training behind you but you still did it. You stopped them. Same as you stopped that gang . . .' She stops and flashes a dazzling grin of white teeth. 'I've been in a fight with Harry Madden *and* Ben Ryder . . . and those things you said to Roland yesterday . . .'

'It wasn't like that,' Ben starts as Harry bustles back into the room.

'Got 'em,' Harry booms. 'Now these,' he says, proudly holding a pair of heavy-looking, battered old leather boots, 'are proper boots. Feel the weight of them.' He hands them to Ben. 'Eh? Feel that?'

'They're really heavy,' Ben says dutifully.

'How're you supposed to stamp a man's head in wearing them things?' he asks, flapping a disdainful hand at the modern boots. 'You'd hurt your foot,' he adds, nodding seriously. 'And a sore foot is no joke.'

'Get changed and we'll go outside,' Safa says, scooping her pile up.

'Outside?' Ben asks, rising from the chair. 'What about the bacteria?'

'Oh, they've got a decontamination thingy by the back door.'

'Technical,' Ben says.

'S'what I said,' Safa says. 'Malcolm and Konrad know how it works.'

'What about the wildlife? There's dinosaurs out there . . . big fucking dinosaurs.'

'You'll be fine,' she says with a smile as she walks into her room. 'We'll feed Harry to them if we get trapped.'

'Roger,' Harry says, walking into his room and closing the door.

Ben scoops his pile up and heads into the room with his name on the door that isn't his room because he does not belong here. This is a mistake. They think he's something special, somebody who can do incredible things. *Ben Ryder.* He's not Ben Ryder. He is Ben Calshott, who was going to get married to Steph but Steph was having an affair. The thought of her sends his mood plummeting into a state of despair that grips his insides and sends a rush of nihilism coursing through his body with a deep longing to be surrounded by things he knows. He doesn't care about what happened when he was seventeen. He had years of psychological treatment but in truth, the fact he killed never really bothered him. He could justify it in his head. They would have killed him, that woman and her child, so therefore the actions he took were right. What *did* bother him was the fact that killing *did not* bother him. Everyone told him he should be upset and traumatised, but he wasn't. He was upset that it happened in the first place, and he felt awful that the woman and her child had such a thing happen to them. In the end he faked it, as it was the only way he could end the treatment. He told the therapists he felt bad and let them convince him that he should not feel bad. The same with Holborn, even though it only happened a few days ago. The fact that it happened is awful. The fact that people died is terrible and he feels every emotional reaction one *should* feel to such a thing. The lives he took, though? No. Nothing. Again it was justified. They would have killed him and many others. What is fact is that neither of those things he did makes him a hero in his mind. Harry and Safa are heroes because they dedicated their lives to protecting and defending others. He didn't do that. He only reacted to a threat in front of him and that was it.

He goes back into the middle room with a feeling of panic starting to rise in his chest as Harry finishes tying the laces on his old boots and stands straight, fingering the black material of his trousers then his top. 'Good stuff,' he mutters.

'I can't do it,' Ben says quietly.

'Both ready?' Safa strides out, looking and feeling entirely comfortable in the new clothes. 'Ben? You're not dressed.'

'I can't do it.'

'Can you rip this for me?' she says, handing her grey tracksuit top to Harry. 'Need a hair-band about this thick,' she says, holding her thumb and forefinger slightly apart. 'Get dressed,' she says to Ben gently.

'Safa, I can't. I can't do what you do—'

'I'll train you,' she says, cutting him off. 'You'll be okay, I promise.'

'I just can't.' He flaps his hands and feels lost in the room with two such incredible professionals. 'I want to go home.'

'Ben, we're staying,' she says, keeping that same gentle soft tone. 'Just get dressed.'

'But . . .'

'Please,' she says, locking eyes on him.

'I don't know what to do,' he says pointedly. 'You both look normal in those clothes. I won't. I'll look stupid because I don't belong in them.'

'Ben, get dressed.'

'Safa, I can't . . .'

'You can and you will,' she says, taking a step closer to him. 'You'll be okay. Christ, you're Ben Ryder,' she says again with her dark eyes locked on his. 'Think of the incredible things you've done.'

'That stuff doesn't bother me,' he says desperately.

'What does then?' she asks questioningly.

'I don't know, like . . . being away from home and . . . not being at home . . .'

'That's homesickness. That's normal. Everyone gets it.'

'But this is forever and . . . we're not going back.'

'Okay,' she says. 'Sit down for a minute.'

'Safa, I'll sit down but—'

'Good, then do it.' She guides him to a chair as Harry starts shredding her grey top into hairbands. 'Break it down into an hour at a time.'

'I don't understand.'

'We've got to disconnect from what we were. We're here to do this. We died. We do not belong to the places we came from. So,' she says, pausing while leaning towards him on the edge of her chair, 'worry about the next hour and just that next hour. Get through that and worry about the next one. Do that and eventually all those hours roll into days and this feeling you've got will ease up.'

'How do you know?'

She shrugs, remembering what she had to endure at Downing Street and that fourteen days had seemed like a lifetime but she knew she would get through it. 'Because it will,' she says.

The way she speaks to and looks at him, the tone of voice, the care in her eyes and genuine concern in her manner all work to push that panic away until he starts to feel settled and calm again.

'Okay,' he says, more to himself. 'Hour at a time.'

'Hour at a time,' she says.

'Okay. Sorry.'

'Don't be sorry,' she says, quickly reaching a hand out again, and for a second he thinks she'll grip his hand in a comforting gesture but she stops and pulls back at the last second. 'I'll get you through this, Ben. Now get changed.'

He returns to his room and tries suppressing the emotions. *Just do what she says.* He tugs the tracksuit off and starts getting dressed. *Just do what she says.* Trousers on. Shirt on. Belt through the loops but he leaves the shirt untucked and starts pulling his new black socks on. *Do what Safa says.* The boots are weird with side zips and laces made of strange material that he guesses isn't flammable or likely to break.

'The trousers are too short,' he says, stepping into the main room with the bottom of his trousers an inch above his boots.

'No,' she says as Harry grins. 'They've got tie bottoms,' she adds.

'What are those?' he asks.

'I'll show you.' She drops down to his ankles and feels for the bottom hem of the trousers. 'See this?' she says, tugging a thread of material out to the side. 'Two of them. You pull them to tighten the bottom of the hem but they go inside the boots.'

'Oh right,' he says, staring at the top of her head and noticing her hair is now tied back in a ponytail held secure with a torn-up bit of grey tracksuit. 'I always thought they just tucked the trousers into the boots.'

'Prevents the material from snagging on anything,' she says, working to tighten them. 'That's it, let's have a look.' She stands up and steps back, giving him an appraising look. 'Very good. Feel alright?'

'Blurgh,' he says, shoving his hands into his pockets.

'You'll wear it all in,' she says. 'Ready?'

'Blurgh,' he says again.

Eighteen

It looks enormous. It is enormous. The grain of the wood shows clear from the base of the stock to the underside of the long metal barrel.

'That for me?' Harry asks, picking it up from the table. That the rifle is for him is beyond doubt. Ben watches him slide the bolt back and check through the barrel while getting the balance and weight of the weapon. Harry grunts in approval and pulls the bolt back several times to feel the action.

'Winchester Magnum four five eight bolt-action hunting rifle,' Safa says. 'They make bigger and more powerful now, but I figured you'd be used to something like that. Apparently it's big enough to bring an elephant down with one shot.'

'They weren't elephants,' Harry mutters, holding the rifle one-handed while he opens the cardboard box containing the huge brass bullets.

'Well, we're a bit short on tanks right now,' Safa says, picking up the holster containing the squat black Glock pistol.

'What's that?' Harry asks, nodding at the pistol in her hand as she checks the weapon.

'Glock. Nine mill.'

'That bring an elephant down too, will it?'

'No, but I'd be on my arse if I fired that thing,' she says easily, glancing at his rifle. 'I'll need to practise before I use something like that.'

Ben watches them. The sudden seriousness of it all slamming home at the sight of the weapons. Real guns with real bullets. Safa attaches the holster to her belt, puts a magazine into the pistol and slides it in as Harry pockets a load of the bullets before slinging the rifle across his back.

'You not loading it?' Safa asks him.

'In here?' Harry asks. 'I'll load it outside.'

'Ben,' Safa says, holding out the binoculars. 'You get these.'

He takes the black binoculars without comment but feeling incredibly inadequate. Malcolm and Konrad watch from a short distance, both silent and obviously nervous of Safa. Malcolm shifts position and clears his throat, getting ready to tell them they shouldn't really shoot dinosaurs because the bullet could be found later. He doesn't say that though. Instead, he opens his mouth but stays quiet.

'Ready,' Safa says, looking at them both.

The two workmen lead them from the main room through the corridors to the back door and the stainless steel panels that form the porch effect.

'That it?' Safa asks, as blunt as ever. 'Looks like a metal detector.'

Malcolm nods as Konrad presses a switch on the right side panel. Lights come on. Small blue LEDs on all three panels.

'They use them in labs,' Konrad explains. 'Like computer labs and places that need to be sterile.'

'This isn't sterile,' Ben says quickly.

'Works though,' Konrad says, pressing another switch. A low hum sounds from the panels with the noise of air hissing. Like a much quieter version of the hand dryers in public bathrooms. Ben goes forward, holding his hand towards the door and feeling air being blown from the three panels.

'That's it?' he asks with a frown.

'That's it,' Konrad says. 'Go through it on the way out and same when you come back in.'

'You know what happened when Columbus landed in America, right?' Ben asks. 'They killed millions with diseases. What if we do that here? What if it's us that ends up wiping out the dinosaurs with a bloody head cold virus?'

'We've been outside,' Malcolm says. 'Loads of times. We had to when we built the bunker . . . the meds we took and that thing stops anything on us hurting anything out there.'

'Fuck me,' Ben says, shaking his head. 'That is the least scientific thing I have ever heard. Have we got those meds in us?' Malcolm nods. Konrad looks down at his feet, actively avoiding looking anywhere near Safa. 'Do we have to take more meds or is it just once?'

'Um . . . just that one time,' Malcolm mumbles.

'Right,' Ben says for lack of anything else to say. The whole of this is staggeringly awful. Guns. Wearing black combat clothes. Two idiots injecting them with God only knows what and a fucking hand dryer that's meant to stop them causing inadvertent mass extinction. The despair comes back. That *whatever* sensation that makes him shrug and go passive.

'Let's go then,' Safa says, seeing the change in him. 'Do we stand under it or just walk through?'

'Er, well, the manufacturer said you just need to walk through it, but me and Kon stood for a couple of seconds . . . you know . . . just to be sure sort of thing.'

'Did the manufacturer know it was for the fucking Cretaceous period?' Ben asks, switching back on for a second.

'Er, no, no, we just read the instruction book,' Konrad says quietly.

'Sod it. Let's just go,' Safa says, once again taking the lead. She waits for Malcolm to pull the locking bar out of the clasp and slide the big bolts back on the top and bottom of the door, which he pushes open.

The sinking feeling of spiralling depression evaporates the second Ben steps through the door. The sheer wonder of the moment is of a magnitude too great to be dwelling on anything other than the instantaneous sensory overload. His eyes go wide and open a clear path to his brain that translates each visual spectacle with a rapidity that feels fluid and organic.

All three of them feel instantly alive and thriving. They see the grass is green but the stems are thicker, broader, and give resistance to each step they take.

Ben is walking on thick weeds that refuse to be cowed but fight back to hold him up. Horsetail is everywhere. So distinctive with the green stems intersected by black and white stripes at the joining segments and the small heads pushing up from the bushy foliage. They're low and spread in every direction. Growing freely through the grasses that surround the bunker on the ledge on the side of the hill that forms one side of the valley.

In nineteen ninety-three a song came out that Ben loved and used to play over and over. 'Insane in the Brain' by Cypress Hill. The words stuck in his mind, as did the distinctive name of the group. Years later he was investigating an insurance claim of a fire to a garden shed that also damaged a cypress tree. He didn't know it was a cypress tree but read it on the claim form. He connected the tree to the words from the song he loved and now, standing here, he can tell that the big tree growing from the side of the hill is a cypress. The trunk is growing sideways out of the hill before forming a right angle and shooting up to the helicopter landing pad foliage at the top, and the branches up the trunk are short and weak, giving it an almost barren look. He looks round and sees more of them growing out in patches from the hillside as it sweeps down to the valley floor, which looks dangerously far below.

The hillside is staggered with ledges and varying gradients of rocky outcrops with trees, ferns and wild flowers growing here and there. Ben turns round slowly, staring in wonder. It looks so normal yet slightly off-centre. Like trying to read classical literature when you're half-drunk. You can see the words but by fuck they don't make any sense. Not that he has ever read classical literature, but he can imagine that's what it would be like.

The valley floor is beyond big. It's enormous and given scale by the forests they can see within it. Thick wooded glades stand distinct and separate from the others with wide open, barren-looking plains between them. Lakes too. Huge glittering lakes of blue water that seems to shimmer and ripple. Trees grow from the lakes and again Ben spots the distinctive swamp cypress trunks so huge at the bottom with striations of roots bulging out that sweep up to a narrow, long trunk. They grow in water and thrive in marshy conditions of high humidity and warm air. At least that's what the owner of the garden shed that burnt down told Ben when he asked him about the cypress on the claim form.

The grazing dinosaurs they saw from the window are there too. A herd of them off to the right and more herds at the lakesides, by the glades and wading through swamps, and yet more further down to the left. Different sizes and makes too, or species, or subspecies, or whatever they're called. Some are just gigantic, but those are fewer in number. The bigger herds seem to be of smaller ones, which are still big but just not as big. They've all got long necks, small heads and long tails, but they differ in thickness of body and the length of the tail and height too. Some are eating from the ground while others stretch those necks up to reach low branches. They look mostly grey but Ben spots areas of darker and lighter shades amongst them and some that border more on browns and greens, but all natural and subtle.

'This is unbelievable,' Safa states, tutting and shaking her head. 'I mean, no warnings, no lists of what is dangerous or what could hurt us, no idea of the time of day or how far we can go. No instructions. It's bloody awful. Harry? Don't you think it's bloody awful?'

'Aye,' he says simply and slides the rifle from his shoulder. He takes one of the huge bullets, pops it in the rifle and operates the bolt to make the weapon ready. He lifts the rifle to stare down the scope towards the plains below, using the magnification to gain a closer view.

Words and phrases like 'ecosystem', 'microclimate', 'biology' and 'hereditary traits' swim through Ben's mind. His history, geography and biology teachers would be wetting themselves right now. He moves off down the side of the bunker, which is nestled perfectly into the hillside and painted shades of green and brown to make it blend so well. No sharp edges either, everything is rounded and seemingly organic in design and he guesses from a distance you'd struggle to even see it. He passes the bit where Roland's office must be, then the main room, and works out that the next section is the corridor leading to their rooms.

Past the bunker, the ground remains flat from a natural ledge that tapers off hundreds of metres away. The first thing that springs to Ben's mind is a roof garden with a safety balustrade and white-shirted waiters serving chilled drinks to people sitting in bamboo chairs enjoying the view down below. Instead, he spots more cypress trees, plants, weeds, ferns and rocks of a world that has already been forming for hundreds of millions of years and is forever continuing to form. Time has no meaning at this point. It is nothing. Time does not exist. Just the sequential transition of the sun following the moon as the planet rotates and spins through space.

The one thing he does remember from school is that continental drift was happening in the Cretaceous period. The land masses of the Americas were joined to Europe, Africa and Asia, which all formed some supercontinent, the name of which escapes him. Pang? Pangle? Pangea? Something like that. They could be anywhere in the world. They could be in the spot of what later becomes the Atlantic Ocean or Beijing or bloody Battersea Dogs Home for all he knows. That's happening now though. The continents are moving apart right now. They could walk or drive for thousands of miles and recognise nothing. The coastlines would be completely different. Everything is different but exactly how you would expect it to look. Get an artist to read some dinosaur books and ask them to paint a picture from the image formed in the mind and this vista is what you would get. Swampy, hot and green.

The irritation Safa felt at the lack of protocols soon passes. The feel of the sun is gorgeous. The view is amazing. The air is so thick and clean. She breathes in a deep lungful and almost feels giddy for a second. Ben said there was more oxygen here but then Roland said they had been medicated. She watches Harry scoping the wildlife down in the plains then glances over to Ben and smiles at the look of rapture on his face. He seems so different again. Like he's come alive and can't move his head fast enough to take everything in.

She motions for Harry to walk down the side of the bunker to join Ben and she stares down as mesmerised as he at the commanding view, which no person ever born could ever tire of seeing. Safa was right. Ben's mind opens completely. Thoughts whirl and spin through his brain as he tries to gain perspective and context.

'Up?' Ben blinks back to the now and looks at Harry motioning up the bank that rises behind the bunker.

'We should,' Safa says, turning her back on the valley to stare up at the bank. How can she do that? How can anyone turn away from that sight? 'Ben?' she calls.

'Coming,' he mutters.

This time Harry takes the lead and threads a staggered route up the steep bank. Within minutes, Ben is breathing hard with sweat beading on his face.

'Moss,' Harry says from up front.

'What?' Safa asks. The big man comes to a stop and points over at a collection of rocks and ferns.

'Moss,' Harry says again.

'Okay,' Safa says slowly.

He looks at her then at Ben. 'Moss grows on the northern side. That way's north,' he says, pointing back towards the bunker.

'Oh right,' Safa says casually with the corners of her mouth twitching.

'What?' Harry asks.

'Nothing,' she says lightly. 'Good skills.'

'Hmmm,' Harry grumbles, giving her a thoughtful glance before walking on a few steps then stopping again. 'What?' he asks her.

'Northern hemisphere,' she says with a smile. 'Moss grows on the north in the northern hemisphere and it's not always accurate.'

'I don't think that's right either,' Ben calls forward. 'I read it somewhere that it's got something to do with moisture and the sun?'

'That's north,' Harry says, pointing again.

'Okay, Mountain Man,' Safa says. 'Lead on.'

They carry on ascending to the top of the bank and come to a stop again at the sudden view opening out. A clearing several hundred metres wide and long bordered by a fluctuating treeline that bulges out in places but recedes in others. It's just like the valley floor too, with swampy patches of gloopy-looking water here and there and big boulders, rocks and stones littered between the horsetails and fern grasses.

'Look at those.' Safa points down to a group of plants that look like tropical houseplants of the type you'd expect to see in Mediterranean hotel foyers. Long, spiky-looking branches that are actually soft to the touch and bushy too, with leaves and stems of almost perfectly identical length and size. In the middle there are weird seed fruit things that look like pine cones with overlapping Roman armour except they look softer and even edible.

'Flowers,' Harry says, giving voice to the things he sees. They look round, spotting flashes of colour amidst the sea of greens and browns. Whites, reds and all manner of shades in-between. Yellows and purples of things that look like roses and sunflowers and magnolias but clearly are not any of those things. They have cup shapes with petals fanning round to entice insects to pollinate and feast. Some are tubular like trumpets, others are more straight or like the rose formation of concentric circles of petals growing tight together.

They get that jarring sensation again. Safa looks at a broad-headed flowering plant, with her brain trying to interpret the sight as a sunflower. But it isn't a sunflower. She doesn't know what it is. Ben doesn't recognise any of the flowers either, but he can see evolution in action. That thing will *become* a sunflower. That will be a rose, but not yet, and not for millions of years either.

The static vision is one thing, but the smells, sounds and feel of the place are an altogether different set of sensations. The heat is close, like a jungle, and the air is filled with thousands of noises of insects buzzing and chirping and other creatures squawking and crying out.

They follow Harry picking a route towards the trees and spot beetles climbing up plant stems and more shoving their faces into the sticky pollen. Small flying insects are everywhere too. Wasp-type things with yellow and black bodies but bigger and much tougher-looking. For a second Ben thinks they must be what bees come from until he actually sees bees and mutters in shock. They're bloody huge things. Much bigger than any bee he has ever seen, with legs like saddlebags weighed down with pollen and broad wings that vibrate as they hover to lift or sink towards the flowers. On sight of the creatures Safa draws her pistol, holding it down at her side. Her thumb resting on the safety switch as she tracks and follows the huge bees buzzing through the air. Harry just watches. He served in jungles across the world and although seeing new creatures is amazing, it does not hold the same shock for him as it does for the other two. Mind you, they didn't have dinosaurs in Africa. Big bugs, but no dinosaurs.

Things scuttle between rocks and plants and are gone from sight before they can turn and lock their eyes on them. They see a column of ants marching along that sends a shiver down Ben's spine. Each one must be over two inches in length, some look bigger and thicker with bulging back ends. They look nasty too, like they would cause damage if they bit you, and there's hundreds of them just in that snapshot of a glance.

A splash of water makes them all look round in time to see a small thing flying up and away towards the treeline and it's at that point that they gain a sense of the scale of the trees standing sentinel on that line.

Ben recognised the cypress trees, but the ones forming the forest are much bigger and must be standing at over fifty metres in height easily. Some look like sycamores or the London plane trees he and Safa are so used to seeing in parks and open spaces. Thick, dense trunks sweeping up to the enormous branches, which stretch out in decreasing size from the bottom to the top with dense green foliage. Conifer-type things too, but again they get that jarring sensation of expecting to see one thing but actually looking at something different.

The closer they get, the more the scale of the trees increases. They have huge gaps between them, forming lanes and avenues threading round the trunks. The noise gets louder too. The clearing is like the quiet section and the forest is the main attraction, where everything that can make noise lives.

Screeches and squawks from everywhere. Branches rustling with scampering noises of things chasing and things being chased. A burst of activity and the sound of twigs snapping bring them to a halt as they listen to the death screams of some creature being chomped.

A thing flies into view. Like a bee with broad stripes, but these are red and black instead of yellow and black. The size of a rugby ball with wings the length of Harry's arms, but it moves like a bee, buzzing towards the nearest flower and hovering above as though scenting to see what's on offer.

It glides away and the noise increases to a pitch like an electric drill that revs louder as it rises and reduces when it sinks down towards the next flower. They watch mesmerised as it drops to land lightly in the middle of the blossoming flower, which hardly moves from the weight bearing down. A big head stuffs face first into the middle and as the buzzing noise dies down so they hear a sucking that's like a dog cleaning itself. Suck squelch swallow. Suck squelch swallow. Then the buzzing increases as the engine pitches to give lift and it soars up freshly drunk on pollen to zigzag along in the air.

A screech rips the air apart, making them duck down. Safa and Harry both raise their weapons. The rugby ball bee pays no heed as the treetops explode with leaves bursting up and twigs falling down.

The three get ready to flee for the bunker as a drumming noise that's fast and furious comes from the foliage high up in the tops of the trees. Wood splinters and branches snap as a black object breaks free, soaring up on wings that beat furiously to gain height, and even from this distance they can see the immense size of the thing. It flies up as though desperate to be away from the trees as another beast of the same ilk explodes out in a shower of broken foliage that drops away as it soars to catch the first.

With enough height gained, the first creature flips in the air to point down and torpedo drops at an angle away from the one chasing it. The wings open wide and long like the sails on a yacht that catch the thermals. The second creature immediately copies until they're side by side, soaring playfully on vast appendages that seem solid yet transparent and the closest thing to a dragon's wings they can possibly imagine.

Undoubtedly the creatures see the people, for as one they adjust aim and glide lower through the sky, heading straight in their direction, but they're so entranced that they don't run or burst away, but stand staring with mouths hanging open. The creatures have long curved beaks and legs with vicious-looking talons clear against the sky and what looks like a long body coated in both feathers and scales: a seamless, beautifully woven tapestry.

The creatures swoop down, letting the warm air do the work as they drop closer, and only at the last second do the three realise the danger and burst away in all directions as the flying things glide powerfully overhead and down into a steeper dive towards the valley floor.

Ben runs to the edge to watch them drop with laughter coming from his mouth at the sight of them in mid-air tumbling and rolling for a few seconds before gliding away in opposite directions then coming back together in what can only be a mating ritual of airborne dance.

'Ben!' Harry shouts in warning. Ben spins round and locks his two eyes on the hundreds presented by the rugby ball bee as it flies towards him. He spots Harry and Safa going wide to the sides with weapons aimed.

'Don't shoot it,' he calls out softly, taking in every detail of the hairy legs, the bulging saddle bags and the wings beating faster than the eye can see. How it gains flight at such a size is beyond his imagination, but then his mind is constrained by the world in which he lived, and this world is not his world.

It slows down, the buzzing becoming deeper as though it's changing gear to hold stationary, assessing, scenting, smelling, seeing and then deciding that it doesn't want whatever pollen Ben might have and round it turns, moving almost lazily to Harry and Safa, who get the star treatment next, and then it's done. They are not interesting. They are not food, therefore they are dismissed.

A black cloud of reverberating wings suddenly bursts from the ground with a sound like angry whispering that builds to an all-out screaming of beating wings, deafening and thunderous. With no scale at first they simply watch, then the size of the insects hits home. Dragonflies with a double-layered wingspan of over a foot and bodies even longer and there are hundreds of them swarming up and around like a school of fish gathering together and moving almost as one organism. They move closer and yet more rise to join the rest, gradually gaining height so as to evade the three figures coming towards them.

The insects swarm round, their heads dropping and lifting and moving so fast but never colliding into each other. They are thick enough to be substantial but light enough to be easily recognised as insects, with blues and reds glinting from their bodies and faint rainbows showing in their wings, like washed-out butterflies.

There's no threat here. None of them feel in danger but in awe at the life in this place and they stare up into the black cloud as if in prayer, then stagger back in shock at seeing one of the flying beasts they saw bursting from the trees go slamming through the insects with its mouth open, snapping left and right. One dragonfly is snatched from the air with a quick rag of the creature's head and the insect is swallowed. The second creature, having gone higher and further out to catch those bursting away, glides down as well, snapping to the sides until it snags a dragonfly for lunch.

The three stand watching. Rooted to the spot as the two creatures soar higher then spread their wings to turn lazily in the air before they commence the next torpedo run back down through the now crazily humming cloud of insects.

Screeches come from the flying creatures. A sound of excitement, of pure thrill mingled with a calling out. They stay together this time, dropping rapidly until they hit the outer edges of the swarm and only then do their wings open to lift them up, into and through the dragonflies that get snagged and gulped down time and again. Ben realises that already the presence of humans has caused an effect that otherwise may not have happened. If not for them, these two flying animals may not have enjoyed this meal and in turn so the insects may have rested hidden in the long-stemmed grass through the heat of the day.

The swarm goes for the trees as the only obvious point of cover and the predators give chase, swooping and rising to bank sharply for another run through.

They go slower this time, advancing step by step towards the treeline as the power of curiosity overcomes common sense. They *should* stay in the open near to the bunker so they can turn and run if they need. Except they aren't those types of people. Ben just witnessed life and death with flying dinosaurs dominating this place as they snacked on giant insects that died to give life that died to give life and forever on it will go. That humans have conscious thought is the one thing that separates them from everything else, but that conscious thought has wrought more damage than all of the combined life that went before them. Ben sags on the spot with a crushing weight pushing him down. Sweat pouring down his face. Whatever happens in twenty-one eleven is probably deserved. *Fuck it, I'm amazed we got that far.*

'Is that a caterpillar?' Safa asks in simple curiosity. Ben and Harry glance over, expecting to see something big and grotesque, and they're not disappointed to see a big, grotesque, hairy, bulging, striped thing stuck on the side of a tree. Over a metre long and with a body as thick as one of Harry's legs. 'I'm allergic to caterpillars,' she says conversationally. 'I get a rash.'

'You'll get more than a rash from that thing,' Ben says in a voice that also sounds entirely too normal and disconnected from the weirdness he still feels inside.

'Big, isn't it?' she says, staring round in what must be the most awesome understatement ever made.

'Noisy,' Harry remarks. 'Malaya in forty-one . . . that was noisy too.'

'Bit further?' Safa asks them both. Harry nods. Ben shrugs, almost fatalistic in mood.

They stop talking as an armoured thing waddles from the undergrowth. Like an armadillo crossed with an anteater and bred with a tank, but it doesn't pay them the slightest attention. They turn constantly at the sounds of motion around them. Ben jerking nervously, Harry and Safa both calm and assured. They move on, stopping every few steps to stare and gawp at something else, like the thickness of the vines climbing the trees and the oversized ferns and other flora abundant everywhere the sun can penetrate.

Butterflies too. Bigger than they are used to, but not as big as the caterpillar they saw, which makes Ben think it wasn't a pre-metamorphosis caterpillar at all.

'Head back,' Harry says, breaking the reverie. He stretches his back out, looking up at the canopy. 'I can normally tell the time of day, but getting nowt here . . .' he trails off quietly.

'What's that?' Ben asks, pointing off to the right to some black things hovering in the air and juddering with a movement that's frantic and panicked in a way he recognises but can't seem to understand.

'Don't know,' Safa says, walking towards the objects. 'What are they?'

A dozen or so of them seemingly vibrate in mid-air in the space between two trees. The three stay side by side watching until a subtle but distinctive sound brings them to a stop.

'That was a step,' Safa mouths, turning slowly to look at Harry, who nods and holds a hand up, signalling them to be quiet.

'Could have been anything.' The words leave Ben's mouth with the air from his lungs vibrating through his voice box, which creates the sound and formation of words that are projected across the distance and used by whatever is behind them to mask another step being taken. Silence again and they hold position with Harry inching slowly round to stare behind.

'Anything?' Safa whispers. Another shuffling step is taken as she speaks.

Movement catches Ben's eye. Sunlight glinting off something that dazzles for a split second. He turns to see rays of lights penetrating the canopy, glinting on the golden strands of a web that hold the objects he thought were caught in mid-air, and as he sees the web so he grasps the shape of the insects and makes out a dozen or more dragonflies caught and trapped. Another step is taken in the undergrowth. The tension mounts. A screech overhead and tiny scuttling sounds of insects moving with claws scraping rough on the tree bark and the dragonflies buzzing in panic at being trapped. Everything feels so close now.

Movement again, but this time from a spider that abseils down on a strand of web to hang with eight segmented, sharply angled legs hanging in perfect symmetry from a bulbous body the size of a closed fist.

A grunt from Harry, who takes an involuntary step back at seeing the spider dangling near the web. His knuckles turn white on the rifle and a look of pure hatred morphs his normally genial face. Another step from the undergrowth as Safa catches sight of the spider. They turn about. Scanning and peering into the shadows all around. Scuttling from a bush nearby and they lock eyes on the undergrowth as the new noise joins the steps being taken and all the time the dragonflies buzz with increasing pitch while frantically fighting to get free from the sticky strands.

'SHIT,' Harry booms with a voice bordering on panic. He starts backing up with a look of fear as Safa and Ben glance round to see another spider coming from the bush making that scuttling, dragging noise. As it pushes through so they get a glimpse behind it of strands of web snaked over the ground and a hole the size of an entrance to a badger set. This thing is enormous. From a nightmare with a black body covered in stubbly hair and nasty-looking pincers at the front that waggle up and down. The back end is brown and striated with lines that look like veins bulging from the skin. Spiders don't normally bother Ben, but this thing does and something about it sends a signal to his brain that screams to either kill it or run away as fast possible, but instead, like a fool, he remains rooted to the spot next to Safa. They watch as the monster goes across the ground to the base of a tree and starts climbing with wickedly sharp claws that dig into the bark. It climbs quickly too, getting faster as it aims for the web holding the dragonflies. The dangling spider carries on dropping to the highest trapped insect until it lands deftly on its own web and digs its pincers into the creature, injecting venom that liquidises the insides.

Another step is taken but closer now, and with a soft blast of air that silences the entirety of the vicinity. Everything freezes. The climbing spider holds perfectly static. The one on the web holding the now dead dragonfly in front does the same. Silence everywhere. Even the trapped dragonflies go silent and unmoving. Fear grows. Something bad this way comes. Something these creatures know and fear. Time pauses. The continental drift ceases. The earth stops spinning. Nothing moves. Another snort of air. Deep and hungry, then it bursts into action, running towards them with pounding feet that no longer remain stealthy.

They run. They run without warning or words needed, but simply breaking from static to all-out sprinting as they charge frantic through the undergrowth.

Harry turns to look over his shoulder and stops dead to stare back with a grin stretching across his face. 'Slow down,' he calls out softly to the other two still blundering on. Safa looks back, seeing Harry staring, and reaches out to touch Ben's arm. Bringing him to a gradual stop. They look back at Harry, Safa breathing easily while Ben gulps for air with his hands on his knees and the binoculars hanging from his neck.

'What is it?' Safa calls back softly.

'Come and look,' Harry whispers, motioning for them to go back. They go carefully, picking a quiet route back to Harry, who is grinning widely.

Every image they have ever seen of bipedal dinosaurs is right there, with two strong back legs holding it upright, a long tail for balance and a head like a lizard with two cunning eyes. Lizard-like but less reptile and more animal with two forearms stunted but fingered with digits that twitch.

'Oh my God,' Safa mouths in delight. 'He's gorgeous.'

The dinosaur is tiny. Standing no higher than Safa's waist as it stops beneath the dragonflies caught in the web.

'Watch,' Harry whispers. The dinosaur back-steps a short distance while staring up at the dragonflies. Intelligence in its eyes. It runs, jumps, snags another one and lands to chomp and munch in apparent bliss with eyes rolling happily. The mini creature takes a quick and darting step as it spots the huge spider on the side of the tree. The fingers twitch. The eyes blink and focus. It swallows what it already has as its tail lifts from the ground. The speed it then generates is stunning. Going from standing to full-on charging in the blink of an eye. At the last second it launches up, snaps the spider cleanly in its jaws and drops down to the ground. It lets go instantly, jumping back like a dog does when it's scared of something. The spider rallies, spinning on the spot with the huge fangs held up as the bipedal creature simply jumps up and lands down, bursting it apart underfoot with a sickening crunch of shell mingled with the sound of legs snapping. The final touch is a twist of the foot and it steps away, turns and looks down at its handiwork before dropping to devour the mashed-up remains. Lip-smacking noises soon fill the air. The dinosaur chomps away then flicks a big chunk up into the air, letting it fall down into its open mouth before crunching the bits up.

Goo dribbles down its chin and the eyes roll back in an obvious display of enjoyment, so animal-like as it eats fast like this could be its last ever meal.

'Fuck,' Safa whispers.

'We should go,' Harry adds in his deep voice. The dinosaur looks over on hearing Harry. Those cunning eyes staring with obvious curiosity before it goes back to eating the spider.

They start back through the forest. Ben sweats and looks round, feeling the weight of everything pushing down again. They do not belong here in this world. They caused those dragonflies to scatter.

They caused them to get trapped in that web, which caused the spider to climb the tree and brought the dinosaur over. Infractions of the timeline. Those thoughts bring the despair and homesickness back.

They get inside the bunker and through the decontamination hand dryer in silence. Each of them absorbed in what they saw. Ben walks to *his* room and that simple last journey from the exit door to their rooms brings his mood sinking down deeper and harder. He goes into his room and closes the door, feeling the distance of a hundred million years or more between him and anything he knows. He curls into the foetal position, clutching the pillow beneath his head while squeezing his eyes closed. He does not want to be here. He cannot stay here.

I want to go home.

Nineteen

'Done it?' Alpha asks.

'Not yet,' Bravo mutters pointedly, tapping on the screen of the tablet held in his hands before freezing to sniff the air. He turns to Charlie on his left then Delta on his right, sniffing through the balaclava covering his face.

'Him,' Alpha says, nodding at the man on his knees. 'Pissed himself.'

'Please . . . I'm begging you . . .'

Bravo tuts and steps away to stop the puddle of piss reaching his boots.

'Done it?' Alpha asks again.

'Not yet,' Bravo mutters again.

Hans Markel thought he was a tough man. He was in the army. He served in conflict zones. He was versed in weapons and tactics and was security-minded. His home was secure. The locks were solid. The windows were triple-glazed and the alarm system was state-of-the-art.

'Done it?' Charlie asks.

'Nope,' Bravo mutters, tapping away.

'Please . . . I have money . . .' Hans sobs. On his knees in his bedroom. He has no idea how the five black-clad, balaclava-wearing men got in his house, only that they did. He's already told them what he knows, that the twelve men were hired for a prototype detention centre, that three were dead on arrival at the clinic and three more died soon after. Hans has already told them two men and a woman beat his twelve men in an underground bunker. One was called Harry. They were English. The woman was very attractive.

Now he doesn't know what they want. Only that four of them are waiting for the fifth to write something on the tablet device.

Alpha sighs and adjusts his grip on the pistol held at Herr Markel's head. Bravo is the best at this but he takes so long. Alpha sighs again and casts a look at Bravo, who pauses, cocks his head to one side then carries on tapping. Charlie exhales noisily. Delta taps his foot. Echo looks round at the room. Bravo tuts at them trying to rush him and continues tapping for a few more minutes while Hans sobs and begs for his life.

'Done,' Bravo says, looking up and round, and although the thin black material of the balaclava covers his face, they all know he is looking smug and satisfied.

'Finally,' Alpha says, lowering the pistol. He looks down at Hans and switches to fluent German. 'Herr Markel, do you want to live?'

'Yes!' Hans gabbles urgently. 'Yes . . . anything . . . I have money . . .'

'This,' Alpha says, nodding at Bravo to hold the tablet screen so Hans can see it, 'is a legal authority from you for your six men to be transferred to a state-of-the-art private facility where their medical treatment will continue. We need you to sign it.'

'Yes!' Hans blurts, nodding eagerly while shuffling towards them on his knees through the puddle of urine.

'Thank you,' Bravo says politely in fluent German. 'Sign here.' He holds a black-clad finger over a dotted line while offering a stylus to Hans. Hans snatches it then apologises for snatching it and signs the section indicated. 'And here,' Bravo says, still politely, now pointing at a different section. 'And finally here . . . thank you . . . and my stylus?'

'Sorry . . .' Hans passes it back. His knees hurt from the stress position. His hands shake.

'Done?' Alpha asks, staring at Bravo, who checks through the form he just downloaded, changed, doctored and made to appear legal.

'Er . . . yes, yes, all done,' Bravo says, lifting his covered head to nod at Alpha.

The shot is quiet. The round travelling from the barrel through the silencer and into the forehead of Herr Markel.

Alpha twists the silencer from the pistol, staring down at the corpse while the others do a forensic sweep to ensure nothing of theirs is left behind. 'There was a camera on the door,' he remarks casually.

'I wiped the system on the way in,' Echo says. 'Uploaded a corruption file.'

'We done?' Alpha asks, tucking the silencer into a pocket. The rest nod.

The two private ambulances stop outside. Five men dressed in the green jumpsuits of paramedics disembark, chatting noisily as they stretch from the long journey.

Alpha walks round with a tablet and thumbs the screen as he checks inside the back of both vehicles. The men joke with him. He smiles and chats for a few seconds before heading inside the reception.

'Hi.' Alpha beams at Clara.

'How can I help you?' Clara asks, without a flicker of reaction.

'We're here for them,' Alpha says, as though they should be prepared and waiting.

'Who?' Clara asks.

Alpha frowns and smiles as though somewhat confused. He checks his tablet screen. 'Didn't Herr Markel update you?'

'Er . . .' Clara hesitates, showing some mild confusion.

'Damn it,' Alpha tuts. 'This always happens. Mind you, he's got a lot on . . . you know . . . with the families of the deceased. Anyway, yes, we're here to transport the remaining six patients to another facility.'

'I am sorry, sir. I have not been informed of this. We cannot release the patients without—'

'Got it right here,' Alpha says, smiling at the pretty receptionist as he hands her the tablet. She takes it in her perfectly manicured hands and scrolls down the authority form.

'I shall require a copy.'

'Of course,' Alpha says with the air of someone who has done this hundreds of times and is used to the bureaucracy.

Clara connects the device to her system. A copy of the form is shared directly into their database. A second later the printer spews a hard copy out under the desk. She reaches down, smiling at Alpha, who smiles back. He is really quite attractive. 'What company are you from?' she asks casually.

Alpha holds the smile. He saw the look in her eye, the tiny nuance that telegraphed her reaction to his physical appearance.

'Medicare patient transport services,' he replies with that same air of someone who has said the same thing hundreds of times. He has, too. He has said it hundreds of times over the last few hours until the words came out so easily it conveyed that exact air. 'You, er . . . you full-time, then?' he asks, equally as casually.

'I am,' Clara says, seeing the overt look he just shot her.

'Might have to come back then,' Alpha says quietly, smiling coyly.

'I think you should,' Clara tells him, nodding wisely with a glint of mischief in her eyes while she goes through a series of system procedures to release the patients. 'Okay, that seems to be in order . . .'

'Great. Karl?' Alpha calls out. 'Karl?'

'Yeah, what?' Charlie asks, coming to the door. 'They ready, are they?'

'Yeah, give them a hand,' Alpha says, winking at Charlie in a way he knows the receptionist will see. 'I've, er . . . got to do the paperwork.'

Charlie nods, rolls his eyes and motions for the others to follow him. 'Paperwork . . . course you have,' he mutters.

'So,' Alpha says, turning back to Clara as the other four file into the hospital, tutting and rolling their eyes. 'Do you enjoy working here?'

The art of flirtation. The subtle mastery of conveying an interest by asking mundane, boring questions to work out if the other person is returning the interest. Clara knows he isn't actually interested in the questions he asks, like how long she has worked here or if it's a good job and whether she enjoys it, but that he is asking them to see how she responds. She asks her own questions too, and conveys the same subtle interest.

They smile and make eyes. Their tones drop quieter. She leans closer and lifts her head to show the length and shape of her neck. He leans closer too and rests his hands on the top of the desk to show his lack of a wedding ring.

The six are taken from another exit to the waiting ambulances. The six men had no idea this was being done, but Hans did tell them he was getting a lot of attention so they figure he is moving them somewhere else for greater privacy. Not that they can argue or question anything that much. The pain medication is too strong. They are too woozy, sleepy, drugged, passive and in shock, even now.

'Done,' Charlie says, leaning in through the door to tut and roll his eyes at Alpha again.

'Best be off,' Alpha says, smiling regretfully.

'Sure.' Clara reaches out with her phone to press it next to his, which bleeps once. He smiles at her and presses the 'Accept' button that automatically uploads her contact information into his directory. 'If you fancy a drink one night,' she says quietly.

'I will,' Alpha says, holding her eye contact. 'I, er . . . best go then.'

The would-be lovers part reluctantly. He casts a last look over his shoulder. She smiles and waves with a blush in her cheeks. He laughs softly and turns away as his men jeer and make remarks that she can hear and laugh at. He waves again as he climbs in and offers one last smile as they drive off. Only once they are out of sight does that smile fade.

'Her phone was encrypted,' Bravo says quietly.

'Let Mother know,' says Alpha.

Only when the ambulances are gone does the smile fade from her face. She activates her phone and checks round to make sure no one can see her.

Five men just took them in two ambulances. Medicare patient transport services. The form is legal. One of the men was very flirtatious. We swapped numbers.

She sends the message and goes about her duties. The manager of the hospital had told all the staff that the twelve men brought in were getting a lot of attention, but their rules were to remain the same as ever. No information was to be given out under any circumstances.

Two days ago, she was at home. A courier delivered a package. Inside was a phone. She was puzzled and switched the phone on. A message told her to log in to the website of an established bank. She used the log-in information and gained access to a bank account in her name that held funds of one million euros. The next message told her to check the phone directory. She did so and found it was a replica of her own phone. Every contact, every message, every photo held in her own phone was now in this new one. This was surprising in that it had happened to her, but the technology of phone cloning had been around for years. The next message told her she had nothing to fear. *You are not at risk. We will not harm you.* The message said she could throw the phone away right now and keep the money, or she could provide information and see that balance increase. *Reply now if you are interested.* She wrote back. *I am interested.* The balance of her new account immediately increased to two million euros.

Now she goes about her duties behind the reception desk of the private hospital. Her phone beeps. She casually checks round to ensure privacy.

Good work. Payment made to your account. Send a copy of the form. Inform immediately if the man contacts you. Stay at your job.

She checks her account. It is now at six million euros. The increase from two to five came from simply sending messages about what she knew. Now it is up by another million.

She thought that the six men leaving her facility would end the deal. She was already thinking of handing her notice in and starting a new wealthy life in the sun, but the message said to stay at her job. She muses on that and decides it does actually make sense. To leave straight away would be suspicious. Another week or so won't hurt. Besides, that man was very attractive and there might be a way to get more money. She feels like a spy. Like a secret agent. Those thoughts send a thrill through her. Being a spy is sexy.

Twenty

'Ben, you awake?'

'Yeah,' he croaks, coming awake to the persistent yet gentle knocking at his door. The night was awful. Truly bloody horrible. He kept waking not knowing where he was and rolling over expecting to feel Steph's warm body at the same time as knowing she wouldn't be there. Even with the shutters down on the window, the piercing wails and screeches from outside got into his nightmares.

He gets up in a mood so foul he feels numb but with the added pleasure of the same depressing sensation of utter homesickness pulling even harder than yesterday. He cannot stay here. He does not want to stay here. He needs his home, his world and the things he knows.

'Ben! Are you up?' Safa calls again, thumping on his door.

'I said yes,' he snaps, glaring at the metal-riveted thing balefully.

'Good, get showered. We're going for a run.'

He pauses midway through pulling his first boot on and launches it across the room.

'I don't want to go for a run,' he says, wrenching the door open to see Harry in his room towelling his hair dry and Safa pulling hers back into a ponytail using the same torn-up shred of grey material.

'Tough,' she says gently. 'You were blowing out your arse yesterday just from walking up that bank.'

'That's because I AM NOT a soldier or police officer . . .'

'Ben,' Harry warns from his room.

'Fuck's sake.' Ben feels the first bite of anger flashing through him. 'I am not fucking staying here, therefore I do not need to go for a fucking run . . .'

'You'll die then,' she says with that same caring look. 'Your choice.'

'Train or die?' he asks with a sneer. 'What kind—'

'Man up,' Harry booms with such force it snaps Ben upright in shock. Harry flaps the towel out, snapping it straight, before flicking it up to rest on the corner of his open door.

'I can't,' Ben says, shaking his head imploringly. 'I can't. I can't do this. I'm not you.'

'They'll take you back to your death,' Safa says gently. 'Drugged . . . or knocked out . . .'

'Not if the three of us . . .' Ben stops talking, the last ounce of pride holding the words in.

'Listen to me, Ben. We'll carry you, okay, we'll do the work. Harry and me, we'll do what's needed, but if you don't go with us, they'll send you back. Roland doesn't have a choice.'

'I'm not a bloody child . . .'

'No, you're Ben Ryder, who saved hundreds of people from being killed and for that,' she says, holding a finger up, 'I'll do what it takes to keep you going.'

He flails for the right words and wants to scream that she's got it wrong, both of them have. He did what he did in the heat of the moment without thinking, acting on instinct, but this is not his instinct. He doesn't want to go with them. He doesn't want to be here but he doesn't want them carrying him either. He heads into the bathroom, closing the door gently behind him, and goes through the motions of urinating, brushing his teeth and showering like an automaton before going silently into his room to get dressed.

'You decent?' she asks from outside his door.

'Yeah.'

The door swings open. Safa leans through with that worried smile. 'It'll be a hard day but I think it will be good for you. Just say if you need to stop, okay?'

'Okay.'

'We'll run first then have something to eat . . . drink some water.'

'I'm fine . . .'

'Drink water, you'll need it.'

He shrugs, nonchalant and unbothered. He is not here. He does not belong here. He wants to go home.

Ben follows them down the corridor and through the main room and waits while Safa stops to give Malcolm a new list of things they need. He zones out and idly looks at the way Harry stands easy, dressed in black combat trousers and a tight black wicking top like something from the SAS, but then he is the equivalent of Special Forces. He is the real deal and everything about him oozes quiet but overwhelming confidence. Safa leads them on to the external door, pausing to activate the decontamination unit, then through and out to a beautiful day of glorious sunshine that makes them squint.

'Warm up, then we'll stretch,' she says, moving to the corner of the bunker. 'We'll use the length of the building for now. Right, steady jog up and down.' She stays slow, trudging more than jogging, and two more times they go up and down before she gives the next instruction. 'Heels to arse.' She goes first, still jogging but flicking her feet up behind to touch her hands pressed to her bum cheeks. Harry gives her a look, a shrug, then sets off, with Ben bringing up the rear already feeling out of breath. The same back down and Ben is sweating by the time they reach the end.

'Sidesteps.'

Sidesteps they do.

'Knees up.'

'Heels to arse.'

'Jog normally.'

For a few minutes, it actually feels nice to Ben, using muscles and doing something.

'Stretches,' she says, moving them away from the bunker towards the open space at the end. They start with arm circles. Small rotations that grow larger but too slowly and within seconds Ben's shoulders are burning from the exertion. They stop and reverse the cycle, which gives a second or two of respite before the pain kicks in. They bend over, stretching hamstrings, lifting feet to clutch and stretch the front thigh muscles. Arms spinning again then stretching overhead side to side and by that time the sweat is running freely down Ben's red face.

'Line up.' She motions to the imaginary start line at the end of the bunker. 'Jogging again.'

They set off just a smidgen faster than the last time, reach the end and jog back down. 'Faster.'

They go to the end and back down.

'Faster.'

Up and down.

'Faster.'

The jogging becomes running then just short of a full-on sprint but she keeps them going until Ben's legs are hurting and his chest is clamouring for air.

'Rest.'

She stops for a minute, hardly showing signs of exertion apart from her face holding a layer of glistening sweat. An assessment undertaken. Harry's fitness is very good. He is breathing hard but then he's a big man. Ben has no fitness. None at all. How far will he push himself?

'Ready? Again.'

They jog up and jog down. They run up and run down. Ben can't keep up with them. His chest hurts. His legs feel like jelly.

'Back up,' she says, reaching the start line and twisting on the spot. Ben turns and runs, pumping his arms while gasping for air. Harry breathing hard and his face flushing from the heat but he keeps pace with her to the end.

'Back down.'

They turn and run. Ben's head starts to swim. He staggers with a wave of dizziness going through his head until gravity takes over and brings him down to the soft grass, where he lies panting and feeling like he is going to die.

'That's enough,' she says from somewhere nearby. 'Take a couple of minutes. I'll get water.' She heads inside, leaving him flat out on the grass and Harry leaning with his back against the bunker, panting through an open mouth. They don't speak. Ben is in too much pain. She comes out carrying three big cups of water. Ben gulps his down, feeling the coolness of the water cascade down his parched throat.

'Over here,' she says as soon as his cup is drained. He rises up and staggers towards her.

'Circuits, ten push-ups, ten sit-ups, rest, repeat, ten push-ups, ten sit-ups, rest, repeat . . . got it?'

'Only ten?' Harry asks, dropping down into position.

'For now,' she says, nodding for Ben to copy her. 'Three, two, one . . . go!'

Ben gets the press-ups done, then ten sits-ups, and for a second thinks maybe he's not as unfit as he thought, but the rest is too short and he's soon back holding his weight on his hands and starting again.

The next round is much harder. He gets nine in before she tells him to switch to sit-ups. He does ten and feels a pain in his stomach. Rest. Repeat. They rest and they repeat. Ben's shoulders and arms burn. His stomach muscles scream out to stop. He flops down in the grass and by the fifth or sixth round he is gasping for air with his eyes burning from sweat.

Safa and Harry keep going while Ben feels like he is being sucked into the earth, dreaming of being at home on the sofa watching television with Steph. Steph was having an affair.

'Enough,' Safa says, rolling on to her back and finally breathing hard. She smiles at the familiar pain. The buzz is there. The endorphins are already being released. She recovers quickly. Her breathing coming back under control as she rolls on to her front and jumps lightly to her feet. 'I'll get water.'

'Bring more,' Ben croaks.

'You're weak,' Harry says, making him look up at the casual tone.

'I'm not a soldier. I work in an office.'

Harry doesn't reply but looks away.

'I'm not staying here, Harry.' Harry still doesn't answer but stands up as Safa comes out carrying the cups of water.

'Have two,' she tells him. 'I drank mine inside.'

Ben takes the cups and downs them both in a few big gulps. Immediately he wants more and gets to his feet. 'Want another?' he asks Harry.

'No.'

'No more for a minute,' Safa says.

'Why not?'

'You'll get a cramp. We'll warm down first.'

'But I want more water,' Ben says obstinately.

'Ben, please . . . you'll pull a muscle if you don't warm down properly.'

They repeat what they did before but she makes them hold the stretches for longer, which just makes Ben's muscles scream in agony.

'Wait here.' She heads back inside as Ben flops down on the cooling grass again.

'I'm not staying here,' Ben says again to Harry, who stays quiet. Ben shrugs and turns away. 'I'm not staying.'

'Put it down over there,' Safa says, holding the door open for Malcolm and Konrad. She doesn't say 'please' or 'thank you' but speaks in a curt, commanding tone.

She places a black bag on the table and calls the other two over. 'Harry, I know you saw mine yesterday, but have you handled semi-automatic pistols before?' she asks, pulling a squat black pistol from the bag.

'Berettas.'

'You've handled Berettas?'

He nods. 'We had Brownings too,' he adds, hefting the gun.

'Ben, yours,' she says, holding one out. 'None of them are loaded.'

'Malcolm and Konrad get these?' Ben asks, taking the pistol.

'Yep.'

'Where from?'

'I don't care.'

'No, seriously, where the hell do they get guns from so easily?'

'Again, I don't care,' she says. 'They've got a time machine, they could take them straight from the factory if they wanted to. Right, this is a Glock semi-automatic pistol that fires a nine-millimetre round. The—'

'What are you doing?'

'Ben, just watch and take it in. This is the safety here, on and off . . . see? On and off.'

'I'm not a soldier,' he says, placing the gun on the table.

'You said you'd try,' she says.

'I did the running.'

'So do this.'

'I'm not a soldier . . .'

'Nor am I.'

'You were an armed police officer protecting the Prime Minister.'

'Ben, please. Just try. What harm can it do?'

If she shouted he could get angry. If she ordered him he could tell her to fuck off, but that kindness sinks deeper and tugs at a deep instinct to do as asked.

'Thank you,' she says as he picks the pistol up.

'You asked for more water, Miss Patel?' Konrad comes out carrying a big glass bottle.

'On the table,' Safa says bluntly. 'Right, magazine goes in here . . . to take it out you press this . . . see?'

Ben flicks the safety on and off a few times then ejects the magazine, which pops out of the bottom too fast for him to catch and falls from the table on to the ground. He picks it back up and takes a cup of water, half-watching as she puts hers back in and ejects it back out. He copies the actions, in and out. Safety on, safety off. Magazine in, magazine out.

'Slide this back *after* ejecting the magazine to make sure no rounds are left inside, see?' She slides the top section of her pistol back, showing him the empty chamber. 'You do it . . . no, like this.' She shows him again and watches as he fumbles with the unfamiliar weapon in his hands, which tremble from the workout. For a few moments he finds it interesting taking the gun apart and seeing how it works. She strips hers down and puts it back together. Telling him how to cock, where the release bits are and showing the internal spring and moving parts. Harry copies and pretty much does it first time while Ben gets stuck on the first bit and has to be shown piece by piece. He drinks more water. It's more complicated than it looks with tiny things called firing pins, an extractor depressor and all sorts of wee, small, fiddly, annoying bits and he's too hot, too hungry, his legs hurt and his face feels like it's burning as he starts sliding back into misery.

'Ben,' she says gently, seeing the expression go blank and bringing his attention back. 'Are you watching?'

'Yeah,' he says, watching her deft fingers pushing a spring thing into the back of something else. They go through it several times and not once does she show any frustration when he slows down and loses his mind to the homesickness or simply turns his head to stare down into the wide plains below.

'Ben.' She keeps that tone so soft. 'Try again for me.'

And it's like that, like he is doing it for her. He nods and tries. Fiddling with small bits of metal that drop from his fingers to roll across the tabletop. She picks them up and hands them back. Harry just works quietly, seemingly learning for himself as he strips and rebuilds several times over.

'Okay, that's enough for today. Let's get you out of the sun for a bit.'

Harry goes to say something but stops with a hard look from Safa, and the fact that a single look from her can bring Mad Harry Madden to a silence is testament to the authority she possesses.

Crash mats lie on the floor in the fruit room. Bright blue and clearly brand new. Head guards, thick padded gloves and other nasty-looking equipment. She nods at the sight of them, grunting in satisfaction as Harry heads straight to the long table to heft a cheesy-feet marrow up.

'We messing now?' Harry asks hopefully.

'Yep, there should be eggs there.'

'Eggs?' He looks round and fixes his eyes on a wooden bowl. 'Eggs!' he says. 'Where did . . . how . . . eggs! Well I never. Are they boiled?'

He picks one up to tap on the side of the table and quickly shreds the shell away before shoving it into his mouth and chewing with a contented nod.

'Eat some eggs,' Safa says to Ben. 'You'll need the protein and fats, and get some fruit too for the vitamins.'

Ben rises at the motherly tone and goes to say something but stops as that last prickle of pride tells him not to be an ungrateful prick.

'I asked for some cutlery too,' she says.

'Yep.' Harry brings them over, the bowl of eggs, fruits, knives, forks and spoons. They sit at a table slicing fruit like civilised human beings and cracking the shells from eggs to eat them down. They don't talk. Ben wallows in pain and misery. His face and arms feel like they're burning. He would ask for some sun cream or a hat if he could give a shit.

'Ben.' She calls his attention back to her. 'Have some of this,' she says, offering him a slice of the lemon–lime–melon thing. 'It's so nice.'

He takes the piece and devours it quickly, suddenly realising how hungry he is.

'They can bring food back,' she says conversationally. 'So if there's anything you want, just say.'

'Pork chops?' Harry asks.

'Probably,' she says, smiling. 'Can't see why not.'

'Beef steak?' he asks as though testing her.

'Er, yes.' She grins.

'Beer?' Harry asks.

'Don't see why not,' she says, smiling wider.

'Woodbines. I'm gagging.'

'What?' she asks.

'Woodbines. Smokes. Cigarettes.'

'You smoke?' she asks in genuine shock.

'Of course I smoke. Everybody smokes.'

'Nobody smokes now . . . or only fucking idiots smoke now. They're dangerous as anything.'

'Ah, get off,' he says, waving a hand at her. 'That's not proven.'

'It bloody is,' she scoffs. 'You haven't asked before, so why now?'

He shrugs and eats. Sometimes you can't smoke. Sometimes you can't do the things you want. That's life and what war means. 'Beer and smoke at the end of the day is nice.'

'Okay, I'll ask, but you're not smoking them in the bunker. Ben? What about you?'

'Not bothered.'

'Okay, well, if you think of anything, just say, yeah?'

'Okay.'

The afternoon is as hard, if not harder than the morning. From eating they go on to the crash mats, where Harry and Safa seem to have the greatest fun in the world showing each other a whole range of killing moves while Ben takes a seat and zones out, settling into a festering pit of misery. When they finish he is summoned over and ragged about, learning nothing apart from that the crash mats are soft and when he goes down he stays down until one of them tells him to get back up.

Afternoon to evening and eventually, finally, and with everything hurting and his brain still numb, Safa brings it to a close. They eat again. Fruit and eggs. Vitamins, protein and fats.

Back in their section he freezes in the doorway to his room, seeing folded clean grey tracksuits on the bed next to new socks, underwear, wicking tops and trousers.

'Well done, Safa,' Harry booms from inside his room.

'You got them then?' she shouts from her room. 'Ben, you found yours?'

He goes to snarl to tell her to fuck off and stop mithering and talk-ing to him like a child, to leave him alone and not to bring new things because he is not staying. But he doesn't say any of that.

'Yes, thank you,' he mutters instead.

'Ben, you showering first?' she asks, crossing from her room.

'Ablutions,' Harry calls out.

'Okay,' Ben says dumbly.

'Need anything else?' she asks, hovering there watching him.

He shakes his head. 'No, thank you.'

'Books or something? I remember Wikipedia said you loved to read—'

'Safa,' he snaps this time, glaring at her with a deep, bubbling anger threatening to blow, but all he gets back is a strange look that morphs into a wry smile twitching at her lips and the tiniest look of hope in her eyes.

'I'll get you through this, Ben Ryder.' She locks her gaze on his. 'Soak your muscles in the shower. Tomorrow will be harder.'

She leaves him to it. His fitness is appalling and his moods are a big problem but that flash of anger is a good sign. He needs patience, time to heal and for that anger to come out once it's ready.

Twenty-One

'Ben, you up?'

He rolls over, closing his eyes against the banging at the door.

'Ben? Are you up?'

'Yes,' he shouts too loud and too angry, but the night was worse than the one before and plagued with bad dreams that he can't bring to mind and the noises outside spoke of monsters and war, not a gentle-looking valley.

He sits up and gasps from the pain radiating through his stomach muscles. He breathes it out like a woman in labour while shifting his legs over the edge of the bed and yelping at the pain in his thighs and calves. Then it hits his shoulders and arms and he sags down, feeling like he could cry.

'Ben? You okay?'

'I said yes.'

'You decent?'

'Fuck's sake, yes, I am decent,' he groans, wondering how the hell he is meant to even stand up.

'Morning,' she says, leaning round the door. 'Aching?'

'No,' he lies.

'You're not aching?' she asks with a sharp look.

'No.' What the hell? Why is he saying no?

'Well, okay then,' she says, clearly not believing him. 'You must be aching a bit. I am.'

'Shower free?' he asks, glancing up to see her hair is still wet and guessing Harry has already done his.

'Ablutions,' Harry calls.

'Not a soldier,' Ben shouts back. 'Is the shower free?'

'It's free,' she says and waits. Ben waits. She waits. Expectation in the room for him to move and therefore show the pain he is in. He could tell her he hurts, that his body is screaming out in agony and he needs more sleep. He could lie back down and tell them to fuck off and leave him alone. Instead, he walks and his top lip twitches against his will at his thighs begging for mercy.

'Soak,' she says, as he closes the bathroom door.

'Stretch lightly,' she says when he goes back into his room to get dressed.

'Drink,' she says, placing a large cup of water in front of him in the main room. He doesn't ask where the new larger cups came from, or the bowls, or the plates, or the napkins, or the loaf of bread.

'Eat,' she says, pushing eggs and already sliced fruit towards him.

'Take these,' she says, giving him two white pills. He doesn't ask what they are. He doesn't care. He swallows them with water.

'Drink more,' she says. He drinks more water. 'Stay hydrated today.'

He finishes the water, stares round at the crash mats and notices the head guards and boxing gloves have moved. Maybe Malcolm and Konrad had some fun last night. Either that or Safa and Harry came out for a few more rounds after he turned in. He doesn't ask because he doesn't care.

'Put this on when we go outside,' she says, handing him a black cotton baseball cap. 'Keep the sun off your face.'

'Stop mithering him,' Harry mutters, tucking into his cheesy-feet marrow and looking ridiculous with his baseball cap perched on the back of his head.

'Mind yourself,' she says in a biting tone, but Harry just shrugs and carries on eating like nothing was said and if Ben gave a shit he'd notice the dynamics of their trio are changing.

'Both of you go outside, I'll be out in a minute.'

Ben follows Harry through the doors and corridors. Outside the view is as glorious as before.

'Up there,' Harry says. Ben follows his line of vision to the sky above and several of the flying creatures they saw bursting from the forest canopy the day before yesterday. Shit. This is the third day here already. No, the fourth. They were drugged for a day or two so it could even be the fifth day. Five days away from home. Five days of being dead. Have they had the funeral yet? Do they have funerals without a body? *I think they do.* Like symbolic or something. Steph must be in pieces. His parents too. Steph was having an affair. Christ, that thought hurts deep in his gut, a pain that will never go away. Is five days too late to go back? He could say he was knocked out and crawling about the tunnels in the Underground for a few days. They'd believe it.

'Give me a hand, one of you,' Safa says, pushing through the door carrying the black gun bag in one hand and a large, stainless steel flask in the other with three steel mugs hanging from her fingers. Harry goes over, taking the flask and cups to the table while she grimaces and tugs the black bag off her shoulder.

'I'm aching a bit,' she says. 'You?' she asks Harry.

'No,' he says. 'Coffee?'

'It is,' she says. 'No milk though . . . and no sugar either.'

'Fine by me,' he replies, lifting the flask to inspect the outside. 'This is clever.'

'You didn't have flasks back then?'

'Not like this.' He unscrews the top and sniffs the contents with his eyes showing his appreciation of the aroma.

'I'm pissing Roland off,' she says conversationally, watching Harry pour the black liquid into the mugs. 'He's got no idea,' she adds, 'completely no idea of what he's doing. He's asked me three times since yesterday when we'll be ready.'

'And?' Harry asks.

'Told him to fuck off and it could take weeks or months and that he has a fucking time machine so he can doubly fuck off.'

'Safa,' he tuts.

'What? You asked. *And* I said I'd punch him in the mouth if he asked me again.'

'Fair enough,' Harry says, pulling the corners of his mouth down in agreement. 'Take it well?'

'Blah,' she says. 'Who cares? How's the coffee, Ben?'

'Fine, thank you.'

'We'll do skills training today.'

'Okay.'

'Seeing as we're all in pain from yesterday.'

'Okay. I'm fine now,' Ben says, tensing his thighs, which no longer hurt.

'The pain is just masked,' she says. 'Grab a pistol from the bag and field strip it for me.'

Repetition of motion. Slow but progressive.

'Assemble it for me.'

Repetition of motion makes him not think about everything else.

'Strip it.'

Repetition of motion. Thinking of the movement now and what comes next to place the hands in preparation. He makes mistakes constantly and waits for her to tell him what to do.

'Assemble the weapon.'

I am warm. I am fed. I am hydrated.

'Strip it.'

I am dead. I died on the tracks.

'Assemble.'

Repetition of movement.

'Field strip the weapon.'

Her voice becomes the only real thing in this place. The gentleness of it, but a tone of command that makes him want to do what she says. She is kind. She is patient. She is solid and unwavering when he loses focus and forgets what he is doing as his mind opens up to the pain in his heart.

'Ben,' she says, moving into his eyeline.

'Okay.' He starts again. Stripping and putting it back together. Harry strolls over to sit with his back against the bunker and dozes off with his cap pulled down over his eyes.

'Drink,' she says in the main room, placing a large cup of water in front of Ben.

'Eat,' she says, giving him eggs and fruit.

'Drink more,' she says.

'We'll go back outside and carry on.'

Outside back to the table. Malcolm comes out with a fresh flask of coffee.

'Field strip the weapon,' she says, and so the day wears on and all that matters is her voice.

Twenty-Two

Water pours into his mouth and nose. Choking him. Drowning him. His senses shut off. The room is pitch black but the light shining in his eyes is powerful enough to induce intense pain in his retinas.

The soaking-wet cloth over his mouth prevents him breathing in. Tilted at an angle, almost upside down on a hard board. Strong hands gripping his arms and legs.

He cannot speak or say anything. He tries screaming but that just opens his airway. He retches, trying to vomit, but that means another intake of air, which means more water.

The board slams upright and the light shines in his eyes, forced open by rough, black-clad fingers.

The confusion is almost as great as the fear. He undertook some basic interrogation training in the military so he understands being waterboarded. What he doesn't understand is the lack of questions, or, to be more specific, the lack of *any* questions. Not one of the five men has asked a single question.

As the immediacy of the threat of drowning abates, so he coughs to clear his airway in order to ask what they want but the gun rises, presses to his temple and fires before the words form.

The lights come on. Harsh overhead strip lights that show the body of the man just killed in the dingy room.

Five remain. All of them have broken noses, contusions and the after-effects of concussions. One has a broken arm. Two have broken wrists. One has a ruptured testicle. One has a dislocated shoulder.

It takes seconds for the pain in their eyes to ease so they can look round and see that death for themselves.

Like Hans Markel, they are hard men. Ex-military. They have seen conflict and bodies before, but being forced to remain kneeling with their arms bound behind them while listening to one of their own being silently waterboarded was an assault to the senses none of them ever expected.

The five look round the room, blinking rapidly as they adjust to the bright lights. As one they spot their mate now dead on the floor, lying in a pool of blood that is turning pink from the puddles splashed during the torture.

Five men in balaclavas stare at them. Five men dressed in black from top to toe.

The five men walk to stand in front of the five kneeling men. They stop with one in front of each from Alpha to Echo in one line.

They have the height advantage, which they know adds to the intimidation and perception of threat. They fold their arms and widen stances. They remain quiet. Not a word spoken.

One of the kneeling men coughs to clear his dry, parched throat. Another groans from the agony in his joints and the fact his broken arm has been forced behind his back. Another sways on the spot. The pain from his shoulder threatening to render him unconscious.

Alpha nods to Delta. Delta draws his pistol and shoots the swaying man in the head.

Four remain. Four that gibber in absolute terror. Still not a question has been asked. Not a word uttered. They were in the two ambulances. The paramedics were really nice and made sure they were comfortable.

The offered water and made small talk. The ambulances stopped. The paramedics got out. There was silence but the injured men did not question it, such was the state of them. Five men wearing balaclavas came back. The operatives were dragged, beaten, thrown and pushed into the cellar of the abandoned warehouse and forced to kneel in the pitch black while the first one was dragged away.

Terror grips them. The lack of questions. The lack of any human interaction from the men in balaclavas renders them as monsters.

Alpha waits. His men wait.

'We don't know anything,' the man kneeling in front of Bravo blurts. The sound of his voice invokes a response and the other three sob and cry out. Pleading for their lives. Begging not to be killed.

'I promise,' the man in front of Bravo sobs. 'It was a job . . . just a job . . .'

The five men in balaclavas stay silent, but as one they turn to look at him. That tiniest motion spurs him on. He nods at them. Staring up and round while gasping in fear and pain.

'We got picked up . . .' He nods again, he keeps nodding. 'In a van . . .'

'Blindfolded,' the man in front of Echo whimpers.

'Yeah, blindfolded,' the man in front of Bravo says. 'Said we couldn't see the location. Said it was secret . . . prototype detention centre . . . Hans said they paid well . . . said it was an easy gig . . .'

The five stay silent but show they are listening by simply watching the man. That gives him hope. That small glimmer of hope that he is doing the right thing and he rushes on, speeding up to get the words out.

'Was, er . . . was underground . . . a bunker . . . concrete . . .'

'Fruit,' the one in front of Echo says.

'Fruit!' the one in front of Bravo exclaims. 'They had fruit on a table . . . er . . . tables and chairs made from wood . . . big room . . .

English guy with black hair . . . another German guy translated . . . said they had three prisoners . . .'

'Detainees,' the one in front of Echo adds.

'Yeah . . . he said that . . . he said detainees . . . said they might be violent so we had to be ready and just wait . . . he was giving the brief when the three came in . . . two men and a woman . . . big man called Harry . . . had a beard . . . he told us to fight him . . . told us to fuck our mothers . . . he was English . . .'

'Said it in German . . .'

'Yes! He said it in German . . . told us to fight him and fuck our mothers in German.'

'Woman was . . .'

'Fit . . . like pretty. Really pretty. Dark hair. Dark eyes . . .'

'Hard as fuck . . .'

'They were.' The one in front of Bravo keeps nodding and swallows quickly. 'The big one . . . Harry . . . he went nuts. He attacked us . . . the woman joined in . . . ragged us senseless . . . then the last bloke came in . . .'

'Drugged them . . .'

'We did . . . they had needles . . . they injected them in the neck . . . we were fucked. Like, three dead and, and . . . and, like, they took us out in the van and, like . . . we were so fucked-up but they put the blindfolds on again . . .'

'That's it . . .'

'It is. I swear it. I swear on my mother's life. I swear it . . .'

'I know.' The man in front of Charlie coughs the words out. He lifts his head. His eyes baleful with hatred. He looks round at the five men staring down at him. 'I took my blindfold off . . .'

The five look at him. They stay silent. An air of expectation hangs.

The man in front of Charlie shakes his head. 'Fuck off,' he spits. He has worth. He has value. They need him alive. It's the only hope he has.

Alpha pulls his pistol and shoots the man in front of him through the head. Bravo shoots next. Echo fires.

One remains. He sobs and squeezes his eyes closed. The smell of blood, piss and shit hangs in the air. The corpses of his mates on the ground next to him. Charlie pulls his pistol and aims.

'NO! Please . . .' The threat is too great. The fear too much. The intensity of the situation grips his mind. These men are ruthless beyond anything he could ever imagine. 'Warehouse . . . back street in central Berlin . . .' He clams up. Holding back in the desperate hope they will not kill him.

Alpha nods. Bravo moves away. The man sobs. Snot drools from his nose. Everything hurts. Bravo comes back holding a briefcase, which he holds flat towards Delta, who presses the two locks and lifts the lid. Bravo shows the kneeling man the banknotes stacked neatly inside.

The man swallows at the lifeline thrown his way. The sheer need to survive suddenly has a glint of greed. He locks eyes on the money, swaying with adrenaline and gut-twisting fear.

'Where?' Alpha speaks for the first time.

'You promise me?' the man asks, turning towards Alpha with a rush of terror-induced rage pulsing through his body. 'PROMISE ME.' He screams the words out, snot and spittle spraying from his mouth.

'Where?' Alpha asks as Bravo takes a small step closer with the briefcase.

The man heaves for air. His eyes darting to the briefcase then round to his dead mates. They will kill him. He knows that. He only has one bit of information left and if he tells them they will kill him.

'I don't know Berlin.' The man whispers the words out ragged and broken. 'We went through a hundred streets and . . . it was down a back street and . . .'

Alpha nods. Bravo starts closing the briefcase. Charlie lifts his pistol.

'NO . . . er . . . oh shit . . . grey bricks! The warehouse bricks were grey . . . oh fuck . . . please . . . you promised . . .'

He has nothing left to give. Alpha senses it. A grey-bricked warehouse down a back street in central Berlin. Not much, but enough.

He nods. Charlie fires. The man's screams cut off. Bravo closes the lid. The others look round then over at Alpha, who shrugs. 'Looks like we'll be out on foot then.'

Twenty-Three

Remove the magazine and check the chamber. Release the slide. Point the weapon in a safe direction. Pull the trigger. Thumb under the slide round the back of the grip, fingers over the slide. Pull back and pull down while pulling down the slide. Remove the slide. Take the spring assembly out. Remove the barrel. The weapon is field stripped.

'Assemble it.'

Ben works the parts, listening to the satisfying clunks and clicks as the gun becomes whole again, and only when it's done does he glance over to see Harry dozing again on a wooden chair underneath a large sun parasol with his arm resting on the wooden table to the side of the bunker door. Ben turns round to stare down into the valley and feels a rush of emotions pouring through his mind. Like they've been held back by being occupied with working the gun, but now, with nothing to do for a minute, they come rushing back, and the sudden onset makes everything feel worse than before.

'Ben.'

He turns back to see her smiling warmly and motioning for him to continue.

It's been a week now. A week of running and circuit training. A week of physical exercise and healthy food. Chicken, rice, vegetables, fruit and more water than he has ever drunk in his life. Some of the food comes precooked and hot. He doesn't question it or ask where it comes from. He doesn't care. Harry had a plate full of pork chops two nights ago with a bowl of chips to go with them. Ben eats what Safa tells him to eat. Ben drinks what she tells him to drink. He sleeps when told. He is a man–child slipping further down a black tunnel of depression. It's been a week of nightmares and waking up bathed in sweat feeling terrified.

'Ben . . . keep going.'

'Okay.'

The day ends. The seventh day since they arrived. She packs the pistols away as Harry heads inside. Ben stands by the edge, staring down into the valley.

'You did really well,' she says, checking each pistol before placing them in the bag. 'Ben?' she calls when he doesn't respond.

'Huh?' He turns round, that expression back on his face. The one she keeps seeing when he drifts off and she has to call him back to the now.

'You did well today.'

'Oh, thanks.'

'Getting there,' she says.

He nods.

'One week today,' she says conversationally. 'Goes quick, really.'

He nods and pushes his hands into his pockets. She looks at the stubble on his jaw and the bags under his eyes and notices the weird contrast. He is already healthier than he was a week ago. He is eating good, nutritious food and drinking plenty of water. He's exercising and has colour in his cheeks but the broken sleep and poor mental health are having an effect too. She smiles warmly. 'We should celebrate.' She winces inwardly at the crass word. 'Well, not celebrate, but . . . you know . . . mark the occasion.'

He doesn't nod this time. He shrugs instead.

'Maybe join me and Harry for a beer tonight.'

'Ah,' he says, looking down at the ground. 'I'll probably turn in.'

'Have a beer with us. The sunsets are amazing out here.'

'Maybe,' he mumbles.

'I'll make you,' she says, still smiling. 'At gunpoint.'

'You don't need a gun,' he says with a weak smile. 'You could beat me up with your eyes closed.'

'Ooh, give me a few months and you'll be beating me up . . .'

'Eh?'

'I've no idea what I just said,' she admits, feeling him coming back and wanting it to continue. She thinks fast, biting her bottom lip. 'Oh, I was going to ask your advice.'

'Me?' He blinks and looks at her.

'Yeah, er . . . do you think it's weird sharing a bathroom with me? You know, like . . . should I use another set of rooms or is it okay to share with you and Harry? You know, we've got loads of rooms and . . . er . . . what do you think?' She trails off, knowing it was the weakest request for advice ever thought up on the spot. For a second she wants the ground to open up and feels a rare blush coming into her cheeks. He stares at her. She's sure he can see the awful question for what it is. He rubs his chin and nods.

'Up to you really,' he says, drifting back off. A double-edged sword. On the one hand she feels relief that he didn't pick up on her ham-fisted attempt to keep him talking, but on the other she feels frustration at his loss of attention again.

'Carry this for me?' she asks, holding out the bag of pistols while picking up the empty mugs of coffee and thinking to tell Harry off again for not taking his empties.

He takes the bag and waits like the puppy he has become for her to go through so he can follow and wait and follow and wait. She passes him the mugs while she locks the back door then takes the mugs back off him. Anything to keep the interactions going. Anything to find a spark of conversation.

'Got steak tonight,' she says, walking with him through the corridors. 'Lean steak, of course . . . and I asked for a nice garden salad. Nice and cleansing. Do you like wine? What about beer? You a lager or bitter man?'

'Er . . . not, er . . . pardon?'

'Lager or bitter?'

'Er, not that bothered really.'

She hides the frustration. She knows more about him than any person has a right to know about someone else. She spent hours of her life reading and re-reading every word about him ever printed and she knows he preferred lager but also really liked real ales.

'What about real ales? I used to love a real ale.'

He shrugs and nods. Hands in pockets as he shoulders the door open to the main room.

'Empties,' Safa says instantly, giving Harry the look as he hovers near the food table.

'Aye,' he says. 'We messing now? Is this steak? It smells like steak. Is it steak?'

They eat. Safa and Harry making conversation that Ben hears but doesn't take in. He eats his steak and salad. He drinks the water then sits waiting quietly. Steph was having an affair. He would never have got married anyway. It doesn't matter that he is dead because she was fucking someone else. He died. He is dead. He misses his life and his fiancée even though she was about to tell him it was over.

'Ben?'

'Huh?'

'You coming for a shower? Shit, I mean going for a shower. Not coming as in coming with me . . . I didn't mean that . . . I didn't mean coming . . . fuck it. I meant are you going for a shower?'

'Yeah, sure.' He gets up as she lifts her hands at Harry, who shakes his head and sighs. He showers. He dresses in the grey tracksuit and heads back to his austere sterile room with the single metal bed and the glaring light.

'Come for a beer.' She leans round his door to see him sitting on the edge of his bed.

'Nah, I'm going to—'

'Fuck that,' she says, venturing into his room. 'Come on . . . you promised . . .'

'I just—'

'Nope. With me. Come on. Just one.' She takes his wrist and laughs as she pulls him up on to his feet. 'Watch the sunset. Have a beer. It's like our Friday night so . . . actually, I wonder what day it is here. Do you know what day it is?'

'Er, no . . . listen, I just want to . . .'

'Fuck that. Fuck off. Get fucked and just have a fucking beer,' she says, still holding his wrist.

He smiles at her profanity and the way she says it. She smiles back, seeing the spark come into his eyes.

They head back outside to three chairs set side by side. Bottles of beer in a cooler box on the gun table. Harry already with a beer in one hand, a cigarette curling smoke in the other and his long legs stretched out, barefooted in the warm evening air.

'Beer,' she says, handing Ben a bottle.

Ben sits and doesn't notice that he's the only one in the grey tracksuit. Safa wears loose linen trousers and a white sleeveless top. Harry in the jeans and T-shirt he wore in Rio.

'I was just asking Ben what day it is,' Safa says, taking a beer and sitting down.

Harry sips from his bottle and thinks for a second, 'No idea,' he says after that whole second's worth of deep contemplation.

Ben drinks his beer but doesn't taste it. He doesn't even register what beer it is. He doesn't *think* to register what type of beer it is. His mind is not here in this place.

'I'll, er . . .' He stands up and places the empty bottle on the table. 'I'll turn in . . .'

'Ah, have another one,' Harry says.

'Nah thanks, mate.' Ben pauses, hesitating and awkward. 'Tired . . . I'll, er . . . see you in the morning then . . .'

They watch him go and hear as he pauses under the hissing air jets then walks down the corridor to the doors. Safa sighs.

'Only been a week,' Harry says quietly, nodding at Safa to pass him another beer.

'Get your own, you lazy shit,' she says, arching an eyebrow. 'Oh, stay there, old man,' she huffs as he makes a meal of preparing to stand up. She grabs two more bottles and sits down in Ben's vacated chair.

'Ta,' Harry says, taking the beer.

'He'll be fine,' she whispers, taking a swig from the bottle.

Harry nods, staring down into the valley. 'I'm sure he will be.'

'He will,' she asserts, shooting him a hard glare.

Harry pauses. His silences speaking as much as ten sentences sometimes. 'We had chaps join up . . . tough chaps too . . .'

'Save it. Heard it. He'll be fine.'

He swigs from the bottle. No offence taken at her blunt tone. 'How long you going to give him?'

She swigs from her own bottle. He is Ben Ryder. He was seventeen when he took on a gang of hardened men high on drugs. He could have run away. He could have hidden. He was terrified but he still did it. Same with Holborn. He was terrified but he still did what hundreds of other people couldn't do. While everyone else ran away, Ben ran towards. That means something.

'Long as it takes.'

Twenty-Four

'It's been almost four weeks.'

'I'm fully aware of that.'

'And he isn't getting any better.'

'He'll get there.'

'Harry?' Roland says, looking from Safa to Harry across his desk. Harry stares ahead, wanting to say something but abiding by his sense of loyalty to Safa. In the end he says nothing, which again speaks volumes.

'We're running out of time,' Roland says heavily. 'You've had him running and training and stripping those blasted guns apart every day.'

'Time?' Safa asks, Roland groans and sags back in his chair.

'Time, Safa! Time.'

'Got a time machine.'

'Again? Is that going to be the answer every time we have this conversation?'

'Got a time machine.'

'Four weeks. It has been four weeks—'

'*Almost* four weeks and, er . . .' She pauses, looking him in the eye. 'We have a time machine. We could take four years and it wouldn't make a fucking difference. We can go back to *any* point in history . . .'

'Yes, but at some point you will have to make the decision that Ben is just not suitable.'

'HE IS BEN RYDER,' she shouts with sudden ferocity. Roland flinches, the words stilled on his tongue. 'It takes as long as it takes. You're feeling the pressure because you think nothing is happening, but it *is* happening. Harry and I are training and learning to work with each other and Ben is adapting to his new environment. He just needs time.'

'How much time?'

'Ask me that again and see what happens . . . go on . . .' Safa growls the words out, the intent clear on her face. A shift at her side. A slight motion from Harry that makes her ease back from Roland's desk.

The heavy silence stretches. Roland waits for the tension to abate. The same as last time and the time before that. That Safa is right is just another irritation. In theory they *can* take as long as they need, but the lack of progress is eating away.

'Are you under pressure from someone else?' Safa asks, breaking the silence.

'Pardon?' Roland asks, caught off guard by the question.

'I said are you under pressure from someone else? Do you want me to explain why it takes this long to train someone?'

'No no.' Roland waves a hand at her. 'Nothing like that. No, you are right. It's my perception at the lack of progress. I apologise.' He exhales long and slow. The weight of the world on his shoulders and showing once more in those deep worry lines. He smooths his hair back and rises from the chair, walking over to the window under the open shutter to stare out into the valley. 'It's just me,' he says after several quiet minutes.

'Just you?' Safa asks.

'Just me and the inventor . . . well, one other person too, but—'

'You're gabbling,' Safa says.

Roland stiffens at her tone. 'The inventor told me when the end of the world was realised. It's just me. I am the one running this. I arrange the financing for it. Me. Just me. So yes, there is no one else to report to, nor is there anyone else putting pressure on us, but I still wish to make progress and to do so as soon as humanly possible.'

Who exactly is Roland? How does he arrange the finances? Who is the inventor? Why did the inventor ask Roland for help? What did he mean when he said one other person?

'So we have time then,' Safa says as bluntly as ever as Harry stares forward and waits passively.

'You asked Malcolm to get sandbags ready for a firing range. Why aren't you using them?' Roland asks, changing the subject.

'He's not ready.'

'Not ready? How many times does it take to strip a weapon down before you can use it?'

'It's familiarity.'

'I know exactly what it is,' Roland says, turning from the window and speaking gently. 'You're worried about giving him a loaded gun.'

She looks up sharply as Harry stares ahead at the spot on the wall.

'Ben wouldn't do that . . .'

'No? Then why hasn't he fired it yet?'

'We're doing other skills sessions,' she says in explanation. 'Physical training and unarmed combat.'

'I've seen,' Roland says carefully, 'and he's hardly applying himself.'

'And Harry and I have both been conditioned by the jobs we did in the services and police,' she pushes on doggedly. 'Ben doesn't have any of that.'

Roland goes to reply but stops and sits back down heavily. 'He looks awful,' he says quietly. 'Is he sleeping?'

'No,' Safa sighs, shaking her head.

'Then tell him,' Roland groans, rubbing his face that shows the stress of days spent waiting and worrying.

'No,' Safa replies instantly.

'Safa,' Roland pleads. 'You have to do something. Tell him what Steph did and take away his desire to go home. Force a reaction. Provoke him so he can channel that anger.'

'Yeah, why not?' Safa says with disgust etched on her face. 'We'll take a man already suffering and make it worse. Yeah, that'll be such a nice thing to do.'

'At some point, which will be sooner rather than later, we're going to have to make the difficult decision that Ben just isn't right for this project.'

'He will be fine. I promise.'

'Okay,' Roland says, sensing the temper in her is threatening to come up again. 'Fine. Just keep me posted.'

Neither of them know where he goes and they have no idea of anything Roland does away from the bunker and although they are curious, they are both too deeply conditioned by their former lives to question such workings. You focus on your job and let someone else worry about where the pens come from.

Safa was a uniformed armed police officer. Every bit of kit she carried came from somewhere else and was organised by someone else. Her service sidearm was maintained by someone else. The vehicles were serviced by someone else. Her uniform was organised by someone else. The canteen was stocked by someone else. Even the bullets for the weapons were sorted by someone else. She was there to protect and worry about the finite details of her job.

It was a single act but it was enough to shape Safa's life from that point on. It seemed like the whole world became obsessed with Ben Ryder after Holborn and even more so when it came out that he was the same man who killed five gang members when he was seventeen. Then Steph tainted it, but not for Safa. She had seen greatness and knew without doubt there were decent, honourable people in the world and it was the essence of Ben that she held close when she was being touched and groped in the private rooms in Downing Street.

There was something else too, something deeper than all of that. A snatch of a view as she held eye contact with him from the platform while he dragged the dead man down the tracks, but in that second she saw someone of immense power and life. It struck her then and it stayed with her.

He's still Ben Ryder though. She can see it. She saw it before and can tell it's there in the tiny bursts of anger that surge up to give life to his eyes and it's thrilling to see, but it dies so quickly and he slumps to become passive and inert, like a child hanging off her every word.

She pours coffee from the flask in the main room and moves to slump into a chair. Harry pauses, wondering if he should leave her alone, but decides on the other option, pours himself a cup and sits down in a chair across the table.

She sips and thinks, remembering seeing him when she staggered from her room and knowing instantly it was him. It was Ben Ryder. She knew it. She couldn't believe it but she knew it. Even now she has to remind herself that this is reality when she's watching him strip the weapons and guiding his arms round her neck to show the best grip when snapping someone's spine.

'He is getting fitter,' she mutters, glancing across to Harry, who nods benignly and sips his coffee. 'And he can strip every weapon we've got here.'

'Aye,' Harry says.

'His reflexes are incredible. What do you think?' she asks sharply.

Harry shakes his head then sips his coffee.

'Go on,' she says, nodding at him. 'What do you think?'

'You've not asked me before,' he says quietly.

'Because I know what you'll say.'

'Aye, you do.'

'You don't think he will make it.'

'No.'

She watches him, sensing he wants to say more but is stopping himself, and instead he sips the coffee with that benign, easy expression. 'You never ask anything,' she observes.

'Nothing to ask,' he replies.

'Harry,' she says firmly.

'Safa,' he says easily, with a smile that makes her pause and take a breath that softens the harshness in her eyes.

'Why do you let me take charge?' she asks, voicing another question that's been quietly nagging at the back of her mind for the last few weeks. 'I'm a woman.'

'You are.'

'You're from nineteen forty-three. You didn't have women officers then.'

'We did.'

'Not in combat roles though.'

'True.'

'So they weren't in charge of you.'

'No.'

'Whatever,' she huffs as he refuses to take the bait and be drawn into an argument to vent her irritation. 'We'll just keep going then.'

'Aye.'

'He'll be fine.'

'Aye.'

Twenty-Five

A war of attrition. A war of trial and error where the front-line soldiers drink coffee, eat junk food and wear jumpers in windowless rooms. A war of hacking, of firewalls, of fingers blurring over keyboards using every method and technique known and inventing more as they go along.

Berlin is a thriving metropolis of over ten million inhabitants, but where there are people, there is crime.

Nearly every business has CCTV. High-quality, real-time, full-colour footage that has to be retained for thirty days to comply with insurance policies. Such large data volumes mean that the only viable storage method for most businesses is cloud storage. A virtual bank where the footage can be uploaded and held for the required time in exchange for a monthly fee. The cloud storage operators promised state-of-the-art security and impenetrable systems.

The soldiers aim their weapons at those systems. They hack and find engineer access points. They delve, look, seek, search and slip out as unseen as their entry.

The private hospital does not have CCTV, but they know a van delivered the men. Where did the van come from? They have the end destination so they work backwards. Hacking businesses to view footage to see angles of roads and junctions in the hope of catching a glimpse of the van.

It works too. They establish the make and model of the vehicle. They establish the colour. They write code and algorithms to embed in hacked systems to do the work for them at a processing speed far higher than the limitations of the human brain permit. They scour, dismiss, negate and pass over thousands of hours of footage from tens of thousands of cameras.

They quickly establish that the van took a very circuitous route and appears to have travelled random roads in an impulsive manner. That suggests a very basic awareness of surveillance. They know this, as an advanced state of surveillance awareness would mean the van never appearing on any footage anywhere. Which would be hard but not impossible. There are crime prevention and detection websites that show maps of the known fixed points of cameras within predefined areas. Simply open the map and pick a route that goes past the least number of cameras. The van has not done that. Instead, it has simply driven round Berlin for a while before heading to the hospital.

The method is not perfect, but it helps.

A grey, brick-built warehouse on a back road in central Berlin.

The van is tracked to the very centre of Berlin. To the old part of the city. Architectural historians are consulted.

Not all brickworks made grey bricks. Some made red bricks, and those red bricks generally ended up in certain areas. Others had a yellow colour. They ended up in other certain areas. History shows us these few brickworks made grey bricks, which served these geographical sections of the city.

That information is applied to the intelligence gained from the hacked CCTV that shows the locations of the van.

The geofencing closes in yet again. The invisible circle on the map grows smaller.

From those sections, they analyse industrial zones, commercial zones, warehouses in current operation and warehouses refurbished as dwellings but that still retain the appearance of warehouses.

It is hard work. It is gruelling work. But they are highly motivated to get results and earn more money. Mother wants results. Mother has made it clear she will reward those that get her the results.

```
Hi Alfie. I hope you are enjoying your trip
and not drinking too much! I was chatting to
my friend just now. She said the old centre
of Berlin is very nice. The area west of
the cathedral has plenty of old buildings
that survived the war. I know you love
architecture so I thought I would mention
it. Anyway, stay safe x

Hi Mother! Yes we are having a lovely time,
thank you. That is very interesting about
the old part of Berlin. We will surely take
that area in. The chaps are as excited as me
at seeing the Gothic architecture. Love to
you and Father x
```

The simplest method to find a grey, brick-built warehouse on a back road in the old part of the centre of Berlin west of the cathedral would be to wave cash at cops, drug dealers, prostitutes, pizza delivery drivers, couriers, taxi firms and anyone else that spends the hours of their lives amongst the city high-rises and blend of Gothic and new architecture. However, it would only take one of those to mention that someone was interested in a grey, brick-built warehouse on a back road and then everyone would be looking for it.

The five go old school instead. Boots on the ground. The section is broken into sizeable chunks and worked through methodically. Every street is checked. Every avenue, road, alley and underpass. They become tourists walking with maps and brightly coloured rucksacks. They stop at the sights and marvel at the things they should be marvelling at. They sleep in low-cost hotels. They blend in and do not draw attention.

The race is on and the prize at stake is worth everything.

Twenty-Six

There is no change. Time does not exist.

He wakes. He trains. He sleeps. The depression becomes worse, stripping him of any shred of the man he was. He doesn't think for himself and as that lack of cognitive challenge continues so he simply cannot think for himself.

The spiral starts. Severe shock means his head produces chemicals that upset his ability to feel evenly balanced. Too much adrenaline. Too much testosterone. Not enough serotonin and a hundred other factors all work to make it so there is nothing Ben can do to stop that spiral becoming worse.

Pull yourself together. Man up. Stop worrying. Don't panic. Stop thinking bad things. Snap out of it. Calm down. Day after day of plummeting down into an abyss of self-pity. Steph was having an affair because he deserved it. He died because he has no worth. He is here to be punished. The self-pity mutates into self-loathing.

The two people next to him are the best in their fields of expertise. Consummate professionals who excel at what they do and make it look effortless in the process. He compares what he is to them. He takes his lack of worth and holds it stark and obvious against Safa and Harry, but that only serves to strengthen his self-perception. He is weak. He is haggard. Look at Harry. Be like Harry. Be like Safa. Snap out of it. Be a man.

His life around him changes without a flicker of reaction that he even sees it. The bathroom they share fills with objects. New towels in different colours. Different toothpastes and brushes. A mirror that he doesn't look at. Razors for Safa. Scissors for Harry to trim his beard. A light over the mirror. Shampoos and conditioners in the shower. A toilet brush. Cleaning materials and products. Shelves. Rails. He doesn't notice when the shower starts producing hot water and doesn't notice the air of victory Malcolm and Konrad have at finally figuring out how to do it.

A rug on the floor in the communal room. Clothes draped on the back of the blue chairs. Books stacked on a low table. Boots, trainers and flip-flops outside their rooms in the corridor.

The three austere, sterile rooms become one austere, sterile room. Safa's and Harry's rooms gain rugs and clothes rails. They gain side units next to their beds on which rest more books, drinking glasses and battery-operated soft lights. Dimmer switches for the glaring lights appear on the walls. Shelving units filled with deodorants, hairbrushes, hairbands and personal objects that are gained over the days, weeks and months of their existence in the bunker.

Ben walks through it but sees none of it. His room remains as it was. Sterile and cold. Empty and austere. He has no worth so therefore he does not deserve any softness. His life becomes empty and meaningless.

The fat disappears from his body. He becomes lean and hard. The muscles show in his limbs and torso. He weathers and browns. His beard grows, his hair becomes unkempt. The bags under his eyes darken and grow too. The haggard look intensifies week by week. The battles are at night. The worst of times. The most awful of times, when he fights to prevent sleep while feeling so tired that all he wants is sleep. Sleep brings the nightmares. The ever-worsening terrors in his head. They become confusing and jumbled. Steph becomes Safa. Safa was having an affair. Safa was going to leave him. Steph is here. It is Steph making him cling to a life he does not deserve. He killed Safa and Steph when he was seventeen. He tried to save Steph and Safa when he was seventeen but Roland killed them while Harry laughed.

The main room changes around him. The chairs and tables broken during the big fight are replaced. The food varies. The uniqueness of people living in a place starts to show. Stains on the tables. Circle marks from the coffee mugs. The mark on the floor where Harry knocked the jug of coffee over.

Malcolm and Konrad move around them. Fixing, repairing, fetching and carrying. Waiting and watching.

Roland frets. His nerves fraying with every passing week. Safa remains brutal and never before has a person guarded another as she does Ben. Never before has such a protective energy enveloped another as hers does him. The others don't speak to Ben. *Don't speak to him. Don't even look at him.* Roland stops asking because to ask will invoke her wrath and they all get caught up in the challenge of waiting for Ben to snap out of it.

Safa's dedication becomes a thing. An entity. An almost living object to be discussed and thought about. Wherever Ben goes she is there. At his side. Behind him. In front of him. She knows what he did. He saved that woman and child. He killed so they could have life. He did it at Holborn. He killed so others could live and for that, her energy seems endless. She will never tire. She will never submit. Ben has worth. Harry retrains with eighty or more years of new skills, weapons and tactics to play with. His proficiency in his art is sublime. He is perfection at what he does. He gives calm to Safa. He gives patience and can say more in one nod than Roland, Malcolm and Konrad can do with many words.

Safa tries repeatedly to bring Ben out. To draw him from himself. And in those months that pass, she has hope only once and cries only once.

Four months in. She was lying in bed unable to sleep with her black and white mind having made a rare foray into the murky world of theoretical science. She was confused and that confusion caused irritation. She wished she had not even started thinking about it but the thought was there. She tossed and turned, huffed and puffed and finally sat up to scowl at the room before marching from her room to knock on Ben's door.

'You up?' she asked.

'Huh?' Ben said. He was still awake, lying on his bed, and showed surprise at the soft knock and her tone, implying a sense of urgency. 'Er, yeah . . .'

'Thank fuck,' she said, marching into his room and not stopping until she reached the end of his bed, where she plonked down and lifted a hand as though ready to make a point. He scooted his legs out of the way and sat up. His eyes flicked to her body and the fact that she was wearing only a bra and a pair of tight-fitting shorts.

'Right, you're smart as fuck,' she said, still holding that hand out. 'So . . . if I went back and killed me as a baby, would I still be here? And would it be me that went back and killed the baby me? And how would that work because I would have been killed as a baby by the me later but then how would I go back and kill myself as a baby if I died as a baby?'

'What the fuck?'

The planets aligned. The ambience. The surprise at her marching into his room in her underwear and the convoluted question all served to bring his faculties back in one glorious, beautiful moment of full cognitive function.

'Is it possible?'

'What?' He snorted a laugh and shook his head. 'Is what possible?'

'Listen,' she said, whacking his bare leg gently and only then registering that he was also wearing only a pair of boxer shorts. 'So right . . . I'm a baby, okay? I go back and . . . so . . . I'm me now and I go back and kill me the baby . . . can I do that?'

'Er . . . fuck,' he said, thinking hard. The room was dark. His light was off and only the soft glow from her bedside lamp was spilling in. 'Er . . . yeah, yeah it must be possible but . . .'

'But how?' She asked in that tone that instantly demanded the answer. 'If I was dead as a baby how could I go back and kill me?'

'That's kinda straying into parallel world theory but yeah . . . think it through . . . by the very fact that you *could* go back and kill yourself as a baby means that it is possible. So if it is possible then yes, you could do it.'

'Eh?' she said, shaking her head in confusion.

'Okay,' he said, leaning forward towards her. 'You're here, right? So you *can* use the time machine to go back and kill the baby you. Just by the fact that *is* possible means that, yes, you *could* do it. But it would also mean that by killing the baby you, you would not cease to exist. Because if you ceased to exist at the point of killing the baby you then it would mean me and Harry never met you. Which means you never grew up, never joined the police, never got brought here and so on . . . but that would mean you would then never be here in order to go back and kill the baby you.'

'What the fuck did you just say?' she asked with a laugh at the utter confusion in her head.

'No, think about it. You would have to continue to exist,' Ben said. 'Because otherwise you would never be here to go back and kill the baby you . . . which would mean the baby you grew up and came here . . . so that must be like parallel worlds or something.'

'Parallel worlds?'

'Yeah. Like . . . infinite worlds all together. See, we think of time as linear, right? That it only goes forward? But the time machine breaks that belief because we can go back . . . but what if we haven't gone back or we have gone back but not to our past. See what I mean?'

'No. Not one word,' she said, no longer interested in what he said but only seeing that spark in his eyes. The same spark she saw during the first few days when he questioned everything and was working things out. The change was profound. His whole manner seemed alive and animated. The proper Ben was there.

'So, right,' he said and reached out to lift her hand. 'This is you here.' He waved her hand up and down, making her smile at the feel of it. 'So we have Safa here now . . . but if we take *Safa* – he waved her hand again – 'and go back to kill baby Safa . . . then maybe we are not killing the baby Safa that you were . . . but another baby Safa . . . like . . . like . . . so every time you do anything . . . anything at all, right? You make a decision and do something, but what if you made a different decision and did something else? *That* life continues to run.'

'I'm so lost,' she said, still not listening but wholly and utterly absorbed in watching him.

'Ah okay.' He smiled. He actually smiled. A flash of teeth showed through his beard as he waved her hand up and down. 'So, er . . . you wake up in the morning and the first thing you do is . . . is what?'

'Er . . . have a piss.'

'Right.' He blinked and smiled again. 'But what if you didn't have a piss? One of you has a piss and the other brushes her teeth and the other uses the shower and the other decides to go for a run and another decides to take a shit on Harry's bed and—'

'What?' She laughed.

'You get what I mean? You do one thing but *anything* you could possibly do is still done but by infinite yous . . . and it stretches off infinitely. Like every person that ever lived all having infinite variations of every possible decision and every possible way of living. So . . . the you now and here' – he waved her hand again – 'goes back and kills the baby you but who knows if it is the baby you from you now or the baby you from another you? Make sense?'

'Not one word,' she said.

'In which case,' he said, 'I cannot answer your question.'

'Well, thanks for trying,' she said, thrilled at seeing him back.

'Welcome,' he said.

A pause. A hesitancy. A sudden awareness of near nudity and the darkness of the room. She is beautiful. Stunning. Flawless. He is not worthy. He is haggard and weak.

She saw it happen. She saw the change and swallowed to cough. 'Er . . . so . . .' She saw him slipping and the dark shadow crossing his face. Her mind raced to think of something to continue the conversation but it was too late. She hesitated too long. 'Thanks,' she said instead.

He nodded. His eyes once more devoid of that spark.

'Much clearer.' She smiled and stood up. 'I'll come back if I get stuck again.'

'Okay.'

'Night, Ben.' She crossed to the door, wondering if his eyes were watching her backside. She turned at the threshold to glance back but couldn't tell if he was looking her way or not.

That night gave the hope. He came back. Not for long but it proved the proper Ben was still there. It was a magical few minutes and an experience that stayed with her over the next weeks.

It stayed with him too, and it made him worse. He'd felt alive for the first time in months but that made him feel guilty. He also saw her body and felt the reaction inside and that made the guilt multiply a hundredfold. How dare he feel alive? How dare he even consider looking at Safa that way? Steph was having an affair. Steph was leaving him. He is dead. He is worthless. He is nothing.

It was also that night of hope that made Safa cry for the first time since arriving.

As tough as Safa is, she is still a beautiful woman who knows all too well the way men react to her physical appearance and she saw a hint of that reaction in Ben that night. Only for a split second and she knew it was in surprise at her marching into his room in her underwear and not once did she feel threatened or sense anything predatory in him, but seeing that reaction in him planted a seed. The proper Ben was still there. The man was there.

It was not a decision taken lightly, but his decline was worsening. He was so withdrawn it was painful to watch. Like he was dying ever so slowly and they had to just stand by and let it happen. Something had to give. It was desperate. She could sense Harry's frustration growing. Harry was ready to go, she was too. Enough time had been given. The seed grew into a plan.

That night, she waited for the hours of darkness to come. She fretted and worried and panicked at the thought but was determined to see it through. Besides, if she was completely honest she knew that, deep down, it was not entirely selfless. Ben had to come back. It was this or nothing. She had no more ideas. No more hope.

With Harry's snoring rattling the bunker, she slipped into the bathroom and stared at her own reflection properly for the first time in months. She looked at the shape of her eyes and pulled her hair out to let it hang down to her shoulders. Her hands trembled as she got ready. Nerves mostly, but with the tiniest, almost unseen hint of excitement. She was doing this for Ben. He had to come back. He was going to die. His life would end either here by his own hand or by going back to perish on the tracks at Holborn. He just needed to remember what it was like to feel alive.

She swallowed, took a deep breath, sniffed her armpits, nodded and tugged her bra down a touch to show a bit more of the tops of her breasts.

'You up?'

Ben snapped awake. His eyes instantly going to the door at the strange tone of voice. Like she was worried.

'Ben? You up?'

'Yeah,' he croaked. He'd started to doze off and the traces from the nightmare were still evident in the panic and fear he felt.

The door opened. She turned the dimmer switch of his light just enough to bring the tiniest glimmer of light into his room. She closed the door and with her heart thundering in her chest she walked towards his bed.

'What's up?' he asked, his voice low.

She didn't know what to say, so said nothing. She stopped next to his bed. Her arms at her sides and her eyes searching his face.

He couldn't help but look. She'd walked in, turned the light on low and stopped right next to his bed. He blinked and flicked his eyes quickly up over her body to her eyes and stopped. His heart reacted. Thudding harder. He swallowed, blinked and moved to sit up higher.

She didn't say a word but waited, watching, searching and seeing it. Seeing that flicker right there. It strengthened her resolve and made that small sense of excitement grow bigger, and quickly too. She moved deftly. Easing on to his bed to lift one leg over to straddle his thighs. He froze instantly. His eyes widening. His mouth instantly dry. He blinked fast. She rested a hand on his naked chest and felt the thudding of his heart. She smiled nervously, suddenly vulnerable and exposed. His eyes remained locked on hers. His mind whirling as she lowered down so slowly it took forever. Her hands moved out to find his. Her fingers entwined with his. No words were said. No words were needed. She moved up higher from his thighs towards his groin. He drew breath, fast and sudden. She felt him stiffen beneath her and again it strengthened her resolve and made that small sense of excitement grow further.

Eyes locked. Hers so dark and stunning. His so blue and full of pain and hurt and possessed of a depth that seemed endless and made her sink lower with her lips forever moving towards his. He moved up too. He reacted to lift towards her. His stomach muscles now strong enough to hold that position without shaking or feeling pain. At that last second she paused. Her lips but a fraction from his. She didn't know why she paused, only that she did. Perhaps it was to savour the feeling of the moment, perhaps it was to reflect, perhaps it was to think that despite the reasons for coming in here to do this, she actually really wanted him to kiss her right now.

That pause broke the spell. He looked down to see the perfection of her form. The flawless skin tone, the raven-black hair spilling down and he felt more worthless in that second than in all the previous seconds of his depression combined. It was the lowest. He was being pitied by someone he respected and admired more than anyone else he had ever met and that single thought was the catalyst.

She felt it change. She'd seen his eyes look down and she wanted him to look. She wanted him to see. She wanted Ben to feel desired, valued, to feel like a man and come back to what he was because he'd taken life so others could live and he'd done it again. She wanted him to look and be turned on. She wanted him to feel the tenderness of intimacy. He had dignity and pride. He was something so special and for that he should not be left to die so alone and frightened. It was when he looked up back at her eyes that she knew it was wrong. A mistake made, something that was suddenly stupid and cheap.

'Get out,' he whispered, the words trembling and full of emotion. 'Get the fuck out . . .'

She moved fast. From his bed to the door to her own that was closed quickly as the tears spilled down her cheeks. Humiliation. Loss. Rejection. She wept then. She wept for the first time in years and she did it quietly, almost silently, as Ben lay on his bed with his own cheeks glistening.

Twenty-Seven

The morning is the same as every other morning. He wakes up to Safa knocking on the door and goes through the motions of showering, brushing his teeth and getting dressed.

'Drink,' she says bluntly in a tone he doesn't register.

'Eat,' she says. He takes a freshly baked croissant from the bowl and goes through the motions of putting it in his mouth.

'Ben!'

'What?' He looks up, startled at the glare coming from Safa.

'You didn't even notice.'

'Notice what?'

'The croissant,' she snaps, getting up from the table.

'Eh?' he asks, confused until he realises this is the first time they've had them, plus the fact that he used to love fresh croissants, which no doubt was on Wikipedia.

'I'll wait outside,' Safa says, getting up and taking the black bag with the pistols with her. Ben watches her go, knowing he should say something, but he doesn't.

'She got them for you,' Harry says.

'Yeah,' Ben says for lack of anything else in his head.

'She's trying.'

Ben looks at him, sensing a build-up to something else. Harry shifts on his chair and bites into a croissant that flakes apart with crumbs falling lightly to the plate in front of him. 'What happened when you were seventeen?' Harry asks.

'Safa ask you to ask me? Get me talking?'

'I'm interested,' Harry says.

'Not much to say. I was walking home on a country lane. Car pulls up. Five blokes attacked a woman and her kid . . .'

'And?'

'That's it.'

'You killed them?'

'Yes. Killed three outright, another died while we waited on the ambulance. The last was DOA.'

'How?'

'Knife.'

'How did it play out?'

'Dunno.'

'What happened after?'

'Got arrested but they let me go. The blokes were gang members . . . like gangsters?'

'I know what gang members are.'

'I had therapy. They gave me a new name and that was it.'

'Therapy?'

'Yeah. They thought I'd be messed up in the head for killing a bunch of people.'

'Were you?'

'Nope.'

Harry eats the croissant and stands from the table. 'You ready?' he asks, but doesn't wait before walking off towards the door.

Ben watches him go, feeling like a complete wanker for refusing to engage in conversation. Fuck it. Instead, he eats slowly and drinks water, staring round in baleful hatred at the bare concrete walls and the bare concrete floor while thinking back to Safa last night.

Eventually, he heads outside to both of them waiting at the table with three pistols already on the top. Ben sighs and picks one up.

'Field strip?' he asks sarcastically. Seconds later the gun is stripped and in parts on the table. 'Reassemble?' he asks and clicks it back together. 'Field strip?'

'No,' she says, staring at him with an altogether new expression. She places a box on the table with a factory-printed logo and the words *9 millimetre* etched on the sides and top. Then he notices three sets of ear defenders on the table and looks past them both to the high wall of sandbags stacked further down the ledge.

'Rounds cost money,' she says, opening the first box to reveal the shiny brass bullets. 'In the police we were limited to what we could fire in practice . . . but now' – she ejects the magazine in her Glock and starts feeding the rounds into it – 'now we don't have to worry . . . and can fire as many as we want. Look over there.'

Ben looks over to another table to see every type of pistol they have stripped and rebuilt resting on the top with cases of bullets next to each.

'Put these on,' she says in a blunt tone after showing him how to load a magazine and handing him a set of ear defenders. 'Keep the safety on until you're ready to fire. Slide back to bring the first round up into the chamber. Keep a two-handed grip and do not ever point the weapon at me or Harry. Point it down when you turn. Face down the range.'

Ben picks the weapon up and adopts the two-handed grip that she and Harry are using while noticing the way she looks at him is different and the gentle tone in her voice has gone. He moves round the table carrying a loaded gun. They both track every movement he makes until he's staring down the ad hoc shooting range at the wall of sandbags. She glances to Harry. He nods with an almost imperceptible movement. She places her gun down on the table and moves in close behind Ben, tugging the ear defender back from his right ear as her foot moves between his legs and starts kicking them out to widen his stance.

'Open your legs. Bit more . . . stop, that's fine.'

'Are you okay?' he asks, turning towards her. 'The croissants were really nice.'

She doesn't look at him. 'Face down the range,' she says curtly and leans round him until her body is pressing into his back. She reaches out to adjust his grip on the pistol. 'Left hand here, right hand here. Relax and breathe normally. I'm going to watch you fire. If I tap your shoulder then stop firing. Understood?' She doesn't wait for the reply but pushes the defender back over his ear and taps his shoulder.

He fires the weapon, feeling the immense jolt travel through his arms into his shoulders. The noise is incredible too, and far louder than he remembers from Holborn. He adjusts his grip a little and shuffles slightly then fires again and this time he notices the little puff in the air as the bullet hits the sandbags. He keeps going, feeling that violent recoil in his hands until the weapon clicks empty. He turns to notice they're both watching him intently.

'What?' he asks, seeing her mouth move but not hearing the words. She tugs the defender from his ear again.

'I said you don't flinch,' she says.

'Am I meant to flinch?'

'No.'

'Okay.'

'Keep going.'

'I've run out of bullets.'

'Rounds.'

'What are?'

'The bullets are rounds.'

'Oh. I've run out of them anyway.'

'Load more then.'

'Are you okay?'

'I'm fine. Keep going.'

'Thanks for the croissants—'

'Ben!' she snaps in irritation. 'Focus.'

'Okay, sorry.'

'Don't be sorry, just bloody focus on what you're doing.'

He goes back to the table with his cheeks stinging from the rebuke and feeling even more childish. He loads up the magazine while they watch him closely. Safa now holding her pistol down at her side, one-handed, and just from the way she holds it you can tell she's been around weapons a lot. Harry looks entirely at ease apart from still tracking every move Ben makes.

Back at the line, Ben gets the grip, adjusts his feet and fires into the sandbags. He doesn't really aim but more points and pulls the trigger. It's a novelty and something different for a few minutes.

'Try and aim now,' she says. 'Line the sights up like I told you before, you already know how to hold it. Squeeze the trigger, don't pluck it or snatch it. Squeeze. Be confident but not cocky and aim properly.'

'Okay.' He loads up, turns back and shoots the sandbag wall.

'I said try and aim,' she says tightly.

'I was.' He shrugs and goes back for another go. The top tier of sandbags has the sky behind it so he sort of aims for the third tier down.

'That's not aiming. That's pointing and shooting. Do it properly.'

'Why are you snapping at me?' he asks while pushing the little brass bullets into the magazine.

'Because you're not trying.'

'I am. I'm trying.'

'Try harder.'

'What for?'

She draws breath and looks away as though counting to ten before answering. 'Because you need to learn how to shoot, that's why.'

'Why do I?'

'Know what?' she says, giving him a withering look. 'Do what you want.' She lifts and fires. Emptying her magazine with perfect shots that seem timed and precise. Harry does the same. Firing into the wall of sandbags with tiny adjustments made to his grip and stance.

'Good,' Harry shouts when he finishes the first magazine, nodding at the pistol in his hands. 'Good weapon.'

The morning passes. All three shooting sandbags as they work through the pistols on the table.

Safa pins targets on to the sandbags but doesn't give any instruction as to what Ben should aim for. He shoots them anyway and learns how to aim to get the bullet closer to the thing he wants to hit.

At lunch they go into the main room. Ben sits down at the table in the usual funk of complete depression. It takes over five minutes before he realises she's got a bowl of food for herself and is eating quietly. He feels the blush of shame in his cheeks at the expectation he had that she would get the food and drink for him. He feels so stupid that for a few seconds he doesn't do anything but stay still and look down at his hands in his lap. Then time passes and it becomes too late to get any food as that would signify that he was waiting all this time for her to get it.

'You not hungry?' she asks eventually, but doesn't look at him and in that second he gives up caring completely.

'Yeah I am,' he says, reaching out for a croissant. He does not give a shit. He never asked for this and he does not want to be here. He shifts the responsibility away and stares round in disdain at the fucking bare concrete walls he hates so much.

'We're staying in this afternoon,' she says.

'Awesome,' he replies, not bothering to look at her.

'We'll do unarmed combat.'

'Yeah?' he asks, faking a sudden interest. She looks at him sharply, narrowing her eyes. 'Enjoy that.'

'Ben . . .'

'What?' He stares over the table at her then sees Harry shift position, hunching lower over his food with a grunt. 'Problem?' Ben asks him.

Harry doesn't reply but focuses on his food. They fall into silence. Ben drinks water, feeling a strange sense of liberation at not giving a flying fuck any more.

'Ready?' she asks once his water is drained.

'No.'

'Come on.' She starts to rise as Harry scrapes his chair back.

'Have fun,' Ben says, pushing his chair back.

'Where are you going?'

'Outside to shoot paper targets.'

'We've got work to do.'

'Like I said, have fun.'

'What the hell is your problem?'

'Nothing.'

'Ben, they'll kill you. Is that what you want?'

'Maybe I do.' He pushes through the door into the corridor.

'What the fuck is wrong with you?' she shouts, running after him.

'Nothing.'

'Don't walk away from me.'

'I'm going outside.'

'You selfish prick.' She grabs his arm, spinning him round on the spot. 'We are training inside.'

'No.'

The fury in her face shows clear and true and the muscles in her jaw twitch as she grits her teeth. 'We. Are. Training. Inside . . .'

He leans forward in emphasis of expression. 'No.'

'Ben.' She grabs his arm again, refusing to let him turn away. He doesn't fight against her but stays passive and non-committal.

'Go play heroes with Harry. I'm not interested.'

'They saved your life.'

'Then they can unsave it.'

'Ben. You will die. Make no mistake about it. They will take you back and leave you there then it's done. Over. You're dead.'

He shrugs and pulls a face, which just sends a deeper shade of red into her cheeks.

'Selfish,' she says, shaking her head with disdain. 'You are a selfish man.'

'Who cares?'

'I DO.' She flashes into rage, prodding him in the chest. 'You will work. Do you understand? You will work.'

'Stop pushing me.'

'You will work to stay alive.'

'I choose death.'

'Grow up!'

'I don't want to be here . . .'

'I don't care what you want. You have to work.'

'Stop fucking pushing me,' he growls, but she jabs harder and faster.

'Stop me,' she shouts and jabs him into the wall. 'Stop me. Do something. Get angry. React, for fuck's sake.' She jabs harder, driving him back so hard he bounces off the wall.

'I do not want to be here.'

'You are here.'

'What do you care? Leave me alone. Go train with Harry and save the world because I ain't doing it . . . stop it . . . stop pushing me, Safa. Stop fucking PUSHING ME . . . WHAT THE FUCK DO YOU WANT?'

'YOU . . . I WANT YOU TO WORK!'

'I won't,' he snarls, forcing his body against her finger that jabs into his chest. 'I won't work for you. I won't work for Roland.' He pushes forward again, forcing her to take a step back. 'I won't do it. I don't want to do it. I want out. I'm sick of running and jumping and taking those fucking guns apart and being thrown on the mats and doing wristlocks and armlocks and eating fruit and eggs. I hate it. I hate this place. I want my life and if I can't have my life then I'll take my fucking death.'

'No.' Her turn to give the one-word, stubborn answers now, and they reach an impasse with her driving that finger into his chest and him pushing against it.

'Get away from me, Safa. Get Harry. Get the other men and come back with the drugs. Do me in the neck and take me back because that's better than being here.'

'No.'

'It's not your choice.'

'No.'

'Stop saying no. It's my life and my choice.'

'No, you're staying.'

'I am not staying. GET AWAY FROM ME . . .' He screams the words into her face but she doesn't flinch. 'I don't know what you think I am. I'm not a cop or a soldier. I'm a fucking nobody . . .'

'You aren't a nobody.'

'I am. I am a fucking nobody that did something weird once—'

'Twice.'

'Fine . . . I did those things, but the second one got me killed and I ended up here . . . that's failure. I failed. I cannot be what you want me to be.'

'Be Ben Ryder.'

'Safa . . .'

'Just be Ben Ryder,' she says in a voice quavering with emotion. 'This isn't Ben Ryder . . . this isn't you . . .'

'This is me,' he says in exasperation. 'This is who I am . . . I want my life . . . I want to be with Steph and I don't need a mercy fuck in the . . . holy fuck, what was that for?' He reels back from the stinging slap delivered hard across his face, but the next one comes faster and harder than the first. Everything she has done for him. The support she has given him. The belief and energy and offering herself to him last night all so he can say that whore's name and lash out with hurtful words. She batters him back into the wall with open-handed hits, striking him over and over.

'Do something . . .' she pleads. 'Fight back . . .'

'No,' he growls and stands upright to take the next slap that stings to hell. They lock eyes. Hers dark and full of rage and his full of self-pity. She hits him again and he takes it. Again and he takes it. The sound of flesh on flesh rolling down the corridor. She purses her lips, furious at the lack of reaction. She hits. Something inside him snaps. When her hand comes at him again he catches it mid-swing and grips hard as he pushes her back with forceful steps.

'You don't know the impact you had on people . . .' she whispers angrily. 'The whole world knows your name . . . you meant something. You are something.'

Still the rage in him builds and rushes through. Her eyes change from angry to imploring to a glimmer of hope that offends him. The trite bollocks spilling from her mouth and that earnest look trying to goad him into reacting like he is something special that deserves all this treatment. He hates it. He hates himself for what she did last night. He hates himself for feeling this way. The self-loathing consumes him and makes him hate everything. The repugnance at his own existence renders her words meaningless.

'You're more than you know. You gave hope to so many. You meant courage and decency. I saw you . . . I saw you, Ben. Be that man now. Be Ben Ryder . . . for fuck's sake . . . BE BEN RYDER . . . BE MY BEN RYDER . . .'

'What?' He stops suddenly with the shock of her words banishing the hate-fuelled anger from his mind. In that second he becomes very aware of the grip on her hand and slackens it off as a crimson blush grows in her cheeks.

'Safa . . .' He blinks at her in confusion.

'Fuck yourself,' she snarls, stepping away from him with a look of disgust on her face. 'You're not Ben Ryder . . . go fucking die . . .'

'Safa.' He starts after her but she goes fast. Marching back down the corridor, leaving him in a silence that rings in his ears and feels like the sting in his cheeks.

He heads outside and grabs a pistol from the table. Safety on. Magazine out. He feeds rounds into the top and slams it back into the butt. *Be my Ben Ryder.* He moves to the line. Safety off. Arms raised. Firing. *Be my Ben Ryder.* He empties the first magazine before realising he doesn't have ear defenders on but it feels nice. Like the recoil and noise are blotting the thoughts out from his head.

He reloads, but this time he loads several magazines and pistols at the same time and carries them over to the table next to the firing line. *Be my Ben Ryder.* He fires. His mind replays every word they just said and the look in her face when she told him to go and die. He deserved it. He is a selfish, horrible man. He fires into paper targets and changes weapons to feel the difference in weight and recoil, adjusting to aim so he can get the holes nearer the centre. Safa is carrying him. She's done everything to get him through this and for what? For someone she glimpsed once dragging a corpse down a train track?

He fires faster. Plucking the trigger to fill the air with the booming explosions and feeling the jolt carry through his body. He sees Safa's face imploring him and the feel of her hand within his grip as he pushed her down the corridor. His cheeks still sting but he deserved it. He fires and switches guns to fire again as Steph's image fills his mind. The last time he saw her was in their bedroom. They had sex that night. *Fuck me, Ben. Fuck me harder.* She took her towel off then got cross with him when he got turned on. He will never see her again. He will never go back. He is dead. He fires and fires. The bullets hit the centre. He twitches and aims for the outside rings, striking home. The depression rushes back in. He turns and aims for Safa's target. Firing at an angle and finding he can still hit the bit he is aiming for and feeling irritated that he is good at it. He shouldn't be good at anything.

It goes black inside again. Safa's face morphing with Steph's who was cross with him that morning.

He becomes lost to his own misery and slides down to a darkness of mood that doesn't abate but gets deeper and worse and he can't stop it. He wants to stop it. He does not want to be here but he doesn't want to fail Safa either. Why did she offer herself like that last night? He fires with tears tracking down his face and he fires until the sobs threaten to come and for a second he wants them to come so he can let the emotion out.

Except the emotion doesn't come out. It goes away and he becomes numb once again.

I hate it here.

I can't stay here.

I don't belong.

Twenty-Eight

She wakes naturally from a body clock honed from years of discipline. That and the tablet device bleeping softly on the table next to her bed.

She gets her legs over the side and reaches down to slide the screen, silencing the alarm. Another day. A new day. She stands and stretches, feeling the pull of muscles worked hard and the pay-offs of good food and solid sleeps. That she is in the best physical shape of her life is not missed, but the sadness inside overshadows everything else.

It was two days ago when the words fell from her mouth in the corridor and she winces at the thought of it. *Be my Ben Ryder.* She has tried everything. *I want to be with Steph.* Of everything, that hurts the most. Ben doesn't know what Steph did though. She wanted to tell him right then at that point but still she held back.

They haven't spoken since and the awkward silence grows by the hour. Ben stayed outside the rest of that day. Firing hundreds of rounds until there was nothing left of the paper targets. He did the same the next day too. Stripping weapons. Cleaning weapons. Loading and firing weapons.

'You ever seen that before?' Safa asked Harry later that day.

'No,' Harry admitted honestly.

Ben's ability to place the shot was outstanding. Truly exceptional. He was a natural at firing and that just made it worse. He even went further back to extend the distance but still learnt to hit where he aimed.

Harry said something else too. He said it was time. *Cut the apron strings. Let him be a man. Give him his dignity.* Simple words spoken honestly.

She didn't wake Ben yesterday. She wanted to and still felt that instinct to protect and nurture. Instead, she and Harry ran the course outside, did circuits, practised firing, did unarmed combat and ate food. She knows they are ready and she knows it will just be her and Harry doing the work now. That still leaves the problem unresolved.

She goes into the main room and looks at Ben's door. Maybe she should wake him this morning. Maybe he'll be different. Changed. Ready to work. She moves towards it, lifting her hand as Harry opens his door behind her. He doesn't say anything but he doesn't need to. She holds still, her hand inches from Ben's door, and turns to look at Harry, who shrugs and goes into the bathroom.

He *is* Ben Ryder. She knocks and waits. He saved hundreds of people. She knocks again and waits. 'Ben? You up?'

Nothing. She knocks again and frowns at the door. 'Ben?' Still nothing. She feels the first tremor of worry and pushes the handle down to crack the door open an inch. 'Ben?' She opens it fully to stare at the bed and the empty sterile, austere room. 'Oh no . . . no no . . .' The bed is made. Unslept in. His clothes folded neatly on the floor.

She's away in an instant. Running down the corridor to the main room, which is empty. Nothing touched or used. No cups on the tables. The chairs all pushed under the tabletops. She goes on, running with fear in her heart through the door and down the corridor to the room holding the device. It's locked. She goes on, checking Roland's office but knowing with a sinking sensation exactly where he will be. She runs hard. Bare feet pounding the concrete to reach the exit door and out into a driving rain that soaks her clothes in seconds.

'BEN?' she shouts, heading round the end of the bunker to the tables and the containers used to hold the pistols. One of them is partially open. She wrenches the lid off, seeing the empty space where the Glock should be.

'BEN?' She screams his name. Her hair plastered to her scalp. She runs down the slick grass past the end of the bunker as Harry runs out from the bunker. 'BEN?' she shouts harder, louder, desperate and worried sick. The rain drives hard. Pelting against her face and drumming noisily on the concrete sides of the bunker. He isn't here. She goes to the edge and peers down. Nothing. She spins round, searching for anything. Wet tracks in the grass going up the bank. 'BEN?' She runs up, planting her bare feet into the grass to gain traction to reach the top. She slips and slides. Cursing but working furiously to gain the crest. Please no. Not this way. Not like this. He doesn't deserve this. To die alone like this.

She reaches the top and spots him instantly. A grey figure on his knees with his back to her. The pistol held in his right hand at his side, resting on the ground.

'He there?' Harry behind her coming up the bank. She waves for him to stop.

'BEN.' She runs hard, heedless of the sharp stones digging into her feet. She spots his chest heaving with sobs. His head bowed in submission to life. 'Oh God . . . Ben . . .' She reaches him as he turns to look at her and never before has she seen such misery in a person. His eyes red from sobbing with thick bags underneath. His hair straggly and plastered down from the rain. A picture of abject dejection. He goes to speak. His jaw working silently. The pistol lifts an inch then drops.

'I can't . . .' he sobs.

'Oh Ben.' She drops behind him, wrapping her arms round his shoulders.

'I can't,' he whispers with pain driving through his heart that she feels pounding within him. His left hand reaches up to grip her arm as it holds him close. 'I can't, Safa . . . I can't do it . . .'

'I know.' She sobs, tears spilling from her eyes to roll fat with the rivulets of rain pouring down her face. She grips him harder, kissing the side of his head and feeling the heaving sobs travel through his body. 'Not like this . . .'

'I've got to . . .' He sobs again. His hand on her arm. She feels him pushing back into her. Desperate for human contact.

'Not like this,' she whispers into his ear. 'Ben . . . not like this . . .'

'Let me . . . help me . . . I can't . . . I . . .'

'Not like this,' she cries into him, pressing her cheek into his head. Her arms wrapping and holding. Rocking him as their knees soak into the mud. Harry watches from the edge of the bank. His face as impassive as ever.

Ben tries to speak but breaks off to let the sobs come thick and fast. An outpouring of grief and loss and utter dejection. He tries to lift the pistol but she grips his arm, forcing it gently back down and sliding along to take the gun from his hand that gets flung towards Harry.

'I can't . . . let me go home . . .'

'Okay,' she whispers, remembering the man she saw on the track that day. His right arm comes up to touch her shoulder. His hand gripping with emotion.

'Go home . . .' he sobs. She turns him slowly, easing him round to draw him close so her arms can go round and hold him tight.

'Okay,' she says again.

'Send me home . . .'

'I will.' She lifts her head, sobbing as much as he. Rocking back and forth in the mud and rain. The man on the tracks was decent. This was that man. This is Ben Ryder.

'I'm so sorry.'

She whispers down with a hand on the back of his head, pushing him into her. 'It's okay . . . you can go home.'

'Home . . .'

'Home, Ben. You can go home.'

Give him his dignity. Give Ben Ryder his dignity. Let him be a man. Let him choose death over life. There's honour in that. There is. She nods and kisses his head as the tears soak into his hair.

Twenty-Nine

'Where is he?'

'In his room,' Safa replies.

'Christ,' Roland says, walking to the table to grab the flask and several cups, which he carries over. 'Is he okay?'

'No he isn't,' she says darkly.

'Why didn't he shoot himself?' Roland asks softly. Harry shakes his head, his mouth turned down at the ends. Malcolm and Konrad watch on, unsure how to act in the charged atmosphere of the meeting.

'Still a survivor,' Safa says, lifting her head to look at Roland.

'Of course,' Roland says, nodding with understanding. 'Poor chap . . . I wish there was something we could do. Is there anything we can do?' he asks the group.

'Did you ever see the footage?' Safa asks, looking round to Malcolm and Konrad.

'Course,' Malcolm says softly.

'Konrad?' Safa asks.

'Years ago, when I was young,' Konrad says.

'I want you to see it now,' Safa says to them all. 'To remember him as he was and not like this. So we know who we're . . . who he is. We owe him that.'

'Course,' Malcolm says again. 'I can get it.'

Silence at the table. Coffee poured and cups lifted. Konrad swallows and draws breath. 'How do . . . I mean . . .'

'I have no idea,' Roland says. 'I never planned to have to take someone back.'

'Fuck,' Safa mouths and looks away.

'Sedate him,' Harry says after a pause. 'I'll carry him back.'

Another silence. 'If you think that is best.' Roland breathes the words out.

'Aye,' Harry says firmly.

'We've still got his clothes,' Malcolm says. 'We can time it so you arrive just after we've taken him.'

'Fuck,' Safa mouths again at the idea of it. It felt right outside but now it feels wrong again. This can't be it. It can't, but it is. It's what he wants. 'Malcolm, can you get the footage?'

'I'll do it now.' Malcolm eases from the table, leaving them in a silence broken only by swallows and throats being cleared as coffee is poured and cups are lifted. A few minutes is all it takes and Malcolm rushes back with a large-screen tablet, which he places on the table. He thumbs the screen while the others wait and drink coffee.

'It's ready,' Malcolm says. 'Er . . . you want 3D or . . . ?'

'Stick with normal,' Safa says. Malcolm nods and turns the device so the others can see the front.

Harry stares at the image and the weird triangle showing in the middle that Safa leans forward to touch lightly. The image changes, showing pin-sharp, high-definition, real-time footage of a train platform. Dense crowds waiting and, despite the years between them, Harry immediately recognises the unique style of the London Underground and the sign emblazoned with 'Holborn' on the back wall.

'That's Ben,' Safa says, pointing at Ben walking out of a side door at the end of the platform. 'He'd just had a meeting with the works manager and Ben being Ben he'd pissed the bloke off enough to get kicked out in the middle of the Underground. See, the door slams in his face.'

'That's Ben,' Harry says in shock at recognising Ben so easily.

'Yeah.' She freezes the image of the footage she's watched so many times. 'See this woman?'

'Yes.'

'She's one of the environmental activists. This guy here, the tall one with ginger hair, this woman, this man at the back . . . there's one behind this crowd kneeling down and another one over here. They're all wearing *I Love London* T-shirts and rain jackets.'

'Pretending not to be together,' Harry says, clocking the distance between them.

'I'll play it through. Keep your eyes on Ben.' She presses the 'Play' button and watches the famous footage she has seen hundreds of times, but now the impact is even greater. She's met this man. She's met and spoken with Ben Ryder. She held him as he sobbed and asked for death over life. She knows every second of this video clip but watches it with fresh eyes as if seeing it for the first time. She knows his voice now, the tone in which he speaks and his humour. The way he walks and that genial manner that masks the utter brutal capability of the man. She was the last person to see Ben Ryder alive. They locked eyes and in that second she saw a man full of honour and integrity. A man who would never grope her, force her to do things or take what he could through power. His was a power restrained that was ready to be used when it was needed. She knew Ben Ryder would laugh easily and be full of humour and fun.

She saw the same Ben Ryder during those first couple of days. The way he took everything in his stride and didn't panic and the way he stood back until she got hit then ploughed in and the violence he used. Untrained but devastating. Ruthless yet human. Not a monster but a hero.

The attack Ben stopped when he was seventeen was sexually motivated, but even so, the fact that a white youth stopped a gang from attacking an Indian woman and her child stuck with Safa. Safa had seen racism first-hand. She suffered it growing up, the insults, the taunts, the bullying, but she knew there were decent, courageous people in the world. She knew she would protect people and stand up for what was right. Years later, she witnessed what he did at Holborn and saw the world react as they learnt the connection between that man at the train station and the boy on the country lane so many years before. The name Ben Ryder came to mean decency, moral fortitude, honour and courage. She joined the Diplomatic Protection Squad because of what he did. She devoted her life to the protection of others *because* of Ben Ryder. Harry understood this and gave the patience he had shown over the months on the basis of her words.

Being told something and seeing it for yourself are two different things and Harry doesn't show a flicker other than leaning closer to the screen. Safa watches him for a reaction but the soldier gives nothing away. Her eyes go back to the footage and Ben running towards while everyone else runs away. People falling on the tracks, dying from electrocution. Smoke hanging in the air and body parts strewn across the ground. The ginger man trying to detonate his vest and Ben running towards him. The dark-haired man using a sawn-off shotgun to devastating effect and the speed at which Ben switches from running towards the ginger guy to heading into the blonde woman firing the two pistols. He takes her down, driving her hard into the floor as she screams at the man with the shotgun. An instinct in Ben to stop that communication between the attackers and he kills the woman with the pistol taken from her hand. A split second later and he's up, firing into the man with the shotgun, killing him outright, before spinning round to scan for the ginger man now throwing people on to the live rails.

Another attack, this one from a woman lunging at Ben with a knife. The speed of reaction and sheer aggression shown by Ben is staggering. They watch him slipping and sliding but his reactions are perfect and the reason this clip is shown to specialist firearms officers all over the world. *Be this man. Match his aggression.* Ben shoots the woman in the head. Another split second and that threat is negated, and so Ben switches back to the primary target and somewhere in his untrained mind he knows the ginger man has a bomb and therefore poses the greatest risk. Running and firing with a face snarling with determination and fear. *We can train you not to miss, but only you can match the aggression and instincts of Ben Ryder.*

Even when the pistol clicks empty Ben doesn't falter, but takes the bomber down on to the tracks with a show of absolute, extreme violence, pinning the man down while driving fists into his face. They could never ask Ben, but the analysis produced after suggested that Ben knew the train was approaching, which is why he tore the suicide vest open and switched from punching to stamping, in so doing delivering the killing blow and rendering the man unable to detonate himself.

Still that threat assessment continues. On his feet, dragging the dead man down the tracks, desperately trying to get the bomb away from the train. He almost makes it too. Another few metres and he would have survived.

'Is that you?' Harry asks, blinking at the younger Safa on the screen, running on to the platform in full uniform.

'Yeah,' she whispers. She can smell the chemicals in the air. The dry heat of air blasted through the tunnels. The smell of iron in the blood and the stench of faeces from bowels opening on death and locking eyes with Ben running backwards, dragging a dead man. She didn't know who he was at that point, or why he was pulling the man, but she caught sight of the suicide vest and the connection was made. She ran screaming at the driver, who slammed the brakes on but too late. The train goes in, blocking the view of Ben as it fills the station, and a few seconds later the explosion tears through the tunnel, bucking the train backwards and up on to the platform as she runs back to the safety of the exit.

Her heart hammers in her chest as the footage ends and Harry sits back, folding his arms across his chest in contemplation of the event he just witnessed.

'Christ,' Roland says again. He too knows Ben now. He knows the man, and to see Ben at work is something else. Malcolm and Konrad feel the same and every bad thought they had of the man that refused to work vanishes. Safa was right. They have to remember him as he was and not how he is.

'Okay,' Harry says, still with his arms folded.

'There it is,' Safa whispers as the footage ends, changing to a black screen.

It's said of the commandos during the Second World War that you cannot fictionalise anything they ever did because they would have done it in real life, and Harry knows good work when he sees it. His eyes narrow and he blasts air out through his nose. That man he just watched is not the man here. He thinks of Ben outside placing the shots with an almost casual manner. He thinks of the first day and the intelligence in him. He thinks of the fight in this room and how Ben ran in despite being terrified to the core. Some soldiers are made and some are born.

Harry never says much but he speaks now. Mad Harry Madden, who brought a German base to its knees, and when Mad Harry Madden speaks out, others listen.

Thirty

They have already been paramedics for this mission and now they are tourists. Bearded, unshaven, clean shaven, tidy hair, messy hair. Neat clothes, slightly creased clothes. They blend in and do not draw attention. Their clothing is carefully chosen to be loose-fitting to hide their muscular forms and they constantly check each other for visual clues that could suggest a military background.

They drink beer but not copious amounts. In public, they chat amiably as old friends. They tell jokes, berate each other and discuss buildings, art, road layouts, the youth of today, sports and every other normal topic of conversation.

The five work the city thoroughly, varying the teams to disrupt their profiles to avoid easy recognition.

A bearded man with a clean-shaved man wearing dark blue waterproofs and stout walking boots one day will be two cleanly shaven men wearing checked shirts, jeans and trainers the next day. Hats are used to limit profile awareness. They are German with varying dialects. They are English and politely spoken. Some are French and display the typical nuances associated with that country. They are what they need to be.

Alpha and Bravo drink coffee in a café. It has been a long morning already and they spread the tourist map open on the table to idly peruse and quietly discuss the sights they should see next.

Bravo eats a cake. Bravo doesn't actually like cake but it fits the profile so he eats the cake. Alpha hums softly as he flicks through the guidebook and glances between the pages and the map on the tabletop.

The café is either half-full or half-empty, depending on the way you view life. To the men, the café is at half capacity of occupancy, such is the manner in which they think.

Bravo ignores the door opening. His instincts tell him two people just entered but his training prevents him from immediately looking. Instead, he drops a crumb from his mouth on to his shirt and rolls his eyes as he brushes it off, giving him a plausible reason for glancing over to see two average-looking men walking to the counter. They look entirely normal. Average height. Average build. Short hair. They also look intensely worried. Like they've just had very bad news. One rubs the back of his neck and sighs deeply while the other orders two coffees in fluent German that bears a trace of an English accent somewhere within it.

'*Danke*,' the German man with the hint of English says at the counter as he takes the two mugs.

'That footage was forty-six years ago,' Malcolm says, rubbing his neck as they walk past the table.

'Yeah,' Konrad says. His tone is sad, worried. 'Can't believe we've actually met him . . . She was right to show us.'

'Oh, definitely,' Malcolm says emphatically. 'You think Harry's plan will work?'

They walk on down the café and the words are lost. Bravo eats his cake. Alpha thumbs through the guide.

'*Kaffee*?' Bravo asks in perfect German after finishing his cake.

'*Bitte*,' Alpha says amiably, also in fluent dialect-worthy German.

Bravo gets two fresh coffees and returns to the table. They converse quietly about the buildings, the area, the hotel they stayed in last night, the food they ate, the price of public transport.

Alpha pulls out his phone and thumbs the screen with a roll of his eyes. '*Meine mutter*,' he says, as though ever so slightly irritated at having to write his mother a message.

'Ah.' Bravo smiles benignly.

Alpha writes the message.

```
Hi Mother, we are having a nice coffee and
cake in a lovely little café in central
Berlin that is really quite interesting. The
weather is fine. How is Aunty?
```

He sighs when he finishes and sips his coffee. The phone bleeps softly.

```
I am fine, dear. Aunty is recovering from her
operation. Your café sounds lovely. I shall surely
try it the next time I visit that area.
```

'*Mutter?*' Bravo asks, nodding at the phone in the manner of mocking his old friend who has a worrisome mother.

'*Ja*,' Alpha tuts, knowing their location is being sent from the signal within the phone.

'. . . Safa will be heartbroken. She's tried so hard with him . . .'

'But it's down to him now. We can't do anything more for him, Malc. *Danke*,' the German-speaking Englishman calls out to the girl behind the counter as the two men head to the door.

Alpha and Bravo gather their maps and groan like middle-aged men as they stand up and politely take their cups back to the counter. '*Danke*,' Bravo says, handing them over.

'*Bitte*,' the girl says, marvelling at how polite middle-aged German men are.

The two tourists head outside. Bravo turns the map round as though perplexed as to why he was holding it upside down. Alpha idly watches the direction taken by the two men.

'Ah,' Bravo says, finally getting his map the right way just in time to allow the correct foot follow distance to form. 'Which way?' he asks in perfect English.

'This way I believe,' Alpha replies, also in perfect English.

They match pace. Not closing the gap or widening it. There is an art to foot follows and they show their mastery by perfect motion and an almost sixth sense with regards to guessing when to stop and turn and when to keep forward momentum.

They follow the men along the busy main road, jammed full of noisy people. The general hubbub of a city centre so conducive to hiding in plain sight. Electric cars hum as they go past. The rare sound of a petrol or diesel engine interspersed here and there. People chatting seemingly to themselves using ear inserts and wireless microphones to carry out perfect conversations with perfect clarity. Other tourists wear digital glasses showing the route they need to take on the interior of the lens. Others stop to read messages only they can see and speak the responses to be sent.

'Is that a Chinese restaurant?' Alpha asks, as though pleasantly surprised to see such a thing.

'I believe it is,' Bravo says. 'Is it open?'

'We'll have a look, maybe we could eat there tonight.'

'Absolutely,' Bravo says with mild enthusiasm.

Konrad and Malcolm reach the Chinese restaurant and turn right into the back road. The tourists amble after them and stop to read the digital menu displayed on the screen inside the window.

'Now that's old Berlin,' Alpha remarks casually, having glanced down the back road to the grey, brick-built buildings.

'Hmmm?' Bravo says, absent-minded as he reads the menu. 'What was that? Oh, I see, yes, yes, it is rather. Maybe pre-Second World War. Shall we have a look?'

'Would you mind?' Alpha asks.

'Not at all. It is rare to see existing industrial buildings still intact after that period.'

'Gosh, look at that one. Nice Gothic drainage systems.'

'The cornice is very good if slightly eroded.'

'Good brickwork I might add.'

'Indeed. I do like the transition from city centre to quiet back road and the way the buildings seem to morph from office to dwelling and light industrial usage. I say, is that a storage warehouse?'

'Certainly looks like it.'

'Is it in use?'

'I couldn't say. It certainly looks very secure.'

'Well, we are in a central location and I should imagine crime rates are significant.'

'Oh, indeed. Stout doors and, oh yes, those two men are operating an alarm system as they enter.'

'Yes, so they are. That is worrying, isn't it? I do hope this isn't a high-crime area.'

'Oh, bother. My mother is emailing me again. What shall I tell her this time?'

'Tell her we may have found a suitable location to rest and recuperate.'

'I will tell her exactly that. Shall we go back and look at that menu again?'

'Gladly.'

Thirty-One

The door opens without a knock. Ben looks up to see Harry staring at him. 'You ready?' he asks bluntly. His face impassive as ever.

Ben nods. There isn't much else to say. It's done. He is going back. He is empty inside and ready. He has nothing left.

'Follow me,' Harry says and walks off. Ben gets up and follows him dumbly through the room with the blue chairs and out into the corridor full of doors to rooms ready to be used. He will never see this place again. He will never be here again. He doesn't feel anything. Nothing. He is devoid of feeling. He does not belong here.

They reach the end of the corridor. Harry pushes the door open and nods for Ben to go first into the empty main room. Ben doesn't ask where everyone else is or how they are going to do this. He does not care. He cannot bring forth any sense of caring about anything other than the fact he died at Holborn and everything since then has been wrong, like he is a ghost left behind in a world that no longer needs or wants him.

The sound of liquid being poured brings Ben to a stop. The sound of a heavy flask being placed back on a wooden table and a cup being lifted with the gentle noise of a sip being taken. A sense of foreboding, of something happening that wasn't expected. Ben turns round to see Harry standing with his back to him at the main table. Static charge fills the air. Ominous and heavy.

'We going?' Ben asks.

'Minute,' Harry says without turning. 'Nice coffee this.'

'Safa said—'

'Safa isn't here. I am.' That dangerously low tone that Ben recognises from the day they had the fight in here.

'What?' Ben asks, blunt and uncaring. He wants to go. Get this finished. End it. Harry doesn't answer but sips again from the cup that's hidden from Ben's view by his broad back and wide shoulders. Ben sighs. An exhalation of air into the otherwise silent room. His feet shuffle on the bare concrete. Harry sips from the coffee. Ben sags and does not care, then an instant later he feels an absurd flush of anger at being delayed, an instant after that and the energy ebbs away, leaving him uncaring and unbothered again. Ben frowns and tries to grasp at least one coherent thought but everything in his head is jumbled up.

'Safa said I should try and talk you out of it.'

Ben looks up and blinks as Harry turns to face him with the coffee cup looking tiny in his massive hands, and in that surreal second Ben wonders why he's holding it in a double-handed grip.

'Don't bother,' Ben mumbles. 'We going then?'

'Said it might be better coming from me,' Harry continues.

Ben shrugs and stares back. Eyes locked. Harry sips. Ben stares. Harry lowers the mug from his mouth.

'Are we going?' Ben asks as that anger starts seeping back in at the way Harry is giving him the evil eye because Harry perceives him as weak and a coward and because he's let Safa carry him and not *done his part*. Fuck Harry. Fuck his values and his sense of right and wrong. Ben is done. Ben wants it finished.

Still Harry stares. Unblinking and expressionless, but within that passivity there is a whole bunch of meaning telegraphed. Harry sips again in an act designed to show he is taking his time, which reflects just how poorly he thinks of Ben.

Ben takes a step towards him. 'Are we going?'

Still Harry sips and stares. Ben feels stupid and angry and confused and sad all at the same time. He feels lost and forlorn and full of hatred for everything and within that maelstrom of emotion he also feels hurt at this last show of power from Harry.

'Fuck's sake,' Ben growls, petulant and getting irritated. His mood plummets down to despair then back up with a flash of rage that has him locking eyes on Harry for a second before Ben blinks away and shuffles impatiently. Ben is losing it. His mind is going. He can't cope. He can't be here. The walls are suffocating him. He feels trapped.

'I have to go,' Ben whispers, staring round with a chest starting to rise and fall quickly. 'I can't be here.' His mind whirls and spins. His heart beats faster. A rush of adrenaline, then fear and dejection. 'Please . . . can I go? Safa said I can go.'

Still Harry stares. Harry doesn't blink or move apart from lifting that fucking cup a few inches to sip with a noise like nails down a blackboard. Ben takes a breath and forces a calm tone into his voice. 'Harry, Safa said I can go . . . stop sipping that fucking . . .' Ben wants to ram it into his bearded face. He wants to rage and smash and destroy everything and himself at the same time.

'Where's Safa?' Ben asks instead, sounding like a child. He turns and heads for the door. Harry doesn't go after him. Ben will find Safa or Roland and make them take him back. He will go through that blue light and walk into the flames of the train explosion without a second thought.

Ben stops and sags. The door is locked. He pushes it. Pulls it. Hits it and kicks it. He hammers his fists on it but it doesn't yield and no one comes to open it. Ben stalks back into the room and grabs a chair that is slammed against the door but nothing happens. The chair is solid wood. The door is solid metal. Rage builds. Ben swings the chair from the side, then overhead. He does it again and again until the chair breaks apart but the door remains intact.

'WHAT?' Ben screams as he turns to Harry, but the big man stands sipping from that cup.

'WHAT?' Ben screams and rages and picks up a chair leg that he grips while he walks towards Harry. 'Open the fucking door,' Ben growls, pointing the chair leg at him.

Harry sips. Ben kicks chairs and turns a table over. He throws more chairs across the room as his mind crumbles into tiny pieces. He wants to tear his own eyes out. He wants to rip his tongue out and gouge his wrists open until he finds a vein then sink down into oblivion. Ben wants to cry and scream but Harry just slurps from that coffee cup and stares at him.

He wants to fight me. Ben can see it. Harry is staring at him to goad him. Harry slurps again, louder and longer. Ben flinches and feels the rage pounding through his skull. Harry swallows. Ben grimaces and winces and screws his face up with every ounce of his being focused on not attacking Harry.

A second of frozen time. Two seconds. Eyes locked. Intent clear. Ben doesn't blink. Harry doesn't blink. Ben grips the chair leg. Harry holds the coffee cup, which he lifts to his mouth. Ben winces and curls his upper lip back. Harry pauses, staring, provoking, goading. His lips reach the rim of the cup.

'Don't.' Ben gives the warning fair and clear with his knuckles turning white from the grip on the chair leg that is now a weapon and in that second Ben finally sees the key hanging from a large metal ring hooked over a finger on Harry's left hand.

'Give me the key,' Ben says instantly. 'I'm going. Give me the key.'

Harry moves his head a fraction side to side.

'Key,' Ben growls and takes another step towards him. Harry slurps and inside Ben feels only hatred for him. 'What . . . ?' Ben tries to speak but his voice breaks with tension. He coughs, clearing his throat.

'Fucking key . . .' He holds his hand out in expectation for Harry to throw it.

Harry looks down casually at the key hanging from his finger then back at Ben and sips from the mug.

'I'm taking that key,' Ben tells him with another step. He drops the chair leg that lands with a dull thud on the ground. Ben stops in front of him. Within arm's reach and so close he can see the flecks in the irises of Harry's eyes. Harry doesn't move. A strange sense of calm descends and Ben knows exactly what will happen if he tries to slide that hoop from Harry's finger or even reach out to touch it. It's not a foretelling but fact, an absolute certainty, and Ben knows within the chaos of his mind that he does not stand a chance trying to snatch it so he lifts his hand slowly and stares at the key.

Ben gets within an inch of the key. Harry's right hand flashes out, slapping him with an open-palmed strike that snaps Ben's head over. Ben blinks and looks back to see Harry holding the cup with both hands again.

He tries again and gets slapped again. The speed of Harry is shocking, his arm a blur of movement. Ben's cheek stings. He goes for the key and gets slapped with a noise that's dull and flat. His face burns. He tries again and Harry hits harder and between each slap his hand goes back to the cup. Ben moves faster, trying to snatch the key, but the slaps make him stagger to the side. He recovers and blinks. His face already swelling. Ben turns and reaches for the key in one very slow motion and gets hit harder.

Red mist descends with emotions of hurt, loss, rejection, grief, mourning, self-pity and abject misery all focusing down to a single beam of pure rage that makes Ben charge at Harry with a dull thought that he wants to die so being killed here is just as good as dying at Holborn.

Ben goes fast, throwing fists the soldier swats away with ease. Finally Harry drops the coffee mug and shoves Ben away.

'You're untrained,' Harry says as though bored.

Ben throws rights and lefts that Harry dodges and moves away from with ease.

'Undisciplined . . .'

Ben lashes out with hard punches but his arms get knocked aside as Harry pushes him in the chest, sending him back several paces.

'Come again and I'll beat you,' Harry says so casually, so easily it sets Ben's rage off even worse.

Ben charges. Incandescent with fury. Blinded by his own impotent rage. Harry shows no reaction until the very last second, then he shrugs and goes to work.

After that is a blur.

Ben can fight but Mad Harry Madden batters him round the room. Punched, pushed and thrown bodily into chairs and tables that splinter into weapons that he grabs to swing wildly, but Harry's skill is far beyond anything Ben can throw at him.

Ben goes down but keeps getting back up until his eyes are swelling and his nose is broken. Still he gets back up. He hates this place. He hates Harry. He hates being dead. He didn't ask for this and he doesn't know what else to do so he keeps getting up so Harry can kill him and the pain gets worse and the blood comes faster but still he keeps getting back up.

Harry doesn't speak but stalks about the room waiting for Ben to rise and charge before whipping left and right and smashing fists into his head. A hard punch to Ben's stomach makes him puke on the ground with acidic bile burning his throat but he gets back up because the rage inside is so strong he cannot deny it.

'Steph sold you out,' Harry's voice booms from somewhere close by. 'Five days after you died she went to a newspaper. Told them you beat her.'

Ben reels on the spot. His mind trying to understand what Harry is telling him. He gets punched again in the side of the head, then a flurry of blows makes him sink down to his knees with blood and snot drooling from his mouth.

'She knew you were Ben Ryder. Said you threatened her. Said you'd kill her if she ever told anybody . . .'

'No.' Ben gargles the word out and shakes his head but still rises.

'I don't like wife-beaters.' A hand grips Ben's hair and snaps his head back. Harry's mouth close to his ear. 'Steph said you beat her. She said Ben Ryder was a violent man . . .'

'No.' Ben tries to shake his head but Harry grips too hard and yanks back while his knee drives forward into Ben's spine, pinning him in place on the blood-soaked floor.

'. . . Said you hit her. Said you beat her. Told the world you beat her . . .' Harry rasps the words out with almost malicious delight. 'She was going to leave you the day you died . . .'

We need to talk tonight.

'. . . Was having an affair . . .' *We need to talk tonight.* '. . . leaving you for him . . .' *We need to talk tonight.* '. . . wife-beater . . .'

Ben flails side to side as chunks of hair are ripped out. Harry tries to pin him but he thrashes and breaks free with fresh energy pulsing in his body. On all fours and with blood pouring from his face Ben crawls away but Harry stalks after him. Kicking him over on to his side then planting a big foot on his chest.

'I don't like wife-beaters . . .'

'I didn't . . . Steph . . . loves . . . I love . . .'

Harry drops down, his face hovering a few inches above Ben. 'You beat her. You hit her. Worthless maggot. Said you forced yourself on her the night before you died . . .'

'NO!' Ben screams at him, spraying blood from his mouth that flecks Harry's cheek. He wipes it away and glares down.

'Said you forced yourself. Said you beat her. Told the world . . .'

Fuck me, Ben. Fuck me harder.

'Said she . . . was in love with someone else but was too scared to tell you . . . said you threatened her . . . said you . . .'

Images flash through Ben's mind of Steph in their bedroom turning away to look at her phone. Pulling her towel off. Her text messages. The sex they had the night before. Safa came into his room. Safa smiling at him as he held her hand to explain parallel worlds. Safa and Steph.

'Worthless maggot . . .'

'I didn't . . .'

'Wife-beater. Coward . . .'

'I didn't . . .' Ben tries to rise but Harry leans harder on his leg, pushing his foot into Ben's chest.

'You're nothing. You deserve to die like a wife-beating maggot that—'

'I DIDN'T,' Ben screams at him.

'WIFE-BEATER,' Harry's foot lifts and the big man bends down in one smooth motion to grip Ben's top and lifts him bodily with one hand to hold him an inch in front of his face. 'COWARD . . . MAGGOT . . .' Spittle hits Ben's lips. 'WORTHLESS LITTLE MAN . . .' He shakes Ben, one-handed and with ease. Ragging back and forth. 'RAPIST . . .'

Ben reaches the nadir of despair. Time slows to a state that he's had three times before. Everything in perfect clarity but fuelled by unspent rage, loss, rejection and hurt. He snaps with pure, unbridled fury that has his fist smashing into Harry's nose and following through with lashing blows one after the other. Harry staggers back from the unexpected onslaught. Up to now it was easy, but now it becomes work and the soldier rallies to counter with more devastating punches that hammer into Ben's already bruised and battered head. Months of training. Months of being thrown about by Safa and Harry and although there was no effort from Ben, the lessons sunk in. The constant reminders to lift his guard. To block and counter. To aim and pivot when he hits. To move and weave. To grip, twist, heave, throw and fight like a professional.

The juxtaposition is stark. Ben's ability to fight and stay coldly detached are mixed with the wild rage driving him on and it makes Harry fight harder and harder still. For minutes they go at it. Moving round the room with brutal explosions of violence that slam fists into faces, heads, bodies and limbs. Locks are applied and countered. Throws are attempted and thwarted. The blood flows and mixes with the sweat pouring from their faces. This isn't a beating now. This isn't a lesson being given. This is a fight. A hard, gritty, nasty fight between two men who know what they are doing. The years of experience and the lack of rage give Harry the edge and he is forced to inflict injury to slow his opponent.

Confusion grows inside Ben. Fear and worry. Steph told everyone those things? She knew he was Ben Ryder? It fuels him. The idea of it, but as shocking as it is, somehow it makes sense. He asked Safa to tell him about Steph and she clammed up. Ben knew Steph was having an affair and figured that was the thing Safa was holding back. A swirling mix of memories and emotions. Safa and Harry teaching him how to fight. Steph's coldness and biting tone. Safa refusing to talk about Steph and becoming almost aggressive every time Ben mentioned her. *'This is who I am . . . I want my life . . . I want to be with Steph.'* Safa hit him. She hit him across the face when he said he wanted to be with Steph. Safa came into his room.

Those thoughts create enough distraction and lack of focus for Harry to strike hard. The lights go out and Ben feels the floor coming up to meet him. He comes awake, slurred and slow. Pain in every part of his body. Thoughts so confused that he can't function. He rolls over and starts rising. Unable to see through one eye. His mouth so swollen he can't speak. Where is he? He is fighting someone that hits him over and over until the pain is so intense it becomes a new dimension within his range of senses.

'Stay down man!' Harry pleads. Ben doesn't stay down. He clambers to his feet, sucking ragged breath and fixing Harry with his right eye. Ben spits blood and puke and feels his teeth rattling loose but staggers towards Harry and flails into him.

'Enough, Ben . . .'

Not enough. Never enough. He has to die. He is not meant to be here. He has to go back to . . . *I have to go home to* . . .

'For the love of God . . . Stop it, Ben.'

Home. Steph. Safa. Steph didn't love him. Steph sold him out. Steph told the world he beat and raped her. Safa came to his room. Safa carried him.

'You fool.' The voice comes plaintive and whispered but Ben turns towards it and swings an arm that gets gripped and held, so he headbutts instead and blacks out again. Flashes of images. A bearded man looking at him with real worry in his features. Ben hits him. Harry takes the hit and stares down with a rare show of emotion.

'I take it back,' Harry says in a tone full of regret and remorse for something Ben doesn't understand. 'You're not weak.'

Ben blacks out again and this time he doesn't get back up.

Harry stands over the unconscious, broken body of Ben Ryder. His own face bruised, bleeding, swollen and sore. His chest heaving. Sweat pours to mingle with the blood. He looks down at his bloodied knuckles then down again to the inert body lying in the pool of blood.

A metallic clunk, the door swings open as Safa pushes into the room to look round at the broken furniture then over to Harry standing over Ben.

'Jesus, Harry,' she cries out, rushing over. 'Is he dead?'

She drops to a crouch and pushes her fingers through the blood smeared on his neck to feel for a pulse.

'I said your way wouldn't work,' Harry says, wiping a bloodied hand across his battered face. 'Is he alive?'

She nods. 'Pulse is there, but weak.'

'What happened?' Roland demands, striding into the room and stopping to first stare open-mouthed at the sight of Ben and then do a quick double-take at Harry's bloodied face. 'Good God,' he blurts and looks slowly round the room, taking in the devastation and blood trails. 'He fought you? Ben fought you?'

'Aye,' Harry says, hardly believing it himself.

'Is he dead?' Roland asks.

'No,' Safa says.

'You've got to break a man before you can rebuild him,' Harry says weakly.

'Rebuild him?' Roland asks in a tight voice. 'He's going back before he dies . . . Malcolm?'

'Behind you.'

'Get Konrad, take Ben back to the tracks at Holborn.'

'You'll not be doing that,' Harry whispers hoarse and low.

'Harry,' Roland blurts, 'the man is spent . . . you've beaten him half to death already.'

'He'll be needing a doctor,' Harry says, staring down at Ben.

'Look at him,' Roland says, holding a trembling hand out to point at Ben then round at the mess in the room. 'He's finished . . . he has to go back . . . he can't die here. Where would we put the body? He can't go back dead either. The autopsy will . . . he needs to breathe the fumes in the tunnel to get them into his lungs . . . God, Harry, he has to go back before he dies.'

'Aye,' Harry says, stretching his back. 'I've beaten men, but none like this . . .' He turns to look at Safa. 'You were right.' Safa shrugs, of course she's right, she's always right. 'We'll be keeping Ben,' he adds. 'Right man for the job after all.'

'Can you get a doctor?' Safa asks.

Roland groans. 'Are you sure, Harry?'

'Aye,' Harry says.

'Harry,' Roland says gently. 'Look at him. He's done in . . .'

'Did you tell him about Steph?' Safa asks.

'Aye,' Harry says. 'Never fought a harder man, I don't think,' he muses, shaking his head. 'He came back at the end . . . reached the bottom, he did.'

'You sure, Harry?' Safa asks.

'I am,' Harry says with brutal honesty. 'Get him a doctor, get him fixed and he'll be the man you need . . .'

'We've got a doctor in the folder,' Malcolm cuts in.

'Folder?' Safa asks.

'In the office,' Malcolm says with a glance at Roland.

'It is the list of people with skills for extraction,' Roland says.

'I'm not getting anyone else though,' Malcolm says quickly. 'Konrad won't go back again either . . .'

'We'll go,' Safa says quickly. 'We'll get the doctor . . .'

Thirty-Two

Hope. There is always hope. Deep down he knows he will die. Hundreds of miles from any living person in a sea that two hours ago was as flat as a millpond but now rages with waves cresting metres high and bursting white froth into the wind-whipped air.

He is a good yachtsman. Experienced and risk averse, but lately his mind has been unsettled and gradually getting worse. Forgetful sometimes, absent-minded often. Recognising faces but unable to recall the name of the person. Older in years, with a bald head framed by salt-and-pepper-streaked hair and a beard to match. His lined face makes him look older, but that's what booze does to you. Wine at dinner and whisky for supper and so his nights passed pleasantly, but then she died and those nights were not pleasant. They were long and lonely and soon the whisky was being taken at dinner, then at lunch, and so a drop of whisky for breakfast wasn't that much of a step to take.

Alone now and nothing makes sense any more. Confusion at everything. The world moves too fast for him to keep up. New technology, new rules, new laws, new faces, new everything.

The sea will always be the sea and to this place he goes when the demons threaten to take over, but now, staring death in the face, surrounded by walls of water looming overhead, he should be quietly accepting that fate. But he doesn't. In that second as the yacht lifts he wants life. As the boat rallies to surge up the near-vertical wall, so he wishes to reach the top and sail safely down the other side.

For over an hour now he has kept the boat facing into the waves. Climbing and dropping, rising and falling. His hands making deft adjustments to the wheel, causing the rudder to turn here, slack there and the half-empty whisky bottle rolls forgotten in the well by his feet.

He grins wide and full of terror, but feels more alive than he has done in years. His old face shedding the years of stress and depression and those lines now speak of experience and wisdom instead of worry and alcohol. Regret is there too. Regret that he has thrown the skills of his trade away to lapse into a luxury lifestyle in which he has greater concern for his social standing than for the people he could help. He wasn't born rich and this was never the plan, but he was gifted and that gift was recognised, and only a fool turns down such a high salary, and with that salary came the perks. The house, the cars, the beautiful wife. The holidays and restaurants.

A vow is made, a prayer to the gods above and one that is as fool-hardy as it is impotent. *I will go back to my trade. If I survive I will work to be the man I dreamt of being.* An offering, a sacrifice, and in his mind the lifestyle can go to hell.

Alas, the dream is too late. The hope diminishes as the waves grow and wind screams through the rigging on the yacht. Sails torn and flapping. The boom loose and swinging with every pitch and toss. He fights just to keep a course into the waves, but each one becomes a monster to be defeated in a never-ending battle.

The crest is reached, buying him another few seconds of life, and in those seconds he teeters on the crest, holding position on a centre point of balance that enables him to see the miles of raging sea in every direction. Such a sight. Such a thing to see. It's time. Minutes maybe. Say your prayers to the gods you choose for your time is done.

Down. Swooping with such speed that the air smacks into his face and he screams out in terror and joy at the sensation. Crashing into the bottom, sending a surge of water high into the air that rains down soaking him, but he lives and another monster is defeated.

Every seventh wave they say. The seventh is the biggest. He hasn't counted them off but that thought enters his mind as he turns forward to face the next monster coming, craning his head up and up but the top cannot be seen. This is it. This monster cannot be beaten. Sailing up a skyscraper but to hell with it, he'll be damned if he won't die trying.

'COME ON,' he screams. The words are whipped away but my God it feels good to scream. 'COME ON,' he cries again, louder, and the grief bubbles to the top of his soul and he bellows at the wave still coming towards him and growing with every passing second as he sinks deeper into the valley. Loss, mourning, a life of excess and regret, all channelled to the vocal chords of his throat and with veins bulging he vents his fear to gain the first peace in many a year.

The bow hits and lifts, the sturdy yacht struggling valiantly to do the job it was designed to do and it goes up, dragging the middle and stern with it. Gravity-defying but still she goes on. He screams for her to keep trying. His fist pumping the air and she goes, she gives it everything she can, but the sea takes what it wants. The point of no return is reached. A single solitary second of contemplation and with respect he bows his head with a hat tip at being bested and the yacht begins the slide back down the wave. They sink stern first but the boat is not designed to move this way and she shifts to turn dangerously side on as the bow struggles to gain the lead. The wave bites, a gentle nip, but enough, and the boat is tumbling down and over on a wall of water. His life flashing in a sequence of images.

Thrown clear of the boat he gains the sensation of air then water and plunges down into the darkness. The buoyancy aid pulls him up and he gasps air but that wall is still coming and this monster hasn't finished toying with him yet. He goes up, pulled by the suction of the wave and the life jacket keeping him on the surface. Water. Air. Water. Air. He takes both in but feels the height being gained. Near the top he snatches a fleeting glimpse of his beloved yacht that fought so bravely and in that moment he prays she will survive.

'We're going to land in the water, right?'

'Yep.' Malcolm nods, dragging one of the poles out.

'Fuck it,' Safa says. 'How big is this storm anyway?'

'Big,' Malcolm says apologetically, as if the storm being big is his fault.

'Right.' She tightens the life jacket then flexes her arms in the wet-suit clinging to her frame before fingering the thick rope tied to the harness under the life jacket. 'How much rope have we got?' she asks, looking to the huge reel at the back of the room. 'Right,' she says again without waiting for an answer.

'You go through in the boat,' Malcolm says. 'Land in the water with the engine running and go *into* the waves. Remember that.'

'Ah,' Harry frowns, sitting in the rear, holding the twist grip of the rudder stick. 'When you've been in a few storms,' he says.

'Mr Madden,' Malcolm says politely, 'the engine on this is really powerful, like . . . so much more powerful than you're used to . . . like, ten times more powerful . . . you twist that grip and she'll bite . . .'

'Less talking, more let's get going,' Harry says, staring ahead at the bare concrete wall, then blinking and looking at the oversized, swollen rubber skirt of the boat. 'What's it called again?'

'RIB, Rigid Inflatable—'

'Got it, RIB.'

'Interestingly, we actually had a boat when we extracted you, Harry, but someone said to get rid of it as we wouldn't need another boat . . .'

Malcolm says with a look at Roland, who suddenly finds his feet very interesting.

'We'll pull the device over you,' Konrad says to both of them. 'As the blue goes over you so you'll appear in the time and location chosen . . . er . . . which is the sea . . . in a storm . . .'

'Yes, got that bit,' Safa says through gritted teeth from her position at the front of the RIB, staring at the same bare concrete wall.

'RIB,' Harry says again.

'Yes,' Malcolm says. 'Land in the water, turn into the waves, find the doctor, get him aboard and get back through the blue light . . .'

'Got it,' Harry says, hunkering down to face the wall with a look of serious intent. 'Water, doctor, blue light, back for tea and cake.'

'And in the event you can't get back to the blue light,' Malcolm says, wide-eyed at the lunacy of these two, 'we'll give it five minutes then pull you both back on the ropes.'

'Ropes, got it,' Harry says, rising up so he can hunker down again. 'Water, doctor, blue light, rope, tea and cake . . . RIB.'

'Five minutes isn't very long so you'll have to move fast,' Malcolm says. 'You'll land at the GPS signal recorded from the distress signal when the boat capsized but you'll have to search visually.'

The last two hours have been frantic, with Malcolm and Konrad rushing through the device to get the equipment needed while Roland strutted and blustered about.

A high-sided rigid inflatable boat. Wetsuits. Life jackets. Rope and reel. Water goggles. Gloves. And Ben being carried gently to his bed by Harry and Safa and the threat made that everyone here will die horrible, painful deaths should he not be alive and in the same bed when they get back.

'This is madness,' Roland mutters, tapping at the screen of the tablet. 'Complete madness. Powering up.' Red lights blink on the black boxes and the room fills with a low thrumming sound. 'Calibrating . . .'

314

he says and waits. A few seconds and he starts tapping his finger on the side of the screen, humming a tune.

'Water, doctor, aboard, light, get back,' Harry says. 'You want this engine on now?'

'Oh, good idea,' Malcolm says, blinking in surprise. 'Didn't think of that . . . you know how to do it?'

'Pull cord?' Harry says, staring at the big engine.

'Er, no,' Malcolm says carefully, 'we don't have pull cords these days . . . press that button.'

'This one?' Harry jabs the button. The engine starts instantly, coughing thick black smoke into the room before rising in pitch to a dull scream that only gets louder when Harry test twists the grip on the rudder stick.

Roland coughs pointedly. 'Ready,' he says, and rolls his eyes when no one hears him. 'I SAID IT'S READY.' He waves.

Harry nods, giving him a thumbs up. Safa follows suit then grips the safety ropes to hold her position at the front of the vessel.

The blue iridescent light fills the room. A solid thing of shimmering beauty that bathes them all in deep hues of colour. Malcolm and Konrad grip a pole each, ready to pull the light over them from front to back.

'GO,' Roland shouts and tuts to himself at not being heard. 'I SAID GO,' he shouts again, waving at his two workmen.

Safa stares mesmerised as the front tip of the boat simply disappears from view into the blue wall. Like it's being pulled through a curtain. The poles move, the blue light slides and the boat disappears inch by inch.

'FASTER,' Roland bellows, knowing the danger of what's on the other side. They burst into a run, dragging the poles down as Safa's eyes widen at the wall of blue light coming at her.

One second she's in the warm, dry room and the next she's staring at a wall of water looming overhead with spray and wind whipping into her face. Noise everywhere from the angry thrashing of the sea and wind. She glances behind, watching the blue light move down the vessel, which appears as quickly as it disappeared. Harry comes into view, grimacing and twisting the throttle, filling the room behind him with more choking black smoke. Then it's done and they drop a foot to land in the water with Harry already opening the engine to turn the boat into the huge wave bearing down on them.

Malcolm was right. The engine does bite. A second later the propeller is pushing the prow into the base of the wave. Harry doesn't falter. Not a flicker of surprise shows. He works with instinct and feel. The wave is big but not too big to be a problem, and he senses the power at play in the engine behind him. He twists more, powering gradually as they start the incline. Safa grips the ropes, swallowing at the experience and the sight. From a room in the bunker in the Cretaceous period to a raging sea somewhere in twenty thirty-two.

It takes seconds for her mind to process the change and in that time Harry gets the boat to the top of the wave, where they hold for a precious few seconds.

'CAN YOU SEE IT?' Harry bellows, quickly turning to see the blue light still holding position at the bottom of the valley as the wave swooshes through it and wondering if the water will end up in the room.

'THERE,' Safa shouts, pointing to the left. 'BOAT.' A white yacht that looks tiny as it reaches the top of a wave and starts racing down the other side and a clear view of a man grinning wildly at the helm. Bald with greying hair round the sides and back and a beard the same colour. He's still alive, the boat is upright and she watches as the yacht powers down the bank of water and hits the valley, pluming up a spray of water.

Harry steers the engine, knowing he has to either stay on the top of this wave or go down nose first into the valley. He opts for the second and sends them over the crest, plunging with a stomach-churning drop as Safa keeps her eyes locked on the yacht.

In the trough Harry takes advantage of the time before the next wave and slams the boat hard over while opening the engine fully. It bites to scream along the surface. Safa pointing at the yacht while he glances to the next wave and up at the sheer bloody size of it. No matter. He waits until the last second and forces the nose into the bank as it swells and starts to lift them higher. Easing the throttle, he lets the engine power them up until gravity starts to tug, then twists more, forcing the boat up.

Safa watches the yacht and the man pumping his fist into the air. He'll make it. He'll get over the wave. In that second, she sees the battle at play and the determination of the doctor as he tries to make his yacht do the impossible, but without power or sail the yacht cannot surmount a wave so high and it stops, pauses and sinks back. Turning side on as the bow tries to take over and it rolls over and over down the cliff face of water back into the valley beneath.

'HE'S DOWN,' she screams at Harry, who nods calmly and keeps the RIB going up the side of the wave, knowing that to try to turn now will also see them tipping over. He forces to the top then a hard yank of the rudder and along that bursting froth of raging sea he powers the boat. Deft touches left and right, riding the wave as it sweeps on its journey. Safa keeps her eyes glued on the spot where the boat first tumbled, scanning the dark, roiling, seething mass for the doctor.

'FIND HIM?' Harry shouts over the noise, sensing they can't hold this position for much longer.

'THERE.' She points down the wall to the valley beneath and a flash of orange breaking the surface with two arms flailing about. Harry peers over the edge, showing teeth in a humourless smile. Ah well, died once and lived. He turns the rudder to start the descent while powering off the throttle and letting nature pull them down. The speed they reach is incredible. Hair flying free and tears whipped from eyes but neither of them think to tug the goggles down over their eyes. The doctor sinks from view as he starts the climb up the same wall they're coming down.

Harry watches ahead, already planning on reaching the bottom and using the pit of the valley to turn and come back up.

The doctor sinks down out of sight then comes up again. Drowning with each lungful of water sucked in. Safa watches closely, praying he'll stay alive long enough for them to reach him and cursing when they fly past.

'GO BACK UP,' she shouts at Harry, pointing at the doctor. Harry keeps going, swooshing down into the base before powering on to turn and come back up the incline while nodding in satisfaction at the ability of the boat.

She'll have one chance to grab him. She knows that. The wave is so steep that to try and stop will cause the boat to plummet back down. Harry judges the approach, watching both the wave ahead and Safa's arm pointing to the spot to aim for.

She scrabbles forward, landing with her belly on the inflated rubber skirt as the water pummels into her face. Snatched glimpses now. An orange blob in the water and the realisation hits her. Leverage. She has nothing to pull against. The man will be heavier than her and if she pulls him, she'll just be pulling herself into the water. She peers round searching for something she can hook her feet into but the handgrips are too far apart. There's nothing to grip or hold. No way of dragging him in. She can't even try to do it one-handed because there's nothing for her left hand to hold.

Harry powers on, driving the last few metres then easing the throttle as they reach the orange vest and the doctor, now face down in the water. Safa reaches out as Harry notices with alarm she has nothing to secure herself with and he can't release the rudder or lose the power either.

'SAFA, NO,' he bellows, but too late. She lunges over, grips the vest and tries to heave the doctor up using just the strength in her arms but the man is too heavy and she slips into the water. Harry twists the grip as hard as he can, making the boat surge past them both, then dives over the side and into the freezing, turbulent waters. Instantly he feels a complex assault to the senses of plunging down into violently moving water while gaining the sensation of rising up the wall of the wave.

His head breaks the surface, driven up by powerful kicks of his legs. He spins round, seeing Safa grappling to turn the doctor on to his back.

Harry swims hard against the current, forcing his body down the wall as they rise up and into his arms. He grips them both in a bear hug, lifting them up and out of the water while Safa gets the doctor's face free of the water. She gasps ragged breaths, spewing the gag-inducing seawater from her mouth and throat. Eyes stinging from the salt and all the time rising higher and higher with the rope trailing loosely behind them. The RIB, having reached the apex of its climb, now plummets down the wall, aquaplaning on the smooth underside and buzzing past their heads so close they could have caught hold if not for the speed of the thing.

Rising higher as they're pulled up the sheer side of the wave stretching to reach the sky and Harry uses just the power in his legs to keep them all afloat. Closer to the top now and the white foam at the pinnacle whips high into the wind.

'Where's the light?' Safa gasps, coughing mouthfuls of water out.

Harry cranes round trying to see the blue square, but seeing just shades of darkness in every direction. A hint of something, a flash of light, but gone again and so far away now. He locks his eyes on the spot, straining to see, then shouting out when the iridescent light shows true at the bottom of the valley with the yacht see-sawing towards it but it might as well be a mile away for all the hope they have of swimming down this wave.

Stomachs flip and churn as they reach the dizzying top and for a second all is calm and clear and they catch a view of a huge sky full of roiling grey clouds shooting jagged bolts of lightning across the heavens with the deep roar of thunder booming in rage and anger. Riding on the crest, holding position as the wave carries them along for a precious few seconds, but the inevitable must happen and when it does they feel the plummet of a rollercoaster ride sinking on the terrifying decline. Plunging down a mountainside of water that bursts and slams into their faces. Screaming from fear, panic and the utter, sheer terror of sliding down a wall with increasing speed as Harry kicks to keep them above the surface, clutching Safa, who clutches the doctor, and the three are hopelessly outwitted by the power of nature.

Going down the wave is bad enough. Going sideways is worse, but sideways they go as the rope snaps straight and taut and they feel the pull dragging them feet first along the side of the wave. All control is gone and they plunge down into the depths as the rope drags them mercilessly through the thick, wide body of the wave back towards the light.

Into darkness and a wave too thick for the light to penetrate, but the roar of the ocean fills their ears as much as the blood pounding through their skulls, urging them to breathe. They hold fast, clinging to the hope that they'll be dragged fast enough to get through the light before their attempts to hold their breath render them unconscious enough to try and draw air.

Safa clamps her mouth closed. She can't see or hear. She can't reach out to touch anything and gets dragged so fast she has no hope of maintaining conscious thought. As her body starts to fight against her to draw air she feels only hope that the doctor will get through and save Ben. He must survive. Ben must live. He is Ben Ryder. He means something. The Prime Minister groping her. Other men that only saw her as a sexual object, but she knew there were decent men in the world and she saw one once.

They break free from the side of the wave into a second of blessed air that they suck into lungs begging to be used. Down they go, falling back into the water as the rope drags them towards the square of light at the base of the wave.

The blue square is so clear but the white hull of the yacht is also so clear. The torn sails hanging from the masts as the vessel shoots down the wave aiming for the portal. Harry screams out as though to give warning but his voice is whipped away by wind and sea. The yacht goes through into the bunker, disappearing from view with the mast cut clean in half by the upper edge of the blue light. An instant later the sensation of being dragged ceases with a sudden loss of forced motion.

'Swim,' Harry snaps the word out, gasping for air as he kicks with his legs, driving them down towards the light. She joins him, kicking hard with one arm holding the doctor and the other stroking through the water.

Get the doctor through. Get the doctor through. That's all that matters. Get him through and give Ben a reason to live. Ben has to live. Get the doctor through.

They swim and kick and paddle against the force of the wave that keeps threatening to pull them back up the rising wall. They swim and kick and paddle with the weight of the doctor held in their hands. Eyes burning, mouths and throats stinging. They puke and retch and cry but swim all the same, but it's not enough and the strength goes from Safa, her limbs refusing to work or do as bid.

'Go,' she pants and simply lets go of the doctor, knowing Harry has the strength to get him through, but the big man falters, snapping round as she fights just to keep her head above the water.

'SAFA,' Harry roars, holding the doctor one-handed as she sinks beneath the waves. He waits, praying she'll come back up, then spotting her form metres away being swept by the waves. The mission has to come first, the mission always comes first. Get the doctor back. They are soldiers and the lives of a few do not matter against the lives of so many. He swims, hating himself but knowing this is what must be done. He swims, aiming for the light, but wishing above all else to ditch this man and go back for Safa.

He gets closer. Rising higher with the current and dropping back down the wall by twisting his body just so and letting gravity do the rest. He times the approach with a plan in mind, rising and falling as the square light shimmers closer and closer with every kick of his legs. He sinks down, sensing rather than knowing when to kick and when to let the wall of water lift him higher until he's about to sail past the shimmering light. He twists and grips the doctor with both of his hands while rolling on to his back. A huge heave and he forces the man up into the air as he sinks from the explosion of force generated. The doctor goes through the light but he does not. Instead, he goes down deep past the light and that explosion of energy drains the strength from his limbs and the air from his lungs. He tries to draw air in but only water comes. Choking water that fills his lungs. Panic sets in with legs kicking and arms flailing and in that panic so he breathes in again, worsening the damage as his body dies from lack of oxygen.

A raging sea with mountainous waves rolling to a far and distant shore. An empty RIB bouncing from peak to trough and two corpses floating face down as they lift and fall in the dark green depths and a blue shimmering light that is suddenly no longer there.

Thirty-Three

The empty building opposite the warehouse is bought outright with cash paid through a property development company that is owned by a finance company that is working for an investment firm that may or may not be registered under an umbrella corporation that might be registered in the Bahamas.

The five men gain access one by one, dressed in exactly the same kind of workmen's clothing. The shade, the fit, the style is identical. It isn't five men that go inside one by one. It is the same man coming and going.

A tradesperson entering a property has reason to carry bags and equipment. He has reason to park his van outside and potter about, taking in large pots of paint and boxes of supplies. He has tool cases, wiring looms, ladders, power tools and a stylus for his tablet tucked behind his ear. He huffs and puffs, slightly harassed, overworked, underpaid. He looks about for the parking attendants and curses softly under his breath. He does it five times.

The five gain access and take up position within. The windows are done first with exceptional attention to detail. A special film is secured above each window and stretched out at an angle into the room. Anyone looking in will see a partial reflection of the room and the outside. Anyone on the inside can stand and stare out without fear of being seen.

High-powered lenses are made ready. High-powered directional microphones are positioned towards the warehouse opposite, aimed in particular at the alarmed front door and the windows to the front. The right-side windows on the warehouse offer glimpses of large and seemingly unused rooms. The windows on the upper levels on the left are blacked out. The three windows on the ground floor to the left are grimy. Two give light to the hallway inside the main door. The third gives light to a room in use. Shelves fitted to walls. Some chairs and a table, but the whole of the room cannot be seen. It is that window that is their focus.

As the last film is fitted to the last window, they observe a RIB being delivered on the back of a trailer towed by a van driven by the German-speaking Englishman seen in the café.

It's a good RIB too. Very high specification. The outboard motor is immense. The German-speaking Englishman opens the alarmed door and is joined by the proper Englishman. Together they carry in wetsuits, diving equipment and a huge reel of rope attached to a motor. Then they huff and puff to get the RIB inside the wide main door.

A weird blue light then comes on. Distinctive and reflecting in the glass of the windows. It goes off within a few seconds then comes again, but this time in the inside room of the far-left grimy ground floor window. Blue light on and off.

When the German-speaking man comes out to move the van, the RIB can no longer be seen in the hallway inside the main door. The RIB is big. It couldn't fit through the door to the room on the left. The van is driven away and a few minutes later the German-speaking Englishman rushes back to get through the alarmed door and inside the room. The blue light stayed on while he was gone, and a few seconds after he goes back in it goes off.

'Mother will be pleased,' Alpha says quietly to the other four. 'I think we've found it.'

Thirty-Four

'Ben . . . Ben . . . can you hear me? Ben, open your eyes . . . that's it. Look at me now. Look at me, Ben. That's good.'

Ben blinks up. A man blinks down at him. Bloodshot eyes in a face filled with broken blood vessels across his nose and a salt-and-pepper-streaked beard.

'Ben? Can you hear me?'

Ben wonders where the hell he is this time. That this man is a doctor is obvious just from the tone of voice, and of course the white lab coat and stethoscope give it away. For a second Ben thinks he is back in the real world in a normal hospital until his eyes start focusing properly and he looks at the bare concrete ceiling above his head. *I'm not dead.* Harry didn't take him back. A weird feeling of relief rushes through him.

'Are you in pain?' the doctor asks him in a deep voice that sounds somewhat rough, like he's got a bad throat.

Ben goes to speak but his mouth and throat are too dry. The doctor helps him sit up a bit and presses a cup of water to his lips with trembling hands. Ben gulps greedily with an increasing thirst but the doctor pulls the cup away.

'That's enough for now,' the doctor says firmly, taking the cup away from Ben's hands as he tries to pull it back.

'Thirsty,' Ben says, staring at the cup.

'Good. That's a good sign,' the doctor says, putting the cup down. 'You can have some more in a minute when I've assessed you. Now, do you feel pain anywhere?'

'Everywhere,' Ben says instantly before actually checking to see what hurts and what doesn't. He tries to focus on his body, gently tensing the muscles in his legs and arms first then tentatively shifting position before glancing back up at the doctor. 'Not really,' he admits.

'Good. That's a good sign,' the doctor says again. 'Follow the light.' He hovers a small torch in front of Ben's eyes and moves it left and right a few times as he tracks the beam. 'Good. Stay still.' He shines the torch into Ben's ears then comes back to his eyes, examining him closely before putting the torch away and reaching out to grasp Ben's skull between his hands that start to probe as though checking for bumps.

'Who are you?' Ben asks while getting his head groped.

'John Watson.'

'Huh?'

'And no I am not making that up,' the doctor says in a tone that suggests he's said the same thing many times. 'It's a common name.'

'Doctor Watson?'

'Yes. I am Doctor Watson.'

'Oh.'

'My father was called John.'

'Oh.'

'And my grandfather.'

'Oh.'

'My great-grandfather was called—'

'John?'

'Hamish.'

'Hamish?'

'Doctor Watson's middle name.'

'What is?'

'Hamish.'

'Hamish is Doctor Watson's middle name?' Ben asks, fighting the confusion to keep up with him.

'Yes. Doctor John Hamish Watson.'

'Oh. Your family liked Sherlock Holmes then,' Ben remarks as the doctor's fingers probe about and start pushing into Ben's stomach and ribs while he watches Ben for a pain reaction.

'Indeed.'

'Is your middle name Hamish?'

'No.'

'Oh.'

'It's Sherlock.'

'You are shitting me?'

'Yes.'

'Eh?' Ben blinks at him.

'I am shitting you. My middle name is not Sherlock,' Doctor Watson says while working down Ben's legs.

'Oh . . . what is it then?'

'Holmes.'

'Seriously?'

'No.'

'What the fuck? Who are you?'

'Doctor Watson, I just said that.'

'No . . . I mean who are you? Like . . .'

'Ah,' the doctor says knowingly. 'I see we have a loss of cognitive function.'

'Do what?'

'What is your name?'

'What?'

'Hmmm, quite a serious loss of cognitive function it appears,' Doctor Watson says with a serious nod at Ben.

'Ben.'

'What is?'

'My name. I'm Ben.'

'Nice to meet you, Ben. I'm Doctor Watson,' he says, holding a hand out to shake.

'You're fucking weird is what you are.'

'Do you know where you are?'

'Do you?' Ben asks.

'Do I?' he asks.

'Yeah, do you?'

'I do. Do you?'

'Maybe. Do you?'

'Hmmm,' the doctor muses, looking at Ben intently.

'We're in Roland's Batcave in the dinosaur times.'

'Hmmm.'

'So who are you?'

'Nice to meet you, I'm Doctor Watson,' Doctor Watson says, holding his hand out again.

'Er . . . we just shook hands,' Ben says, shaking his head again.

'Did we?'

'We did.'

'Sure?'

'Yes, I am sure.'

'You are sure we shook hands.'

'Yes.'

'Hmmm.'

'Okay, weirdo, why are you here?' Ben asks.

'Checking on you,' the doctor says, looking down at him as though the answer is obvious.

'Not here in this room, but why are you here? In Roland's Batcave in dinosaur times?'

'I just said. I'm checking on you.'

'Fuck me, you're a one, you are,' Ben says, getting up into a proper sitting position and reaching for the cup, which is on a newly installed bedside table, or rather a rough-hewn bit of wood on legs.

'Did I say you could have more water?'

'No,' Ben says, taking the cup and downing it in one smooth motion. 'So . . . why are you here?'

'Ah,' he says in a voice that makes Ben realise he was pissing about before, but this new voice is serious, deep and full of gravitas. 'Mind if I sit down?'

'Crack on.'

'Is that a yes?' the doctor asks.

'Yes.'

'Thanks.' He sits down on the edge of Ben's bed and sighs deeply in that way doctors do when they're about to tell someone they've got fourteen seconds left to live.

'You look like shit,' Ben says with a wince.

'I feel like shit,' Doctor Watson says. 'I'm an alcoholic.'

'Oh.'

'Haven't had a drink for four days though.'

'Good for you.'

'Thanks.'

'Why four days?'

'I got here four days ago.'

'You got here four days ago?'

'Yes.'

'I've been out of it for four days?'

'You have been in an induced coma to allow your body to heal past any point of danger. You were on a drip until a couple of hours ago. Medicine has come a long way since your times, Ben.'

'Oh.'

'And other than needing complete rest, you're fine.' The doctor sighs again, that precursor to bad news. 'However . . . I have some bad news.'

'Okay.'

'Miss Patel and Mr Madden came for me . . . I believe the term used here is *extraction*? I was on my yacht when a storm hit and I am given to understand that I died in that storm.'

'Right,' Ben says, feeling his heart rate increasing.

'A doctor was required to give medical aid to you following the beating given to you from Mr Madden. I was the doctor chosen and your colleagues came for me to extract me from my point of death to bring me back here to administer to your injuries.'

Ben stares, mesmerised by this strange man speaking so bluntly but in a way that ensures his rapt and unwavering attention.

'They did not make it back,' the doctor says, staring at Ben. 'Miss Patel and Mr Madden both perished in the storm.'

Ben stays silent for a long second. Staring unblinking and unmoving. 'But . . . how did you get back?'

'I don't know. I was unconscious. All I know is I got through and they did not come back.'

Ben swallows, feeling the world as it spins dizzyingly the wrong way, making him want to grip the bed for fear of falling off. Safa and Harry are dead. Both dead.

'But . . .'

'This is a shock,' Doctor Watson says gently, 'and I apologise for the way in which I spoke to you, but I needed to be sure you were able to cognitively absorb and deal with the bad news.'

'Safa?'

'Yes, Ben. Safa did not make it back, and neither did Harry. I am sorry.'

'I . . . but . . .'

'I understand that Harry beat you,' he says, still looking closely at Ben.

Ben nods, unable to say anything.

'I think it's important for you to know that Harry was trying a last resort to save you. Roland wanted to send you back, but Harry had told him you've got to break a man before you can rebuild him. That's why the beating was given . . .'

'I attacked him,' Ben says stupidly.

'I think, from piecing everything together, that perhaps you were provoked to have that reaction so that the beating could be given. I understand you were not applying yourself to the tasks required.'

Ben sits stunned to the core as his system dumps adrenaline into veins that surges through his body, snapping him wide awake with his mind racing. 'Fuck me . . .'

'Indeed,' the doctor says, gravely bowing his head in respect.

'It was wrong . . . the whole fucking thing was wrong . . . Safa was right . . .'

'I don't follow you,' the doctor says gently, as though prepared for a shocked patient gabbling nonsensically.

'This. All of this . . . bringing people here with no expectation of how they would react and . . . Safa was right . . . I had to disconnect . . .'

'Yes, yes indeed,' Doctor Watson says, letting him vent his grief.

'Oh fuck, what have I done?'

'You must not carry the personal responsibility for the decisions made by others—'

'Fuck off,' Ben snaps, shifting his legs over the edge of the bed. 'I've killed them . . . I fucking killed them . . .'

'Ben, you did not kill them. The storm did that. You must rest. Please, get back into bed and I'll give you something to help you sleep.'

'I'll kill him.' Ben seethes with anger, pulling his grey tracksuit off and stripping naked in front of the doctor without registering the bloke is still there. 'I'll bloody kill him,' he mutters, reaching down to pick up his black clothes, still folded neatly on the floor, and tugging them on.

'Ben, the shock is expected, but you're still healing. You must rest.'

'Safa was right. I had to disconnect but I didn't. I wallowed in self-pity like a selfish fucking twat . . . Jesus Christ, what have I done? Why did he let them go back?'

'Ben, please . . .'

He gets the boots on, lacing up quickly before striding towards the open door with the doctor in hot pursuit, pleading for him to go back and rest.

'Ben, you must listen . . .'

Ben gets through the door and into the corridor, heading down into the main room with a thunderous rage building in his gut.

'ROLAND?'

'Ben, stop this.' The doctor bustles behind him.

'ROLAND, WHERE THE FUCK ARE YOU?' Ben roars louder as his mind finally awakens to where he is and what should have been done. Roland was right when he said he didn't have a clue. The man is incompetent beyond words and because of that Ben was allowed to get so bad he needed a beating to snap him out of it, and his own stupid selfish stubbornness made him keep getting back up when Harry was begging him to stay down. Harry hurt him, but every punch he gave was deserved. Ben caused this. He made this happen. He made them go for that doctor and he made them die and that cannot be forgiven, but it was Roland that brought them here and Roland that didn't factor in the reactions people would have, and it was Roland that let them go back to get the doctor.

Through the next doors and Roland walking towards him with a conciliatory smile on his face. 'Ah Ben, I am glad you're up—'

'You fucking prick,' Ben snarls, closing the distance between them.

'Ben, stop now,' Roland says, firmly holding a hand out like a policeman, and that thought makes Ben think of Safa and no sooner does that hand come out than Roland is gripped, turned and pushed down with the wristlock that Ben was made to practise over and over. Roland tries to say something but Ben doesn't give him a chance.

'You fucking piece of shit.'

Rage inside. Rage at everything, but this man here becomes the focus and that rage explodes out, but it's refined now and targeted with a mind finally running clear and free.

'You let them go back . . .'

'I had no choice,' Roland bleats.

'You did. You bloody did. Harry follows orders . . . he would have done what you said . . .'

'He wouldn't, Ben,' Roland gasps.

'Ben!' Malcolm comes into the corridor with the doctor and Konrad close behind him.

'Harry's a soldier,' Ben growls. 'He follows orders . . . why did you let them go back?'

'I—'

'WHY?'

'Ben, stop that . . .' Malcolm comes forward to grab his arm, his actions prompting Konrad and Doctor Watson to approach him too. The men usher him away from Roland, who rolls over groaning at the pain in his arm.

'Why?' Ben asks again as the other three men gently guide him back.

'To save you,' Roland gasps.

'I was going back,' Ben mutters.

'We watched the footage,' Malcolm says quickly. 'Harry saw it. He changed his mind about you. Said he was going to try it his way . . .'

'But . . .'

'We were desperate,' Malcolm blurts. 'We didn't want to send you back . . . Safa suggested we watch the footage so we'd remember you at Holborn and not like . . . not like here . . .'

Ben sags against the wall, groaning at the thought of it. 'What have I done?'

Roland gets to his feet, wincing audibly as he rubs his painful wrist. 'Safa tried everything to snap you out of it,' he says into the charged atmosphere of the room.

'You shouldn't have brought us back the way you did,' Ben replies in a voice whispered but clear. 'A sterile bunker.' He looks round in disgust. 'It . . . you . . .' He falters and stops to bring his thoughts to order. 'No. No, this is my fault . . . how long have we been here?' Ben asks, looking round at the others.

'How long?' Malcolm asks, confused at the question.

'Weeks? Months? How long?' Ben asks, his memories of being here hopelessly blurred together.

'You don't know?' Konrad whispers in shock.

'Six months,' Roland says, standing straight.

'Six months?' Ben reels back. 'No . . . no way . . . that's not possible . . .'

'Six months, Ben,' Malcolm says, his face showing the worry he feels.

'Oh fuck . . . fuck no . . .' Ben sags against the wall. It can't have been six months. It's not possible. He's been here six months? Everything is a blur, like time is blurred and weird in his head.

'I've said the same thing,' Doctor Watson says, casting a look at Roland.

'Huh?' Ben asks, blinking at the doctor.

'Bringing people back like that,' the doctor says. 'It induces shock and that, coupled with the medications and sedatives given to you, plus the adrenaline and chemical releases, would put anyone into an awful state of mind. It could have equally caused anxiety to the extent of psychosis just as much as severe clinical depression. The doctor, or rather *I* should have been first . . .'

Roland stiffens at the repeated rebuke. His face showing the strain. 'There is no precedent for this . . .'

'There is,' Doctor Watson says, not unkindly. 'Not extraction for time travelling, but there is precedent for isolation from society. Prison? Solitary confinement? Persons trapped for long periods of time? Persons kidnapped? There is a great deal of precedent.'

Ben listens. His brain no longer trying to work through a fug of confusion. He swallows and nods at the doctor in agreement of everything said.

'Can you send me in?' Ben asks as the others look at him in confusion. 'To Safa and Harry. Can you send me there?'

'Ben,' Roland says gently. 'They're gone. It's too late.'

'I'm going back for them,' he says with firmness building in his tone and a resolve hardening by the second.

'You can't . . .' Malcolm says.

'I am,' Ben cuts him off with a firm nod as he stands up from the wall. 'Send me back . . .'

'Ben, please,' Malcolm protests. 'Please listen . . .'

'I'm going back.'

'Please listen,' Malcolm asks. 'It was bad . . .'

'What was?'

'We opened the window but we did it in the storm and the waves came through the window into the room . . .'

'So?'

'Tons of water,' Malcolm gabbles, desperate to get the words out. 'We were too low down and the doctor's yacht came through . . .'

'What the hell are you on about?'

'Listen to him, Ben,' Roland pleads. 'Safa and Harry were attached to ropes. They had five minutes to find the doctor before we pulled them back but the doctor's yacht crashed through the window, jamming everything. The water was everywhere . . . we couldn't get it out the room fast enough . . . look at the walls.'

Dark patches on every wall. The water stains solid from three feet down, giving an indication of the sheer volume of water coming into the bunker.

Malcolm rushes on, taking advantage of the brief silence. 'It's too much out there. No one can get through that and survive.'

'Show me.'

'You can't see through it,' Roland says.

'Show me.'

'Ben, please,' Malcolm whimpers.

'Just bloody show me.' Ben's turn to plead.

'Show him,' Doctor Watson says. 'Let him see for himself.'

'Roland?' Konrad asks, turning to Roland, who just nods and blows air out through his puffed-out cheeks.

Malcolm unlocks the door with the red light over it to reveal a room that now stinks of seawater and seaweed. Holes and dents in the walls speak of things smashing into them. Deep gouge marks everywhere.

'Ben.' Ben turns to see the doctor standing a few feet away. 'I was there. I saw how bad it was. You will not survive.'

'You survived,' Ben says bluntly, turning back to watch Malcolm and Konrad adjust the poles while Roland thumbs the tablet device to life.

'Okay,' Malcolm says as Ben hears the low thrumming sound coming from the speakers that show red lights flashing on. A second later and the blue light is there as beautiful and mesmerising as it was before.

'Where's the water then?' Ben asks, looking round the room, then at Roland.

'We're not set to that point,' Malcolm says. 'We're on the settings from the last time I used it.'

'Get to the . . . where Safa and Harry are . . . make it go there.'

'Ben,' Malcolm says, swallowing with a nervous glance at the blue light. 'Waves will come crashing through that window with a force that will take everyone off their feet. We barely escaped when the yacht came through.'

'But you *did* survive,' Ben points out. 'Make it go to Safa and Harry.'

'You are not listening,' Roland says.

'You brought them back once so we can do it again.'

'Not from there,' the doctor says urgently. 'The waves were ten metres high at least.'

'Okay.' Ben looks round at the faces staring at him. 'Everyone keeps telling me I am not listening. Safa kept saying it all the time. This time *you* are not listening, but you *will* fucking listen and take this in. I am going to bring them back. You are going to make that window at the point it needs to be. I am going through it. I am no good here. You need Safa and Harry, not me. If you do not do this I will start hurting people.' He pauses, making sure the words are going in. 'But please . . . please do not make me do that. Help me. Work with me. Tell me what I need to do. Make this work.'

Silence in the room, but a shift in energy tells him the cogs are slowly turning as Malcolm glances towards Roland.

'Help me . . . please . . . you need Safa more than you need anyone else here . . . and that includes you.' He points at Roland. 'What use am I?' Ben pushes on, desperate to make them understand. 'Harry beat me because I was shit and wouldn't listen or do what they said. I was going to be sent back and killed anyway, right?' Ben asks them all. 'Right?' A few nods, reluctant but honestly given. 'So fuck it . . . please let me try. Please . . .'

'Roland?' Malcolm asks, clearly showing that he wants to do it but giving way and allowing the final say to go to Roland, who rubs his wrist and stares at Ben.

'Fine,' he grunts. 'It's your death.'

'Thank you,' Ben says with real meaning. 'What do I need to know?'

'You should rest,' Doctor Watson cuts in. 'A few more days won't make any—'

'Now. We're doing it right now. What do I need to know? Tell me. Big waves, you said,' Ben says, looking at the doctor.

'Ben,' Doctor Watson says, his voice deep and gravelly. 'You have just come out of a medically induced coma. If you go now you will pass out within a few minutes. That is fact. Do you understand? As strong as your will is, it cannot defy the capabilities of your body.'

Ben swallows again. The urgency inside pushing him to do something now. To dive through and put right the wrongs. 'What did you do last time?'

'They went through in a RIB,' Konrad says. 'But something went wrong. We waited five minutes then started pulling them back on the ropes but the yacht came through and jammed the winder . . .'

'Did they have air to breathe? I mean scuba tank things?'

'Didn't think of it,' Malcolm says with an expression of grief and pain.

'We'll learn from that mistake . . . I'll take three tanks of air . . . can you get small ones?'

Malcolm nods, casting a look at Konrad. 'We can use compressed air tanks . . . really small,' he says, holding his hands apart a few inches.

'Three of them . . . rope . . . and flotation devices like lifeguard rings or something they can grab . . .' Konrad says.

'I'll need a bit of time,' Malcolm says, looking back at Ben.

'We don't have time,' Ben replies with a growing sense of urgency.

'They're dead, Ben,' Malcolm says, swallowing and blinking hard. Ben goes to reply but his words strike deep.

They're dead.

They died days ago.

Ben reels back, suddenly unsteady on his feet. The world spins. Adrenaline spikes. Shock hits. His inert body slumps as Doctor Watson rushes to prevent the fall he could see was coming.

Thirty-Five

'M and K out,' Echo says. Delta feeds it into the tablet, tapping on the screen.

Malcolm and Konrad. Names learnt by eavesdropping on snatches of conversations over the last four days since the RIB was delivered. Sometimes Malc. Sometimes Kon. Once it was Malcolm and three times it was Konrad.

Roland. They have not seen that person. Ben. They have not seen Ben. Safa and Harry. They have not seen them either. Safa and Harry both died.

'*. . . can't believe they're both dead . . .*'

That one sentence fragment heard, but since then they have learnt Ben is alive and Roland is alive from the way in which they are spoken about.

'*. . . Ben will be devastated . . .*'

'*. . . Roland's under so much pressure . . .*'

Present tense remarks.

Someone new too. *Doc Watson.* Doctor Watson is caring for Ben. Harry beat Ben.

'*. . . Harry almost killed him . . .*'

Intelligence gained. A picture being built and fed back to Mother. They suspect the blue light is connected. The light comes on before K and M come out. If only K comes out the light may go off, but then it comes back on. The five have worked out the light operator doesn't know when K is coming back as sometimes K waits for a few minutes and sometimes the light comes on just before he gets back. That means there is no communication between K and the light operator. The five also surmise that M operates the light because when both K and M go out the light stays on until they go back.

'He must be mad,' Malcolm says to Konrad, shaking his head, oblivious to the surveillance. 'He only woke up two days ago . . .'

Ben must be awake. Harry hurt Ben. Ben was unconscious.

'Training hard though, so he's determined,' Konrad says.

Ben is training for something.

'When's the swimming tank getting here?' Malcolm asks as they walk down the street.

Alpha nods to Charlie and Bravo, who move off towards the back door to thread down through the maze of alleys to the main road to begin the foot follow.

'In an hour,' Konrad says.

Alpha listens through the headphones. *Swimming tank.* They said *swimming tank*, not *swimming pool.* A swimming tank is a single-person training device equipped with a current generator to allow a person to remain static and swim against a flow of water pushed from a machine. Ben is training. They are waiting for a swimming tank. Ben is training to swim for something.

'He's a different man,' Malcolm says, the voice now fading as they walk down the road. 'Like when he first got here . . .'

Konrad replies but the words are lost to a static hiss.

The intelligence picture grows. Pieces of a puzzle that are fed into the system and put together by experts under the ever-watchful eye of Mother. Harry and Safa went into a water environment using the RIB.

They did not survive, but straight after that is when Doctor Watson was first mentioned. It is suspected Harry and Safa rescued the doctor but died in the process.

Alpha, Delta and Echo wait. Bravo and Charlie foot follow. Malcolm and Konrad go to the café. They drink coffee. They come out and walk further into the city to a specialist diving store. They purchase small tanks of compressed air. Three of them. They purchase flotation devices, wetsuits, diving knives, rope, flippers, diving masks and all manner of equipment associated with scuba diving.

'M and K back,' Echo says, watching the end of the road.

'. . . but it feels horrible without them,' Malcolm says, grimacing at the weight of the bag on his shoulder. 'Like empty . . . six months they were there . . . six months . . .'

'Ben shouldn't be doing it,' Konrad says. 'If he dies it'll be me and you back to bloody extracting people again . . . either that or we go back to before Ben goes and tell him he'll die and scrap it . . . but then if he never goes after them, then we'll never know that he dies? Fuck me, this shit is confusing . . .'

Alpha lifts his head and quickly types Mother a message.

`We have time, Alfie x`

It is confirmed. That conversation just confirmed that the device is within that warehouse. Ben is going to try to rescue Harry and Safa using the device.

`Well done. Mother x`

Thirty-Six

Time gains a whole new perspective. It does not exist but it does exist. It is not linear except it is linear. He can go back in time. He can go forward in time. But the one thing he cannot do is make time pass faster. There are still sixty seconds in a minute, sixty minutes in an hour and each day is filled with twenty-four hours. Actually, he does recall that the Cretaceous period may have had longer or shorter days or something to do with the spinning of the world or something else? He frowns and tries to remember but dismisses the notion and goes back to thinking about time.

Ben woke from his medically induced coma four days ago. He got up, threatened Roland, told everyone he was going to rescue Harry and Safa then promptly passed out.

Ben woke up again three days ago and realised that, despite a cast-iron will, he still has to rely on his physical body. Which is still very weak. Hence the time issue and the perplexing, frustrating paradox that he has to bloody wait until he gets better before he can go and rescue them. He did think, for one flawed second, that he could simply use the time machine to go forward one week but then it would be the weak him going through the device and the weak him coming out the other side in the future. So that wouldn't work. He then thought that by using the device in such a way he would come face to face with himself. The weak him now and the not-so-weak future Ben. Which would make two Bens. He then considered perhaps he could give himself a hand to rescue Harry and Safa and then had a wild few seconds of wondering how many Bens he could get to help him.

What he did learn was that six months of healthy eating and constant physical training are paying off. His body, it seems, is actually in great shape. His heart is strong. His lungs are good. His blood pressure is fine. There is nothing actually wrong with him other than he took a massive beating from a very big man which caused a great deal of shock to his system. Then being bedridden for several days meant he weakened. His energy levels lowered. His internal resources focused on healing and mending the damaged bits, which in turn left him tiring easily.

Despite all of that, and despite the utter desolation of knowing Safa and Harry are dead, his mind is once more his own, and to compensate for the sense of bereavement he reminds himself constantly that he has a time machine and will go and get them back.

That thought drives him, generating a relentless, unstoppable energy. He trains. He eats. He sleeps. The swimming tank is fantastic. Ben only ever swam for leisure and the tank, as small as it is, means he can build up his technique for powering through an ever-increasing current. It also means he gets used to the mask, the flippers and exerting himself while having the mouthpiece of a breathing tube between his teeth.

He also runs. Not far at first, but as the days go on, so he covers more distance. Up and down the side of the bunker, where Safa and Harry drilled him relentlessly. He remembers the lessons. He remembers the warm-ups, the stretches, the warm-downs. He remembers the circuits and the types of food that Safa told him to eat. Proteins, carbs, fats and nutrition.

Ben knows, despite the urge gripping him to go now and dive through the portal to save them, that he has one shot and one shot only. Malcolm and Konrad will never come after him. Roland has made that clear. Roland will not risk losing them in addition to Harry, Safa and Ben if he doesn't make it back. So that means Ben has to get it right the first time.

The evenings are the worst. In the day, he can focus on the training. He can swim, take a break, swim more, do some other exercise then go back to swimming. He can fire pistols at targets and use the metal detector to hunt for the casings on the grass. He can find focus and things to occupy his mind, but when night comes, so the emptiness of the bunker becomes striking.

Instead, he takes a bottle of beer and sits outside to watch the sunset that Harry and Safa watched so many times. He sits next to two empty chairs then returns to their rooms that have changed so much but that still hold the smell of them. The bittersweet scents that invoke too many emotions.

He sleeps soundly now. The dreams still come but the terror of them is less and the noises outside are more homely now, more normal and organic, like they belong to this place and his life. Like people who live near busy roads who say they get so used to the noise they can't sleep without it. The meds given by Doctor Watson help. They take the edge off and aid his production of serotonin, which serves to improve rationality and well-being, and to rationalise is to know where you are in time and space.

'Beautiful, isn't it?' Roland said, stepping out from the bunker one evening a few days after Ben woke up.

Ben nodded. 'Is,' he said.

Roland turned to look at Ben. Smiling politely but very clearly examining the other man. 'How are you feeling?'

'Fine,' Ben said. 'Tired . . . still sore . . . getting better though,' he added.

'I see,' Roland said.

'You're here late,' Ben said. Roland was rarely in the bunker. Ben had noticed Roland's lack of presence even when he was in the grip of his mental deterioration, but it was something he never thought to question or could be bothered to ask about.

'Indeed,' Roland said while looking at the bottles of beer in the cooler. 'Mind if I join you?'

'Carry on,' Ben said. He almost said *it's your bunker*, but stopped himself at the last second.

'Malcolm and Konrad needed some money,' Roland explained as he selected a beer, unscrewed the cap and took the first swig. It didn't look right somehow. Roland was too stiff and too formal to drink beer from a bottle. Ben's curiosity prickled. His investigative mind moved into gear. He showed no reaction on his face but inclined his head as though to show interest in the conversation and by not speaking he invited Roland to fill the silence. 'Costs a fortune,' Roland said, feeling a need to fill that silence.

'What does?' Ben asked.

'This,' Roland said. 'All of this.'

'Oh,' Ben said blandly. He paused, swigged his beer and exhaled to show a relaxed state, telegraphing that any questions he asked were purely conversational. 'You must be wealthy.'

Roland snorted with a dry laugh. 'God, no. I died in twenty forty-six. Committed suicide. Walked into the sea and drowned myself.'

The sudden information flow surprised Ben. He was expecting a gentle flow of conversation but the shift in pace told him Roland had something he wanted to say.

'Go on,' Ben said gently.

Roland cast him a look. Weariness in his eyes. Weight on his shoulders. Ben felt the urge to ask why, where, when and what happened but resisted asking any closed questions that invited single responses.

'Business folded,' Roland said, nodding morosely at his bottle of beer. 'Financial ruin. Had an insurance policy that paid out in the event of my death and, fortunately, it covered suicide.' He stopped to swig from his beer. 'My death paid for my children's education.'

Ben nodded. His mind working clear and free. Conclusions drawn. Suspicions formed. Connect the dots. Follow the breadcrumb trail. One of Roland's children extracted him. Why? Roland is working for one person. Who? Roland is rarely here. Why? Ben rubbed the back of his neck and smiled wryly. 'Ah,' he said.

'Ah indeed,' Roland replied. He did not look at Ben but stared ahead.

'Son? Daughter?' Ben asked.

'Son,' Roland said.

'Got it,' Ben said.

'Do you?' Roland asked. He shifted position to look at Ben. 'Do tell me.'

Ben prickled at the tone but suppressed any show of irritation. 'You died. Your kids got a private education. Your son invented time travel to save his father but fucked the world up then went back to actually save his father, who is now trying to fix what his son fucked up. Which is why you are never here. Because you are spending time with your son.'

'You are astute, aren't you?'

Ben did not hide the irritation that time but inclined his head to offer a hard glare. 'So now you play God with people's lives to fix the fucking mess your son made. Like I said. Got it.'

Roland stiffened. A blush spread through his cheeks. 'I . . .'

'What?' Ben asked coldly.

'My apologies.'

'Where does the money come from?' Now was the time for specific questions.

'Pardon?'

'The money. You said this place costs money to run and you said you are not wealthy. Where does the money come from?'

'I would rather not . . .'

'Yeah, I'm not giving you a choice. Where does the money come from?'

'Ben, what is—'

'I will throw you off that fucking ledge in a minute you nasty, vile, selfish, egotistical prick. You brought three people into a sterile bunker. You shoved them in rooms like cells and expected them to be heroes because a fucking computer program told you they would be okay and you left them to it while you went to the park with your son—'

'Now listen here—'

'I investigated suicides. I had to look into the lives of people to validate the claims and nearly every single one of them were cunts like you. Rich fucking bastards that bankrupted themselves through greed and couldn't face a life of poverty and not being able to drive a fucking Porsche. People like you have no concept of the misery you cause. You fucking killed yourself for money? You abandoned your family for money? You brought us here and dumped us in the fucking dinosaur times to alleviate your own guilt? Fuck you. Fuck you and what you stand for. This is too big to be left in the hands of a fucking idiot like you. Where does the money come from?'

Roland swallowed. The intensity of the words pouring from Ben wilted him. The ferocity of the glare together with the calm tone of the voice was frightening. 'Investments,' he said weakly.

'Investments? What investments?'

'We can't just take money. The impact on the timeline would be . . . I mean. In theory I could use future knowledge to gain a fortune but that could influence the timeline. I invest in stocks and shares that I know will do well. Some small amounts here and there that pay out but that do not upset the natural—'

'Just steal it. Find a drug or gun smuggler and fucking steal it . . . actually, tell me where one is and I'll go do it right now.'

'We can't! You can't . . . I mean . . . think about it. The smuggler wakes up to find his money gone. Who does he blame? Who does he kill in revenge? That is influence on the timeline.'

'Gold then. Go back in time and find gold or diamonds.'

'Again, we cannot. What if that gold or diamond is used later in the timeline?'

'There you go. Right there,' Ben said darkly.

'What?' Roland asked.

'You place higher regard for material wealth than you give value to the lives of people.'

'I beg your pardon?'

'You killed yourself for money. You dumped me, Safa and Harry here and fucked off to play stockbroker and you care more for a lump of gold or a cluster of diamonds than the entirety of the human species . . .'

'Okay,' Roland said as he stood up. 'I think this conversation is over.'

'You extracted me from my death—'

'I did but—'

'But that does not make you God. It does not mean you get to control everything said and done by those you extracted.' Ben was up, on his feet and stalking hard towards Roland, who backed away in alarm. 'You do not get to come out here, boast about your life and fucking end the conversation when you see fit. Safa and Harry died. Even if I bring them back . . . which, according to Doctor Watson, is highly unlikely, they will have still died. They died because I suffered a mental breakdown. I suffered that mental breakdown because of your actions and what you did and the way you did it.'

'Ben please . . .' Roland stopped with his back to the side of the bunker.

'You do not pay me. You do not own me. You do not control me. The second you brought us back and explained why is the second you gave us the responsibility to deal with the problem. Can you understand that? You do not run this. This is not yours. This problem is bigger than you . . . the lack of care you have shown is staggering. I suggest, Roland. I really . . . really fucking suggest that from now you focus solely on providing the money and do nothing else that you can fuck up.' Ben stopped an inch from Roland. Nose to nose. Threat and malice in every word spoken. Roland swallowed.

'Find someone with a military intelligence background,' Ben said, his eyes locked on Roland. 'Find someone who knows what they are doing, because you don't.'

That conversation ended with Roland rushing off but it left Ben fuelled by an anger inside that would not subside. He missed Harry and Safa. He drank another beer and paced up and down as the sky above him grew dark and the noises of the night grew louder.

He went inside and stared down the corridor. The bunker felt so empty. So lonely, sterile and cold. The blue light from the device was spilling out from the room holding it. He headed down and stared into the room at the shimmering, iridescent square. Roland gets to go home. Roland bends the rules to suit himself. Ben knew, without doubt, that should he go after Roland right then he would see a home of luxury. The lure of wealth is too great for people like that. Roland doesn't sleep in the bunker. He creams the stock markets and plays God instead while letting the little people do the dirty work for him.

Anger inside. The unfairness of it. He marched in and snatched up the tablet left on the side next to the device. A simple PDA thing. Easy to use. He lifted his head at hearing Malcolm and Konrad talking in their rooms. He scrolled through the screens. Figuring out the workings as he swiped. 'History'. A simple button that he pressed to reveal a long list. He scrolled down seeing the words *Berlin* and *Roland* appear time and again. *Berlin* must be where Malcolm and Konrad go to get the things they need. *Roland* must mean Roland's home. He scrolled down further until he saw it and froze. *Rio 1999.* Fuck. He swallowed and, without thinking, without thought, he pressed it. The screen changed. *Set portal to Rio 1999?* Fuck. He pressed the green 'Accept' button. The blue light flickered and went off, a second later it flickered and came back on. He stared at it. His heart hammered in his chest. His mouth suddenly dry. Rio was right there. The implications hit home. The crossing over of time travel. If he went through he would meet his former self. He would see Malcolm waiting on the other side for the rest to come back. The lure was there. The lure to go through and see Harry and Safa again. Just for a minute.

He ran quickly to his room and grabbed his black baseball cap. He put his jeans on and the grey tracksuit top he used when he first got here. His hair and beard were long and thick. He put on the baseball cap and tugged it low. He looked so different. He ran back. Still fuelled by the idea.

In the device room he stared at the blue portal but knew he could not go through. Malcolm was on the other side but there was a risk that by setting the portal again he was overriding the previous one. That thought made him swipe the screen and switch the device off but his mind had not finished with the idea. Instead, he found the settings and located the GPS coordinates for *Rio 1999.* The six-digit latitude and longitude numbers were there. All he had to do was adjust the last digit of each to move the position along. The original portal would be unaffected. He would simply be creating a new portal from this time through to that time but to a new location. He did it. He deleted the last number of the latitude and increased the value by two. He did the same with longitude and pressed the buttons to make the beautiful blue light fill the room. He took a tentative step forward and eased through his head, which bounced off the wall the portal was set against. He adjusted the values and tried again, leaning through. Sound filled his ears. Hot air hit his face. The carnival was close. The smell of Rio that he instantly recalled from six months ago. He looked round while leaning through. There off to the left was the telltale glow of the other portal, out of sight round the corner of the alley. He realised he must be further down the same alley. He crept out and paused to listen. The feel of it was incredible. The humidity, the smells of life, the sounds of people and music. He eased to the corner and peeked round to see Konrad leaning against a wall smoking while staring down at the main road. The blue portal right next to him.

Ben's heart thudded. That was Konrad six months ago. The concept was too much but the lure and temptation were also too much. He went the other way and wound through the long alley, which fed on to the same main road further down. He stepped out to lights and music and people dancing. He stepped out to crowds cheering, whistles, klaxons and the thrumming beats. He spotted a gap in the procession and sprinted across the road to the other side then started down through the crowds. He was jostled, pushed and bumped into but it was wonderful. He smiled and nodded at people. They smiled and laughed back. The atmosphere was electric, pulsating, and it gave energy to his already excited state.

He spotted the awning of the bar through the gaps in the procession but the crowds were too thick on both sides to allow a clear view. He moved up and down, trying to catch a glimpse, but it was no good. He went further down, waited for a gap, ran across to the other side and started moving up towards the awning. He tugged his cap down lower and kept his head lowered, looking up under the rim towards the thick crowds outside the bar.

A gut punch. A surge of adrenaline. Harry being pulled into the road by a scantily clad dancer. Harry. Ben stopped right where he was to stare. Harry. The big bearded man laughing and turning on the spot with a bottle of beer held over his head. He scoured the crowd and saw Roland standing stiff and worried, tightly clasping a bottle of beer. Then right there. Right in front of him suddenly in clear view was him talking to Safa. The sight made his heart lurch. His stomach flipped. His legs wobbled but the feeling was nice. It was more than nice.

He looked so different. Short hair. No beard. Fat too. Well, not fat, but not fit like he is now. The old Ben looked puffy and just different, but as great as the desire was to stare in fascination at himself, he found his attention pulled to Safa. She looked the same. The exact same. The same raven-black hair. The same stature. The same poise and stance. He felt both sick and ecstatic at the same time. Just the sight of them, of her. Harry and Safa. The music. The sounds. The heat. The laughing people. Seeing his old self and knowing what Ben had to go through. There was an urge in him then, to intervene and say something, to tell them to do things differently, but again the dangers of meddling screamed in his mind.

He went closer. Drawn to them. He wanted to hear their voices. He needed to hear Safa. Hat low, peak down, head lowered, he slouched and changed his gait to shuffle as though tipsy. He fed into the crowd and weaved to get stupidly close.

'Oh my God, Ben! Look at him.' Safa's voice drifted over. Her raucous laugh that he remembered so clearly. He closed his eyes and just listened. Just for a second. Just to know she was there. Right there. 'Need a piss, hold that . . .'

Shit. He snapped his eyes open. Safa had gone to the toilet in the bar. He was in the way. He turned round and dropped his head as Safa moved round him, her shoulder brushing against his. 'Sorry,' she said, lifting a hand. He lifted a hand and turned to watch the procession while suddenly feeling like a voyeur. Fuck. This was wrong. This was so wrong. He moved away quickly and crossed the road to sprint down back to his alley then down and through his portal that was deactivated the second he got into the bunker. He breathed hard. His chest rising and falling. For a second he felt sick to the stomach at what he had just done. Then the humour of it hit him and he burst out laughing. He saw Harry. He saw Safa. Safa touched his shoulder!

If he wasn't forged mentally prior to that, he was from that point on.

Thirty-Seven

He fixes his gaze on the blue square. 'I just run through, yeah?'

'I would dive through,' the doctor says behind him. 'Not that *I* would actually dive through as only a maniac would actually go through that thing into—'

'Got it. Dive through,' Ben says, casting a worried glance at the doctor, still muttering to himself. 'Can I look now?' he asks Malcolm.

'Of course,' Malcolm says. 'Just be careful in case a wave comes through.'

Ben sticks his face through and screams at the huge wall of water inches from his face. He gets one step back before it hits. A surge of violent, seething water that pummels him back off his feet into the wall.

'Shit,' Ben says and starts fumbling to put the mouthpiece of the air bottle into his mouth.

'Ben,' Malcolm says from the doorway with everyone else having run from the room. 'Maybe this isn't a good idea . . .'

With grim determination, Ben walks back to the portal and sticks his head out to a sea raging with waves like mountains and a sky torn apart from bolts of lightning and thunder booming overhead. White foam whips up high into the wind at the crests of the waves.

'I can't see the other blue light,' Ben says, stretching his back.

'We've had to move position because of the yacht and getting Doctor Watson through,' Roland calls out from the corridor.

'Do what?'

'Time travel, Ben,' Roland huffs. 'The other blue window is a link from this place weeks ago . . . we have to let Safa and Harry get the doctor through the first window otherwise he wouldn't be here now.'

'Ah right, got it . . . yeah, that makes sense . . . so I can't get them if they've still got the doctor with them?'

'God, no.' Malcolm blanches at the mere suggestion.

'What would happen if I brought all three back here?'

Malcolm shrugs, stunned at the question. 'We'd have two Doctor Watsons.'

'I thought two people couldn't occupy the same . . . same something?'

'That was a movie.'

'So . . . okay . . .' Ben nods, looks ahead, then looks back at Malcolm. 'And that's a bad thing?'

'Two of the same person?' Malcolm asks, staring flat at Ben.

'Oh, oh yeah, of course, totally a bad thing,' Ben says quickly. 'So let them get the doctor through then get them . . . right?' Ben says.

'Right,' Malcolm says with an expression that doesn't convey the same level of confidence.

'Got it.' Ben sticks his head back through and stares round at the nightmare view for any sign of them. 'What's the distance from this window to the other one?' he asks, pulling back into the room.

'The first window should be two hundred metres in front of you,' Malcolm says.

Ben leans through and stares with the rain pelting his face and the wind whipping the tears from his eyes. The sky strobes with bolts of lightning and thunder rolls heavy and deep. Motion everywhere. A seething mass of mountains rolling with deep valleys and sky-high tops.

There. There it is. A square of blue light two hundred metres ahead, which doesn't sound far but in this mess it looks miles.

His heart slams into overdrive at the sight of the RIB powering up the wall of a wave ahead of the first portal and the second he sees it so the noise of the engine reaches his ears. Harry and Safa are alive in that boat and just the sight of them sends a thrill through his body. The crazy bastards attempting something as dangerous as this with just two of them. Jesus, that's bravery right there. Proper heroes doing proper heroic acts.

'Got it . . . I can see them,' Ben says into the howling wind, then realises and ducks back into the room. 'I can see them,' he tells the others. 'They're in the boat going up a wave.'

'They haven't got me yet,' Doctor Watson shouts from the corridor. 'You have to wait for them to get me through the other window . . .'

'Yep.' Ben paces back from the light and gets ready to run.

'How long do you want?' Konrad asks, standing ready at the big reel of rope.

'What for?' Ben asks.

'Before we pull you back?'

'Fuck knows.' Ben shrugs. 'How long did they have?'

'Five minutes,' he says.

'Right, so they've had maybe one minute of that . . . and you're pulling them back when they've got the doc . . . so, fucking hell, I don't know!'

'Ten minutes?' Malcolm asks.

'How long does the air in these bottles last?'

'I don't know,' Konrad says.

'Fuck me, this is a shower of shit. Fine, right, give me ten minutes then.'

'Ten minutes is a long time out there,' the doctor says.

'Oh, for fuck's sake . . . right . . . eight minutes then,' Ben says to Konrad. 'Eight minutes, then get pulling.'

'Got it.'

'And keep pulling until Safa and Harry get through.'

'Got it.'

'And if the other doctor comes through by mistake, then just throw him back out.'

'What?' Doctor Watson says.

'Eight minutes . . .' Ben nods, sticks the mouthpiece in his mouth, nods again and runs for the window with big steps to avoid tripping over the half-size flippers on his feet. He dives forward with his arms outstretched and through once again into another world in another time and place.

'Crazy bastard,' Malcolm says once he's gone.

◆　◆　◆

Life is crazy and nuts and bizarre but fucking hell be like Harry and get on with it. Lock it down. Let it go. Be here in the now and dive through a time machine into a wild storm of an ocean and he would scream except his mouth is full.

He plummets and bellyflops into the valley of two waves and sinks beneath the surface with his stomach churning and his heart hammering. The buoyancy aid does its job. He surges back up, feeling an immense sense of relief. Then he remembers he is breathing from a tank so he doesn't need to hold his breath.

Everything looks different now. He was just a bit higher a minute ago but that height made the world of difference. Now he's at the bottom staring up in awe at the wave rolling towards him and he has to force himself to stay calm and get his bearings.

He twists and paddles for a second until he finds his square of light below and behind him, still in the trough of the waves. With the position of that light in mind, he starts swimming directly away from it, breathing fast and ragged through the mouthpiece.

The sessions in the tank pay off. The ability to withstand the current and not feel as if he is in a totally alien environment. He goes for what feels like a few minutes and glances back to see the square of light still seems to be in the same place so he swims harder and remembers to make use of the flippers properly.

A huge rolling wave starts to lift him with a sensation he can feel and with that height gained he searches ahead. He catches a glimpse of the other square of blue light and a white yacht bobbing along towards it. Harry and Safa are there too, working to rescue the doctor and having no idea that within a few minutes they'll be dead. That thought drives him on harder with a fresh burst of energy. He thinks of Harry and everything he knows about him, of his exploits and the daring missions he did, and now Ben knows him he can't translate the movies and television programmes he has seen to the real man. Harry is real and absurdly easy-going and relaxed, but with a simmering, boiling temper just waiting to be released. The way he took that first drink of water to Safa, going so low and trying to appear less of a threat. If they ever make a list of the top human beings ever to have lived, Harry Madden will be on it.

Ben swims and swims, fighting against the wave trying to lift him up and the current sucking him back. Progress is made but too slow, and so he searches for energy to drive him on and make him faster before they drown. He has to reach them. He has to get the ropes and flotation devices into their hands and the breathing tubes into their mouths. Malcolm and Konrad can do the rest. No matter what happens, Safa and Harry must survive and get back. Doctor Watson told him how hard it would be, but never did he imagine it would be anything like this. The rise and fall of the waves. The wind screaming past him. The rain pelting down. The flashes of lightning. The boom of the thunder. The current is so much stronger than he factored and for a few seconds he realises the hopelessness of it.

Then he remembers that Safa didn't give up on him, not for six months, and never has he felt so sorry for something in his life. He failed. He fucked up and let everyone down and they died because of that, but he will not let it happen again. So he swims. He refuses the pain starting to burn in his already exhausted limbs and he swims harder and faster while sucking air through a rubberised mouthpiece and all the time he stares at the spot where the blue light appears.

The yacht is closer now, see-sawing and spinning as it clashes with the currents, waves and wind. Thrown about, and for a few seconds it looks like the yacht will be lifted by the wave, but it drops down into the trough and starts what can only be the final run before it crashes through.

He can see he is still too far away. *Swim, damn you, and for once do something properly.* Thank God he listened to the doctor and didn't attempt this when he first woke up. He'd be dead already. Even now, with ten days of healing, he is struggling. Pure rage hits at his own failure. That drives him on through that seething, constantly moving water. He stretches out with powerful strokes. The flotation devices hamper his motion. The water drags and throws him about. He breathes hard and worries about using too much of the air. He should have used a boat, used a rescue service, used the bloody navy or tried anything other than this stupid idea. If he dies then they all die and there is no one left to come and rescue them. It gets desperate. The lack of progress and the constant sensations of rising and falling, then he sees a flash of orange and three heads bobbing on the surface close together, but a split second later everything moves and the view is lost.

The sight of them gives him what he needs and he powers through that water with his eyes unblinking while his mind blots out the pain blooming through his body. He will not fail. He will not give in. Failure is not an option. The life of one for the lives of many. He understands that now.

He sees them again. Harry holding Safa, who holds the doctor, and all three of them going slowly down the wave towards the light, but even he can see they won't make it. They're too slow. He has to get to them so he uses the wave to take him up that sheer wall so he can gain height.

Safa stops and pushes away, waving at Harry to keep going with the doctor. Harry shouts back through the maelstrom. Ben hears his voice but watches as Safa sinks down and although Harry hesitates, Ben knows he will keep going because the mission has to come first. Harry does. Harry roars and kicks and gains speed while dragging the doctor towards the blue shimmering light as Safa comes back to the surface but she's not moving. Ben lets the next wave take him up and spots Harry doing the same thing and using the lift of a wave to rise so he can fall back down and get through the light. Except Ben knows he won't get through. Harry will get the doctor through then go back for Safa.

That means Safa is the priority. Ben starts working to descend. He twists and rolls to help gravity take over and pull him down more than the wave is lifting him up and the energy he expends in doing so drains him to the core. All he can do is roll and force his body to fall down that wave as he plummets towards her sinking beneath the surface. She doesn't swim or thrash now but is inert and lifeless as though already a corpse.

Closer but not close enough. Ben drives forwards with legs thrashing and arms going wild while biting down on the mouthpiece. He almost reaches her but the water pulls him away at the last second. He tries again and kicks, swims and fights against the world and all it has to get to that woman, looking strangely serene with her eyes closed as though not even death can taint her.

He reaches again, stretching with wild desperation. His fingertips brush against her buoyancy vest so he thrashes and flails until suddenly she's in his grip. A violent wrench brings her through the water into his arms. He taps the side of her face, willing her eyes to open while he gags and spits the rubber from his mouth.

'SAFA,' he screams out while trying to get one of the bottles from his wrist. 'You're okay now . . . you're okay, Safa . . . you'll live . . .' He keeps speaking with gasping, ragged lungs and gets the strap over her face. 'Open your mouth, Safa . . . it's Ben . . . open your mouth . . .' She does. Her mouth opens and he feels a surge of hope that somewhere inside she can hear him. 'You're okay . . . bite down now . . . bite down . . . BITE DOWN, SAFA.'

She bites hard, clamping her teeth on the rubber bit. Safa will live. She will not die. He draws her closer and feels her arms reaching up round his neck but her eyes stay closed.

Working to hold her steady he takes a breath and drops beneath the surface to find the rope still attached to her vest. Everything takes so long, fumbling with the knife and finding a way to hold the rope so he can cut it, but eventually he does it and goes back up to suck air in as her face presses close against his.

'Got to get Harry . . . got to get Harry . . .' He blurts the words, the wind whipping his voice away. The rain driving down. The waves lifting them together in a sickening motion. He gets the flotation device and pushes it into her hands. 'Hold this . . . grip it . . . grip it Safa.' She holds on to his neck, gripping him closer. 'Not me . . . fuck it.' He struggles to get the rope from the flotation device round her body and tie it off. 'You bite down . . . you hear me?' He shouts the words, willing his words to be heard. 'They'll pull you back . . . just hold on and bite down . . .'

He forces her arms from his neck and feels a sudden urge to keep hold until she's safe. She can breathe. She is tied on. He has to let go. He grabs his mouthpiece and before he can push it into his mouth he pulls her close and gently kisses her forehead. Then he is away, turning and swimming like a crazy man.

Harry is nowhere to be seen. Just a surface of immense water rippling and moving with the tide and wind. Ben dives down, heavier now from having got rid of one flotation device. Nothing. He goes deeper, working down into the depths that seem so dark, but still nothing. He turns and searches in every direction but still nothing. Where is he? Ben pushes on, looking and staring and hoping he will see a flash of movement or a shadow. Something. Anything. Please. *Please, I have to find him.*

The tug comes. The rope on his vest plucking that tells him they will start pulling soon. He hasn't found Harry yet. The rope tugs again, harder and drawing him through the water a few feet while he searches and looks for a shadow or a flicker of light or something.

Then it hits him. He is looking down. He should be looking up. Safa was floating from the buoyancy vest and Harry must have been wearing the same thing. He twists to face up and spots him instantly. A dark mass of a shape metres ahead. Ben fights on but he has nothing left to give. His limbs are so heavy. His head pounds. He feels sick, weak and dizzy, but the man he is trying to save is Mad Harry Madden so he must work. He must work and train and do what Safa tells him. He must not be selfish. Don't be selfish, Ben. Be Ben Ryder. *I am Ben Ryder.* He claws energy from deep within. Ben gets closer. So close now and like Safa, Harry is lifeless and still in the violence of the water.

Ben swims into the big man's legs then up his body and just about grabs his vest as Harry's rope goes taut and away they go. Cutting through the water again with that almighty pull drawing them both down into the depths as they are dragged through the body of the wave to the other square of light, where the old Malcolm and Konrad are operating the winch.

Ben's rope goes taut as the Malcolm and Konrad from now operate the winch from the other portal. Two ropes. One to the past. One to the now. Both pulling. The violence they inflict is staggering. Wrenching the two grown men down through the thick bodies of waves. Harry's rope has to be cut. Harry needs to breathe. Which one first? Get the mouthpiece in or cut the rope? Ben tugs the knife from the sheath on his thigh and feels for the taut rope. He goes to cut then checks again to find it's his own rope. He flails again. Still pulled, still battered, still knowing Harry cannot breathe. He finds the other rope and slices the sharp blade through the rope that pings apart. A sudden variance in direction. Ben's rope takes the strain, heaving them both through the water.

He lets go of the knife and works to force the mouthpiece into Harry's mouth. Hammering his clenched fist into the end to force it in. Finally it goes. Finally Harry opens enough to get the thing in. He has to tie Harry on. He has to secure Harry to the rope but he is fading fast. He can feel it. His mind is not far from closing down and falling into blackness but if that happens he will let go of Harry, who will be left here to die.

Ben can't grip him anymore. He cannot hold on. Ben wants to hold on. More than anything he wants to hold Harry, but the strength is going from him so fast he is blacking out. Ben gets the flotation device between them while the water surges past their heads and bodies. He pushes the soldier's hands on to the grab handle and wraps his fingers over his, telling him to hold on. Harry does. He grips sudden and hard with a tension in his hands that Ben feels. He looks to Harry to see bubbles streaming up from the mouthpiece. Harry is breathing. He is holding on. Ben did not fail. Not this time.

A few seconds later Ben blinks his eyes open. He is not being pulled any more. He is floating in an almost pitch-black sea watching Harry stream away towards a faraway blue iridescent light.

It's calm and quiet. No noises now. Just his breathing through the mouthpiece, which sends bubbles surging to the surface above or below him. He does not know. He is spent, exhausted and dying and he blacks out. Seconds? Minutes? Could be hours or days, but he opens his eyes and he is still there in the water feeling his body go limp and the air coming from the bottle has a weird taste to it now so it must be running out.

No matter. Safa and Harry will get back and they'll save the world while cracking jokes and firing guns. Ah, at least he met them, and that on its own is an honour. Just to have known them for those few months is enough and as he blacks out he feels regret that he was such a dick.

He is hit hard by something slamming into him with such force that the now empty bottle is ripped from his mouth. Hands round his waist hold him tight and he looks through his mask into the open eyes of Safa staring at him with that blazing look of utter capability and refusal to be beaten by anything or anyone.

Ben clamps on, pulling her body into his while their eyes stay locked. With the water streaming past them she wriggles one hand free and pulls the bottle from her mouth. For a second Ben thinks she'll pull it from the strap. Instead, she pulls him in and pushes her lips against his. Ben takes too long to respond. Her tongue pushes between his closed lips, forcing them open so she can expel the air from her to him and whether by mistake or design it's a better shock than any defibrillator can ever give and he snaps back to his senses, breathing Safa Patel into his lungs. Taking the life she gives and once again doing what she tells him.

She closes her eyes and pulls back to suck on the mouthpiece. She draws air into her lungs and exhales the stream of bubbles. She inhales again and holds the air while reaching out to guide him in. He goes willingly this time. Her hand on the back of his head. His hands on her cheeks. As their mouths meet her tongue comes out to tell him he can open his lips but they are already opening. She breathes out. He breathes in. The chaos of the moment. The chaos of the last six months. She left Ben severely injured in the bunker but now he is here, holding her, staring at her, and even through that water she can see the spark is back in his eyes. It is a crazy second. It is a second of life and death, of being pulled through the body of a huge rolling wave towards a time machine. His mouth is open. Hers too. She can exhale into him. He can inhale from her. It is confusing though. She knows that. The mischief in her eyes tells him she knows that. They might both die right now. Her tongue finds his. His tongue finds hers. Be heroes and do heroic things. Go through the ocean towards a time machine while kissing because later, if you survive, you can say it was an accident and you didn't know what you were doing. It is brief. It is fleeting. It is over in a second. Did it even happen?

The wave and the rope take them through the portal with the thick body of water losing hundreds of gallons a second to a window giving entry to a concrete bunker a hundred million years ago. They sail through water and air wrenched by a motor giving power to a reel and the action is so violent they are ripped apart.

Ben spins and falls, swept along by water pummelling him into the hard wall and so great is that tide that he remains pinned in place, unable to stand or do anything. People scream out as someone lands on top of him, driving him harder into the corner of the room. He wriggles and fights to free himself of the tangled limbs and somehow grabs whoever it is and forces them upright to get their head out of the water. Still the water comes through. Wave after wave crashes into the room, filling it quickly and causing a jet to surge through the open door. With the mask still on, Ben gains a view of the motor on the reel still dragging Safa and Harry across the room, threatening to suck them in. He lurches away from the wall against the tide, wading and diving while scrabbling for the knife on his leg that is no longer there.

He reaches Harry and pulls the knife from Harry's sheath to slice down, severing the rope, which whips away into the reel with a greater speed. Harry instantly drops down under the water but with the bottle mouthpiece still clamped between his jaws.

Ben turns looking for Safa as the next wave slams into him from behind, taking him from his feet and into the wall with bone-jarring speed and again he slumps down with the wind knocked from his lungs.

He is thrown and dropped, lifted and slammed, but all the time he looks for Safa and he finally sees her at the reel with her arms locked out trying to prevent the thing pulling her in. Veins bulge from her neck. She screams out in exertion. The air tank hanging from the strap round her neck.

Ben dives towards her, grinding his feet into the ground and wading through thigh-high turbulent water that forms whirlpools and eddies from the suction created by the open door.

Harry surges up. The huge man appearing like Poseidon himself with water pouring from his beard. He loops one huge arm round her waist and heaves back. She screams as the motor on the winch grinds noisily. Ben fights through the water. Wading hard as another wave crashes through. Harry's hand shoots out. Ben grabs it and uses it to lever himself closer and get in front of Safa to flail the blade of the knife at the rope. One touch from the sharp steel and the rope pings apart. They fall back into the water as the next wave batters into the room.

Konrad fights to keep the tablet above the water as he slips and flails about. He tries again and again to jab at the screen but each time the waves come and he's pulled off his feet by the suction of the eddy flowing through the door. As he goes down, Ben snatches the tablet from his hand and grabs his collar to heave him up. Konrad comes up gasping for air and spewing seawater and puke. The next wave comes in. The power of it sweeping them through the open door. Rip tides and counter-swirls. Waves bouncing from the walls. Voices screaming out. The water in the corridor is already at waist height with more coming in faster than it can empty into the other rooms.

They fight together. Ben and Konrad doing everything they can to keep the tablet above the water. Malcolm flows past them. Screaming and flailing to try to stop himself. Roland already lost from view.

'Hold it up.' Konrad grunts the words out. He surges up as Ben holds the tablet and swipes at the screen. His fingers frantic and rushed, but the red 'End' button shows. He hits it hard, swiping and swiping as Ben screams for him to stop the water coming through.

'DONE IT,' Konrad roars in relief. An instant sensation of the power of the water ending. Konrad sinks. Ben retches saltwater from his guts. The water flows out, the level sinking down as the rooms absorb the flow. The end door opens. The water rushes past the doctor.

'Where are they?' Doctor Watson yells, which he doesn't need to do as the noise is all gone now.

'In there.' Ben waves an arm behind him towards the door and manages to keep hold of a conscious mind for about another five seconds before he sinks down and finally lets the pain and exhaustion pull him to the wet ground.

Thirty-Eight

'Just rest for a few minutes,' Doctor Watson says, standing up.

'Thanks, doc,' Harry grunts.

'You seem fine. Nothing damaged.'

'What was the thing you called it?' Harry asks.

'Acute respiratory distress syndrome. It's caused when you take water into your lungs but there's no signs . . . that's why I kept you under for a couple of days. Safa will be waking up . . . you'll be okay?'

'Fine.' Harry waves a hand.

The miracles of modern science, the wonders of modern medications. Timed to perfection and Safa starts rising from the induced coma state as Doctor Watson stops next to her bed. Her eyes flutter. Motion in her limbs.

'You're okay,' Doctor Watson says deeply, his voice giving reassurance as she comes back to the land of the living. 'Safa . . . you're okay . . . just wake slowly . . . everything is fine. I'm going to take your wrist for a minute,' he says. Malcolm, Konrad and Roland have all told him how fast her reactions are and that she hates being touched. He lifts her wrist, detects the pulse and stares at his watch.

'Who the fuck are you?'

'Good morning,' he says with a smile.

'I said who the fuck are you . . . ?' Safa glares up at the craggy face then down to his hand holding her wrist.

'Doctor Watson,' Doctor Watson says. 'No relation. Nothing to do with Sherlock Holmes . . .'

'Who? What the . . . ?'

'Never mind. Pulse is fine. I'm going to check your eyes and ears.'

'You fucking—'

'Oh shut up,' he says with a huff, silencing her instantly. 'Follow my fingers.' He waves his hand past her eyes. 'Good. Any blurred vision? No? Good. Ears.' He shines a torch in and dares touch her face to move her head to see into the other one. 'Good . . .'

'Are you the doctor we saved?'

'Good detective skills.'

'I'm shit at investigating.'

'Clearly.'

'I prefer hitting people until they answer me.'

'Really? Does that work for you?'

'Dunno, want to find out?'

He smiles and chuckles. 'I am the doctor you saved. Thank you,' he adds with sincerity.

'Where's Ben and Harry? Ben came and got us . . . so he's alive then . . . is he okay now? Where's Harry? HARRY? BEN?'

'Good Lord, you are impulsive.'

'Here,' Harry calls out from the middle room. 'Don't beat the doctor up.'

'Ben?' she asks, sitting up.

'You should rest,' Doctor Watson says. Knowing she will ignore him the same way Ben ignored him and Harry ignored him.

'BEN?'

'He is fine,' Doctor Watson says. 'He wanted to be here but I made him wait in the dining room.'

'Dining room? Have we got a dining room now?' Safa asks, still glaring at him.

'The room with the food.'

'The main room.'

'Or the dining room,' Doctor Watson says. 'Does it hurt when you breathe in? Which I'm assuming it doesn't seeing as you are shouting perfectly well.'

'I'm fine,' she says. 'Thirsty though . . . can I have some water?'

He passes the cup. 'Just sip it . . . sip it . . . I said SIP IT . . . oh, for the love of God, you people are just impossible to treat.'

'What?' she asks, lowering the now empty cup. 'I was thirsty.'

'I did that and got told off too,' Harry calls through.

'You seen Ben yet?' she calls out.

'Wow,' Doctor Watson mutters and waves a hand in front of Safa. 'Can you see me? Do I exist? Am I ghost? Perhaps you have brain damage and need medicating again . . . I said Ben is in the dining room . . .'

'Main room.'

'Fine! Whatever,' Doctor Watson says.

'Can I get up?' she asks. 'I'm getting up,' she tells him and gets up. She looks down at her bra and knickers then up at the doctor with a face like thunder before deciding that he is a doctor and therefore she should probably not kill him for undressing her. She dresses in joggers and a T-shirt then heads through into the communal room to see Harry sitting in one of the blue chairs.

'Morning,' he says.

'Morning,' she says, walking straight past him to Ben's door that she opens. 'Oh,' she says dully. 'Seen this?'

'Seen what?' Harry asks.

'This,' Safa says, nodding at Ben's room.

'No. What is it?'

'Ben's room.'

'What about it?'

'Get up and have a look you lazy shit.'

Harry rubs his beard while contemplating this request. He comes to a decision. 'No, just tell me,' he says.

'Bedside table . . . lamp . . . rug on the floor . . . got some shelves for his clothes,' she says, looking round at the stark change inside. She sniffs the air a few times. 'He's using deodorant too.'

'Thank God,' Harry mutters.

'Well,' she says, turning back to Harry, realising the doctor must have left. 'It worked then.'

'Seems that way,' Harry says.

He pauses in the corridor at the metal-riveted door marked with the names *Harry Madden*, *Ben Ryder* and *Safa Patel*. A quick, deep breath and he heads inside.

'Morning,' Ben says, his voice catching from both nerves and anticipation.

'Ben!' Harry grins, getting to his feet. Safa looks round in surprise with a slow grin forming.

'Stay there,' Ben says, waving for him to sit back down.

He gets up anyway and squashes Ben's hand while shaking his head and smiling. 'Aye, it's good to see you, Ben. You okay?'

'I'm fine,' Ben says, staggering to the side from the enormous pat on the shoulder. 'How you feeling?'

'Ach, fine.' The big man beams all toothy and happy.

'Safa? You okay?' Ben asks as she steps away from his door.

'Fine,' she says with a broad smile. 'Look at you being all sheepish and shy . . . your room looks better by the way. Where's your beard? You shaved it off? I liked that beard. Are you wearing jeans? You look better. Doesn't he look better, Harry?'

'Aye.'

'You do. Got colour in your face,' she says, examining him closely while smiling and talking non-stop without any sense of shame. 'Yeah, I did like that beard, but then it's nice to see you shaved again. Your hair's a mess though. Anyway, stop fucking yacking on and get the brews in.'

'What the fuck?' Ben says, shaking his head at the onslaught.

'Shit, and I thought I was slow at investigating,' she says, still beaming at him. 'Oh, for fuck's sake . . . come here . . .'

'Eh?' Ben says as she flies at him.

'I hate hugging people,' she says, hugging him. 'I would literally only ever hug you or Harry . . . like, no one else ever . . .'

'Okay,' Ben says, looking at Harry, who's still smiling.

'Well hug me back then, you fucking dick.'

'Sorry,' Ben says, bringing his arms round her body.

'Get off now.' She pulls back to stare at him then at Harry. 'Sorted. Right,' she says, nodding as though a little embarrassed at her show of affection. 'You're still a dick though.'

'Probably,' Ben says.

'Stop yacking on. So? Was it Harry beating you up or did we die?'

'Er . . .' Ben says. He had wondered how to tell them they had died but then he remembered they were Harry and Safa and tiny things like death didn't bother them. 'Both . . . like . . .'

'Ah now, about that,' Harry says seriously, pushing a hand through his beard. 'Didn't expect you to keep getting back up.'

'Had it coming,' Ben says before he can continue.

'Aye,' Harry says.

'Did the doc tell you what happened?' Ben asks.

'No . . . but you came back for us,' she says. 'On your own? Is that right?'

'Yeah, but hang on,' he says. 'I've got something I want to show you. The doc said I wasn't to get you excited but it's only next door so . . .'

'What is?' Safa asks.

'Come see. You both okay to walk? I could get wheelchairs and wheel you about if you want . . . ?'

'Funny,' Safa says, marching past him to the main door. 'Which way? Left or right?'

'Hang on,' Ben yelps, rushing after her.

'I'll try left.' She heads left as Harry smiles at Ben and makes his way over.

'Nope,' Safa says, looking into the room on the left. 'Must be right then . . .'

'Will you just slow down a bit,' Ben says, as she strides past him to the other side.

'Ah,' she says, coming to a stop at the next door. 'Ah yes, yes, that's really nice. Did you do it?'

'Um, well . . .'

'Harry, come and look at this. Ben? Did you do it?'

'I just—'

'Isn't that nice?' Safa says, cutting across Ben as Harry joins her at the next door down.

'Aye,' Harry says, staring inside.

'So who did it? Did you do it?' she asks again.

'Fuck me,' Ben says, walking down to squeeze past them to get inside the room. 'Yes, I did it . . .'

The rooms are the same as theirs. Three bedrooms. One bathroom. One communal central room. But there the similarity ends. The three go inside to peer through the doors into the bedrooms. Big, deep rugs on the floors. Bedside tables. Armchairs, shelving units, paintings and pictures on the walls. Soft lighting and soft furnishings. The blue chairs in the communal section are replaced by armchairs, more rugs on the floor. The walls painted off-white with pictures and paintings hanging. Shelves fitted to the walls. The bare light overhead now covered by a shade. The bathroom is softened too. More fittings, more softening of the harsh concrete and stainless steel. The window shutters are up. Natural daylight streams in. The rooms look inviting, warm and homely.

'There was precedent,' Ben says as they look round. 'Doctor Watson has torn Roland up for arse paper over the way he did things. Roland said there was no precedent, but he was only thinking of time travel and not the taking of someone from their environment. Prisons have been doing it for centuries. Same with accounts of people stranded on desert islands and the methods they used to survive the mental anguish. Kidnappings, solitary confinements, social deprivation experiments, even those reality television programmes like *Big Brother* provided some level of scientific study. This,' Ben says, turning slowly to wave his hands at the rooms, 'alleviates the initial shock. The doc also said the sedatives, coupled with the meds we were given to prevent harm from the environment and oxygen toxicity, can all contribute to severe mental decline. We were in high-stress situations of life and death. You two were both trained, so your mental state was already sort of prepared for those situations. Mine wasn't, plus I'm just one of the percentage of the population susceptible to side effects from the drugs. The doc has already changed the meds to be used if we bring someone else back.'

'Shit,' Safa murmurs, blinking as she takes it all in.

'Sorry,' Ben says, lifting his hand. 'You've both just come round . . .'

'It's fine,' she says, shaking her head at him.

'Roland seriously does not have a clue, and with it being his son that invented the device it means he's off playing with—'

'What?' Safa says.

'What?' Ben asks her.

'What did you just say?'

'Which bit?'

'Roland's son? Seriously? It was his bloody kid?'

'You are joking, right?' Ben asks, looking at them both. 'You didn't know that? You didn't know it was his son? Six months and you didn't ask him?' They both shake their heads. 'Did you ask where he goes? Where the money comes from? Did you ask him anything?'

'You're the investigator,' Safa says, thereby disclaiming any responsibility.

'Right,' Ben says, nodding slowly. 'Fair one then . . . anyway, I've told him to find someone from military intelligence or that kind of background . . . someone who knows how to run something this size. Roland can't be left to do it.'

He stops to let them take it in and say something in reply. Harry heads for the closest armchair and sinks into it with a heavy sigh and a satisfied nod. Safa follows suit, taking the middle one, which she slumps into, grooving her backside into the soft seat.

'Very nice,' she says.

'It's like you said,' Ben says slowly, watching them get comfortable. 'You said I have to disconnect and that's it, I couldn't disconnect and it took a beating from Mad Harry Madden and you two being killed to make that happen.'

'We can't beat people as they get here,' Harry says thoughtfully.

'And I'm not drowning every bloody time we rescue someone either,' Safa adds.

Ben tuts and keeps going. 'Look at the bunker. Everything is bare concrete and sterile. It's like a prison or something . . . but here at least . . .' He looks round the room. 'Here there are things we can relate to. Does that make sense? Like windows and leather chairs and coffee tables . . .'

'We changed our rooms but you didn't want to,' Safa says.

'I was having a mental breakdown. I didn't know what I wanted. Listen, it might have happened regardless of what anyone did but . . . it might not had it been dealt with properly.'

'No, I agree,' Safa says.

'Aye, good work,' Harry mumbles, stretching his legs out and looking round.

'So has Roland got someone in mind then?' Safa asks.

'No idea. I haven't seen him for a couple of days. Malc and Kon said he's here less and less . . . almost like he thinks you two are back and I'm now fine so he doesn't have to worry . . . *or* he's so worried he's off doing something else. I don't like him. I don't trust him either. The sooner we run it the safer it will be . . . but, and no offence when I say this, but we can't oversee the whole thing. It's too big. The bloody portal they use to get the things for this place is in the same fixed place in Berlin in twenty sixty-one. They've got no concept of security or surveillance. Christ, his son invented time travel then failed to secure it properly.'

'Ben?' Malcolm calls out from the corridor.

'In here, mate,' Ben says, turning to watch Malcolm walk into the room holding a tray with three big, steaming mugs of coffee.

'Harry, Safa,' he says, nodding at both in turn, 'good to see you back up . . . like the rooms then?'

'Very nice,' Harry says, taking a mug from the tray. 'How are you?'

'Fine, fine,' Malcolm says, holding the tray out to Safa. 'It is much better . . . me, Ben and Kon got some good ideas for the main room and other sections . . . and did Ben tell you what the doc said about the meds?'

'Yeah, just told them, mate,' Ben says.

'We didn't know,' Malcolm says, offering an apologetic wince at Harry and Safa. 'Anyway, we'll leave you to it. We're popping into the city for an hour, Ben. Need anything?'

'Nah, it's fine. See you later.'

'Thanks,' Harry says as Malcolm leaves.

'Right,' Safa says, fixing Ben with a firm look that immediately makes him squirm. 'Elephant in the room.'

'Eh?' Ben asks.

'What elephant?' Harry asks, looking round.

'I'll just come out with it,' Safa says, looking at Ben. 'Get it behind us now . . .'

'Oh,' Ben groans. 'Don't . . .'

'What?' Harry asks.

'Steph,' Safa says.

'Bollocks,' Ben mutters.

'Oh,' Harry says. 'That.'

'Well?' she asks. 'You over it?'

'Safa,' Ben groans and shifts at her penetrating gaze as Harry eases subtly back on his armchair to disengage from the conversation.

'Are you?' she demands.

'Guess so,' Ben says quietly, looking away.

'Harry, close your ears for a second. She was a fucking bitch, Ben. An absolute nasty, cold, money-grabbing whore bitch shit-head fucking bitch . . .'

'Okay . . .' Ben mumbles.

'I haven't finished. She was a dirty, nasty, fucking bitch. Harry, really close your ears now . . .'

'Closed.'

'She was a cunt.'

'Safa!' Ben and Harry exclaim, but she just glares without a trace of apology.

'And I hate that word,' she adds emphatically. 'So for me to use it means she really was a cunt . . .'

'Yes, alright,' Ben says quickly.

'Oh, you don't know,' she says darkly. 'You were dead.'

'Yes, yes I was,' he mumbles, slightly alarmed.

'Honestly, there are two people in this world . . . our world . . . the old world . . . anyway, there are two people I hate. Like really hate. To the point I would actually murder them and sleep soundly, and she is one . . .'

'Christ,' Ben mumbles again and looks at Harry, who pretends he's not there.

'Seriously,' she continues. 'She tried to ruin what you did . . . what you did twice. You did it twice and she tried to take it all away from you. Did Harry tell you she knew you were Ben Ryder?'

'Er, I think so . . . I don't remember all of it but I got the gist,' Ben says with a frown as he tries to think back.

'She said you raped her.'

'I didn't,' Ben says, his tone instantly hardening.

'Oh, fuck off,' she tuts. 'I know you bloody didn't. Everyone knows you didn't.'

'Huh?'

'Long story short. You died. Someone recognised you from the footage as Ben Ryder. Word got out. The press went into meltdown. The whore already knew you were Ben Ryder as she'd overheard you talking to your mum and dad about telling her who you were and she was already having an affair with her boss, then when you died she sold her story for a fortune. The press went into meltdown again but then every single person that ever knew you came out and called her a lying fucking whore . . .'

'They said that?' Ben asks.

'Words to that effect,' she says, waving the question away. 'Then your parents re-mortgaged their house to pay for the best private investigations agency in London, who bugged her and finally caught her blackmailing her boss over dinner in a restaurant.'

'Do what?'

'The boss wanted to leave her. She couldn't handle it so tried to blackmail him but . . .' she says, shuffling to the edge of her seat. 'The whore admitted, during that bugged conversation, that she'd lied about everything . . .'

'Fuck.'

'Press went into meltdown for a third time. She was ruined. A newspaper paid the detective agency fee and your parents paid off the debt on their mortgage.'

'I—'

'So she was a whore.'

'I'm—'

'Complete bitch.'

'Er—'

'Enough said,' she says firmly and sits back. 'But she was a cunt.'

'But—'

'Done now.' She holds a hand up. 'We don't need to talk about the bitch whore slag ever again.'

Ben exhales slowly and tries to get his thoughts in order. One pops into his head. 'Who was the other person?'

'What?' Safa asks.

'The other person you hate. Who? Christ, Safa.' He reels back again, and if he thought he saw hatred in her face talking about Steph, he was wrong. The look she has now is venomous.

'Doesn't matter,' she mutters.

'Safa. You don't get to—'

'I do,' she cuts him off with a dark look. 'Leave it.'

'Okay.' He holds his hands up in retreat.

'I'll tell you one day.'

'Fine.'

'Not today though.'

'Okay.'

'Or tomorrow.'

'Noted.'

'So don't ask me again. I'll tell you when I'm ready.'

'Yep.'

'Which will be never.'

'Fine.'

'Got a time machine,' Harry says, glancing at her casually.

'Two steps ahead of you,' she replies.

'What?' Ben asks, shaking his head in confusion.

'What?' Harry asks in return.

'Do you know what she's on about?' Ben asks him.

'No,' he says simply.

'I'm so fucking lost,' Ben groans.

'Blimey, Ben,' Harry says with a gently chastising tone to his voice. 'We've got a time machine.'

'So?'

'Safa has something she would like to rectify . . . and I want to see Edith again.'

'Fucking hang on a minute!'

'What?' Harry says.

'What about the timeline and all that arse about not going back and disconnecting?'

'Christ, Ben,' Safa groans. 'Harry isn't talking about leaving . . .'

'But . . . you said . . . I said . . . fucking hang on a minute!'

'Wikipedia said Ben Ryder was intelligent,' Safa points out.

'Yeah, but . . . I got beat up for saying I wanted to go back . . .'

'No,' she says. 'You got beat up for being a dick. Harry is merely suggesting that should an opportunity present itself whereby we can make a wee trip . . . for him to see Edith and for me to . . . do what I need to do . . . then, you know . . . fuck's sake, Ben! We've got a time machine right there.'

'Timeline,' he blurts.

'Yes, which is why we haven't already done it until we know what we can do without breaking things,' she says.

'Have you discussed this?' he asks, looking at them both.

'No,' she says honestly. 'I just figured Harry was thinking the same.'

'Aye, was,' Harry says.

'I don't know what to say,' Ben says indignantly.

'*If* an opportunity presents is all we're saying,' Safa says. 'But not yet.'

'I'm so shocked right now.'

'Man up,' Safa grunts, but smiles at him.

'Mission comes first,' Harry points out.

'So you'd go back and see Edith then come back here?'

'Aye,' he says with brutal honesty.

'Fuck me,' Ben mutters. 'I think I'll stick to soft furnishings . . .'

Thirty-Nine

'They loved it,' Malcolm says.

'Yeah? Really? Did they say anything?' Konrad asks. Malcolm smiles and goes through. 'Did they?' Konrad asks again, stepping into the warehouse in Berlin from the bunker in the Cretaceous period.

'Not in words, but I could tell,' Malcolm says, leading the way across the room to the door at the end.

'How did they look?' Konrad asks, waiting for Malcolm to unlock the door then following him out to the street door.

'Er . . . alright actually,' Malcolm says, tilting his head side to side. 'Yeah, like, same as normal, really.'

'Can't believe Roland didn't come back to see them,' Konrad says, tutting as he stands waiting for Malcolm to lock the street door. He stares over to the buildings opposite, seeing only the same windows and doors he has seen nearly every day for over six months. 'He was always like that though,' Konrad adds, his tone dropping to a grumpy moan. 'Always had big ideas then got bored and lost interest. *His* son fucked it up, so you'd think he'd stick with it . . .'

'He's getting the money,' Malcolm says in a tone that suggests this conversation has been going on for a while.

'Yeah, still,' Konrad says sulkily.

'Come on,' Malcolm says, walking past him to head down the street. 'We'll get a cake with our coffees. Hey, should we take them something back? Like a big cake or something? What do you think?'

'Could do,' Konrad says, nodding but still sulking a bit. 'Get some paper hats and a few candles while we're at it.'

'Oh, pack it in,' Malcolm tuts. 'They're back. We've got all three now . . . it doesn't matter if Roland is here or not. Let them sort it from—'

A tourist turns to smile at Konrad and Malcolm from the corner at the junction. His tourist guide and map clutched in his hands and his face showing the confused, harassed look of someone lost in a strange city.

'Er . . . do you speak English?' the tourist asks clearly and slowly with hope in his eyes that someone might be able to communicate with him.

Malcolm grins. 'You're a bit lucky, mate,' he chuckles. 'You lost?'

'You're English!' the tourist says with evident relief. 'I have no idea where I am . . . apparently this building should be a museum,' he adds, looking at the building on the corner.

'Let's have a look,' Malcolm says, nodding at the map. 'Where you trying to find?'

'Gentlemen, say a word and you die right here,' Alpha says, showing them the pistol held under the map. The genial look vanishes in a second. His eyes dart between the two stunned men.

'Just stay still,' Bravo says almost politely, walking briskly towards them with his own squat black pistol held partly concealed.

Men come in from all sides. All of them dressed in normal civilian clothing. Malcolm flinches. His heart jack-hammering in his chest. Konrad spins, seeing the net closing in.

'Don't move,' Alpha says calmly.

'Easy, mate,' Malcolm says, rushing the words out.

'Mistake,' Konrad blurts. 'Seriously . . . don't do this . . .'

'Shush,' Bravo whispers, moving to stand behind Malcolm. Echo moves behind Konrad. Alpha holds his pistol under the map, staring at them both with interest.

'Mate,' Malcolm says. 'Don't . . . you don't know who they are . . .'

'They'll fucking kill you . . . all of you . . .' Konrad adds in a rush.

'Do as we say and you live. Understood?' Alpha says, his tone calm, his manner relaxed. All five men are relaxed and calm.

'No.' Malcolm grimaces at having to argue. 'Don't do it . . .'

'Listen to him,' Konrad urges. 'You won't get a—' He stops speaking with a gasp as the ultrathin point of a stiletto blade sinks a millimetre into the flesh of his right thigh.

'Not another word,' Bravo mutters, holding the blade while apparently trying to see between them to the map being held by the tourist. 'The blue light. Is it the device?'

'Shit.' Malcolm sags on the spot. His eyes closing as he realises what is happening.

'Is the device the blue light?' Alpha asks.

'You don't know what you're doing,' Konrad says, steeling himself as the stiletto sinks another millimetre into his thigh. They both breathe fast with panic rising in their chests and tight balls of fear forming in their guts that twist and flip.

'Now gentlemen, you can see we are serious,' Alpha says, smiling benignly. 'Is the blue light the device?'

'Oh fuck,' Malcolm whimpers. 'Please don't do this . . .'

'Killing us makes no difference,' Konrad gasps as the blade sinks further in. Strong hands grip him in place. The pistol pushing in his back prevents him going back.

'Answer the question and you both live. We will pay you. You'll be millionaires within an hour. Your employers will never find you. We will protect you. Go anywhere you want. Have anything you want . . .' Alpha speaks earnestly in a tone honed to perfection, the ultimate expression of believability and sincerity. He moves closer. His voice softens again. 'Please . . . just tell me. Is the blue light the device?' He sounds almost worried, afraid even.

'He's stabbing me, Malc.' Konrad swallows and stares down at the blade.

'Yep,' Malcolm grunts. 'We'll be alright, mate.'

'Really fucking hurts, Malc,' Konrad whispers.

'Malcolm, Konrad. We know who you are. We know who you have inside. Ben, Harry, Safa. Roland. Doctor Watson. We know already. You can be wealthy. Go anywhere. New identities. Don't sacrifice yourselves . . .' Alpha implores them, his face a mask of worry and pity.

Konrad snorts a dry laugh. 'He thinks it's about money, Malc . . . argh, fuck, that hurts.'

'Yeah, millionaires,' Malcolm replies, looking down at the blade sticking in Konrad's leg.

'You want to die?' Alpha asks, puzzled and worried for them. 'Here? In this street? For what? No one will know what you died for . . .'

'Died before,' Konrad whispers.

'Do it again,' Malcolm adds.

'Ben went back for 'em, Malc.'

'I know.' Malcolm nods.

'He got 'em too . . .'

'He did . . .'

'Malcolm, Konrad. See sense. There is no honour dying here. They won't come back for you. We are taking the device before any damage is caused. Help us. Be rich. Save yourselves . . .'

'Malc?'

'Yep,' Malcolm grunts.

'I'll slit you open and stuff your fucking cocks down each other's throats . . .' Alpha switches tone, seeing the resilience within the men.

'Fuck.' Konrad blasts air as the blade digs further, sliding deeper.

'Life or death? Your choice . . .' Alpha says. His tone hard then soft. 'Choose life. Choose living. Be rich . . .' he urges, begs, pleads. 'See sense. Do the right thing.'

'They'll come for you,' Konrad says through gritted teeth.

A soft sound. Like air forced at speed through a small tube. Malcolm sags back, a sudden warmth in his gut. Strong hands hold him steady and he looks down to the crimson blush spreading across his T-shirt. 'They shot me . . .' he whimpers. 'Kon . . . they bloody shot me . . .'

'You're all dead,' Konrad says, grunting again as the knife goes deeper.

Another soft sound of air. Malcolm staggers again. The hands hold him. The blood drains from his face. 'Please stop shooting me,' he whispers.

'What's on the other side of the blue light?' Alpha asks. He lowers the gun and fires into Malcolm's kneecap. A gloved hand comes over Malcolm's face, cutting off the scream. The knife in Konrad's leg twists and saws side to side. 'What's on the other side?'

'FUCK YOU,' Konrad roars. 'FUCK YOU FUCK YOU FUCK—'

The hiss of air is lost under his booming voice that cuts off as the bullet goes through his heart. He slumps down as the pistol is put to the back of his head and fired. Malcolm screams under the hand over his mouth. Pain in his guts. Pain in his knee.

'What's on the other side?' Alpha asks.

Malcolm closes his eyes. Konrad is dead but Harry and Safa were both dead and Ben got them back. This is not the end. They will come. He jerks sharply, yanking his mouth free to scream out. The gun fires. He slumps dead.

◆ ◆ ◆

The assault is coming. She knows that. They are professionals. They move like professionals. They cluster round Konrad and Malcolm like professionals and although she cannot hear the words, she can guess at what is being said. Polite at first, soft and earnest. Threaten death while offering wealth. Play to both fear and greed at the same time.

Now they have blown their cover. They have assaulted two men in a public street. She looks past the cluster of seven men to the junction and spots more operatives. Men and women looking oh-so-casually in every direction except down the back road. She watches as the long truck slides across the mouth of the junction, blocking any passing motorists' view. She nods in a show of respect. That was very well-timed. Getting a truck through a city to arrive the second you need it is no easy feat. That tells her they are big. They have resources. She knew they were here. She knew they were watching the warehouse. She watches as the operatives go to a side compartment of the truck and start drawing long-barrelled assault weapons. More operatives converge. More men. More women. She flicks back down to the cluster of seven and tuts sadly at the sight of Konrad shot dead and Malcolm squirming to break free. He too is executed. Time to go.

◆　◆　◆

Alpha and his four wait. The truck is in position. Operatives come down to scoop the bodies up and carry them back to the truck. Workmen at both sides of the junction unfold huge screens that are fixed from the building line to the sides of the truck, effectively sealing the back road and shielding it from sight of anyone passing.

Alpha takes his submachine gun and works the parts to check the weapon. Bravo, Charlie, Delta and Echo do the same. They strip their tourist outer jackets off to reveal tight black clothes. Balaclavas are tugged from side pockets and pulled down over heads. Holsters fitted. Pistols slid in. Magazines checked. Stun grenades taken from the truck. They work fast and in silence.

Alpha steps away to look down the road towards the warehouse. His men gather round him. The extra operatives brought in make ready, tugging down balaclavas in preparation for the assault.

Bravo looks round. Checking each is in position and ready. He pats Alpha on the shoulder. Alpha raises his right hand and motions ahead. As one they move down towards the warehouse.

She goes back through the warehouse and down the stairs to the ground floor. She stops to collect what she left earlier then moves along the corridor to the door. She stops, slides a thin metal file from her pocket and bends over with a groan at the stiffness in her lower back. She fiddles with, pokes and works the lock. She stands up, twists the handle, pushes the door open with her foot, picks up the two heavy objects and goes inside. She closes the door with her foot, grimacing at the dull pain in her hips. She waddles down the room, swaying side to side from the weight in her hands.

She tuts at the blue light bathing the room. She tuts at the objects left scattered everywhere. She tuts at the metal shelving units bolted to the walls filled with diving equipment, black clothes, grey tracksuits, lamps, furnishings, rugs, food, toiletries and everything else five people need to live in a bunker. She is amazed they haven't put a sign outside saying 'Time Machine in Here'.

Alpha leads. Bravo and Charlie right behind him. Delta and Echo out to the sides. They go steady but swift. No point in running now. Move carefully and approach with caution. Not that they need caution. The people who run this place have no security awareness. They have no surveillance awareness. They have no right to be in possession of such a thing.

That thing is the target. The device must be secured. Above all else, it will be secured.

She is too old for this. She moves round the room, focusing on the shelves then on the stacks of goods next to the portal. She moves steady but swift. No point in rushing. Move carefully and work with caution. She finishes the first and lifts the second to work into the crevices, the nooks and crannies. Do a thing right. Get it right first time. She lifts her head at the dull clunk reaching her ears and starts moving back towards the blue light.

Alpha glares at the operative working the lock on the main door. The dull clunk was a schoolboy error. The operative swallows. He has just secured himself a punishment when this mission is over. It's not his fault though. The lock is really old. He hasn't done a lock this old for years. He nods and moves back. Alpha nods at the next operative, who pulls the door open as the operatives aim inside the corridor. Not that anyone will be there, but they have skills for a reason and precautions count.

The outer door is breached. She looks round the room then unzips the compartment on the small black holdall. She reaches in and pulls the weighty object out. She throws the bag through the portal and moves closer to it. She leans through to quickly glimpse the room in the bunker then pulls back into the warehouse. She gains position. One foot through. One foot in the past and one in the future. She tuts again at the analogy that sums up the last few years of her life. One foot in the past. Always one foot in the past. She presses a button on the object in her hands and makes ready.

Alpha points to the inner door then at the method of entry operative. Alpha motions what will happen if the MOE operative fucks this one up. The operative nods and moves to the door. He drops to a crouch then opens a leather pouch to select the picks he needs. He pushes them into the lock, and barely a click is heard as the lock is undone.

Barley a click heard, but it's enough. She smiles and throws the object. A second later she is in the bunker picking up the tablet, which she swipes to break the connection. As the signal is sent and the blue light flickers off one flame comes through, dying the second the light ends.

Alpha hears the charge being dropped on the floor. Bravo hears it. Charlie hears it. Delta and Echo hear it. They hear it, which is why they are paid more, why they are the elite, why they are selected to do the things they do. They drop as the others move forward towards the door and the room beyond that detonates from the plastic explosives on a timer that ignite the fuel splashed from the cans the woman brought with her. Flame scorches out. The pressure wave is huge. The sound, the heat, the sensation and the vortices created by the explosion kill the other operatives outright. The five move fast. They scrabble to stagger out through the main door as the front wall of the warehouse blows out. Glass and brick flies across the road. The air feeds the flames that roar up into the sky.

◆　◆　◆

She sighs and looks round. Not a tremor of excitement in her manner. Not a flicker of adrenaline. She moves out to the corridor then up towards the doors to the main room. She came here two nights ago. Roland brought her while everyone was asleep. She saw the bunker and listened to what he said. She showed no reaction. She told Roland to go home and stay away. Then she worked out, as Ben did, how to use the tablet to operate the device. She went home and got the charges she had stored. She also got the nine-mill pistol now held on her hip in the holster. She came back and spent the rest of her time monitoring and assessing. She wanted to see for herself. It is always best to see for yourself. What she saw did not impress her. She was not appalled, as to be appalled you have to have an emotional range, which, after the life she has led, she does not have. She prepared and made ready. It was obvious what was going to happen. Using one staging area was a ridiculous idea, but at least that entry point is now negated.

In the main room she nods at Doctor Watson and heads to the big table, where she takes an apple and bites down. She chews methodically as the doctor stares wide-eyed and shocked.

'They awake?' she asks.

He nods. He spots the pistol on her hip and wonders if he should do something, say something.

She clocks what he sees and swallows the mouthful. 'On your side,' she says, her voice deep and very American. Doctor Watson nods quickly. Rendered silent by the sight of her. She is of average height and average build. She looks tanned and healthy but jaded and worn. She could be anywhere from fifty to sixty-five years old. Dark blonde hair streaked with grey pulled back in a simple ponytail away from a face lined from a life lived. Cold grey eyes stare out, but the intelligence is deep.

'You the doc?' she asks.

He nods again. Still unable to find his voice.

'Sciatica,' she says, patting her hip. 'Shrapnel . . .'

He lifts his head. 'Right,' he says.

'Age is a state of mind,' she says, more to herself, as she moves to the door. 'That's what they told me.'

She goes through to the corridor and up towards the door, following the sound of their voices. She goes slow, listening to absorb the conversation. When she gets near she stops.

'Are you sure?' Safa asks.

'Yes,' Ben says. 'From the supermarket. Genetically modified, steroid-injected, DNA something fruit . . .'

'Urgh.' Safa's voice carries from the room. 'Don't know if I still like it now.'

'And the water we thought was super-nice?' Ben says.

'Oh, don't tell me,' Safa moans.

'Tap water. They run a pipe and fill tanks.'

They did, the woman muses to herself, taking another bite of the apple.

'German tap water?'

'Er, yeah,' Ben says. 'It's just water though.'

Three voices tell her they are all inside one room. She resumes walking and swallows the mouthful as she stops to stare in.

The three rise fast. The three rise as one. The three freeze at the sight of the woman eating the apple and the pistol on her hip.

She nods and bites into the fruit. She chews and takes them in. 'Hey,' she says with a mouthful of apple. She swallows and looks at them. 'I'm your new boss . . .'

About the Author

RR Haywood is a long-standing and highly successful Amazon author. He is the creator of the bestselling series The Undead, a self-published British zombie horror series that has become a cult hit with a readership that defies generations and gender.

Living in an underground cave, away from the spy satellites and invisible drones sent to watch over us by the BBC, he works a full-time job, has four dogs and lots of tattoos. He is also a certified, badged and registered hypochondriac, for which he blames the invisible BBC drones.

Should you not have a drone to hand, you can find him at www.rrhaywood.com.